Forever and Ever:
Volume One

E. L. Todd

"What if I fall?

Oh but my darling, what if you fly?"

Erin Hanson

Chapter One

Cayson

I needed to get a new laptop. The damn thing ran so slow at the most crucial times. I was trying to submit my paper to the teacher's website when my computer decided to take a break instead.

I decided to call the one person who knew everything about computers. He worked for a successful software company in New York City, and he was paid big bucks to make sure their servers weren't hacked.

It rang three times before he answered. "Hey, Son. How's college life?"

"Good. How are you?" I thought it would be rude to skip all the pleasantries.

"Great. Your mother and I just got back from the Van Gogh museum."

I cocked an eyebrow. "Haven't you been to that already?"

"Yeah...but your mother loves it." Dad pulled the phone away then whispered in the background. He was probably talking to my mom. "I'll be there in a second." He was back to me. "Any particular reason why you called?"

"My computer is acting weird. Everything is running slow."

"Is it a virus?"

"If I knew, why would I be calling you?" The smartass inside me was coming out.

"You're starting to sound like your cousin, Slade."

"I'm not sure if that's a compliment or not."

"An insult, actually." He breathed into the phone while he moved around. Then I heard typing. "It's probably running slow because you're downloading too much porn."

"I don't download porn," I argued.

"Hey, I'm not judging you."

"Well, I don't."

"Come on...let's be real here," he teased.

"I'm not dumb enough to download it. I stream it."

He laughed. "Smart boy." He typed on his computer. "Let me take a look."

The mouse on my screen started to move. "How the hell are you doing that?"

"Uncle Sean and Uncle Mike don't pay me a fortune just to look like a stud in the office."

"You don't look like a stud. You look like an old man." I watched the mouse move across the screen of its own accord. I had no idea my dad could do this. He clicked on a few icons then accessed my system setup screen.

"I'm not old. Your mother tells me I have the same stamina I did in my twenties."

I cringed. "Let's keep this PG."

He chuckled. "What? You think your mom and I conceived you then we just threw in the towel?"

The idea of my parents doing it was absolutely disgusting. I wanted to gag. "Just fix my computer, Dad."

"Geez, someone's in a hurry."

"I have to submit this paper in..." I looked at my watch. "Half an hour."

"I'll be done long before then." His mouse made a few adjustments before it went idle. "There. Brand new."

I used my mouse to access the website. Then I attached my paper to the correct folder and submitted it. It went through without any problems. "It worked."

"You sound surprised."

I rolled my eyes. "Maybe you should try being humble once in a while."

"No. As your aunt Janice would say, if you got it, flaunt it."

"I think she was referring to something else, Dad." Sometimes my dad was oblivious to other people's meanings.

"So, how's everything going?"

"About the same." I shrugged even though he couldn't see me.

"You're doing well in your classes?"

"Yep. Biochemistry is a snooze fest but I'm passing."

He chuckled. "By passing, you mean getting straight A's?"

I shook my head. "Unlike you, I choose to be humble."

"The most successful people in life didn't stand in the corner and hope their talents would be miraculously noticed. They put themselves out there and blatantly told the world what they had to offer. Keep that in mind."

"Seriously? You're giving me a pep talk?"

"Just some wisdom from your old man."

"I thought you weren't old?" I challenged.

He chuckled into the phone. "Your mother says I'm like wine. I taste better as I age."

I cringed again. "I know you guys still have sex but do we need to talk about it?"

"I know you jerk off but do we need to talk about how you access your porn?"

I rolled my eyes. "Touché."

"Well, I'll let you go, Son."

Thank god. "Thanks for your help."

"Anytime, kid. I love you."

He always said that when we got off the phone. My mom was worse. She would blabber about how much she missed me then she would discuss her favorite baby picture. My dad was the lesser of two evils. "I love you too."

"Call me if you need anything else."

"I will."

"Bye."

"Bye."

I dropped the phone on my desk then looked out the window. Winter was coming to Boston, and it was bringing a deep chill. Soon the ground would be covered in snow. Everyone would huddle near the fires in the student lounge. Girls would don their boots and scarves. But winter was my favorite season. I wasn't sure why.

I walked into the bathroom then washed my face. When I stared at the mirror, I couldn't deny the similarities between my father and I. I had blond hair just like him, crystal blue eyes, and a fair face. I didn't understand how I didn't inherit any of my mother's exotic looks. My sister did. Sometimes people didn't believe we were siblings.

I left my apartment then headed to Skye's, knowing the football game was about to start.

***

"What took you so long?" Slade came up to me with a beer in his hand. Of all my friends, he was definitely the closest one to me. Just like our dads, we were best friends.

"I had to submit my paper but my computer was acting up."

"Too much porn?" he blurted.

I glared at him. "No."

"Because you can put that stuff on a separate hard drive so it won't affect your computer. Or you could just get another computer strictly for porn. Personally, I go with the second route."

"Good to know," I said sarcastically. "My dad said my system setup screen was messed up. A virus or something. He fixed it."

"Uncle Cortland, the Geek Squad."

I eyed the sleeve of tattoos up and down his arm. His entire back was covered with different colors and so was his chest. There was hardly any virgin skin left. "At least my dad knows how to do something other than ink people."

"What's wrong with inking?" He held up his beer. "You know how many tramp stamps my dad does a day? Let's just say he sees a lot of hot ass—and gets paid for it."

"I'm sure Aunt Janice is thrilled about that."

He rolled his eyes. "My mom is annoying. Who cares what she wants?"

I eyed the TV. "What's the score?"

"27-0. Seahawks."

"Ugh. I hate the Seahawks."

Slade shook his head. "Don't let Aunt Scarlet or my dad hear you say that."

I opened the refrigerator then pulled out a beer. The apartment was spotless. The smell of rose hips came to my nose, the distinct scent of Skye and everything she touched. Her white furniture contrasted against her hardwood floors, and the flowers she had arranged everywhere made the place look like something you'd find on Pinterest.

I opened a drawer then grabbed the bottle opener. After I popped the cap off, the smell of rose hips became more prominent.

"Hey." Skye approached the counter wearing a white shirt with a red cardigan. A silver necklace hung around her throat, and the diamond pendant in the center caught the light when she moved. "What took you so long?"

I faced her while I gripped the bottle. "I had to turn in a paper for my theology class."

She cringed. "Sounds brutal."

I smirked. "Why do you think I'm drinking a beer at...?" I looked at my watch. "Noon."

She laughed. The lighthearted sound echoed in my ears. Her perfect teeth were displayed, and the tiny freckle in the corner of her mouth was more noticeable. Her hand moved to her stomach while she laughed. Then she smiled at me. "Would you prefer something stronger?"

"No, it's okay. It would be too easy to become an alcoholic right now."

"True." She leaned against the counter while facing me. Her skintight black jeans clung to her perfect curves. And she was gifted in the chest department, just like her mom. "Business is challenging but I'm sure it's nothing like biochemistry."

I shrugged. "You can't compare the two."

Her eyes twinkled slightly. "Always so modest."

I didn't have a response to that. I drank my beer, not sure what else to do. When I was around Skye, I was nervous. My heart rate was always a little quicker when she was near. It was difficult to pay attention to anything else in the room because she consumed my thoughts. I had her wardrobe memorized, and I recognized her scent from a mile away.

"There's pizza and appetizers on the table."

It took me a moment to process what she said. I was too busy eyeing the freckle in the corner of her mouth. "Thanks. You're always a great host."

She rolled her eyes. "I really am my mother's daughter."

"That's not a bad thing."

"Are you kidding me?" She rolled her shoulders then stretched her neck. "These damn boobs are killing my back. Sometimes I just want to chop them off."

I didn't glance down, keeping my eyes glued to her face. "Most girls would kill for your curves."

"Then they would change their minds when they realized how painful it was."

I put my beer on the counter then grabbed her elbow. "I can loosen things up for you."

"No, it's okay—"

I turned her around then rested my hand on the area between her shoulder blades. I massaged the muscle, feeling the tightness. My hand was large enough to span her entire back. I kept the other one on her hip, holding her in place.

Skye immediately fell quiet, moaning softly at my touch. She rolled her head and closed her eyes.

I was over a foot taller than her, and I was twice her size. Her petite frame made it easier for me to massage her. I could do so much work with just a single hand. I rubbed my fingertips in a circular motion, relaxing the muscle underneath. With her petite waist and small rib cage, I understood why her back hurt all the time. Her breasts were disproportionately large in comparison to her small stature. My hand moved to the back of her neck and I loosened the muscle there. Being this close to her, touching her, made my breath hitch.

I looked past her and saw everyone on the couch. Slade rolled his eyes then acted like he was jerking off with his hand.

I ignored him and kept moving my hands.

After a few minutes, she finally turned around with sleepiness in her eyes. "Now I'm ready for a nap."

I laughed. "It is Sunday. That's allowed."

"It's rude for the hostess to ignore her guests."

I scanned everyone on the couch. Their eyes were glued to the TV. "I don't think anyone would notice."

"They would if the food was gone."

I laughed again. "Animals."

She touched my forearm then dropped it. "Thanks for the massage."

"Anytime."

She walked back to the living room then took her spot on the couch. I stayed behind the counter and drank my beer.

Slade made his way over, standing beside me. "Massive hard-on?"

I didn't deny it. "Yep."

"I thought so."

I stayed in my spot and watched the TV from where I was standing.

"You know what works for me?"

"Hmm?"

"Imagining an evil clown busting the shit out of a piñata."

I cocked an eyebrow. "That's oddly specific."

He shrugged. "I'm telling ya, it works."

I drank my beer and pictured it.

Slade winked at me. "Told ya." He walked back to the living room.

I walked behind the couch then took a seat. "Hey, Trinity."

"Hey." She had a magazine in her lap. Her long blonde hair reached her chest. Gold hoop earrings hung from her lobes, and she wore a purple scarf. Her outfit was usually splashed with color. "How's it going?"

"Good. I'm glad it's Sunday, but it's also the day I'm most depressed."

"Why?"

"Because school is tomorrow."

She smirked. "True. But I thought you liked school."

"I do—for the most part."

She flipped through the magazine. "What do you think of this?" She held up a picture of a woman wearing a poncho. "Do you think that's cute?"

I didn't think anything was cute. I shrugged. "It's cool, I guess."

"Cool?" she asked incredulously.

"Are you asking if I would wear a woman's poncho? I would hope you already know the answer."

She rolled her eyes. "You don't understand fashion."

"I understand jeans and a t-shirt."

"And sports," Slade added.

"And food," Skye added.

"Definitely food," I said.

Slade kept his eyes glued to the TV. "And porn."

Trinity glared at him before she looked down.

I glanced at Skye, watching her play with a long strand of brown hair. "Your brother isn't coming?"

"No. He says he's busy." She had a knowing look in her eyes. "Which means Roland would rather sit in the dark and play video games by himself."

"Video games are awesome," Slade said. "You can kill people and get away with it."

Trinity put the magazine down. "You're twisted, you know that?"

"And you're stupid," Slade said. "Why would you ask a guy if he likes a woman's poncho?" He gave her an incredulous look then turned away.

Trinity and Slade argued more often than they got along. It surprised me they were friends at all. But since our family was so tightly knit, they didn't have much of a choice but to at least be frenemies.

I watched the game, finally starting to relax. That paper was still in the back of my mind. It was my fault for waiting until the last minute to do it, but I didn't care about my non-major courses. They were a waste of time and I wouldn't remember anything anyway.

Spending Sunday with the people I trusted most in the world was my ideal way of using my free time. I could be myself with them, no matter how ludicrous I behaved, and I knew they had my back until the end of time. Even though most of us weren't related by blood, we were still a family.

Zack walked through the door, destroying my high.

"Yo." He grabbed a beer from the fringe then shoved a slice of pizza down his throat instantly. He was like a barbaric caveman, destroying everything in his path with his clumsiness.

Skye left her seat then walked to him. "Hey. I was wondering if you would show."

I didn't turn around to greet him. In fact, I ignored him. Slade pretended he didn't exist and Trinity continued to read her magazine. None of us liked him. Actually, I hated him.

"Hey, baby." He drank his beer then put his hand in his pocket.

I could see their reflection in the screen. Skye wrapped her arms around his neck then gave him a kiss. His thick arms were the size of tree trunks. He had dark brown hair that was almost black and his chin was covered in hair. I despised him.

"How was your day?" Skye asked.

"Good. Yours?" He ate another slice.

"Good. I finished that paper. Do you want to read it and give me your thoughts?"

"Maybe later." He walked away from her then plopped down on the other couch, taking Skye's spot. Skye moved to another seat—on the sofa with no cushion on the back.

Skye never said it, but I knew she always sat in the recliner because the padding felt good on her back. Her chest constantly made her ache. She hardly exercised because her chest would hurt so much after.

I was pissed Zack was so inconsiderate. I stood up and walked to Skye. "Switch with me."

"No, I'm okay."

I knew she would never admit when she was in pain. "I'm not asking you. I'm telling you."

She looked at me then took the spot next to Trinity. Once she sat down, I saw her face relax. Zack's eyes were glued to the screen. He drank his beer then leaned back, oblivious to the beautiful and perfect girl beside him.

Seeing them together was torture. Maybe it wouldn't hurt so much if Skye were with a guy I actually liked. Maybe it wouldn't make a difference at all. I would never know.

Slade leaned close to me. "Don't worry. They won't last."

"Yeah." I watched the game and tried not to think about it. In my heart, I knew it didn't make a difference if they broke up.

Because Skye would never feel the same way.

Chapter Two

Skye

There wasn't much trash after everyone left because Cayson picked everything up. He always cleaned everything before he left, even if it wasn't his own mess. And he always took the trash on his way out. I was lucky I had such an incredible family. They made me feel at home no matter where I was.

"Good game, huh?" Zack asked.

"Yeah."

"I bet a dime on the Seahawks."

"A dime?" *Like ten cents?*

"It's a thousand dollars."

"Oh." *I thought he was broke?* "So, you won?"

"Yep." He rubbed his hands together greedily. "I'm going to buy new lights for my car."

"Why don't you just save it?" That made sense to me.

"Nah. Too boring."

I chose not to argue with him. We both had different points of view when it came to money. Personally, I believed in investing and making a small amount grow. Zack liked to piss away everything he had.

I stretched then rolled my shoulders. "I'm going to bed. I'm tired."

"I'll be there in a second." He put his feet on the coffee table with his beer in hand.

"Like I've asked you ten times, please keep your feet off the coffee table."

He rolled his eyes. "Geez, calm down."

"I asked you nicely."

"Are you my girlfriend or the police?"

He really got under my skin sometimes. "Maybe you should just go, Zack. I don't have the patience to put up with you."

"Fine." He took his feet down. "Sorry."

"It's too late. Just go."

He put his beer on the coaster then stood up. "I said I was sorry. What else do you want me to do?"

"Are you deaf? I just asked you to leave."

He sighed then turned off the TV. "Look, it won't happen again. Don't kick me out."

I rolled my eyes. "You just want to get laid."

"Well, why wouldn't I? Look at you."

That loosened me up a little bit. "I'm going to bed. I guess I'll see you soon."

"Okay."

I walked into my bedroom then set my alarm, thinking about Zack. I had a crush on him since the moment I saw him, but our relationship took a while to develop. He didn't notice me until we had a class together. Then when we bumped into each other at the library, he seemed to become more interested. One thing led to another, and then we were together. I didn't have a great history with relationships, but it didn't seem like the one I had with Zack was how it should be. I had doubts about it but I never voiced them. Even if it was based off physical attraction more than anything else.

Zack came into the bedroom then stripped his clothes. He was packed with hard muscle, and his arms were the size of my head. He gave me a dark look, just like he usually did, and then got into bed beside me.

Just like every other guy I came across, he was obsessed with my chest. It was the first thing he wanted to see during sex. He pulled my shirt off then unclasped my bra. When he saw them, his eyes lit up. Most of the time, he stared at them more than my face.

Zack moved between my legs then did his thing. I admit, I was disappointed with the sex. I expected him to rock my world but he never did. Most of the time, our rendezvous ended without any satisfaction. I lay there, feeling the burn between my legs, and listened to him breathe loudly until I fell asleep.

I eyed Trinity across the table from me. She was flipping through a magazine, licking her fingertips every time she turned the page.

"Don't you have homework or something?" I asked. My economics book was to the side and my business ethics book was in front of me. It seemed like I always had homework or something to study for.

She shrugged. "It's not due for a few days. I still have time."

My cousin wasn't as goal oriented as I was. We were different in that way. I pulled out my glasses because I was having a hard time reading. After I put them on, I returned my focus to the textbook and highlighted a few notes.

"Do you even like Zack?" she blurted.

I stilled, surprised by the unexpected question. "Where did that come from?"

She didn't look up from her magazine once. "It just seems like you aren't as into him as you used to be."

"Well, he gets on my nerves sometimes..."

"Is he at least good in bed?"

I shrugged. "He's alright."

She finally tore her gaze away from her magazine. "Alright? If he annoys you and he isn't that good in bed, why are you with him?"

"I don't know. I used to really like him. I guess I'm hoping it'll go back to the way it was before."

"Wishful thinking..."

"What about you? Are you seeing anyone?"

She looked away again. "No."

"Are you interested in anyone?" She used to be outgoing. She had a different date every weekend. Now she seemed like a nun.

"No...no one has really caught my eye."

I found that hard to believe but I didn't press her on it. "If all you care about is fashion, why are you even in school?"

She adjusted the scarf around her neck. "You know how my dad is. He wants me to work for the company when I graduate."

"But what do *you* want?"

She shrugged. "I don't know. I really like fashion."

"Then tell him. Uncle Mike gives you anything you ask for. You know that."

She sighed. "But it's important to him. You know, keeping it in the family."

"Like I said, you need to do what you want, not what your father wants."

She looked down at her magazine. "I'll think about it..."

I returned to my work and continued to study. Business was interesting to me. When I was little, my father used to take me to work when my mom needed to work from home. Seeing him in meetings and handling a large company motivated me from a young age.

Slade came to our table and plopped down. He was eating a cheesesteak sandwich.

"Wad up, playas?" He chewed his food loudly, smacking his lips. His elbows were on the table and his tattoos were visible. He looked more like a thug than a college student. He wore a short sleeve shirt no matter how cold it was just to show off his sleeves of tattoos.

Trinity eyed him with disdain. "You aren't supposed to eat in the library."

He rolled his eyes. "Like there are police for that."

Her anger started to smolder. "Do you always have to eat like a pig?"

"I'm hungry," he snapped. "Get over it."

"You're always hungry."

The bickering was starting to give me a headache.

"I need a napkin." He set his sandwich down then ripped a page out of her magazine.

She stilled like someone stabbed her in the heart. A gasp escaped her lips. "How dare you!" She hit him in the arm.

"Buy another one, rich brat." He wiped his mouth then his hands.

"Ugh, I hate you sometimes."

"I hate you all the time."

They were driving me crazy. "Are you guys five years old?"

"She is," Slade argued.

"Why don't you just pull her hair?" I demanded.

"Okay." Slade grabbed a handful of hair and pulled it.

"Ahh!" Trinity yelled then swatted his hand away. "Knock it off."

Students from the other tables started to look at us.

I covered my face, thoroughly embarrassed.

"You're such an ass," Trinity hissed.

"You're such a tight ass," Slade countered. "Just let me eat my sandwich in peace."

"Let me read my magazine in peace."

"Keep it down," I whispered.

"You keep it down!" Trinity turned her fury onto me.

I needed to get out of there—quick. "I'm obviously not going to get any studying done with the two of you around." I packed my bag while they continued to fight.

"Why can't you just be nice to me?" Trinity asked. "It's like you're two different people sometimes."

"No, I'm always the same person," he argued. "Don't expect me to treat you like a princess. I never said I would."

Trinity grabbed his sandwich then took a huge bite.

Slade's eyes widened. "You just crossed a line..."

I didn't want to see the end of that fight. I left the table and got out of there as quickly as possible.

I headed to *Manhattan Grub*, the small food joint just off campus. My parents opened it a few years ago, and I ran the register and took care of the bookkeeping. It was a random place to buy, but my parents insisted on it. And it only sold hot dogs. Even weirder.

After I walked inside, I went to the cash register and counted the cash.

"Hey, boss." Adam came to my side and leaned against the counter.

"Hey. How's it going?"

"Slow—like always. I'm not sure why we stay open past five. The students only come for lunch."

I shrugged. "I don't make the rules."

"Your parents probably lose business by staying open."

"I think they have some grand plan in mind but they haven't shared it with me yet...I just work here."

He chuckled. "I guess you can do that when you're loaded."

I ignored his question. I never talked about my family's money. Being rich was more of a curse than anything else. It was difficult to tell if people liked you for you or what you could do for them. Which is why I loved my family even more. Wealth meant nothing to them. "Can you change the bins and restock the chips?"

"Yeah, boss." He disappeared in the back.

When the bell rang overhead, I knew we had a customer. I looked up to see a familiar face. "Hey, Cayson."

"Hey, wiener girl."

I rolled my eyes. They all teased me for working here. "What are you up to?"

"Just got out of lab and I'm starving."

"Well, you came to the right place. What can I get you?"

"You're actually going to make it?" he asked incredulously. "I thought you just did the register?"

"I can make food too."

He gave me a hesitant look. "Are you sure there's no one else...?"

"Oh, shut up. I'm pretty good."

"Unlike your mom, I don't like my food being dropped on the ground."

I laughed. "She's never going to live that down, is she?"

"Nope. My dad talks about it all the time."

I grabbed a pen and paper. "What will you have?"

"The Kaepernick dog."

"You like the 49ers?"

"No. The description just looks amazing. Chili, coleslaw, and jalapenos. I'm so there."

I smirked and wrote it down. "Coming right up."

He pulled some cash out of his wallet. "How much?"

"Don't be stupid."

"Skye, how much?" He gave me that serious look he only did on occasion. It meant he wasn't going to back down. His eyes were wide and dark.

"You're family."

"No, I'm a customer. Please let me pay."

I knew he wasn't going to let this go. "Fine." I rang him up and took the money.

"Thank you."

"Whatever." I turned away and started making the hot dog.

"I'm watching you," he warned.

"If you keep watching me, I'm going to drop it on purpose."

"Fine." He watched the TV in the corner while I finished making it. Then I put it down with a Cherry Pepsi. I knew that was his favorite. I didn't need to ask.

He smelled it. "Wow. It does look really good."

"Why are you surprised?"

He shrugged. "I didn't think you were a cook."

"Well, I can be."

He took a bite then nodded. "Excellent."

I beamed with pride as I returned to the register.

Cayson stayed at the counter and continued to eat. Comfortable silence stretched between us. He watched the TV while he ate and I did the bookkeeping.

Cayson eyed me. "How's your back doing?"

"Fine." I squared my shoulders. "When I wear a sports bra, it's not so painful. Sometimes I consider getting a boob job." I was a C cup so I wasn't humongous. I knew girls had it far worse, but since I was so petite, my back couldn't support the weight of my front.

Cayson didn't try to talk me out of it. "You should do whatever makes you comfortable. But talk to your mom first. There's no one better to ask for advice."

"Yeah. That's true."

He finished half his hot dog then took a sip of his soda. "That hot dog was good."

"You mean that wiener?" I teased.

He chuckled. "Yeah. I like to eat wieners."

"That makes two of us."

He smirked then looked at the TV again.

"I was studying in the library when Slade and Trinity went at it like they were fighting to the death."

"That sounds about right..."

"What's with them? They used to bicker occasionally but now it seems like it's happening all the time."

Cayson shrugged. "I couldn't tell you."

Something wasn't right but I couldn't put my thumb on it. "What's new with you?"

"Nothing, really. My lab partner for analytical chemistry dropped out so now I'm all alone."

Wow. Juicy. "That sucks."

"Not really. I don't like doing partner work. I usually end up doing everything anyway."

"True."

"What's new with you?"

"I have a business conference in a few weeks. I'm presenting my research on economic inflation and how it affects the trickle down theory."

"Cool." He nodded his head slowly. "That sounds like fun."

"I'm excited for it. Plus, there will be food there."

"And your father, I'm sure."

I rolled my eyes. "Of course, he'll be there too."

He caught the annoyance in my eyes. "Uncle Sean loves you, Skye. When you put it in perspective, you have to realize just how lucky you are."

"Your parents love you too."

"I know they do. And I'm exceptionally fortunate. My mom is wonderful, and my dad is the greatest guy I've ever known. You'll hear no complaints from me."

He always knew how to make me feel guilty. Any time I wanted to act like a brat, he stopped me. "He just smothers me sometimes. He does it to my mom too."

"Because that man loves you more than anything."

"He didn't smother Roland nearly the same way."

"Girls are different," he said. "Men feel the need to protect them."

"But I don't need to be protected. I can take care of myself."

"Your dad knows that, but that doesn't make it easier for him to accept." He gave me a firm look. "Just remember he loves you. Everything he does comes from a good place."

I sighed. "How do you always do that?"

"What?"

"Make me feel like crap every time I want to say something slightly bad about my family."

He shrugged. "I guess because they are my family too." He picked up the other half of his hot dog and stuffed a bite into his mouth.

I turned my gaze back to the register. The shop barely made a profit after all the bills were taken care of. It was hard to justify keeping it open sometimes. But my dad didn't care.

The bell rang overhead, and I looked up to see the new customer.

Zack came inside, wearing a tight t-shirt and jeans.

As soon as Cayson spotted him, he grabbed his food and moved to a table in the corner where he could watch TV.

Sometimes I wondered if Cayson disliked Zack. It didn't seem like anyone particularly liked him but I couldn't think of a reason why Cayson would dislike him. He never spoke to him and he never mentioned him. Cayson and I talked about everything, but my relationship.

Zack eyed him in the corner, practically glaring at him.

Okay...

"Hey, baby." He came to the counter then looked down at my chest. He always did, not at all discreet about it.

"Just because I'm your girlfriend doesn't mean you can stare at my chest all day."

"Actually, that's exactly what it means." He gave them another firm look before his eyes met mine.

"Pig..."

"Like you don't stare at my junk," he argued.

I cringed. "Actually, no, I don't."

"Sure..."

I shook my head then made a few notes.

Zack looked over his shoulder and eyed Cayson before he turned back to me. "Every time I see you, he's trailing not far behind..."

"Because we're friends." *Duh.*

"But he's always with you. Seriously, every time I see you, he's there."

I gave him a hard gaze. "Because he's family. Obviously."

"You guys aren't even related by blood."

"We're as good as." I warned him with my look.

He leaned over the counter and lowered his voice. "That guy is so hung up on you. You really don't see it?"

"No, he isn't." I clenched my jaw so I wouldn't explode. "He's practically my brother. We used to bathe together. We used to race our Hot Wheels across the carpet."

"And then you grew boobs and his dick got hard," he snapped. "I don't like this. It makes me uncomfortable and I don't want you seeing him anymore."

I dropped my pen on the counter. Anger coursed through every vein, firing off nerves. I almost sucker-punched him right then and there. "I don't care if it makes you uncomfortable. Whether Cayson has feelings for me or not, which he doesn't, does not make a difference. He's my best friend, he's my family, and he's staying. If you're going to make me choose between you and him, it will always be him."

Anger brewed in his eyes. He clenched his jaw in annoyance. "So I don't mean anything to you?"

"I didn't say that. But if you're going to act like a baby, then I don't want to be with you anyway. So, if this is going to be a problem, let's just end it now and cut to the chase."

Zack wasn't pleased by that response. Sometimes he tried to exert his power over me, tried to call the shots about what I wore and whom I hung out with, but I didn't put up with that shit. I was a strong woman who needed my independence. If he pushed too far, I pushed back.

"Do we have a problem, Zack?" I stared him down, waiting for a response.

He swallowed his pride, but it didn't go down easy. "No."

"Good." I picked up the pen again and returned to my work. "Is there a reason you stopped by?"

"What time do you get off work?"

"I don't know. Nine?"

"Why do you work here anyway?" he asked. "If you're going to inherit a multi-billion dollar company, it's pointless for you to be here."

"Pointless?" I asked. "It'll be pretty hard to run a massive company with absolutely no experience, don't you think?"

He narrowed his eyes at me. "Get experience at the company."

"No. I want to prove to my father I can handle everything on my own. Besides, I don't mind working here. I like having extra money."

"Don't you have one of your father's credit cards?" he asked incredulously. "I'm sure it has, like, a million dollar limit."

"I don't need my father's money," I snapped. "I can take care of myself."

"He pays your tuition, doesn't he?"

"I'll pay him back." Now I was getting pissed. "Why are you being an asshole right now? Don't tell me how to live my life."

"Geez, calm down."

"Geez, don't question my finances. You're the one gambling money you barely have on sports games."

Now he was angry. "Why don't you mind your own business?"

"Why don't you mind yours?" I hissed.

Zack clenched the counter while he stared me down.

"I'm getting sick of your bullshit, Zack. Get the hell out of my store. Now."

"You're kicking me out?"

"No, I'm throwing you out."

"I'm not moving." He stayed glued to the spot.

I stared him down then came around the counter. I grabbed him by the arm and yanked him. He was twice my size and height. He wasn't going anywhere.

"This is pathetic."

Rage burned inside me. I twisted his arm, hitting a pressure point. Then I pressed another one on his neck.

"Shit!" He stepped back. "What the hell did you do?"

I put my hand on my hip. "You want more?"

"Geez, I'm sorry." He held up his hands.

"Now shut up and get out." I walked back behind the counter.

He turned back to me. "Baby, I don't want to fight. I'm sorry, okay?"

"I'm so annoyed with you that I don't even want to look at you right now."

He gave me a sad look. "I'm sorry. I just don't like having you work here by yourself—at night."

"There are other workers here."

"Is that supposed to make me feel better? Guys twice your size while lover boy hovers in the lobby?"

"Don't talk about Cayson like that."

He narrowed his eyes at me. "You defend him like you love him."

"Because I do." I slammed my fist on the counter. "He's like my brother, Zack. Until you're my husband, you'll never compete with him."

"Wow. That makes me feel special." His sarcasm was heavy.

I couldn't take it anymore. "We're done, Zack."

His face turned pale. "What...?"

"You're driving me crazy and I'm sick of your bullshit. All you do is stress me out for no reason at all. I'm perfectly happy being alone. I don't need a man to make me happy, and I certainly don't need one who acts like a five-year-old."

He grabbed my arm across the counter. "Baby, I'm sorry. I'm sorry, okay? It won't happen again." His eyes were pleading. "Come on. I'm sorry."

Cayson approached us. "Skye, is everything okay?" He stared Zack down, ready to punch him in the face and break his jaw.

"Fuck off, asshole." Zack squared his shoulders then turned his look back to me.

Cayson stepped in front of me, blocking me with his immense size. "It's time for you to go."

"Get the hell out of the way, jackass." Zack's eyes burned in hatred.

This is the last thing I needed. "Knock it off. Both of you. Cayson, please sit down. Zack, just go."

Cayson didn't move. He remained idle.

"Cayson, I'm fine." I gave him a hard stare.

After a moment of silence, he returned to the table.

Zack turned his gaze on me. Then he grabbed my arm.

"Just go." I twisted my arm so he had to drop his hand.

"Please don't do this. I'll be better. I just care about you so much."

I sighed and averted my gaze.

"Baby, come on. Talk to me."

"I'm working right now."

"Then I'll be at your apartment when you get off work."

"I don't care. Just go."

"Okay." He backed away. "I'll see you then."

I didn't say another word.

With a final sad look, he left.

I got back to work and tried not to think about the way Zack pissed me off. He could really drive me up the wall. Sometimes I wasn't sure if I wanted to kiss him or rip his head off.

"Are you okay?" Cayson approached me so quickly I didn't even notice.

"Oh yeah. I'm fine."

He stared at my face intently, reading the stress in my eyes. "I know it's none of my business, but if you ever need to talk, I'm here."

My heart warmed. "I know, Cayson."

He cleared his throat. "For what it's worth, you deserve the best. And if he isn't it, then you should keep looking."

Sometimes I felt like no one liked Zack. No one ever said anything bad about him, but they never tried to hang out with him either. "Do you not like him, Cayson?"

He seemed surprised by the question. He shifted his weight for a moment. "It doesn't matter what I think—or anyone for that matter. Your opinion is the only one that counts."

"Yeah..."

"I guess I'm going to head out. But I can stay and walk you to your car if you'd like."

"No, I'll be fine. Thank you."

"Okay. Well, goodnight."

"Night."

Cayson walked out and I got back to work. When I looked at the clock, I realized the shift was almost over. I spent the entire time arguing with Zack over nothing.

Chapter Three

Cayson

Slade met me in the student lounge then sat across from me. "Yo."

"Yo." I leaned back in my chair and sighed.

"What's your deal?" he asked.

"Nothing. So, what are we up to?"

"Conrad has a table at the bar. Let's go."

"Sounds good." We left the student lounge then cut across the grounds, taking the shortest way possible to the bar. We had cars, but we hardly used them. When everything was so close, it was pointless to drive.

"I hear you and Trinity are going at it like enemies across a battlefield."

"Well, she's annoying." He put his hands in his pockets while he walked beside me. "I was just trying to eat a damn sandwich and she was throwing a hissy fit about it. It's like, leave me the hell alone."

Was I missing something? "She was mad that you were eating a sandwich...?"

"We were in the library," he explained.

Oh. Now it made sense.

"Sometimes she just won't shut up."

"Skye made it sound like something was off."

"No." He ducked under a tree. We eventually reached the sidewalk then moved up a few blocks.

I eyed him suspiciously. "If there was something going on, you would tell me, right?"

"Something going on?" he asked. "Like what?"

"I don't know. That you like Trinity or something."

"No," he blurted. "She's got a nice body and a pretty face, but no."

I decided to drop the subject.

"Besides, me being mean to her means I like her?" He shook his head. "That makes no fucking sense."

"I guess."

We walked inside then met Conrad at the bar.

Conrad fist pounded us. "The Steelers are up by a touchdown."

We sat down and waved down the bartender

"What will it be, boys?" She had blonde hair and blue eyes. Her shirt was low cut and she wore a black tie. I glanced at her, noticing her curves, and then looked away.

"Blue Moon," Slade blurted.

"Heineken, please," I said.

She smiled. "A pretty boy with manners...I like it." She winked at me then walked away.

Conrad smirked. "Why do all the girls immediately go for you first?"

"No, they don't," Slade argued. "They only go for him when they realize I'm not interested."

"Dude, she didn't even look at you," Conrad argued.

"She probably assumed a sexy beast like me already has a girlfriend," Slade argued.

Conrad rolled his eyes. "Because the tattoos really say you're a one-woman kind of guy."

He shrugged. "I could be."

I watched the TV, ignoring both of them.

Conrad's phone lit up. "Theo's coming."

"Cool," I said.

The waitress returned with our beers, but she only had eyes for me. "So, who are you cheering for?"

"The Steelers," I answered.

"Good team. Personally, I'm a Chargers type of girl."

"Everyone has their preferences." I didn't know what else to say. She was looking at me with blue eyes that were as clear as a shallow cove. Her make up made them stand out, and her lips were red. Her chest was impressive but I tried not to stare.

She leaned closer to me, ignoring the guys. "So, are you a college boy?"

"I am. How about you?"

"Am I a college boy?" she asked with a laugh.

I smirked. "I misspoke. Do you go to college?"

"No. I'm hoping to attend cosmetology school."

Was that for hair? Or nails? Something like that? "Very cool."

"And what are you studying...what was your name?"

"Cayson."

"Cayson." She said it slowly. "It's got a nice ring to it."

"And yours?"

"Jasmine."

"Oooh...Jasmine." Slade winked at me as he said it.

I shot him a glare before I looked back at her. "I'm majoring in biochemistry."

"Wow." Her eyes were wide. "I don't even know what the hell that is."

"Neither do we," Conrad said with a laugh.

"What do you plan on doing with that?" she asked.

Didn't she plan on waiting on the other tables? "I intend to go to medical school—if they accept me."

Slade laughed while he drank his beer. "If they accept you? Seriously?"

Conrad shook his head. "I doubt they would reject a Harvard graduate with a perfect GPA."

I felt my cheeks start to redden. "Anyway...enough about me."

"Please tell me you don't have a girlfriend," she blurted. "Because you're really hot and I'd like to get your number."

Did she just ask me out? I wasn't sure why this always happened to me. I hardly hit on women because they always beat me to the punch. "I...uh..."

"He doesn't have a girlfriend," Slade said. "And he would love to give you his number."

I never said that. "Whoa, hold on."

Slade took the napkin and wrote down my number. "This is his cell phone. He's out of class by five." He pushed the napkin toward her. "Here ya go."

"Thanks." She shoved it down her shirt. "I'll give you a call." She gave me a flirtatious smile then walked away.

I immediately glared at Slade. "What the hell was that?"

"You were going to turn her down," Slade argued.

"So?" I snapped.

"You always turn them down." Slade took a drink then rested his elbows on the table. "I wasn't going to let you this time. Seriously, people are going to start thinking you're gay if you reject every woman you see."

"I don't care what people think," I argued.

"Give us one good reason why you don't want to go out with her," Conrad challenged.

"I just...she isn't my type."

"Not your type?" Slade asked incredulously. "Beautiful, boobalicious, friendly—what don't you like?"

"I—I prefer brunettes."

Conrad rolled his eyes. "No, you prefer one stacked brunette."

Here it comes...

"Dude, it's never going to happen with her," Slade said. "You need to move on and start having fun."

"But how can I have a relationship with someone when I'm this hooked on someone else?" I asked.

Slade shared a look with Conrad. "Who said anything about a relationship? Just go out and have fun. Fuck her then be done with it."

That wasn't really my style.

"How are you ever going to get over Skye if you reject every woman who's interested in you?" Slade asked. "For all you know, this girl will change your life. Maybe sleeping with other women will make you realize how shitty Skye is. I don't see what you're so intrigued by. She's annoying and talks too much."

"You only see her like that because she's your cousin," I challenged. "Skye is just...amazing. She's—"

"Romeo, knock that shit off," Conrad said. "It's never going to happen. She doesn't see you like that, man. I hate to be harsh, but even if she weren't dating Zack, she wouldn't date you. You need to let it go and just move on."

Slade gave me the same firm look. "Now move on with Jasmine."

They were telling me something I already knew. Skye and I would never be together. She didn't look at me the way I looked at her. When I stared at her, I examined every feature. The freckle in the corner of her mouth drove me crazy. I'd give anything to taste it, to feel it with my tongue. When she looked at me, all she saw was a friend. Life didn't always give you what you wanted, and I needed to make my peace with it. Skye was the one woman I wanted but would never have. She was off the table. "You're right."

"Damn right, we are." Conrad clanked his glass against Slade's. "We finally got through to him."

"It's a miracle." Slade set down his glass then wiped his mouth with the back of his hand.

Theo came to our table. "You guys are already drunk. Typical."

"How else are we supposed to stand you?" Slade asked.

"Shut the hell up," Theo said. He rested his elbows on the table and watched the game.

"How was practice?" I asked.

Theo was a martial arts student. After he got more black belts than anyone could remember, he started teaching as a part-time job. "It's good. Most of the people are idiots though."

"Including you," Conrad said.

"You want me to kick your ass right now?" Theo threatened.

"You want me to slam my glass over your head?" Conrad challenged. Conrad and Trinity would inherit half the software company, and Skye and her brother Roland would get the other half. Conrad had the same beefiness as Uncle Mike, and dark eyes.

"You want my famous dad to write a parody of your dad?" Theo snapped. "Maybe your dad has more money, but mine has more intelligence."

I rolled my eyes. "Why don't we just ask our dads to take a picture of their dicks and we'll compare sizes?"

Conrad cringed. "Nah, I'm good."

"Me too," Theo said. He eyed Jasmine across the bar. "The bartender is cute. She has a nice rack."

"She belongs to Cayson," Slade blurted.

"You're hooking up with her?" Theo asked like it was the highlight of the year.

"Slade gave her my number," I explained. "She may not even call me."

"Oh, she'll call you," Slade said. "I can tell she wants to fuck the shit out of you."

I felt dirty just thinking about it.

We turned our attention to the game. Whenever the ref called the wrong foul, we cursed. The bar got noisier as time went on. I had two beers then cut myself off when I felt a little buzzed. It was a school night and I had class in the morning. When the game was finally over, we headed out.

"Cayson?"

I turned around, seeing Jasmine come toward me with her coat over her shoulders. "Leaving?"

"Yeah. The game is over."

She nodded. "Well, I just got off work. Maybe we could hang out..."

"Uh..." I turned to the guys, but they were walking away.

Slade winked then mouthed, "Fuck her or I'll kill you." The rest of the guys walked with him, ditching me.

"Do you live nearby?" Her voice caught my attention.

"I have an apartment near campus."

She nodded. "Got any roommates?"

I swallowed the lump in my throat. "No..."

"How about you show it to me? I could use some decorating ideas..." She gently placed her hand on my arm, making my hair stand on end.

A lot of women were attracted to me. Why couldn't Skye see me like that? "Jasmine, I have to be honest. I'm not looking for a relationship right now." I couldn't be a dick like Slade and the rest of the guys. They brought women back to their apartments, fucked them, and then kicked them out without ever calling them. I didn't have it in me. The guilt would eat me alive.

She smiled at me. "Any reason why?"

"I'm just...not."

"Well, I appreciate your honesty. It makes me hotter for you."

Seriously? It was that easy?

"Show me your place."

Could I really do this? Have a one-night stand with some girl I just met? I couldn't remember the last time I had sex. It was something I missed in a carnal way. But she was okay with it meaning nothing and I guess I was too. Every time I thought about Skye sleeping with Zack, it made me sick. Maybe this would make me feel better. Make me forget her. I'd do anything to see her as just a friend, someone that blended in with the crowd. I would do anything not to recognize her smell a mile away. Her freckle always caught my attention, and my eyes always took in the beautiful color of her eyes. She was my muse, a work of art I loved to stare at. I wished she meant nothing to me. Because I would never mean anything to her. I took a deep breath before I answered. "Okay."

Slade hunted me down on campus the next morning. "So...how was your night?"

"Fine." I kept walking down the hall, being vague.

"Fine? Asshole, it better have been more than fine. You better have fucked her brains out ten ways to Sunday."

A group of girls passed us, their eyebrows raised.

"Keep your voice down," I hissed.

"Who cares? So, did you?"

I stopped in the hallway then faced him. "I'm not one to kiss and tell."

He smirked. "You dog." He hit me in the shoulder. "Was she good?"

"Yeah. She was great." I shrugged. All a girl had to do to be good was be hot. And Jasmine definitely had that down.

Slade clapped. "About time. Are you gonna see her again?"

"No...I don't think so."

"You're just never going to call her?"

"Well, I told her from the beginning I didn't want a relationship."

"And she still went through with it?" he asked incredulously.

"Yeah."

"Whoa...you have better game than I give you credit for."

"I've always had game," I argued.

He rolled his eyes. "I haven't seen it in so long I can't recall. So, does that mean you really moving on?"

"I've been moving on. I just haven't made any progress until now."

"Well, progress is progress."

"Why is my personal life so interesting to everyone? When was the last time you got laid?"

"Last night, actually."

"With who?" I asked. "You didn't leave with anyone."

"Just because I didn't pick up anyone doesn't mean I didn't find someone elsewhere."

"Like, where?"

"It was a booty call."

"I thought you didn't do back-to-backs?"

He shrugged. "She's good in the sack so I made an exception."

I thought it was odd Slade didn't mention her before. He told me everything.

"Well, I got to run. I'm a busy man with women to please."

"When you say it like that, you sound like a prostitute."

"Maybe I am." He winked and headed down the hall.

I went to class, doing my best to forget about Skye forever.

Chapter Four

Skye

When I came home from class, there was a bouquet of roses on my doorstep.

"Looks like someone is cheating or apologizing." Silke looked down at the flowers with her arms across her chest.

"Since it's Zack, I'm going with apologizing," Trinity said.

"Did you guys have a falling out?" Silke asked. She tucked a strand of blonde hair behind one ear as we walked into my apartment. Even though she and Slade were twins, I didn't see the resemblance. She looked just like her mom and Slade looked like his dad.

"He just...pissed me off." That was the short version of it.

Trinity helped herself to a glass of wine. "Meaning...?"

I sighed. "He thinks Cayson has a thing for me, which is totally ridiculous."

Trinity shared a glance with Silke then smirked.

"What?" I asked. *Was I missing something?*

"Nothing," Silke said. "We've just told you the same thing for years and you never believe us."

I was sick of hearing this. "Cayson isn't into me."

"Why do we bother?" Trinity asked. "You're in denial or you really are as dumb as your brother claims."

"I'm not in denial. I know my best friend better than you do," I said.

"Forget it." Trinity waved her hand. "What were you saying?"

"Zack asked me not to see him anymore. Obviously, I told him to go to hell and get the hell out of my store. The fight just kept building until I broke up with him."

"You broke up with him?" Trinity asked incredulously. "So, you're done for good?"

"No…we didn't really break up." I felt ashamed to admit it. "I know he's obnoxious sometimes but he can be really sweet when it's just us so I figured I'd give him another chance."

"That's too damn bad," Silke said. "If he wants a woman he can boss around, then he needs to find someone else."

"I hope we don't have anymore problems," I said with a sigh. "Otherwise my head might explode."

"Or you could just dump him," Trinity said. "Skye, you're smoking hot. You could get any guy you want."

I rolled my eyes. I never heard anything more untrue in my life. "The only hot things about me are these damn tits. Other than that, I got nothing."

Trinity rolled her eyes. "Not true, but whatever."

"And I like Zack." *For the most part.*

"But do you love him?" Silke asked. "You guys have been together for months. Shouldn't that have been said by now?"

"A few months?" That was way too soon. "No. I like to take things slow. It's way too soon for that."

"You're already sleeping with him," Trinity pointed out.

I shrugged. "Well, I have needs. If I were a guy, this wouldn't be an issue."

"Good point," Silke said.

I put the flowers in a vase with water then left them on the counter. "Anyway, enough with my dull life. Should we have a Halloween party this year?"

"Duh," Trinity said. "Is that a serious question?"

"I'm in," Silke said. "And I know exactly what I'm going to be."

"Let me guess," Trinity said sarcastically. "A slutty bunny?"

"No," Silke snapped. "Something much more creative."

"A slutty nurse?" Trinity asked.

"No." Silke stomped her foot. "It has nothing to do with being slutty."

"That's boring," Trinity said. "What are you going to be, Skye?"

"I don't know..." I rubbed my palms together. "I haven't thought about it much."

"Oooh. We should have a prize for the best costume." Trinity clapped her hands. "That would be so much fun."

"I'm soo going to win that," Silke said.

"We'll see about that," Trinity challenged.

"Should we get everything this weekend?" Silke asked.

"I can't," I said. "I have a conference this weekend in Washington DC."

"A conference?" Trinity asked. "For what?"

"I'm giving a speech about small markets and inflation," I said.

Silke rolled her eyes. "Geek."

"Are you going alone?" Trinity asked.

"Yeah." I hadn't traveled alone often but I wasn't worried about it. I could figure it out.

"Like, totally alone?" Trinity asked.

Yes, Dad. "I can handle it."

"I know that." She waved her hand. "It's just that DC is one of the most dangerous cities in the country. Be careful."

"I'm always careful," I said.

"Can you take someone?" Silke asked. "I wish I could go but I can't. What about you, Trinity?"

"No, I can't go either. I didn't do my homework all week now I have to cram on the weekend."

Shocking.

"Maybe one of the guys could go?" Silke asked.

"No," I said. "I'll be fine—really."

"Does Uncle Sean know about this?" Trinity asked.

"No. But I wouldn't be surprised if he found out. That man knows what I'm doing every second of the day. It's damn annoying."

"Every second...?" Trinity cringed. "I sincerely hope not."

"You catch my meaning," I said. "Uncle Mike is the same way."

"He's protective but...stalkerish? No, I wouldn't say that," Trinity said.

"He doesn't stalk me," I said immediately. "He just knows about all my school functions even though I never mention it. Last semester, I got all A's, and he called me to congratulate me before grades were even posted."

"Probably because he paid the professors to give you good grades," Silke said with a laugh.

I glared at her. "My dad would never do that."

Trinity shrugged. "Honestly, I wouldn't put it past him."

"I earn my grades by my own merit, not with money." I refused to live any other way.

"Miss Perfect is starting to get pissy," Trinity said. "Time to change the subject."

Cayson walked through the door holding pizza boxes. "Delivery boy is here."

"And you're late," Trinity said. "Don't expect a tip."

"Well, I paid for these pizzas so don't expect to eat," he countered.

"I take that back," she said quickly. She opened the lid and took a sniff. "Heavenly..."

Cayson raised an eyebrow then looked at me. "How's it going?"

"Good. You?" I always felt comfortable around Cayson in a way I never felt with the others. I was closer to him than my own brother.

"Good." He nodded his head slowly.

Trinity shoved some pizza into her mouth. "Why don't you take Cayson with you?"

"No, it's okay," I said immediately. "I'll be fine alone."

"Take me where?" he asked.

"I have a conference in Washington DC this weekend and the girls don't want me to go alone," I explained.

"I'll go," he said immediately. "I don't have plans."

"You don't have to study?" I asked incredulously.

"No," he blurted.

"No...I'll be fine. Don't worry about it." I really didn't need anyone to come with me.

"I really don't mind," he insisted. "It'll be fun. I've never been to DC."

"I don't want to ruin your whole weekend or anything..."

"You aren't." He gave me that serious look he did the other day. "It'll be fun."

If I had to pick someone to take, it would probably be Cayson anyway. He was my best friend. "Okay."

He cleared his throat. "Zack can't go...?"

"He can't miss football." I rolled my eyes.

Cayson spotted the flowers on the counter but didn't mention them. "We leave Friday?"

"Yeah. I'll book the tickets."

"Cool. And I'll call the hotel and make sure I can get my own room."

"Good idea."

I jotted down the name of the hotel and handed it to him. He pulled out his phone and walked outside, to make the call.

"Cayson is such a sweet guy," Silke said with a sigh.

"He really is." Trinity pulled another slice out and scarfed it down.

I couldn't agree more. He'd always been there for me since we were little. I couldn't recall a time he wasn't.

"Zack is going to be so mad when he finds out you're going with Cayson." Silke shook her head. "It's going to be World War III and he's going to have to get you some bigger flowers."

I got a headache just thinking about it. Zack's jealousy drove me crazy, especially when there was nothing to be jealous about.

***

"Is this a fucking joke?" Zack's eyes were wide and his jaw was tense.

I crossed my arms over my chest, not backing down. "No. Like I said, Cayson and I are family. I've known him since I was born. If he had feelings for me, he's had twenty-one years to act on them."

"This is unacceptable! How would you feel if I went away for the weekend with a friend?"

"If she was a family friend, I wouldn't care. And we aren't going away for the weekend. It's a business conference."

"And that geek is majoring in science."

I narrowed my eyes at him. "Call him that again and I'll kick you in the nuts."

He gritted his teeth. "You treat him like he's a god."

"I treat all my family like that. I made it clear what they mean to me."

Fury burned in his eyes while he clenched his fists. He moved his hand through his hair, the muscles of his forearm tense. "I'll go with you instead. Now he doesn't need to tag along."

"I already asked you and you said you didn't want to go."

"I'd rather go than have lover boy get cozy with you."

"I told you not to call him names. Ever."

He growled then slammed his fist into his chest. "I'm going."

"No." I stepped closer to him, not intimidated. "I asked you to be there for me and you said no. You don't get to change your mind just because someone else actually cares about what I'm passionate about. That's not how it works. You missed your chance."

"And all your girlfriends weren't available? Your blood relatives? Your damn brother?"

"No, they weren't."

"I thought you could handle going by yourself."

"You would prefer if I traveled alone?" I glared at him. "That's how threatened you are by Cayson?"

"I'm not threatened by him," he snapped.

I laughed. "It sure seems like it."

He growled again then opened his mouth to speak. I cut him off before he could get anything out.

"This conversation is over. I'll see you when I get back."

"I don't think—"

"This discussion is over. If it really bothers you that I spend time with Cayson, then you should just end this relationship. I'm never going to change the way I act with him. So this is an ultimatum; accept my relationship with him or walk away." I watched his face, seeing the darkness in his eyes. I admit it was a little wrong to spend the weekend with a guy I wasn't related to, but if he trusted me, it wouldn't be an issue. I couldn't continue to have this fight over and over again. He had the right to walk away if it really bothered him that much. "What's it going to be?"

He sighed, bottling his anger. "You know what my answer is."

I waited for him to say it. "Yeah?"

"If you think I'm just going to walk away, you're mistaken."

"Then I don't want to fight about this anymore."

"Fine." He clenched his jaw. "Breaking up isn't an option."

I raised an eyebrow. That was an extremely serious thing to say. "We aren't married...couples break up all the time. If you're unhappy, then don't settle for me."

"It's not settling," he said immediately. "It's the opposite."

I loosened up a little. "So, can we put this behind us?"

"Yeah." He rubbed the back of his neck and sighed. "Have a good trip."

"I will."

"And be safe." He put his arms around my waist and kissed me.

I massaged his lips with mine.

Cayson cleared his throat.

I immediately broke the kiss, not realizing he was standing there.

Cayson didn't look directly at us. His eyes scanned the ground and the walls of the apartment. "Ready to go?"

"Yeah." I stepped inside and reached for my suitcase.

"I got it," Cayson said immediately. He grabbed everything and carried it to the car.

Zack watched him like a hawk. His eyes smoldered but he didn't say anything.

Cayson came back. "We should go. We're late as it is."

"Yeah." I turned to Zack. "I'll see you when I get back."

"Yeah." He turned to Cayson. "Take care of her."

"I will." Cayson straightened his shoulders while he stared at him.

Zack looked like he wanted to rip his throat out. But he didn't. "Bye." He walked away, heading to his car.

"Sorry about that," I said.

"No need to apologize." Cayson didn't look at me.

***

After we were in the air, I finally relaxed. Flying wasn't my favorite form of travel but I hid my unease. It was an irrational fear and something I shouldn't be concerned about.

Cayson crossed his ankle at his knee. "Thousands of planes, big and small, take off and land every day. The odds of anything bad happening to you are so low that you're more likely to get hit by lightning and win the lottery on the same day. It'll be alright."

Did I make it that obvious? Or did he just know me that well? "Yeah, you're right. I shouldn't be scared."

"It's okay. A lot of people are."

"Are you?"

"No." He looked out the window and stared at the clouds.

I settled into my seat and got comfortable. "Thanks for coming with me."

"Sure. I don't mind. But Zack didn't seem too happy..." Cayson never talked about Zack. I couldn't even recall a time when Cayson said his name out loud.

"He's...complicated."

"I hope I'm not causing any strain."

"You aren't," I said immediately.

He rested his hand on his thigh and the other on his armrest. The TV in front of the cabin was on and Ben Affleck's face was on the screen. I watched it for a moment before I grew bored. I needed to go over my presentation again but I practiced so many times my head was going to explode.

Cayson looked at me. "Can I ask you something?"

"You can ask me anything, Cay." I assumed there were no secrets between us by now.

"Do you love him?"

Cayson never asked me about my personal life. That was one subject he stayed clear of. Perhaps it was because he saw me as a sister and it made him uncomfortable. Maybe he just didn't know how to talk about it. "I don't know...I think it's too soon for that."

"Haven't you been together for six months?"

"Yeah...but love is such a strong emotion. It's not a word that should be thrown around easily."

"I agree...but you shouldn't need that long to figure out how you feel."

"What are you saying?" I asked.

"Nothing," he said immediately. "If you loved him, you would know. That's all."

I hadn't thought about it much. I had a crush on him from the moment I saw him. We had a good time together, when we weren't fighting, and there were a lot of things I liked about him. But love? I was too young for that. "Love is such a complicated thing. I doubt I'd even recognize it if I experienced it."

"You would," he said firmly. "It can't be described in a way another person would understand. It's totally subjective. And it's illogical. It doesn't make any sense. But the feeling is so paramount, so strong, that it can't be denied. If you felt it for him, you would know. Your heart would burn with pain every time he left you. And it would burn even more when he was near."

I processed his words, trying to sort them out in my mind. He spoke like he knew the emotion intimately, could recognize it even in a dark place. For as long as I could remember, Cayson didn't have any serious girlfriends. Girls popped up here and there, but no one lasted long enough to be remembered. "Have you ever been in love?"

He continued to stare out the window. He was quiet for so long I wasn't sure if he would answer. "Yes."

With who? I wasn't sure. "Who? What happened to her?"

He rubbed his chin while his eyes stared at something only he could see. "She didn't feel the same way." He didn't answer the other question.

Oh. I found that hard to believe. Cayson was the perfect guy. He was a diligent student who was ambitious and successful. He never gloated about his perfection and intelligence. He was polite to everyone who was polite to him. He was humble and down to earth. And he was good-looking. I couldn't count the number of times I caught girls looking at him. And they glared at me when they thought Cayson and I were an item. How a girl wouldn't fall head-over-heels for Cayson was beyond my comprehension. "For what it's worth, she's a damn idiot."

He chuckled. "I wouldn't say that."

"No, she is. Cayson, you're the perfect guy. I see girls stare at you all the time. Every girlfriend I've ever had wanted your digits. Maybe she was a lesbian or something."

He laughed again. "Maybe." He rubbed his chin, where a light stubble of hair was growing. "By the way, the hotel was booked for the conference so I had to make reservations for a place down the block. It's just a cab ride away."

"Down the block? Don't be ridiculous. You can stay in my room."

He stilled for a second. "I would get the floor and you would get the bed?"

"No. My room has two queens."

"Oh. If you're comfortable with that."

"We've slept together before...countless times."

"As long as you're okay with it."

"I am." I pulled a blanket over me and closed my eyes.

"I'll wake you after we land and all is safe."

"Okay." I yawned and kept my eyes closed.

***

We left the cab and walked into the hotel. "Reservation for Preston."

The woman at registration pulled up the room. "Here you are. Two nights in the presidential suite."

Huh? "No, I have a deluxe suite with two queens."

She checked again. "No, it says you were upgraded."

"But I can't afford that," I blurted. Could they just upgrade me then charge me like that?

"It's already been paid for."

Cayson chuckled. "Your father must be here."

I scowled. Only he would pull something like this. "That'll be fine. Thank you."

She handed the keys over. "Have a great stay."

"Yeah." I didn't mean to sound annoyed but I couldn't help it.

The bellman carried our bags to our room on the top floor. When we stood in the elevator, Cayson smirked.

"What?" I said.

"Your dad is hilarious."

"Sometimes I wonder if he just does this stuff to piss me off."

"He probably gets a kick out of it."

"How does my mom deal with him?"

Cayson shrugged. "Love makes people crazy."

"Insane, actually. She must be off her rocker to love such a madman."

Cayson rubbed the back of his neck. "I like Uncle Sean. He's definitely a man who has my respect."

"You're only saying that because he's family."

"No."

I sighed. "Well, Slade really is an idiot. He actually pulled Trinity's hair in the library."

Cayson laughed. "I feel like we are five-year-olds and playing in the sandbox all over again."

"Remember when I put sand down Roland's pants and he cried?"

"Could never forget it." He smirked.

The doors opened and we finally entered our room. The size of the suite was bigger than the average house. It had a full kitchen, two living rooms, and a master bedroom.

I rolled my eyes. "Seriously? We're not even going to be in the room most of the time."

Cayson walked to the center table and saw the enormous bouquet of flowers. "Skye, I think these are for you."

I came closer then stared at the white lilies. They were in full bloom and smelled like a summer day. I opened the card.

Skye

I'm sorry about the room. But my daughter doesn't deserve anything less. I'm flying in tomorrow and I'll see you then.

P. S. I hope you like the flowers. They are your mother's favorite.

I dropped the note on the counter. "He's something else…"

"He just loves you."

"I know..."

Cayson gave me a serious look. "You never let the wealth get to you, and you choose to be independent. You never take that for granted, and I respect you for it. But don't take for granted the most important thing in the world, your father and mother. Sometimes he's over the top, but a lot of daughters would kill to have a father who loved them as much as he loves you. Don't forget that."

I sighed. "I know, Cayson."

"I'm known for my wisdom as well as my dashing looks." He walked away then moved to his suitcase near the couch.

I picked up a lily and brought it close to my nose, smelling it. I knew my father was crazy, but his intensity came from a good place. He could drive my mom up the wall, but he also made her love him even more every day.

"I'll take the couch," Cayson said.

"Okay. Too bad we don't have our original room. It would have worked out perfectly."

"No, this is better. It's a pull out bed."

"Good. That worked out."

Cayson took out his phone and typed a message to someone.

"Hungry?" I asked.

"Starving."

"Want to go out to dinner?"

His thumb hit the screen a few times. "There's a nice restaurant in the lobby."

"Black tie?"

"Yeah." He put his phone back in his pocket. "You want to go?"

"Sounds good to me."

***

After I showered and got ready, I walked out and saw Cayson sitting on the couch. He was wearing slacks and a button up shirt.

"Ready?"

He looked up and took me in. His eyes widened slightly before they returned to normal. He stood up then turned off the TV. "Yep."

I grabbed my purse off the counter then walked in my heels to the door. I was wearing a black dress that only had one shoulder. There was slight padding in the dress to support my chest. But it was nice not to wear a bra.

Cayson opened the door for me then let me walk out first. We took the elevator to the ground floor.

"What kind of food do they have?" I asked.

"Steak, greens, stuff like that."

"Good."

We were led to a table where Cayson pulled out the chair for me. He always did that no matter where we were. I was used to it. When Zack didn't do it, it threw me off sometimes.

I immediately grabbed the wine list. "Would you judge me if I ordered alcohol?"

"I never judge you for ordering alcohol."

"I knew we were friends for a reason."

He smirked while he stared at me.

The waitress arrived at our table. "Good evening."

"Hi," I said.

"Special occasion?" she asked. "An anniversary perhaps?"

I tried not to laugh. "Oh no, we're just friends."

Relief filled her eyes. "Oh, I see." She gave Cayson a long smile before she turned back to me.

Well, at least she made sure he wasn't taken first.

"Can I get you a drink?" she asked.

"I'll have a chardonnay."

"Excellent choice." She turned to Cayson. "And for you?"

"Whatever you have on tap."

"You got it." She walked away.

Cayson didn't stare at her ass. His eyes were glued to mine.

"She was cute." Her blonde hair was in a French braid and she had nice lips. I wasn't gay, but I knew an attractive woman when I saw one.

Cayson didn't respond. He looked at his menu and browsed the selections.

"So, are you seeing anyone right now?"

He stilled at the question. "No."

It was impossible to get anything out of him when it came to this subject. "Do you hit it and quit it like Slade?"

He cocked an eyebrow while he looked at me. "Hit it and quit it?"

"Isn't that what they used to say?"

He smirked. "I'm not like Slade. I thought that was obvious."

"But you never talk about girls with me. You tell me everything else but that."

He shrugged. "There's not much to say."

"Come on. You must have some juicy stories."

He seemed uncomfortable. "I don't have an active personal life like other people do."

"Is it because you're too busy with school?"

"Yeah…"

I looked through the entrees until I selected the New York sirloin. I put the menu aside. "Is there a reason why you're so quiet about it?"

"No. I just don't have much to say."

"Okay, you can't be celibate."

"Well…no."

Why was he being weird about this? "When was the last time you had sex?"

His eyes widened slightly. "Uh...that's a personal question."

"We tell each other everything. Why is this the only subject you aren't comfortable discussing?"

He pressed his lips together but said nothing.

"I'm sorry. I didn't mean to make you uncomfortable." I backed off and looked at the menu again even though I already knew what I was getting.

"You didn't. You're right—we tell each other everything. I guess I'm just not a kiss and tell type of guy."

"It's your privacy and I respect it. You don't have to tell me anything."

He sighed then leaned back. Conflict was in his eyes. He was battling for a decision, trying to make up his mind about something. His fingers drummed the surface of the table. "I had sex last week."

He was finally opening up. "With who? Someone I know?"

"It was a woman I met at a bar."

"How was she?"

His cheeks reddened slightly. "No complaints."

This guy was as unreadable as a tree. "Are you going to see her again?"

"No. She's not my type."

"What does that mean?"

He shrugged. "She's just not a woman I see myself falling for."

"Any reason why?"

"No...the chemistry just isn't there."

I nodded. "I feel like that's all Zack and I have."

He stared at me but kept his mouth closed.

"He's okay in bed. He does this thing that makes me—"

"Stop." He said it like he was in pain. "Sorry, I just...it makes me uncomfortable."

"Okay..." I even told my brother about my sex life and he didn't cringe and practically gag.

Cayson became flustered. "Sorry...I guess I see you as a sister and it's weird..." His voice was at a different pitch and tone. He didn't sound like him.

"It's okay. I didn't mean to make you uncomfortable."

"Let's just...talk about something else."

"Okay."

The waitress returned with the drinks and took our order. She batted her eyes at Cayson then smiled like her life depended on it. When she walked away, Cayson still didn't look at her.

"How's school?" I asked.

"It's good. Pretty uneventful."

"I barely passed my biology class last semester."

"Didn't you get an A?" he asked with a laugh.

"But it was hard. I had to go to tutoring and everything."

He smirked. "Well, you did well and that's all that matters."

"I need to get good grades otherwise I won't get the company."

He cocked an eyebrow. "I'm sure your father would give it to you even if you were an idiot."

"I don't know about that..."

"You're his star in the sky. It's a safe bet."

"He could give it to Roland."

"I'm sure there's room for both of you."

"Actually, I don't think Roland even wants it. I'm not sure what he wants..."

"We all walk our own path."

The waitress set the plates on the table. As soon as the aroma hit my nose, I started to salivate. She gave him a smirk again before she walked away.

Okay, now she was trying too hard.

Cayson cut into his chicken. "How do you like your food?"

"It's good." I was eating too much to pause for a more detailed response.

He smirked. "I can tell."

We ate quietly until our plates were clean. I ate like I hadn't in weeks. That plane ride erased my appetite, but it picked up again once we were on solid ground.

Cayson finished first then looked across the restaurant, staring at nothing in particular.

I wiped my mouth then caught my breath. "Damn, that was good."

He chuckled. "Now I judge you."

I hit his arm playfully. "I hadn't eaten all day."

"Even so..."

I hit his arm again.

The waitress brought the tab. "Thank you. Have a good night."

"Thank you." Cayson took the tab and placed his card inside.

"Let's split it," I offered.

He rolled his eyes. "Ignore her." He handed the tab back to the obsessed waitress.

"You got it." She walked away and headed to the register.

"You should let me pay," I said. "You came all the way here just to support me."

"No. If my father taught me anything, it was to never let a girl pay, whether you are sleeping with her or not." He stared me down. "How long have we known each other?"

I shrugged. "Twenty years."

"And when have I ever let you pay?"

"You let me buy you an ice cream from the ice cream truck one time."

"Besides that."

I sighed. "Never."

"That's right."

I rolled my eyes.

The waitress returned with the card and the receipt. "Thank you. Have a good night."

"Thanks," Cayson said.

She pulled a napkin out of her pocket and pushed it toward him. "Give me a call sometime." She smiled then walked away.

Cayson glanced at it then put his card in his wallet.

"Are you going to take that?"

"No."

"Why?"

"I don't live in Washington DC in case you didn't notice..."

"I have a feeling she doesn't care."

Cayson stood up, ignoring the napkin.

He was an enigma sometimes.

We headed back to the room.

"*I Love Lucy* marathon until we fall asleep?" I asked.

"Which will be in five minutes for you," he teased.

"No," I argued. "I can be a night owl when I want."

"Yeah, right." He kicked off his shoes then sat on the couch. He turned on the TV then leaned back.

I changed then joined him on the couch. My hair was pulled back and I was wearing my flannel pajamas but I knew Cayson didn't care about my appearance. He'd seen me without make up hundreds of times.

I lay down on one side of the couch and pulled the blanket over me.

"Twenty bucks says you're asleep in five minutes."

"You're on." I kept my eyes glued to the TV.

Within minutes, I felt the heaviness leak in. My eyes wanted to close and my breathing changed. I tried to fight it but I couldn't. The darkness descended.

"Good night, Skye."

I wasn't sure if I really heard that.

**

When I woke up, I was in my bed. Cayson must have carried me and tucked me in at some point. Now I owed him twenty bucks. Damn.

I showered and got ready for the conference, wearing a new pencil skirt. I bought a new pink blouse that I liked because it kept everything tucked in and tight. My breasts didn't look nearly as big.

I clicked diamond earrings to my earlobes and made sure my hair was as presentable as possible. My father got me a gold bracelet with my name engraved into the medal, and I usually wore it to any fancy occasion.

When I left my room, Cayson was wearing slacks and a dark blue button up. "You look nice."

"Not as nice as you." He eyed my legs and looked away.

"I hope I can last in these heels. Me and stilettos don't mix well."

"I'll make sure you don't fall."

"Thanks." I grabbed my laptop and placed it into my bag.

"Nervous?" he asked.

"A little."

"Can I get you something? There's a Starbucks down the street. I can get you a coffee."

"No, it's okay. I'm sure there will be snacks downstairs."

"Okay." He stood up and adjusted his tie. "Are you ready?"

"As ready as I'll ever be."

He took the bag off my shoulder and put it on his. "I got it."

"You don't need to—"

"Don't argue with me." He opened the door and waited for me to walk through.

"Someone's bossy today..."

"Someone owes me twenty dollars today."

I blushed. "I guess I was more tired than I realized."

He smiled. "It was a long flight. I'll let you off the hook—this one time."

We took the elevator down to the lobby then headed to the conference hall. The crowd was swarming in the entrance, talking and greeting each other. I didn't know anybody so I kept walking with Cayson.

When we got inside, there was a designated area for coffee and snacks, and the rest of the room was the auditorium with rows of chairs. A chandelier hung in the center of the room, and stairs led to the seating area below. It was fancy for a conference. The hardwood floors contrasted against the white banisters of the stairway, and the dark lighting illuminated the room just right.

Everyone was wearing suits and dresses, looking professional. I read the nametags people wore as I walked by. Numerous influential and inspiring professors and experts were in the crowd.

Cayson whistled. "Wow. This is fancy."

"I know, isn't it?"

"I think I picked the wrong major." He nodded toward the coffee cart. "I don't get free food in the chemistry department."

I rolled my eyes. "What you're studying is far more important than what I'm studying."

"I couldn't disagree more." He eyed the coffee. "Can I get you something?"

"No, it's okay. I'm too nervous right now."

"Alright." He stood with me while we watched the crowd move. He looked at his watch. "It's starting soon."

"Good. I just want to get this over with."

"You voluntarily signed up for this."

"Yeah, but I always get nervous right before public speaking."

"You shouldn't be. You're very good at it."

I rolled my eyes. "You're just trying to make me feel better."

"Would you prefer if I said you sucked and you were going to embarrass yourself?" He smirked at me.

"No, I prefer the other one."

"In that case, you're going to do great."

"I feel so much better now," I said sarcastically.

The crowd suddenly shifted as someone came through the entryway. A few people approached him and shook his hand, talking to him quickly. The room was too saturated for me to get a good look, but he wore a suit and he was fairly tall.

Cayson eyed the door. "Gee, who could that be?"

My dad parted the crowd then spotted me. Looking cool and calm, he kept one hand in his pocket and walked with his back perfectly straight. His tie was dark blue just like his eyes, and his Rolex shined in the light. The white gold band of his wedding ring looked small on his large hands. Like he owned the room and everyone in it, he came to my side then looked into my face, the fondness and affection evident.

Time had hardly weathered his skin, and faint lines that were almost invisible marked the area around his lips and eyes. His skin was fair like he stayed out of the sun, and his shoulders were still broad and muscular. Every day after work, he went to the same gym he'd been going to for years. He was thin and toned, still carrying the vigor of someone in his youth. Our features weren't similar with the exception of our eyes. Those were the same, identical.

My dad wrapped his arms around me and gave me a long hug, squeezing me tightly. "You look lovely."

I pulled away. "Thanks. Mom got me the blouse."

"She has good taste."

"And she knows how to hide a chest."

He smirked. "Yeah, I'm not sure why she bothers." He stared at me like he hadn't seen me in years—like he might never see me again. I recalled the day I left for college. My dad smiled and was supportive, but my mom told me he got teary-eyed the moment I drove away. It was the same look he gave me now.

He turned to Cayson. "It's nice to see you."

Cayson extended his hand. "Hey, Uncle Sean."

My dad raised an eyebrow when he looked at his hand. Then he pulled him in for a hug. "You're getting big."

"Hitting the gym with Slade."

"Because that guy needs to look more threatening," he joked. He pulled away then patted Cayson on the back. "Thanks for coming with Skye."

"I don't mind."

My dad put his hands in his pockets then returned his focus to me. "How's the room?"

"Ridiculous. We aren't even going to be in there very often."

"We?" Hardness came into his voice. My dad was psycho when it came to boys.

"Cayson and I. They didn't have any other rooms available."

His shoulders relaxed visibly. "Oh."

Only Cayson or someone else from the family could get a reaction like that. "Mom isn't coming?"

"No. I wanted it to be just us."

"Oh." My mom was my best friend. She would come down on the weekends from time to time and we would go shopping then stay up all night drinking wine. It was something only she and I did. My father and I shared our passion for business.

"I'm sorry to disappoint you." Sadness was in his eyes.

"No, you didn't," I said immediately. "I was just curious."

His eyes lightened slightly.

"How did you know I was here?" I asked.

"There's nothing my children do that I don't know about." He looked around the room, eyeing everyone in our vicinity. He was like a shark, watching the school of fish around him but not really interested.

"That's not creepy…"

"You know what I mean, pumpkin."

"I didn't even invite you to this. You just show up out of nowhere—like a phantom."

He shrugged. "I'm mysterious. Is your brother here?"

"I thought you knew what we did every second of the day?" I challenged.

He smirked. "I'm not as concerned for his safety as I am with yours."

"Because I'm a girl?" I asked incredulously. "I'm very capable of taking care of myself."

"I know." He kept his hands in his pockets. "But I like to ease my mind."

"No, you're just sexist. You treat Mom the same way."

"If being sexist means I care about my girls, then fine. I guess I am sexist." A flash of irritation filled his body, tensing noticeably.

"You don't care. You're totally controlling," I argued.

My dad clenched his jaw. "I'm just protective. Your mother has been through a lot. It's something I'll never forget."

Been through a lot? What did that mean? "What happened to Mom?"

He looked away. "The conference is starting soon. Nervous?"

Was he trying to change the subject? "Dad, tell me."

"Mr. Preston?" An elderly man came to his side. "It's so nice to see you here." He shook his hand vigorously. "When I told everyone you were coming, a hundred more people registered. Isn't that delightful?"

My dad kept a polite face. "It is. I'm glad to hear it."

"Can we talk more later?"

"Sure." I knew my father had no interest in that.

The man left, leaving us alone again.

"Having a zillion-dollar empire has its drawbacks, huh?" Cayson asked.

"Like you wouldn't believe." My dad's voice was calm but the intensity shined through.

A group of girls approached the food line, talking loudly and not bothering to keep their voices down. "God, he is so hot."

They must be talking about Cayson.

"I'd fuck Mr. Preston in a heartbeat."

What? Eww!

"Too bad he's married," another one said.

"Like I care," the first one said.

If I heard it, so did my dad. *Damn, that was awkward...*

Cayson smirked. "You still got it, huh?"

My dad didn't seem amused. "According to my wife I do."

My dad had always been weird around other women. He was so stern and rigid, like he was afraid to talk to them or even be polite. He wouldn't even reciprocate a hug most of the time. My mom kept him on a tight leash and he was well behaved. Growing up, I had a lot of girlfriends with parents that divorced. The father usually cheated and the relationship unraveled. I was grateful my parents were nothing like that. My dad had money and I wasn't stupid. He went on trips often, but he always took my mom with him. It would be easy for him to have an affair, but I knew he never would. He was too loyal and devoted to his marriage. I respected my dad for a lot of things, but I respected him for that the most.

"Looks like they are about to start." He eyed the stage and the people taking their seats. "I'll see you afterwards."

"Okay."

He kissed my forehead. "You'll do great, pumpkin. I know you will."

"Thanks, Dad."

He walked away, one hand in his pocket. Everyone turned and stared, watching him take his leave. My father had a commanding air about him. He wasn't famous, but he certainly was a celebrity. Being the owner of the third most profitable company in the known world certainly made him an interesting person. And the fact he was so private about his personal life made him more mysterious. I understood why he was so protective of me and my mom. If people wanted something from him, they would go through us. Despite his wealth, money didn't seem important to him. The only things he cared about were my brother and I and our mom. And our extended family.

"Uncle Sean is so cool," Cayson said.

"Why?"

"He can command an entire room with his silence. That's pretty damn impressive."

"It's only because he's rich."

"No. If he were a rich idiot, he wouldn't ring with authority. His intelligence and suaveness is what catches people's eyes. There's nothing that happens under his nose he doesn't know about. Because everything is under his thumb. Being raised by him will make you a relentless businesswoman, I'm sure."

When I thought about it, I realized my father and I were a lot alike. We both craved control and independence. We both commanded respect with little effort. When something threatened us, we didn't take a defensive stance. We attacked. We were both cruel and malicious when we needed to be, but our hearts were golden any time it allowed. Maybe that was why my father and I butted heads more often than me and Mom—because we are the opposite sides of the same coin.

Cayson and I took a seat and listened to the other presentations. A lot of students had interesting research projects, and I learned a great deal about the open market and exchanges. There was a lot to business I wasn't sure about. It was something I had to learn with experience, but hearing tales from other people made me see things in a different way.

When my turn came, I walked to the podium and kept my back straight. Then I set up my laptop and began my speech. Before I spoke publicly, I was always nervous. My hands would sweat and I'd get anxious. But as soon as my mouth opened, that fear disappeared. I owned the stage just like my father did in meetings. I didn't let anyone intimidate me no matter how hard they tried. My father was the biggest shark in the sea, and he taught me to be the same way.

When my presentation ended, I received a loud round of applause. I released the air from my lungs, letting the stress ebb away. It felt good to finish, and even better knowing I did the best I could.

I returned to my seat beside Cayson.

"You were awesome," he whispered.

"Are you just saying that to make me feel better?" I teased.

"Yes. You totally bombed." He smirked at me, his eyes bright. "But I'm still your friend."

"My family, actually." I grabbed his hand and squeezed it.

As soon as we touched, I felt his fingers flinch. It only lasted for a second before his fingers went still. His hand was warm to the touch, and so much bigger than mine. His thumb lightly trailed over my knuckles in the split second we touched. Then I dropped my hold, feeling cold all over again.

We sat quietly while the rest of the presentations continued. My stomach was starting to growl, and I heard it rumble in my ears.

Cayson smirked at me then nudged me in the stomach. "Could you keep it down?" he teased.

"Shut up," I whispered. "It's out of my control."

It growled again. *Damn it.*

He chuckled. "We'll get something to eat as soon as this is over—if you can last."

"I can." I crossed my arms over my stomach, hoping it would drown out the sound.

When the lights flickered back on, the conference was over.

"Thank god. I'm starving."

"What's new?" Cayson joked.

We rose from our chairs then headed toward the exit. Like my father had me on radar, he joined my side and walked with me, towering over me. He didn't speak to me, just moving with the crowd. Everyone stared at him, getting a good look at his face.

When we moved off to the side, away from prying eyes, my father relaxed slightly. Anytime he was in public, he was different, stern. Whenever we were in the privacy of our home, he was relaxed and buoyant. He always had to put on a face for the public. "You did a great job. I'm very proud."

"Thanks, Dad."

He put his arm around my shoulder and stood beside me. Then he pulled out his phone and handed it to Cayson. "Please take a picture of us."

"Sure." He stepped back and held the camera up.

A group of girls walked by. "So cute!"

It seriously grossed me out that the girls were my age and they wanted my dad. Disgusting...

We both smiled and Cayson took the picture.

"Thank you." My father took the phone back and put it in his pocket. "Pumpkin, are you hungry?"

"Do you not know me at all?" I asked sarcastically.

For the first time, he chuckled. "You are your mother's daughter."

"I couldn't agree more," I said.

"Can I take you to dinner?" he asked.

"Sure. Cayson can come too, right?"

"Of course." My dad patted his shoulder. "He's another son."

Cayson nodded. "Thanks, Uncle Sean. I appreciate it. But I'm going to stay in tonight."

"Why?" I asked.

"Spend some time with your dad. He doesn't see you as often as I do." Cayson stepped away. "I'll see you when you get back."

"No, we want you to come with us," I argued.

"Well, too bad." He winked then walked back toward the room.

My dad put his hands in his pockets and waited for another surge of people to pass. "Any requests?"

"Hmm...I eat anything."

He smirked. "Well, that makes it easy." He pulled out his phone and looked at the nearby restaurants. "There's an Italian place just down the road."

"That works for me."

"Then let's go." He walked beside me and held the door open for me as we stepped outside. The valet didn't even ask who he was. "Your car will be here in just a moment, Mr. Preston."

"Thank you," he said politely.

The guy hurried into the underground garage like my dad might shoot him if he wasn't fast enough. My dad intimidated everyone.

A slight chill in the air blew through my hair. My dad took off his jacket and placed it around my shoulders.

"Thanks." I tightened it around me.

"You're welcome."

The car was retrieved. It was a two-seater Sear, the most expensive luxury car in the world. My dad splurged on a new car every few years. He always had to have the top of the line stuff, probably to keep up appearances.

The valet reached for the passenger door but my dad got there first. "Allow me."

"Of course, sir." He stepped away so my father could get me in the car. Then he shut the door.

I saw my dad slip the valet a hundred dollar bill.

He was always a generous tipper.

Once my dad was behind the wheel, he drove to the restaurant a few streets over.

"I thought you flew to DC?"

"This is a rental."

"It looks identical to yours."

"Which is why I got it." He pulled in front of the restaurant and the valet took the car. Like always, my dad opened every door and pulled out the chair for me. His impeccable manners reminded me of Cayson. He was the same way.

I picked up the menu and looked at the selections. I was starving so I would eat anything at that point.

My dad glanced at it then put it down again.

"You already know what you're going to get?" I asked incredulously.

"A salad."

"That's what you always order."

He shrugged. "Your mom likes the way I look. I don't want that to change."

"Mom eats like a pig and she doesn't look different."

He smirked. "She's blessed in a way I'll never be."

I looked at the menu then made my decision. "Where is the waitress? I'm about to eat this table."

"Please don't. Humans are unable to digest cellulose."

Huh? "Sorry?"

"Never mind."

The waitress made her appearance. And the second she saw my dad, she was smitten.

Ugh, this is so annoying.

"Good evening, sir. Taking your girlfriend out?"

Girlfriend? I was half his age. "Daughter."

"Oh, my mistake." She smiled then took out her pad of paper, ready to take our order.

"I'll have the pear gorgonzola salad," my dad said politely.

"You watch your weight," the woman said. "And it shows..."

I'm going to gag.

"And you, kid?"

Kid? "I'll have the meat lasagna."

"Excellent choice." She turned back to Dad. "Anything else, sir? Some wine, perhaps?" She shifted her weight and shook her hips at the same time. She batted her eyelashes and stuck out her chest.

Did she not see his wedding ring? "Could you not hit on my dad for a second so we can have dinner together?" I was hardly catty, but this obvious disrespect really pissed me off. His wedding band was in plain sight.

My dad smirked, amused.

The waitress scowled. "Of course." Then she turned on her heel and walked away.

She was totally going to spit in my food.

"Thank you," he said.

"Does that happen all the time?"

"Pretty much." He said it like he was bored.

"Geez, it must drive Mom up the wall."

He laughed. "No, she doesn't lose any sleep over it. Your mother knows she has nothing to worry about."

My parents were still in love even all these years later. My dad looked at my mom like she was the only thing that mattered. He often tucked her hair behind her ear then kissed the shell. He still held her hand when they walked anywhere.

"If some girl was hitting on my boyfriend like that, I wouldn't be so cool about it."

My dad gave me a hard look, examining me like I was under a microscope. "You have a boyfriend?"

Shit. "No...I just meant hypothetically." I hated lying to my dad. It wasn't something I usually did, but I didn't want to introduce a guy to my father unless he was the man I wanted to spend the rest of my life with. My dad was overprotective to the point of insanity. I didn't want to deal with his aggression every time I was seeing someone. I'd rather only go through it once, and I wasn't sure if Zack was the one... It was too soon to tell.

He continued to stare at me. It was like he could see right through me. If he knew everything about me, he probably already knew I was dating someone even though that would be a huge violation of privacy. But he didn't question it. "Is there a reason why you've never had a boyfriend? Or are you lying to me?" The intensity settled over his eyes and darkness shined.

Sometimes my father scared me. He never yelled or raised his voice, but his quiet intimidation was worse. And the disappointed look on his face just made me feel lower than dirt. "If you know everything about me, you should be able to answer that question."

"I know every professor you have. I know every crime committed on campus and within a three-mile radius from your apartment. I know every single neighbor and their criminal record. I made sure there isn't a single sexual predator within ten miles of you by personally having them removed. I know what your class schedule is, and I know all of your academic activities. Yes, I keep tabs on you. I won't deny that. But I've never stuck my nose into your personal life nor will I ever. Your business is your business."

Now I felt like a jerk. My dad was psychotic but I guess he wasn't as crazy as I thought.

"Being two hours away makes me concerned for your safety. It's my job to take care of you. I—"

"I'm an adult. No, it isn't."

"Don't. Interrupt. Me. Again."

I fell silent, knowing I couldn't match my dad in a fight. Like a lawyer, he could turn everything around on me. And like a genius, he was always one step ahead of me.

"I will always look after you, even if I can't physically be there. That's my job and I take it very seriously. I pay attention to your school activities because I will never miss anything that's important to you, whether you want me to be there or not." He stared me down, not blinking.

"I'm sorry."

"What are you apologizing for?"

I wasn't sure.

"For interrupting me? Or for lying to me?"

This just got tense. My dad could be the scariest guy in the world. He babied me because I was his daughter, but he didn't go easy on me when he was upset. He gave me the same dark look he gave my brother. He was the only person

I knew who was more intimidating when he was calm than when he was angry.

"Skye, why don't you tell me about your school functions? Why do I have to show up uninvited?" He rested his hands in his lap.

"I know you're busy..."

"I'm never too busy for you."

"I know you have a lot going on and I don't want you to drop everything for me."

He paused before he spoke. "You want to know something your grandfather taught me?"

"Sure..."

"Work can never be more important than family. It's just a job, Skye. I will never skip out on my family to work. Nothing is more important than you, Roland, and your mother. I don't come to these things out of obligation. I come because I want to be here. I will never miss a dance recital or a business conference. I will always be there. Don't ever worry about me being busy."

I looked down at the table, unable to meet his gaze.

"Have you ever called me and I didn't answer?"

"No..."

"Have you ever had any event that I wasn't there for?"

"No."

"Holiday?"

My voice became weak. "No."

"That will never change, Skye. You know what I want?"

"What?"

"For you to call me and invite me. I'm sorry I did something to make you think you were bugging me, because you never have. I hope this talk straightened that out."

"It did." I looked up again.

"Skye, I love you so much. Somehow I love you more every day. You're such a beautiful girl, just like your mother. You're smart and funny. Sometimes I can't believe I made you." The affection was in his eyes. "You're my whole world. Somehow, I love you, your brother, and your mother more than anything else on this planet."

"I love you too, Dad." He was making me teary-eyed.

He reached across the table and put his hand on mine. He left it there for a moment before he pulled away. "Now, can we try this again?"

I sighed. "Okay."

"Do you have a boyfriend?"

Ugh. I couldn't lie to him again. "No comment."

He cocked an eyebrow. "What?"

"I don't want to talk about my personal life with you."

"Why?"

"Do I really need to answer that? When my date picked me up for prom, you threatened to kill him if he touched anything besides my hand."

"I just wanted to get my point across."

"So what makes you think I would tell you about a guy I'm seeing?"

He didn't have a response to that. He pressed his lips together tightly. "Do you talk to your mother about it?"

I wasn't sure how to answer that. I didn't want to throw my mom under the bus.

He caught the unease. "I won't be upset if you say yes."

"I do."

"Are you honest with her?"

"Yes." What did that mean?

He nodded. "Okay. I'm okay with that."

Was I missing something? "Okay with what?"

"If your mother thought you were making bad decisions, she would intervene. If she hasn't, that means you're being a responsible young adult."

"Of course, I am."

"So, when will I meet a boyfriend?"

I shrugged. "I don't know. When I find the right one."

He nodded. "Okay. That sounds fair."

"I just hope you don't scare him away."

He smirked. "If he really loves you, nothing will scare him off."

"There's no love strong enough."

The waitress appeared and set my dad's plate in front of him. Then she practically threw mine at me. She gave me a deep scowl then marched away, her anger evident in her swaying hips.

My dad smirked then switched our plates. "I have a feeling she spit in yours."

"And you're going to eat it?"

"I'm certainly not going to let my daughter eat it."

I picked up my fork and picked at the lettuce. "Couldn't you order something...better?"

"Your mom thinks I'm sexy. I want her to keep thinking that."

I cringed. "You're gross."

"I'm gross? How do you think you got here?"

I cringed again. "Let's just eat in silence."

He picked up his fork and took a few bites, eating slowly.

The comfortable silence stretched between us. We ate quietly, just enjoying each other's company. Even though we always butted heads, I was glad it happened. I felt closer to my dad, finally comfortable admitting that I did have boyfriends. And the fact he accepted it made me feel better. The guilt was gone. I didn't feel like I needed to lie to him, which I never liked doing. "Dad?"

"Pumpkin?"

"I don't just love you because you're my dad. You're the best role model I could ever ask for. You're ruthless and ambitious but you're generous and kind. You love Mom every single day and never take her for granted. You raised me and Roland not to be spoiled brats, and you loved us even when we were brats anyway. You put us first every single time, not caring about yourself. I'm so lucky to have you. I know most kids don't have relationships with their fathers. A lot of dads don't care about softball games and dance recitals. They don't make an effort to always be there. But you do." I picked at my salad and looked at my bowl, suddenly feeling self-conscious. When he didn't say anything, I looked up.

A slight coat of moisture was visible in his eyes. Red was stained in the corners, growing more prominent with every passing second. He swallowed the lump in his throat, the emotion evident. When he blinked, the moisture disappeared. It happened so quickly I wasn't sure if I saw it. "That means the world to me, Skye."

I looked back down and ate my salad. I felt my father's gaze burn my skin for a few seconds. Then he turned his attention to his own food, sinking back to the comfortable silence between us.

Chapter Five

Cayson

I ordered room service and ate pizza while I watched TV. I made sure it was charged to my credit card so Uncle Sean wouldn't get a bill for it. I doubt he would notice, and if he did, he wouldn't care, but that didn't matter to me.

My phone rang and I looked at the screen, seeing my dad's name. I rolled my eyes. He called me more often than my mom. "Hey."

"Hey. How's it going?"

"Good. You?"

"Good. I hear you're in DC."

"Sean?"

"Well, we work together. It was bound to come up."

"But I didn't see him until today."

"It's called a text message."

"Dad, are you calling for a reason?"

"Just to check on you."

"I've been out of the house for three years. You don't need to check on me anymore."

He laughed. "Yeah, that will never happen. So, doing okay in the crime capital of the nation?"

"And you think New York is any safer?"

"It's safer than DC. Actually, everything is."

"Well, I'm not sitting on the curb and counting my cash so I think I'll be okay."

"Do you ever get tired of being a smartass?"

"I guess I hang out with Slade too much, right?"

"Just a smidge."

"Well, I'm doing okay so I'll talk to you later."

"When are you going back to Boston?"

"Tomorrow night."

"Can you do me a favor and call me when you get home?"

He was like a mother hen sometimes. "How about I just text you since you're so fond of it?"

"As long as I know you're safe, I don't care how you tell me."

"Okay."

"I love you, Son."

My dad said it every time we got off the phone. "I love you too, Dad."

"Bye."

I hung up.

The door opened and Skye walked inside, her father behind her.

"Thanks for dinner," she said.

"Thank you for letting me walk you to the door."

"Well, you didn't give me much of a choice." She rolled her eyes.

He smirked then hugged her, holding her for a long time. Even if Uncle Sean never said it, I knew how much he loved his daughter. He reminded me of my own father. He pulled away and kissed her forehead. "I love you, pumpkin."

"I love you too, Dad."

He turned to me. "I need a hug before I leave."

"Coming right up." I walked to him then embraced him.

Uncle Sean hugged me just as hard as he hugged his own daughter. "I love you too, kid."

"I love you too."

He clapped my shoulder and stepped away. "Thanks for escorting my daughter. I appreciate it."

"No problem. She's pretty cool— sometimes."

He chuckled. "Good night." He stepped out of the door then shut it behind him.

Skye immediately slipped off her heels. "God, my feet are killing me."

"Foot massage?"

"No, it's okay." She limped to the couch then sat down. She examined the bottom of her feet, rubbing her thumbs into them.

I sat beside her. "Allow me. You just kicked ass tonight. You deserve some respite."

"No, it's—"

I pulled her feet into my lap and rubbed the muscle.

"Fucking amazing..." She leaned back and closed her eyes.

I chuckled then massaged her heel and the pad of her foot. Her feet were so small in my hands. A single hand was bigger than both of her feet put together. She was so petite and small.

She sighed quietly while I rubbed the aches and pains away.

"How was dinner?"

"Good. My father knows I have a boyfriend."

"Because of his spies."

"No. He could tell I was lying."

"That doesn't sound good..."

"He was actually pretty understanding and agreed to stay out of my business."

"I'm sure it was a struggle for him. He's extremely protective of you."

"I know...but it was a good night. We had a heart-to-heart talk. I feel closer to him."

I continued to rub her feet. "You've always been close."

"Yeah, but now in a different way. Oh, and the waitress was all over him. So disgusting."

"Your dad is a good-looking guy."

She glared at me.

"What? He is. You think he's ugly?"

"Well, no. But he's old…"

"Isn't he in his forties?"

"That's ancient."

"Girls like older men—especially when they are rich."

"It just irritates me because he wears his wedding band every where he goes. People don't respect marriage anymore or what?"

"Unfortunately, not everyone does." My hands moved to her calves, massaging the tension away.

"I'm realizing that…" She sighed, closing her eyes again.

"Ready to go home tomorrow?"

"I just have to get through the conference and then we'll leave."

"Sounds good to me."

"Cayson, that feels so good but you don't have to do that."

"I don't mind—really."

She rested an arm over her chest. "I couldn't get Zack to do that even if I paid him."

Why didn't that surprise me? I loathed Zack with every fiber of my being. Not just because I had feelings for Skye, but because he didn't appreciate her. There wasn't a doubt in my mind he didn't love her. I wasn't sure what he felt for her, other than lust, but it definitely wasn't love. I would tell her to leave him, but that would make me a jerk. Besides, I would hate anyone she dated.

Coming on this trip was a bad idea. I was supposed to focus on getting over her, forgetting about being with her. She and I made so much sense. We were perfect together. We were already best friends, and I knew we would be even greater lovers. But she didn't see me that way. And she never would.

But when Trinity asked me to go with her, I couldn't say no. I jumped on the opportunity quickly, knowing I would have a great time. Skye and I clicked on a different wavelength. We could be serious, having deep conversations with multiple meanings, and we could be laughing idiots having too much fun.

Why couldn't she just see me in the same way? It would make my life so much easier. Getting laid was nice but it was still empty and meaningless. I didn't want a one-night stand. I wanted a relationship—with Skye.

I needed to stop thinking like that. It wouldn't change reality. I needed to move on—really move on.

"Can I ask you something?" she whispered.

"What?"

"Would it be too greedy if I ask you to rub my back? It's killing me."

I'd do anything for her. "Sure."

She turned on her side, facing the back of the couch.

The only way for this to work was for me to lay behind her. It was a big couch so we could fit. I lay behind her, feeling my legs touch hers. Then I rubbed her back through her shirt, listening to her quiet moans. The tension was obvious in the muscles of her shoulders. She was tight and rigid. I rubbed her gently before I increased the pressure.

Her quiet moans ended when she fell asleep.

I continued to rub her, feeling my eyes grow heavy. I should've carried her to bed but I was too comfortable. Her hair was near my face and I could smell her scent. I gave into my weakness and did the thing I'd always wanted to do. I hugged her to my chest and fell asleep with her in my arms.

***

The next morning, I woke up to her facing me. Her arm was around my waist and she was hugging me like a teddy bear. Her lips were relaxed and her skin was rejuvenated after a night of rest. Her cheeks were soft and pale. The skin of her neck was flawless. One button at the top of her shirt was broken, revealing the line of her cleavage but I never looked. I knew Skye hated it when men gawked at her chest.

Just for a moment, I pretended this meant something. She and I weren't just platonic friends. We were soul mates, holding each other all night because we couldn't stand to be apart. I was her hero, her everything.

I stared at her face, memorizing it. She and I slept together before, but it was nothing like this. I liked feeling her arm around my waist, anchoring me to her. I liked feeling needed, wanted.

Unable to control myself, my hand moved up and touched a strand of her soft hair. It was smooth like silk, sliding through my fingers easily. Then I leaned in and pressed my lips to her forehead. Her skin was soft, and my lips burned the moment I touched her. It was something I longed to do, something I almost did countless times when she made me smile or laugh. Then I pulled away, suddenly feeling cold the moment my touch ceased.

I settled my head back onto the armrest and stared at her, wondering what the hell she saw in Zack. He was a typical jerk. They fought more often than they enjoyed each other. I'll admit he was good-looking but that was all he had going for him. Skye was deep and selfless. There was so much behind her pretty face. She had a heart of gold and soul of priceless fortune. She was the most beautiful person I knew, on the inside as well as the outside.

Skye took a deep breath and a quiet sigh escaped her lips. Then her eyes fluttered open, taking me in. Morning light filtered through the curtains, making the room slightly lit. When she came around, she pulled her arm slightly but kept it around my waist. "Looks like I fell asleep..."

"Me too."

"Do I owe you another twenty bucks?"

I smirked. "No. I'll let it go because I'm a gentleman."

She pulled her hand away then ran it through her hair. "You're the best masseur in the world. You put me to sleep."

"Well, putting you to sleep doesn't take much work. As long as it's nine o' clock, you're out."

She smirked. "Stop teasing me."

"Never."

She adjusted her head on the armrest and closed her eyes. "I don't want to go back to the conference."

"They have free food." Food was the fastest way to her heart.

"But then I have to wear heels...ugh."

"We could get room service then catch an early flight."

She opened her eyes and they lit up. "Oooh...I like it."

Damn, she was adorable. "Get in the shower and I'll call it in."

"Make sure you get me French—"

"French Toast. I know."

"And—"

"Oatmeal. I know. You're very predictable."

She blushed. "I am, aren't I?"

"A little. But that's okay." It took all my strength to stand up and leave her embrace. I could lay in her arms all day, letting her warmth surround me.

She sat up then adjusted her top. She didn't bother with the top button, which meant she was comfortable around me. Then she walked into her bedroom and shut the door.

With a heavy sigh, I called room service and placed the order.

***

"I love room service." She inhaled her French toast like it might disappear if she didn't eat it quick enough.

"Nothing else can compare." I cut into my pancakes then sipped my coffee.

She drenched her breakfast in syrup, saturating it before scarfing it down. "So damn good."

I glanced at her every few seconds, loving the fact we were having breakfast together in a private room. There's no one else I'd rather be secluded with. It was hard for me to connect to other women. I always found something wrong with them. They were either boring or annoying. There was no place in between. Only Skye seemed to catch my attention in an unshakeable way. Her beauty was unparalleled, her down-to-earth personality just made her irresistible.

I couldn't recall the exact moment when the feelings started. In high school, she suddenly caught my attention. Perhaps it was for a shallow reason, like her breasts started to come in. Maybe it was because she was the only girl I had feelings for and I didn't just want to sleep with her. I didn't know. But as soon as the feelings started, they never went away. I had a few girlfriends on and off, and I had sex as often as I could when I was younger but nothing ever satisfied me. Skye was the prize I had my eye on.

But she didn't even notice me. She slept with me all night and it meant nothing to her. I was practically her brother, a blood relative. She admitted I was a catch and any girl would be lucky to have me, but that didn't apply to her.

I didn't understand. I was a far better guy than Zack. First of all, I was better looking than him. It was a cocky thing to think, but it was the truth. After football ended in high school, I continued to lift weights, making my body filled out and toned. I had fair skin and blue eyes that usually attracted women. And I was funny, down-to-earth, smart, and trustworthy. What more did she want?

"Cayson, is there something on your mind?"

Damn, I was brooding right across the table from her. "I'm not looking forward to the flight."

"I thought you weren't scared?"

"I'm not. I just don't enjoy being in a small enclosure with two hundred people. Not much legroom for a tall guy like me."

"It's one of the times I'm happy to be short."

I finished my breakfast then stacked the plates on the cart. "Are you finished?"

"What do you think?" Her plate was as empty as if it was clean.

I smirked. "Do I need to order more food?"

"I could squeeze in a few more bites, but no. We should go."

I cleared the table and placed the cart against the wall.

Skye's phone lit up. "Guess who it is?"

Probably Zack. "You tell me."

"My dad." She rolled her eyes and read the message. "He wants me to text him the moment I'm in Boston."

"My dad called and asked me to do the same thing."

"Are we five?" she asked. "We don't need to check in with them every hour."

I shrugged. "They just care, Skye. I try not to fight it. Believe me, you'll always lose."

She laughed. "Amen to that."

***

The second we got to the car after the plane touched down, both of our phones went off.

Skye grinned at me. "It's my dad. I'm guessing yours is calling you?"

I glanced at the screen. "Yep."

"So much for letting us call them when we had a chance." She rolled her eyes and took the call.

I answered mine. "Yes, I'm in Boston."

"I just wanted to check. Your plane landed half an hour ago."

"Sorry. I guess getting off the plane, taking a piss, and grabbing my luggage took too long."

He chuckled. "I'll talk to you later."

I hung up without saying goodbye.

Skye looked at me. "They are freaks."

"Of nature."

We drove home and finally arrived outside her apartment. I grabbed her luggage and carried it up the stairs. Like a gargoyle, Zack was leaning against the wall next to her door, his arms across his chest.

I fucking hated this guy.

I dropped her luggage and looked at her. "Thanks for inviting me. I had a great time."

"Me too. Thanks for putting up with my dad."

I smirked. "He's a good guy."

She stepped toward me and gave me a big hug.

I was pleased she showed affection with me despite the presence of her boyfriend. I felt like I always had the upper hand, that he could never compete with me in a twisted way. I hugged her back and smelled her hair.

"I'll see you later." She ended the embrace and pulled her keys out.

"Yeah." I turned away and spotted Zack scowling at me. His jaw was tense like it was chiseled from stone. Hatred burned in his eyes like a spreading wildfire. This guy loathed me, wanted me dead.

But the feeling was mutual.

I wasn't going to leave until I got the last word. "Thanks for letting me stay in your room." I caught the look that spread across Zack's face. He wasn't happy.

With a smirk, I walked away, a skip in my step.

***

Slade sat across from me in the student lounge. His books were laid out in front of him but he wasn't studying. A fire burned to our left, and the windows started to frost as the fall deepened. The leaves were starting to turn blood red before they detached and fell to the ground. I wished I was curled up with Skye in bed, staying warm despite the chill.

"What are you going to be for Halloween?" he asked.

I shrugged. "I haven't given it much thought."

"Well, you're running out of time."

"What are you going to be?"

"A tattoo artist." He grinned.

I cocked an eyebrow. "And how will you dress up for that?"

He shrugged. "Jeans and a t-shirt."

"So...you'll look the same?"

"No. I'll be a tattoo artist."

I couldn't argue with this stupidity. "Whatever."

"What are you going to be?"

"I just told you I don't know."

"Be a clown."

What? "Why the hell would I be a clown?"

He shrugged. "It's better than being nothing."

"Like you?" I jabbed.

"No, I'm going to be a tattoo artist."

"Why don't you just be a moron? You're already dressed for that."

"You're a moron," he countered.

"What a good comeback," I said sarcastically.

"Be a baby beluga whale," he blurted.

I gave him an incredulous look. "What the hell is wrong with you?"

"What? No one else will have that costume. And you're paler than the sun."

"You're just as white."

"But my sleeves bring out some color."

I shook my head slightly. "I'll never figure out how you got into Harvard."

He glared at me. "Hey. I'm smart."

"No, you aren't."

"Well, I'm sure Uncle Sean had something to do with that."

"He had everything to do with it."

"Not everyone can be a genius like you. Hey, be a dinosaur!"

I couldn't follow his thought process. "How did you get from genius to dinosaur?"

"Be a pterodactyl." He spread his arms and acted like he was flying. "Roar! Roar!"

My head was about to explode. "When they roar, they don't say roar. They just roar."

"Roar! Roar!" He continued to flap his arms.

I covered my face with my hands and sighed. "Okay, I'm not going to be that."

"You're going with the whale, then?"

I dropped my hands and glared at him. "No."

He rubbed his chin. "I got it! Be Batman."

"I'm not a twelve-year-old."

"That's arguable…"

Sometimes I wasn't sure why Slade was my best friend. "How about you be Batman?"

He nodded. "I'll be Batman and you'll be Robin."

"Are we going to a Halloween party or coming out of the closet?"

"That's not gay!"

"That's the gayest thing I've ever heard." I gave him a serious look.

"Whatever. It's not like you have any ideas."

"In this case, no idea is better than a stupid idea."

"You're no fun." He rolled his eyes. "So, how was the weekend getaway with that annoying thing?"

"Annoying thing?"

"My cousin."

"She's not an annoying thing."

"Let's cut the crap. She's annoying as hell." He rested his elbow on the table, showing the tattoos of his arm.

"It was fine. And she wasn't annoying."

"The only reason why she isn't annoying is because you like her rack."

119

"Dude...she's your cousin."

"What? I'm not totally oblivious to why men find her attractive."

"And I like her for more reasons than the size of her chest."

He smirked. "Sure, man."

I glared at him. "There's a lot more to her than a pretty face."

"Well, I don't see it."

"Anyway...we had a good time."

"Didn't you go to a business conference?" he asked incredulously. "It must have been extremely boring."

"It wasn't. Skye did a great job on her presentation. She killed, actually."

He started to snore. "Talk about a snooze fest."

Slade could never take anything seriously.

"Did Uncle Sean show up like Batman lurking in the shadows?"

"In fact, he did."

"Cool."

"He got us the presidential suite, which Skye wasn't too thrilled about."

"Us? Did you guys stay in the same room?"

"Yeah."

His eyes widened. "Did you sleep with her?"

I rolled my eyes. "I've been alone with Skye thousands of times and I've never slept with her. A guy and a girl can be alone and not want to immediately bang."

"I've never experienced that." He said it with a straight face.

"You have ten STDs, don't you?"

He glared at me. "No. It's called a rubber."

"Anyway…all the other rooms were taken so I just stayed with her."

"Did anything happen?"

"No. Nothing ever happens. We did sleep together on the couch though."

"Like, you cuddled and shit?"

"Something foreign to you…yes, we cuddled." It was much more satisfying than sex, if you ask me.

"So, she had her arm around you and junk like that?"

"Yes."

He rubbed his temples and sighed. "I'm sorry. Am I the only one who finds that weird?"

"It's not weird."

"Friends don't just cuddle together."

"Yeah, they do," I argued.

"When have you and I ever cuddled?" he demanded. "We're friends."

"But we're both dudes—straight dudes."

"How is it any different?" he asked. "I would never cuddle with a girl who was just a friend. Shit, I don't even cuddle with the girls I tap."

"Well, we've been friends for a long time."

"What does that matter? Plus, she has a boyfriend. I'm finding it hard to believe that she just sees you as a friend."

Hope burned in my heart but I tried to hide it. "Well, she does."

"I don't believe that anymore. Maybe she doesn't realize it or something. Maybe it's a subconscious thing. But she totally feels different toward you than she does to everyone else. She and Theo are friends but they never cuddle."

"They aren't as close."

"She still wouldn't cuddle with him," he argued. "You really think there's nothing else there?"

My heart and mind were at war with each other. Sometimes I couldn't believe we clicked so well and she didn't see me as something more. Sometimes she looked at me like I wasn't even there. My mind told me our relationship was strictly platonic, but my heart told me she was in love with me, in a very complicated way. "Sometimes I think there is...sometimes I don't."

"And I don't know about Zack...every time I'm around them all they do is bitch at each other."

"Does every other word out of your mouth have to be a curse word?"

"I wear sleeves of tattoos for a reason," he countered.

"Do you have to be a stereotype?"

"Yes." He looked at the tattoos on his forearm. A tentacle from an octopus reached down his arm and wrapped around his wrist. His body was a fresco of various images. He kept getting more but was running out of room.

"Your dad does all your artwork?"

"Yep. He's the best in the business."

"I'm sure your mom is happy about that," I said sarcastically.

"Hey, she has a tattoo."

"Of her wedding band. That's pretty tame. And she's a partner at the biggest publishing house in the world. I doubt she's dropping F bombs left and right."

He smirked. "You should listen to my parents fight. My mom is psycho. She rips into my dad and puts him to shame."

"How romantic," I said sarcastically.

"Then they screw like rabbits." He cringed. "Their room is on the other side of the house and Silke and I can still hear them."

"My parents are the same."

He flipped through his textbook. "I hate school. It's not for me."

"Then why are you here?"

"I already told you why. My dad said he would get me my own tattoo parlor if I graduated from college—so fucking stupid."

"I think he wants to make sure you keep your options open."

He rolled his eyes. "Whatever. The only good thing about being in school is all the girls. They think I'm smart and wild. Apparently, that makes me irresistible."

"Or they're just stupid."

He ignored the jab. "Have you talked to Jasmine?"

"No." I didn't plan on it.

"She seemed really cool. Why don't you hook up with her again?"

"Because I don't see me committing to her. I'd rather not waste her time."

"She didn't exactly seem like a girl who cares about commitment." He winked at me.

"I don't want to hurt her."

"Who cares? You were honest with her. It's her own grave she's digging."

"That's what makes me different from you. I'm not a complete asshole."

"At least I'm not a pussy. If you love Skye so damn much, why don't you just tell her? Be a man and be honest."

I narrowed my eyes at him. "She's not just some girl I can avoid and never see again if it goes south. She's in my family. If it gets awkward, our relationship will never be the same. And if I thought there was a slight chance she felt the same way, I wouldn't hesitate. But I know she isn't into me. It would be a suicide mission."

"Then. Move. On." He slammed his palm onto the table. "Start dating and fucking. You're never going to get over Skye if you spend the weekend with her in a presidential suite and cuddle with her all night long."

He had a point. "It was a bad decision...you're right."

"Of course I'm right. Now call up Jasmine and have a beer with her."

"I don't know—"

"If not her, someone else. I'm not trying to get all mushy-mushy on you, but you're a catch, man. You're going to school to be a doctor, you're ripped, and you're good-looking. I see chicks check you out all the time, eye-fucking you. You have your pick of the crop. Now start taking advantage of it."

As vulgar as Slade was, he had a good point. I'd wasted so much time on Skye, someone I would never have. She was just a friend and she would always be a friend. "I guess..."

"You should invite Jasmine to the Halloween party."

"No...I don't want to give her the wrong idea."

"Then you should pick up someone at the Halloween party."

"We'll see how it goes..."

"Now back to your costume...this is what I'm thinking. How about a rabid hippo?"

I didn't understand what went through Slade's head sometimes. "No."

"How about a blimp?"

"A blimp?"

"You know, those big balloons that float in the sky."

I gritted my teeth. "I know what a blimp is. Why the hell would I be one?"

"No one else is going to be that."

I turned my gaze back to my textbook. I had too much to do to entertain his craziness.

***

After my lab, I went to *Manhattan Grub* to get dinner. I usually went every Wednesday night as a tradition. The smart thing to do was to avoid Skye, but of course, that was impossible.

I walked inside and spotted her at the register. "Hey."

"Hey." She gave me a beautiful smile. Her white teeth were perfectly straight, and her lustrous brown hair framed her face. The strands reached her chest, long and silky. Her blue eyes caught my attention, like they always did.

Ugh...why did she have this affect on me?

"The usual?" she asked.

"Yep."

"You never change."

She didn't know how true that was. "How's business?"

"Slow. During lunch hour, the line is out the door."

"Maybe you should close in the evenings."

She shrugged. "A lot of college kids can only work at night. My dad considers it working charity."

"Good man."

"I know." She turned to make the food.

"Skye, you didn't charge me."

"Cayson, you're family."

"No, I'm a customer. Now charge me."

She rolled her eyes. "You're annoying."

"So are you." I put a twenty down.

She took it then handed me my change. "Coming right up."

"Make something for yourself and join me."

"I'm supposed to be working."

I smirked at her. "You call this work?"

She grinned then made my food. When I saw her make another, I knew she was going to eat with me.

We sat across from each other in the corner. Her hot dog was covered in chili, cheese, jalapenos, onions, and relish.

"That looks good," I said.

"It's on the secret menu."

"What's it called?"

She thought for a moment. "The Sky High Dog."

"Naming a meal after yourself? A bit cocky."

"You're cocky," she countered.

I smirked then sipped my soda.

"How was lab?"

"Fine."

"You're always short with me when I ask about school."

"Because it's boring. And frankly, you wouldn't understand it."

"Cockier." She gave me a firm look.

"I wouldn't understand all your business lingo."

"Touché." She ate half her hot dog in just a few bites. Unlike most girls, Skye didn't order a small salad with a side of dressing. She ate like a real person, and as a result, she had real curves. She had a small belly and noticeable hips, but she was gorgeous because of it. I loved her body. The first time I saw her in a swimsuit I almost came in my shorts. "So, what are you going to be for Halloween?"

I still had to figure that out. "Not sure. You?"

"Zack wants to come as Batman and Wonder Woman."

God, that was cliché. "Do you want to do that?"

"Not really. I wanted to be Beatrix Kiddo from *Kill Bill* and have Zack be Bill."

God, she was killing me. She was the coolest damn chick in the world. "And he didn't want to do that?"

"He said he hates that movie."

What the hell did she see in him? "I think you guy should keep brainstorming..."

"At least we have ideas."

I watched her eat the hot dog, sinister thoughts coming into my mind. "Maybe I'll be a wiener."

She laughed. "So you'll be wiener boy?"

"And you can be wiener girl. It'll be perfect."

"That would be awesome. I would love that." She sighed. "But Zack would kill me."

"Why?" I sipped my soda and stared at her.

"He's just...never mind."

"You can tell me anything, Skye."

"He's just a little threatened by you."

He should be. "He thinks you're into me?" *Damn, I wish that were true.*

"No...he just gets jealous that we spend so much time together."

"Would you rather us not spend time together?" *Please say no.*

"Of course not. He can deal with it. I made it clear if he had a problem with you, then he should just walk away. I won't put up with his bullshit."

The aggression in her voice told me they had this discussion several times. "Well, that means a lot to me."

"You're family. No guy will ever be as important unless he's my husband."

"Do you see him as your husband someday?" I sipped my soda again so I could hide my anxiety.

"I don't know. I'm too young to think about marriage."

That was a firm no. Thankfully.

She finished her hot dog then moaned. "That was so good."

"You know your way around a kitchen." I wiped my mouth with a napkin then tossed it aside.

"So, what's Slade going to be?"

I rolled my eyes. "A tattoo artist."

She cocked an eyebrow. "How's he going to manage that?"

"I don't know. He's going to dress like himself."

She laughed. "My cousin is a weirdo."

"You think you're any different?" I teased.

She grinned. "I guess not."

"So, was Zack pissed we stayed in the same room together?"

"Of course he was. But he kept his mouth shut like he's supposed to."

I was glad Skye didn't put up with his bullshit. She was too strong to let a man control her. And she was too independent and smart.

The bell rang overhead when the door opened, and Zack appeared.

Great.

As soon as his eyes landed on mine, a scowl deepened on his face. He didn't like me and he didn't bother hiding it. I didn't bother hiding it either. He came to our table, his shoulders becoming tenser with every step.

"Hey, baby." He leaned down and kissed her, rubbing it in my face.

She ended the embrace quickly. "Hey. What are you doing here?"

"I wanted to see you. I know you get off soon."

"Yeah. Time flies when I'm not working." She laughed at her own joke.

Zack sat beside her and put his arm over her chair, claiming her.

I felt sick to my stomach.

"Baby, can I order some food?"

"Sure. What do you want?"

He glanced at the menu. "The number two."

"Seven bucks." She held out her hand.

"You're going to charge me? I'm your boyfriend."

"So?" She glared at him. "This is my father's business, not mine."

He sighed then gave her the cash.

Skye took it then headed to the register, leaving us alone.

Zack immediately threatened me with his eyes. "You can fool everyone else but you can't fool me, asshole."

I kept my silence.

"If you think following her everywhere she goes and stalking her is going to win her over, you're wrong. She's mine and I'm not letting you take her away from me. If you continue to piss me the fuck off, I'll bash your face in so hard you won't be recognizable."

"I didn't realize I threatened you so much." I leaned back and stared him down, not blinking.

"I'm not threatened by you," he snapped.

"Sounds like it. And I'd love nothing more than for you to throw a punch. Believe me, ripping you apart, limb-by-limb, would give me nothing but satisfaction. And you know what the best part would be? To watch Skye leave your ass for touching me."

Fire burned in his eyes. He clutched his hand and made a fist, and it shook on the table.

"Let's be real here. You'll never compete with me. And every time you try to fight me, you push her further away. You're digging your own grave, man."

He clenched his jaw, telling me he didn't have an argument against that. We both knew I meant more to Skye than he ever would. I was her family, her best friend. I would always be more important until the day she said I do. "She's going to realize it eventually. And what do you think will happen then? She'll turn her back on you and ignore you, trying to get away from you."

"That would never happen."

"Then why don't you just tell her the truth? Huh? What do you got to lose?"

Seriously, this guy was a dick. What did she see in him? "Skye doesn't feel anything for me. She sees me as a friend and a brother. Telling her would change nothing. And even if she did, you should stop questioning her left and right. If you knew her better, you would know how ethical and trustworthy she is. She's not a cheater and she's not a liar. You really should calm the fuck down."

Skye came back to the table and put the hot dog down. "No onions, right?"

Zack didn't look at her. "Yeah."

Skye sat beside him with her clipboard in hand. She made a few notes.

Zack continued to stare at me, probably wishing he could strangle me and get away with it. I wished he would so Skye would leave him.

Skye glanced at Zack. "Are you going to eat that?"

He finally snapped out of his trance. "Yeah..."

I couldn't stand to be around him a second longer. Skye didn't even seem happy with him. He didn't make her laugh the way I did. They didn't have an openness to their relationship, a playfulness. It was stern and serious, almost gloomy. "I have to go."

Skye caught the anger in my voice. "Is everything okay?"

"Yeah. I just remembered I have an assignment due tomorrow."

"Oh." She knew I was lying. "Okay."

"Night." I walked away without waiting for her to say it back.

When I reached the door, I heard Skye speak to Zack. "Did you say something to him?"

"No," he said.

"Because he seemed pissed about something."

"I don't know. And I don't give a shit."

I walked out and shut the door, feeling the anger in my limbs.

***

Slade came to my door, looking like he did every day. "You like my costume?"

"What costume?"

"I'm a tattoo artist. I said that already." He sighed in annoyance.

"Well, it's the cheapest costume in the world."

He looked at my costume, confusion spreading on his face. "Are you...Buzz Lightyear?"

"No. I'm a laser tag soldier."

"Oh!" He nodded his head in approval. "It's not quite as cool as a dinosaur but it works."

"Since I'm not five, the dinosaur costume never would have been cool."

"That's debatable." He stepped inside my apartment, uninvited. "You ready?"

I put my vest on then grabbed my plastic gun. "Yep."

"Now let's talk about our game plan."

"Game plan?"

"You're getting laid tonight."

I rolled my eyes. "If I want to get laid, I will."

"I have a feeling I'm going to have to give you a push. The women are going to be all over us. I'm telling you. You'll have your pick of the crop."

"We'll see..."

"Let's head out." He spotted a bag of candy on my counter and snatched a few pieces. "Expecting trick-or-treaters?"

"There are a few kids in my building."

"What a nice guy," he said sarcastically.

We left the apartment then drove to Trinity's house a few blocks from campus. Uncle Mike bought her a house because he didn't like her being so close to other people. Uncle Sean was protective but Uncle Mike was worse. Much worse. It had a security system and video surveillance. It was a little over the top.

The streets were flooded with cars. Every curb was taken, so we had to park a few blocks away.

"A lot of people are here tonight," I said.

"We know a lot of people."

"Her house is going to be demolished."

"Nothing Uncle Mike can't fix with the change sitting at the bottom of his pocket."

After we parked, we headed to the house. The bass from the music thudded loudly, and the front of the house was decorated for Halloween. Spider webs covered the bushes and skeletons were forked into the lawn.

"So spooky," Slade said sarcastically.

We walked inside and met the smoke from cigarettes and bongs. The music was louder, heavier on our ears. I didn't recognize most of the people, and it didn't seem like Slade did either. We walked until we reached the living room.

Conrad and Roland were both holding beers, checking out the girls in the corner. Each girl wore a slutty bunny costume. They weren't even original. They wore black lingerie with pink ears. They had perfect bodies and nice racks, but they weren't unique.

"Hey." Slade joined the guys. "We got some talent here tonight."

I came by his side and looked at Roland. "Hey, man."

He fist pounded me. "Have fun with my sister this weekend?"

I shrugged. "It was alright."

Everyone knew I was in love with Skye, even her brother. I never admitted it, but I didn't need to. They all knew. It was a miracle Skye didn't know. Like I said, she was blind.

"Was my dad there?"

"Yep. He was a bit of a celebrity."

"When isn't he?" Roland drank out of his red cup. "What are you?" He eyed my outfit.

"Laser tag soldier."

"Cool," he said with a nod.

He was wearing jeans and a t-shirt. "And what are you?"

"Nothing. I'm too cool to dress up."

Conrad was in jeans too. "Everyone knows Halloween is just a night where girls can dress like sluts and other girls can't talk shit about it. And it's a great way for us to determine who really has the nicest body."

Slade nodded. "Word." He eyed the bunnies in the corner. "And it's a tie."

Roland smirked. "All I have to do is say I'm a Preston and the girls come to me."

"All I have to do is show off my tattoos," Slade said. "Girls think I'm dark and dangerous."

"And reckless and stupid," I added.

Trinity came to our group but I hardly recognized her. She was wearing blood red panties and a matching push-up bra. Her blonde hair was curled, and red horns sat on her head. Five inch red heels made her almost as tall as us. "Hey there." She put her hands on her hips and kept her shoulders back. She eyed Slade, watching his reaction.

Slade's eyes widened while he stared at her. "Uh..."

Conrad was the first one to react. He almost spit out his drink. "What the hell are you wearing?"

"My Halloween costume," she snapped.

"No, you're wearing slutty lingerie," he snapped.

"So, the girls you were checking out in the corner can dress like this but I can't?" She glared at her brother.

"Put on some clothes. Now." Conrad clenched his hand so hard he dented his cup.

"No." She twirled a strand of hair then looked at Slade again. I wasn't sure what she was expecting out of him. A silent conversation passed between them.

Conrad pulled his phone out of his pocket. "Fine. I'll just take a picture and send it to Dad. I'm sure he wants to know what his whore of a daughter is doing."

Her eyes smoldered in demonic fire. "Don't even think about it."

Conrad held the phone out to take a picture.

She hissed then grabbed his wrist, trying to yank it away.

Slade and I stood back, staying out of the line of fire. Roland sipped his glass, looking indifferent.

"I'm a grown woman and can do what I want," Trinity snapped. "You can't just tattle on me every time I do something you don't approve of."

"You're wearing underwear in public," Conrad snapped.

"How is it any different than a swimsuit?" she challenged.

"Because we aren't at the damn beach." He yanked his phone away then took a picture.

"I will never forgive you if you send that to Dad!" She was practically hysterical.

After knowing Uncle Mike my whole life, I knew he was someone I didn't want to cross. Sending that picture to him would have dire repercussions for Trinity. I would hate to be the recipient of his wrath.

I snatched the phone away and stuffed it in my pocket. "You guys are both adults now. If Trinity wants to dress like that at her party, that's her right. Tattling on her to Uncle Mike isn't fair."

"Thank you." Trinity gave me a look of gratitude.

"How would you feel if your sister was dressing like that?" Conrad demanded.

"I wouldn't like it one bit," I said honestly. "And I would ask her to change. But I wouldn't tattle on her to my dad. That's not cool." I returned the phone to his hand. "Do the right thing, man."

Conrad growled then stuffed his phone back into his pocket. Then he looked at his sister. "When you dress like that, the only thing guys want is sex. They don't give a shit about you and they don't respect you. If you want to parade around like a whore, fine. But don't expect me to be there for you when the guy doesn't call you ever again." He headed to the booze table and poured himself another beer. Roland went with him.

"He pisses me off sometimes." Trinity crossed her arms over her chest.

Slade kept eyeing her, not bothering to be discreet about it.

I wasn't related to Trinity, but I didn't see her that way. As far as I was concerned, she was a distant cousin.

"You like what you see?" Trinity asked him.

Slade drank out of his cup and said nothing.

These two made no sense. They argued like they hated each other, and now they seemed like friends again. Wanting to stay out of their feud, I trailed away and searched for Skye. I knew she would appreciate my costume...unlike everyone else. And I sincerely hoped she went with the *Kill Bill* outfit.

I moved through the house until I spotted a man wearing a Batman costume. He didn't wear a mask, and I recognized Zack the moment I saw him.

So fucking cliché.

Against the wall was Skye. She was wearing a Wonder Woman outfit, her chest prominent and her legs long and thin. Zack was pressing her into the wall, his face near hers. Then he kissed her, groping her like he wanted her then and there.

Just watching it made me sick. Like a horrific accident that you couldn't stop staring at, I continued to watch their affection. She sucked his bottom lip then kissed him again, her eyes closed. The passion on her face made my stomach turn into uncomfortable knots. The way his hands hugged her hips made me spiral down, making my heart beat slower with every passing second. I was watching my worst nightmare.

"What are the odds you would be here?"

The voice was familiar but I didn't recognize it. "Sorry?" I turned to see Jasmine standing beside me. She was wearing a slutty Native American costume. A tube top with fringe was around her chest, barely containing her voluptuous breasts, and she was wearing a short skirt that barely covered anything. She wore a black wig that was pulled into a braid.

She studied my face, probably seeing the horror in my eyes. I couldn't hide my pain. I'd seen Skye kiss Zack before, but never like that. It hinted at their sex lives, something I found so disgusting it made me want to hurl. I felt alone. I felt hurt. How could I be so in love with someone who didn't even notice me? How could she prefer him over me? Why couldn't she kiss me like that? It wasn't fair. I was better than him in every way.

Jasmine glanced at Skye, seeing her make out with Zack, and then turned back to me. "Now I understand." Pity was in her eyes.

Seeing them together took a toll on my heart. I was sick of feeling this way. It was heartbreaking and exhausting. At this age, I should be dating and having fun. I shouldn't feel this strongly for another person. Sometimes I wished I never met Skye so I could be normal just like everyone else. The pain was digging into my marrow, scarring the bone. "You want to get out of here?"

She smirked. "I thought you'd never ask."

Chapter Six

Skye

Sex with Zack was...okay. When he was drunk, it was worse. It lasted a long time but he was sloppy and bouncy. It took him forever to get off. He made me climax every now and then, but it was hit or miss. But that's how sex was and I didn't complain about it. He seemed to enjoy it more than I did. Every time we fooled around, he was harder than a rock. And as soon as he was inside me, he moaned like he'd never had sex before.

I tried not to think about it too much. Real relationships weren't fairy tales where the guy swept you off your feet and solved every problem you ever had. They were work and time-consuming. There were days when I didn't want to put the work in and there were days when I did. But sometimes I wondered if he was worth it.

I'd been in relationships before, and I never felt the all-consuming love they referred to in novels and movies. My heart didn't stretch so wide that I thought it would give out. My stomach didn't fill with butterflies when he was around. I used to be that way in the beginning of our relationship, but that quickly faded. Now all it seemed like we did was argue and have sex.

Was that normal?

I didn't see Zack much the next week. I had an exam on Friday and I didn't feel prepared for it. Zack was majoring in political science because he wanted to get into politics. I knew he had a long road ahead of him. Honestly, I couldn't see him being a senator or congressman. He just lacked charisma. Perhaps law school was better for him.

After I finished my exam on Friday, I finally relaxed. I had the whole weekend to sit around in my pajamas and do nothing. I had a date with a pint of chocolate ice cream and my TV.

Life was good.

When I got home, I got a text from my mom.

What are you doing this weekend?

Eating ice cream.

I do that every weekend.

I know. I'm your daughter. Did you have something in mind?

Next weekend your father and Uncle Mike are hosting a gala for the company. He would like it if you and Roland came. I thought I could drive up there tomorrow and we could do some shopping.

Gala? Is it for charity?

Yes. And it would mean a lot to him if the two of you came.

Of course we will. Does that mean Cayson is coming too?

I'm not sure but I would assume so.

Cool. I love to shop.

Great. I'll pick you up at noon.

Sounds great.

Okay. I'm excited to see you.

Me too, Mom.

My mom and I were close. She was my first girlfriend and now she was my best girlfriend. I told her everything without feeling judged. And I knew she wouldn't tell my father anything if I asked. She would keep my secrets unless she was concerned for my well-being. She knew how psycho he was.

I texted Cayson next. He didn't come in on Wednesday night like he usually did. Actually, I hadn't seen him all week. We didn't cross paths at the Halloween party either. Not talking to him felt odd. *Hey stranger.*

He didn't respond.

Normally, he returned messages within seconds. It was like his phone was always in his hand. Half an hour went by before he responded.

Hey wiener girl.

Don't call me that in front of my dad. He might get the wrong idea.

And I want to keep my head.

My mom told me there's a gala for the company next weekend. Are you going?

I would never let my father down.

Cool. My mom is coming down tomorrow so we can go shopping.

Tell her I said hi.

I will. There was nothing else to say but I wanted to keep talking to him. I missed him. It was weird not having him around. *You want to carpool?*

May as well.

We can take my car.

Cool.

This was strange. I had to keep the conversation going. Normally it just flowed. It seemed like he was being short with me. *Want to get pizza? I finished an exam a few hours ago and I'm starving.*

I have a date. Maybe next time.

A date? Who?

Some girl I met a while ago.

Oh. He never mentioned that to me. Since he was so secretive about his private life, I wasn't sure why he mentioned his date at all. *Okay. Have a good time.*

Thanks. See ya.

See ya? He never said goodbye over text messages. The conversation was always left open—indefinitely. *Cayson, is everything okay?*

Yeah. He said nothing more.

I put the phone down, unsure what to think.

***

My mom arrived at my door right at noon.

"Hey, Mom." I moved into her arms and gave her a big hug. The scent of vanilla came into my nose, a smell I remembered from my youth. My mom was the kindest person I knew. She had a heart of gold but she was also strong. She stood up to my dad no matter how protective he was.

"Hello, dear." Her hand touched the end of my hair, feeling the softness. "You look beautiful, like always."

"You're only saying that because I look like you."

She pulled away and smirked. "Well, I'm sure it helps. Are you ready to go?"

"So ready." I grabbed my purse and we walked out the door.

As soon as we reached the car, her phone rang.

I already knew who it was before she pulled her phone out.

"Dad?"

She rolled her eyes. "You know your father well." She looked at the screen then took the call. "Hey."

"Hey, baby." His voice carried to my ears. "You made it to the apartment?"

"You have a tracker on my phone so I'm sure you already knew that."

He chuckled. "I just wanted to check in."

"Well, I'm fine."

"Call me when you get back to the apartment."

"I'll think about it." My mom liked to make him squirm.

"Call me or I'll drive down there. Your choice."

"Hmm...which is the lesser of two evils?"

I rolled my eyes while I listened to them.

My dad's voice became firmer. "I'm already going crazy without you so any excuse to drive down there is welcomed."

"I guess I'll call you then."

"I love you." Every time he said those words, his voice sounded the same. It didn't matter if he was angry or tired. He said it the same way every time. The emotion came from his throat, echoing long after he said it. It was almost like he was desperate, like he wanted my mom to know he meant it every single time he said it. While they were gross and disgusting, they also made me long for a love like that. But I doubted a man would ever love me the way my dad loved my mom.

"I love you too." She hung up and returned her phone to her purse.

"He's intense."

"Your father is...there are no words." She started the car then headed to the mall.

When we arrived, we hit the stores.

"When I had dinner with dad a few weeks ago, our waitress practically threw herself at him." I rolled my eyes. "It was totally disgusting."

My mom smirked. "Sounds about right."

"It doesn't make you mad?"

She shrugged. "I have one of the best looking men in the world as my husband. Unlike women, men get better looking with age, and your father has definitely become even more handsome. Plus, he's one of the richest men in the world. I'm not ignorant to the intents of other women. They'll want him. But that doesn't matter because they can't have him."

"Wow. You really trust Dad."

"I have no reason not to."

I'd like to say the same about Zack but I wasn't sure if I could. "How did you guys get together?"

"We met in college, like I said."

"No. I mean how did you hook up?"

"Oh...that's a long story. There aren't enough hours in the day."

"You were friends first, right?"

We walked into a clothing store, eyeing the gowns on display.

"I knew your father for ten years before we had our first kiss. Actually, he was about to propose to another woman."

"Whoa...what happened?"

"She cheated on him," she said with a smile. "And then I got him."

"How could you be friends for so long and not notice each other?"

She walked to a champagne pink dress and felt the fabric. "Well, sometimes it takes just a single touch or look to make you see them differently. I think I was in love with your father long before I realized it. The first time we were...together...I realized it."

"Like, a booty call?"

Her cheeks blushed. "More like a drunken night."

"Mom!"

She laughed. "Honey, I'm not a saint and I never said I was."

"So, you guys hooked up and that's it?"

She laughed again. "No, that definitely wasn't it. We had a very rocky relationship. In fact, I moved to Seattle just to get away from him. In time, we figured it out and made it work. And it only made us fall in love even more."

"So, sleeping with him made you realize he was the one?"

She shrugged. "Sean was always the one. I think having a night of really great sex just made me realize how passionate we were toward each other. Everything changed."

It surprised me they could be friends for a decade but not start a relationship for so long. It was odd to me. Most relationships didn't happen that way. "Did being friends first make you better lovers?"

"Definitely. What's better than falling in love with your best friend? They know everything about you, every strength and every flaw. You never have to fear being yourself. You don't even need to tell them what you're thinking or what you want. They just know." She felt the dress in her fingertips. "I like this one. I think it'll look good on you."

I eyed it. It was beautiful and classy. But it was a tube top. "I'm not sure it'll contain my cleavage—thanks for that by the way."

She smirked. "It will. It has padding inside." She grabbed one in my size then grabbed a white shawl "It'll look great on your skin tone."

"You think?"

"I know. Let's get it."

"Okay."

We headed to the fitting room and stepped inside together. I changed in front of her, unembarrassed about being practically naked in front of my mother. I pulled up the dress then fit the zipper.

My mom smiled. "It's perfect."

I looked at my chest. "They look like they are sitting on a platter."

She rolled her eyes. "Don't fight it. Besides, your husband will love them."

"Every guy I pass in the hallway loves them."

She laughed. "Sounds about right."

I changed then we left the dressing room. At the register, my mom took out her credit card to pay for it.

"I can get it, Mom."

"No," she said firmly. "It's a gift from your father."

"You guys buy me too much stuff."

"Just accept it." She held out a gold bracelet. "Your father bought this for me twenty years ago and he spent way too much on it. I practically ripped his head off but he talked me down. So, you can accept this dress."

"How do you put up with him?"

She handed over the credit card then took the receipt. "Because I love him like crazy."

We headed out of the store.

"Lunch?" she asked.

"Pizza?"

"It's like we have one mind."

We went to the pizza parlor in the mall then sat down with our food. We both ordered slices of combination.

"Dad knows I have a boyfriend and I've had them before." I took a bite then sipped my soda.

She nodded. "He told me."

"Was he mad?"

"No. He understands you're a grown woman that has a personal life. It's just hard for him to accept it sometimes. He just cares about you, honey."

"I know...but he's so psycho about it. Did he ask you anything?"

"No."

"Is he having a PI follow me around?"

She laughed. "No."

I breathed a sigh of relief.

"How's it going with Zack, by the way?"

I shrugged. "Fine."

She eyed me. "Fine? Just fine?"

"Yeah...I don't know. There's not much to say."

"No interesting stories?"

"None that I can think of."

My mom ate her pizza quicker than I did. "It doesn't seem like you really like him, Skye."

"I do," I said quickly. "He just gets on my nerves sometimes. He gets extremely jealous and argumentative. I feel like we argue just as much as we enjoy each other's company."

"What do you fight about?"

"Nothing, really. That's the sad part."

"You know how your father and I get."

"Yeah, but then you guys are love bunnies for two weeks in between. It's not like that with Zack."

"Do you love him?"

I didn't like it when people asked me this. "I'm too young to know love."

She raised an eyebrow. "You're twenty-one. What are you talking about?"

"I don't know. We've only been together for six months. I don't think that's long enough to know."

"I disagree. You know if you love someone immediately. You may not acknowledge it, but that doesn't make it untrue."

"Zack and I aren't that serious. We're just having fun."

"So, he's good in bed?" my mom asked.

I shrugged. "He's alright."

She smirked. "I'm having a hard time understanding why you stick around."

"Well, I used to have a really big crush on him. The moment I saw him, I was dumbstruck like a teenager. But I guess after I got to know him, that excitement wore off. Isn't that how it is in all relationships?"

"No. I feel the same way about your father as the day we married."

"But you guys are weird."

"Then ask that question to any of your aunts and uncles. They'll have the same response."

I knew that too well. Sometimes they didn't understand the boundaries of public displays of affection. "Well, they are weird too." I finished my pizza then felt my stomach. "I'm going to explode."

She shrugged. "I could eat forever."

"You're lucky you aren't a cow. I hope that's something I inherit from you besides these humongous back killers."

She laughed. "I'm sure you will. It seems like the only thing you got from your father is his eyes."

"That's a good thing. Otherwise I would be a crazy control freak."

"There's more to your father than that."

I knew that was true. "I know."

We squared the bill then headed home. My mom usually spent the night at my place before she drove home the next morning, on my father's orders.

We tossed our bags in the corner then sat on the couch, putting our feet on the coffee table.

"How's Cayson?" she asked.

"Good. He's being a geek, like usual."

"And you think you aren't?" she teased. "You went to a business conference to give a presentation."

"But I don't study biochemistry. That's super geeky."

She smirked. "I guess. That was nice of Cayson to go with you."

"Yeah, but it didn't surprise me. He's the nicest guy in the world."

"He is. I know Cortland is very proud of him. Whenever he talks about him, all he does is brag."

"He's something to brag about."

"Your dad mentioned you stayed in the same hotel room?"

"Yeah. All the other rooms were booked."

She nodded. "And how was that?"

"Fine. He slept on the couch. But Dad got me the presidential suite." I had to roll my eyes. "So the couch was practically the size of a bed. After walking in my heels all day, Cayson rubbed my feet. His hands are a godsend."

She chuckled. "He's too sweet."

"He is. But that's why he's my best friend."

"Is he the reason why Zack gets jealous?"

"Don't even get me started… Zack thinks Cayson is in love with me because he's always around."

"Does he know you stayed in the same hotel room?"

"Yeah…he wasn't pleased about that. It was World War III."

"What did you say?"

"That he has to accept Cayson completely or our relationship is never going to work."

My mom raised her hand and high-fived me. "Good girl."

I laughed then pulled a blanket over my legs. "Would Dad react the same way if you and Uncle Cortland stayed in the same room?"

"No. He trusts everyone in our inner circle. In fact, if your father couldn't be there for some reason, he would prefer someone to stay with me."

"Wow. I guess he's not that crazy."

She smirked. "I wouldn't say that..."

Like my dad could hear our conversation, he called her. Her phone vibrated on the coffee table. She grabbed it and sighed. "I forgot to call him."

"Oh no. Where's my helmet?"

She answered it. "Hey."

His voice was audible on the other line. "Are you back at the apartment?"

"Just check the GPS," she said sarcastically.

"You know I'll only do that if I'm concerned for your safety."

"Yes, I'm back."

"Okay. Can you do me a favor?"

"You know I'll do anything for you."

"Can you make sure you get a picture with Skye? I'd like one."

She smiled. "Sure."

"Thank you. Can you do me another favor?"

"Now you're pushing your luck…" A wide grin was on her face.

"Can you call me when you leave tomorrow?"

"I know the drill, babe."

"Thank you, baby. I miss you."

"I miss you too."

"I love you."

"I love you too."

"Bye."

She hung up.

"You just saw him today," I argued. "How can you possibly miss him?"

She put the phone down, a smirk still on her lips. "I always miss him."

When Zack and I were apart, I wasn't going crazy for him. Most of the time, I appreciated the space. "Did you see Roland while you were down here?"

"We had breakfast today."

"Why don't you spend time with us together?"

She shrugged. "I know you both have different needs. I like to give each of you my full attention privately. It makes us have a stronger bond. Besides, your brother isn't going to want to listen to us discuss shopping, boys, sex, and my marriage to your father."

"Yeah…I don't even want to discuss it."

She laughed.

"Movie?" I asked.

"Something with a pretty man."

"We really are related." I turned on the TV and we lay on the couch until bedtime. I wasn't going to make my mom sleep on the couch, so we both slept in my bed. I had a king size bed so there was plenty of room anyway.

When my mom left the next day, I was sad. Saying goodbye was always hard. She was just a two-hour drive away but not living at the house anymore always made me a little teary-eyed. I missed helping her make breakfast in the morning on the weekends. I missed listening to her read to me at night before bed. There were so many things I took for granted in my youth.

"Bye, Mom." I hugged her tightly, closing my eyes.

"Bye, honey. I'll see you next weekend."

"That's so far away..."

"It'll be here before you know it. And the holidays are coming up." She pulled away and gave me a brave smile. "We'll be spending a lot of time together."

"Yeah..."

"I love you."

"I love you too."

She walked to her car then drove away. I stayed outside my door, suddenly feeling alone. Something in my life wasn't right but I couldn't put my finger on it. Something was missing. I had a wonderful family who loved me, I was studying something I was interested in, and I had great friends that would do anything for me. So what was wrong?

***

"What do you think of this?" Trinity held out the dress to me. It was silver with sparkles and was skin-tight.

"It's cute." I stayed on the couch, my computer in my lap.

"I think it'll be good for this gala."

"I'm sure it will be."

"What are you wearing?" she asked.

"A pink dress."

"Short or long?"

"Knee length."

She laid the dress on my counter then sat down on the couch.

"Does your house still smell like a beer factory?"

She laughed. "No. I left the windows open for a few days and that cleared out the smell."

I scrolled through an article I was reading. "That night was a blur. I drank way too much."

"You and Zack were practically having sex in the hallway."

Why didn't that surprise me? "I'm sorry if you saw too much."

"Apology accepted."

"Did you hook up with anyone?"

She grabbed the remote and flipped through the channels. "No."

"Really? That devil costume didn't attract any winners?"

"Nope. They couldn't handle this anyway."

I hadn't seen Cayson in almost two weeks. He didn't come by the diner on Wednesday like he normally did. It was like he disappeared. "Have you talked to Cayson?"

"I've seen him around here and there." She stopped when she found a fashion show.

"Did he seem...different?"

"No. Why?"

"I don't know... I just haven't seen him around much. We usually cross paths every day, but I haven't spotted him in almost two weeks. He didn't come to the diner either. That's two weeks in a row."

She shrugged. "Maybe he's busy."

"Yeah...but it's still unusual."

Trinity watched the show then grabbed the bowl of popcorn off the table.

"I miss him," I whispered.

"When was the last time you saw Zack?" she asked.

"Um...we've both been busy so I guess over a week."

"So, you miss Cayson more than your own boyfriend?"

"Well, I wouldn't put it like that…"

"That's how it sounds."

I scrolled through the article on my computer. "Relationships come and go but what Cayson and I have is for life. That's why it's different."

"I didn't see you all week and that didn't ring any alarms."

I looked at her. "What are you getting at?"

She shrugged. "Sometimes I wonder if you have feelings for Cayson."

What? "No."

"You're awfully close. You do everything together, tell each other everything, and you snuggle together."

"I tell you everything," I argued.

"But I can't recall a time when we snuggled on the couch together."

I cocked an eyebrow. "How did you know about that?"

She squirmed a little bit. "It's not brand new information, Skye. Seriously, you aren't attracted to him?"

"Well…I think he's a good-looking guy."

"You know what I mean, Skye."

"I understand why the girls are so interested in him."

"That doesn't answer my question either."

"I don't know," I said. "He's just a friend."

She gave me a firm look. "You're sure?"

"What do you mean am I sure? I have a boyfriend."

"That you don't even like most of the time."

"That's not true," I argued.

"Yes, it is. He drives you up the wall."

"We have good times too."

"Sure..." She turned her attention back to the screen.

"I don't have feelings for Cayson."

"Whatever you say."

"I don't," I argued.

"It sounds like you're trying to convince yourself, not me."

I turned my attention back to my computer, ignoring Trinity.

She smirked then continued to watch TV.

"You're going away for the weekend?" Zack asked sadly. "You just spent last weekend with your mom."

"It's for my dad's company. I have to go."

He sighed. "Why didn't you invite me? I'd be your date."

"Well...it's a family thing."

He crossed his arms over his chest while he stared at me. "When am I going to meet your family?"

Meet my family? Where the hell was this coming from? "Um...I don't know. But I don't think now is a good time."

"Why not? We've been dating for six months."

"I haven't met your parents," I countered.

"Because they live in California," he snapped. "If you want to make a trip out there, I would love that. But your parents are only two hours away."

Why did he want to meet my parents so bad? "We haven't even said I love you to each other. Don't you think meeting parents is premature?"

He continued to stare at me with intensity in his eyes. "Well, I love you."

What? Did he just say that? "Sorry?"

"I love you," he repeated.

Blurting it out right this second wasn't romantic at all. It felt rushed. "Uh..."

"It's okay if you aren't ready to say it back. I'm not in a rush."

"No, I think you are."

"I just think it's time we take our relationship to the next level. I have a suit and a tie, and I'm not doing anything this weekend. It'll be fun."

I wasn't ready for that. My dad was intense and stern. Meeting a boyfriend was something he didn't look forward to, and I would rather only put him through it once, for my sake and for his. "I don't think it's a good idea, Zack."

He sighed in annoyance. "What more do I have to do, Skye? I said I love you. I treat you right. I don't rip Cayson's head off."

"Have to do for what?" I asked. "What do you want from me?"

He ran his fingers through his hair anxiously. "Nothing. Forget it."

What the hell was going on here? Why did he want to meet my parents so much? "Zack, I told you from the beginning that this wasn't serious. I just wanted something fun. Meeting parents and saying I love you is not something I signed up for."

"So, I don't mean anything to you?" he snapped.

"No, that's not what I'm saying. I feel like you're rushing me. You have from the beginning. I said I wanted to take things slow and just hang out, but you wanted to be my boyfriend. I just wanted to fool around and you pressured me into a commitment. This is as far as I can go—for now."

He clenched his jaw but didn't say anything. "Fine. Whatever. I can be patient."

"Maybe we should just end this relationship..." If this situation was making him unhappy, then he shouldn't be in it. I didn't want to hurt him and I didn't want to string him along.

"No." His eyes shined in determination. "I said that's not an option."

"It seems like you want something more than I can give. If you're looking for a wife to settle down right now, that isn't me."

"I'm not looking for anything. All I want is you." He came close to me and cupped my cheeks. "I'm sorry I pressured you. I am. I'll give you whatever you want. Just don't go. Please." Desperation was in his eyes.

When he looked at me like this, I couldn't say no. He did mean something to me. He did make me feel good. There were times of laughter and joy between us, and the sexual attraction was undeniable. Every time he held me like this, begging me to be with him, I couldn't say no. "Okay."

He breathed a sigh of relief then pressed his lips to mine. The kiss was slow and gentle then escalated into passion. He was an amazing kisser and he knew how to use his hands. He touched me the way I liked, made my legs shake for him.

When we got to the bedroom, we peeled our clothes away and touched each other. His finger slid between my legs and brought me to the edge of a climax. It was so close I could feel it. But then he pulled away.

"I want you to come when I'm inside you."
Ugh. That rarely worked

He slipped inside me and did his thing. Like usual, he didn't make me come. The foreplay leading up to the sex was always the best part. He could get me off with his mouth or his hands. But he could never do it during intercourse.

Oh well. I guess that was normal.

***

I had a SUV so I thought my car would be the best to take on the trip. I piled everything into the truck when everyone else showed up.

Roland tossed a bag on top of mine.

"That's all you're taking?" I asked.

"It's just for the weekend."

"Where's your suit? Is it stuffed in there?"

"Mom will iron it. Calm the hell down."

My brother and I were constantly butting heads. "You can just hang it up in the back."

"You can just stop talking."

I rolled my eyes. "You're annoying."

"And you're a pain in the ass." My brother looked so much like my father it was frightening. They had the same dark hair, the same eyes, and the same build. He hit six feet before he graduated high school, and he had my father's intensity.

"Shut up and get in the car," I said.

"You shut up for the entire drive."

"Gee, this should be fun." Cayson approached us then tossed his bag in the back. "I love hearing you guys nag. It's a hobby." He hung up his suit on the hanger in the back.

I was so excited to see him that I didn't care about his comment. "Hey. I haven't seen you in weeks." I immediately moved into his arms and hugged him.

He flinched, which he never had before. "I've just been busy." He pulled away quickly then stepped back. "How's your mom?"

"Good. We spent the day shopping."

"Sounds boring. But cool."

I couldn't ignore the distance between us. I felt like he was pushing me away but I had no idea why. "How was your date?"

He cocked an eyebrow. "Date?"

"You said you had one a few weeks ago…that's why you couldn't get pizza."

"Oh that. It was fine." He walked to Roland then shook his hand. "Are you dreading this as much as I am?"

"Dressing up nice and pretending to give a shit? Yeah, it sounds terrific." He rolled his eyes. "At least there will be girls there who already want to marry me and will do anything to catch my attention."

"You're such a pig, Roland," I snapped.

"Is that supposed to be an insult?" He snatched the keys from my hand. "I'm driving. You suck at it."

I didn't bother arguing with him.

Trinity and Conrad pulled up in his Honda.

"Wow, everyone is on time today." Cayson looked at his watch.

Trinity carried three bags to the car then started to shove them in the back.

Cayson eyed her. "Um...I'm not sure if it's all going to fit."

"I'll make it fit." She continued to stuff the bags inside. It was almost overflowing.

"And where am I going to put my stuff?" Conrad demanded.

"Like I care," she said.

"Do you really need that much stuff, Trinity?" I asked.

"Does a mule need water?" she countered.

"That's not the same thing at all," Conrad said. "Stick to fashion." He pulled one bag out and tossed it on the ground then inserted his into the pile. "You have to leave one behind."

"No." She picked up the bag. "This has all my shoes."

"We're only going to be there for two days," Conrad snapped. "Why do you need a whole bag of shoes?"

"You never know." She picked it up and almost fell over because it was so heavy.

"Just borrow something from Mom." Conrad snatched the bag with one arm then carried it back to the car.

Trinity pouted. "Skye, why don't you have a bigger car?"

Cayson raised an eyebrow. "Because there's nothing bigger than an SUV..."

"Let's hit the road," Roland said.

Everyone headed to the doors. Cayson sat by the window in the backseat and I moved to the spot next to him.

"What are you doing?" Conrad demanded.

"Sitting next to Cayson. I don't want to sit next to my brother for the whole drive."

"Then I call shotgun!" Conrad got into the passenger seat.

"Sweet." Roland fist pounded him.

Trinity sat beside me then pulled out a pile of magazines.

Cayson stayed quiet, staring out the window.

Roland left my apartment and made it to the freeway.

I looked at Cayson. "I haven't talked to you in a while. I thought we could catch up."

"Yeah..." He looked out the window again.

What was going on? It seemed like he was brushing me off. "Cayson, is everything alright?"

"Yeah...just tired."

"I didn't see you at the Halloween party. Did you go?"

His mood suddenly became sour. "Yeah. I left early."

"What did you dress up as?"

"Laser tag soldier."

I smiled. "How cool. I wish I could have seen it."

He leaned his head against the glass.

"Why did you leave early?"

"I left with someone..."

"Oh." That made me feel awkward and I wasn't sure why. "Why haven't you been coming into the diner?"

"Geez, would you stop interrogating him?" Roland looked at me in the rearview mirror. "Maybe he finds you annoying like the rest of us."

"Shut up and stop eavesdropping," I said.

"It's hard not to when you're less than a foot away from me," Roland said.

Cayson didn't defend me. He kept looking out the window.

Since he was acting so strange, I stopped talking. I wasn't sure how to act around him. He seemed so different and I wasn't sure why. Did I do something? Maybe I should speak to him privately. He was more open with me when it was just the two of us.

***

After Roland dropped everyone off, we finally arrived at my parents' house. I knocked on the door and Roland dropped all our bags in front of the twelve-foot door. Our house wasn't exactly small. We had a country house in Connecticut, just a thirty-minute drive from New York City. It had seven bedrooms, two living rooms, a pool, and it was right on the beach. Every friend I had wanted to come over, and it was easy for Roland to pick up any girl he wanted.

My dad opened the door. "You have a key."

"But we don't live here anymore." Roland shrugged.

"Knock it off," my dad said. "You're always welcome to just come in."

"Last time we did that, you and Mom were going at it on the couch." It was a disturbing image burned into the back of my brain. It wouldn't go away no matter how hard I tried.

My dad smirked, not ashamed. "Just let us know when you're coming." He came to Roland first and hugged him tightly. I watched them, seeing my dad close his eyes while he held my brother.

My mom stepped out of the door then smiled at me. "See? Didn't the week go by fast?" She wrapped her arms around me and hugged me. "You look lovely today."

"I hardly brushed my hair."

"Which makes you even more beautiful." She pulled away then headed to Roland.

My parents switched and my dad came to me.

"Hey, pumpkin." He wrapped his arms around me and gave me a warm hug. When we were in the privacy of our house, my dad was less tense and intimidating. He let his walls down and was carefree. Sometimes I felt like my dad was two different people.

"Hey, Dad."

"Thank you for coming down."

"You never miss any of my things so why would I miss yours?"

He pulled away then smirked. "We got each other's backs, huh?"

"We do."

My dad grabbed my luggage and Roland grabbed his own. Then they carried everything to our rooms.

When I walked inside, I smelled the scent of home. It was decorated for fall. Colors of brown and orange were splashed everywhere. My mom had a red blanket on the back of the couch, and pumpkin scented candles were lit. I loved living on my own but I missed home. There was nothing else like it.

My dad returned then put his arm around my mom's waist. "We've got a few hours to kill. What did you kids want to do?"

"Laser tag," Roland blurted.

"Are you sure?" my dad asked. "Because your mother is going to cream you again."

"Rematch," I said.

"Alright." He kissed my mom on the cheek. "The old married couple versus the brats."

"We aren't brats," Roland said.

"You'll always be brats." My dad grabbed the keys off the hook.

Roland came to him. "Dad, can we take your Sear?"

"It only has two seats, Son. You know that."

"Come on. Mom and Skye can take a different car."

"How about this?" He handed the keys to Roland. "You drive."

Roland's eyes widened. "Seriously?"

My dad smirked. "I think you're responsible enough."

He stared at the keys, in awe.

"Just be careful," my mom said. "Otherwise, I'll be angry."

"Got it, Mom." Roland ran out the door before anyone else could follow.

My dad laughed. "I love it when the kids are home."

My mom wrapped her arm around his waist and squeezed him. "Me too."

I stared at them, wondering if I'd ever find a relationship like that. They never got sick of each other. Despite all the time they spent together, they were still madly in love. Relationships were supposed to get stale and old.

They were supposed to become repetitive and boring. But my parents were never like that. I hoped I was lucky enough to share the same fortune.

***

A limo drove us to the gala. My dad and Uncle Mike were hosting the event, and they had to make a striking appearance. I wore my champagne pink dress and Roland wore a suit with a gray tie. The silver Rolex around his wrist brought out the color of his eyes.

My dad was wearing a black suit with a black tie. He usually never wore any color. His white gold Rolex matched his wedding band. It was the same one he always wore. My mom wore a black dress that had sheer sleeves. The gown was tight around her waist then flared out slightly. It reached the skin just above her knee. Her pumps were five inches tall, and black diamond earrings hung from her lobes. She matched my father perfectly. Her brown hair was voluptuous and curly, pulled to one side to reveal her neck.

My dad kept his hand on her thigh, always touching her in some way. Her arm was hooked through his, anchoring him to her. It was disgusting how affectionate they were all the time, but I admit it was better than having parents who hated each other. Or even worse, a cheating father who despised his wife. One who only stayed married for the sake of the kids, but that just made things worse. I decided not to complain. It could be worse.

When we finally arrived at the hotel, my dad opened the door and helped my mom out. When she was out of the way, Roland stepped out. Then my father helped me out. Photographers were on the sidewalk, taking pictures of us. My father's warmth disappeared. He was tense all over again, his eyes guarded and his back rigid. The only human emotion he showed was affection with my mom.

We headed inside then entered the ballroom. Everything was decorated for a spectacular night. The crystal chandeliers shined bright from the ceiling, and waiters carried glass flutes on trays. It was fancy.

Even when my mother wore heels, my dad was still vastly taller than her. He held her closer to him when he looked at us. "Be on your best behavior tonight. You represent me. Don't forget that."

Roland rolled his eyes. "We know, Dad."

"I have to mingle with your mother. Have fun."

"Okay," I said.

My dad never dropped his touch for a moment. "Come on, baby. You're my eye candy for this."

"You hate when people look at me."

"But they would be stupid to gawk at you in my presence." They moved into the crowd and disappeared.

Roland sighed. "Now where are the hot chicks?"

"Dad said we had to be on our best behavior tonight."

"I am," he snapped. "That doesn't mean I can't hook up with someone."

"Actually, I think it does mean that."

Roland put his hands in his pockets and looked around. "The blonde at the bar is cute."

I turned to see a woman sitting alone. "She looks too old for you."

"Only by a year or so. Besides, I like older women." He wiggled his eyebrows.

"Don't be gross."

"You want to be my wingman tonight?"

"Not really."

He rolled his eyes. "Damn. And Cayson is pretty much good for nothing."

"Why?"

Roland sighed. "Because he's in love with you, like I've said a zillion times."

"Oh shut up. I'm sick of hearing this ridiculous theory." I crossed my arms over my chest.

Roland glared at me. "Whatever."

"Hey." Trinity came up to us, wearing a silver dress. "Man, this party is lame."

Conrad wore a black suit just like Roland's. "There are a few cute girls here. It's not a total bust."

Roland nodded to the bar. "There's a baby cougar over there."

"Baby cougar?" I asked.

"It's a woman who's going to be a cougar but she isn't old enough yet." Trinity said it like it wasn't her first time.

"Oh. Where's Cayson?" I asked.

Conrad shrugged. "I don't know and I don't care. He'll find us if he wants to see us."

The fact Cayson wasn't with us alarmed me. Was he sitting at a table alone?

A man in a suit came to Trinity then handed her a glass of wine. He looked older than us, in his late twenties. But he was cute. "A beautiful woman should never be empty-handed."

She smiled then took it. "Why, thank you."

"I like your dress—especially the back." His eyes smoldered while he looked at her.

"Thank you." Trinity's cheeks blushed again.

Conrad stuck a finger down his throat and acted like he was gagging. Roland snickered while he watched him.

179

A shadow suddenly fell on us, blocking out the light from the chandelier. It was like a mountain had been moved to our vicinity, cutting us off from civilization. Uncle Mike stepped in front of Trinity then stared down the admirer, making him take a step back.

Oh shit.

"Leave." That was all he said. Just a simple word made us all uneasy. Uncle Mike looked similar to my dad, but he had more muscles in his arms and chest. His eyes were darker, more threatening. He looked like a Roman soldier about to gut his enemy.

"Sorry..." The guy held up his hands. "I didn't know she had a man."

"I'm her father." The threat was heavy in his voice. "Now go."

The guy high-tailed it out of there quicker than we could watch. Uncle Mike watched him go until he turned around and faced his daughter.

"Dad, that was totally unnecessary." She crossed her arms over her chest.

"He is too old for you. And don't take drinks from strange men."

"I can make that decision on my own." It was obvious how annoyed she was. My dad was bad when it came to boys, but Uncle Mike was a million times worse.

"I just saved you some time." Like a shark, he moved away slowly, making heads turn.

Trinity sighed and rolled her eyes. "He's just ridiculous sometimes."

"Well, that guy *was* too old for you," I said.

She glared at me. "You better not be taking his side."

"I'm just saying..." I stepped away, not wanting to piss her off.

"He just doesn't want his daughter to be a slut," Conrad snapped. "A reasonable request."

"So you can sleep with every girl in Boston but I can't have a single boyfriend?" she asked incredulously.

"Exactly." He grabbed a glass from a passing waiter. "I guess you're smarter than you look."

I looked around the room, wondering where Cayson was. After scanning for a moment, I spotted him at the bar. He was drinking a brandy by himself, watching the people dance in the center of the room. "What's his deal?"

"What?" Roland asked.

"Cayson is sitting alone at the bar," I said.

"So?" Roland shrugged.

"What do you mean *so*?" I asked. "Why is he avoiding us?"

"Maybe he doesn't want to spend every waking hour with us," Conrad snapped. "Seriously, all we ever do is hang out with each other."

"What's wrong with that?" I asked.

"It's lame," Roland said.

I rolled my eyes then waved at Cayson. "Cayson, we're over here."

"Just leave the guy alone," Roland said.

"Maybe he couldn't find us," I explained. "That makes sense."

Cayson heard me then looked in my direction. He sighed deeply then walked to us, wearing a black suit with a dark blue tie. "Hey, guys." He seemed down, sad.

"I'm sorry my sister is being particularly annoying today," Roland said.

"I just assumed you couldn't find us," I said.

"Yeah..." He drank his brandy then stirred the ice cubes. He looked at the crowd, watching people.

"I think I'm going to make my move for the blonde," Roland said.

"When she turns you down, I'll make my move," Conrad said.

"I'm a Preston," Roland said. "Even if she's married, she'll still put out."

"You better not sleep with married women," I demanded. "That's wrong, Roland."

"Hey, I stay out of your business so stay out of mine." He glared at me for a long moment before he looked away.

"There you are!"

We turned to see Grandpa smiling at us. He wore a dark suit with a gray tie. Lines covered his face and his hair was starting to turn gray, but he was vibrant and buzzing with life. He was never in a bad mood, and he always knew how to make us smile.

"The man is here!" Roland came to him first and hugged him. "You're looking good, Grandpa. The ladies must be swarming."

"They are but your grandmother isn't too happy about that." He pulled away and winked. Then he looked at the rest of us. "I love my grandkids. You guys are the greatest joy in my life." He hugged Conrad next then made his way to me. "Skye, you're more beautiful every time I see you. I'm just grateful you look like your mother and not your father."

I chuckled. "Thanks."

Then he hugged Cayson. "Wow, you're bigger every time I see you."

"I hit the weights every day." Cayson patted his back then pulled away.

"It shows, kid." Grandpa patted his shoulder. "Thanks for coming. I know everyone appreciates it."

"We wouldn't let our dads down," Roland said. "Plus, there's free booze, food, and pretty girls."

"But the girls aren't free though—for you." He nudged Roland in the side.

Roland laughed. "Good point."

"I'm headed back to the dance floor. They can't reenact *Dirty Dancing* without me." He headed back into the crowd and disappeared.

"Grandpa still has game," Roland said. "He's a legend."

"He's adorable," Trinity said.

"Too cute," I said.

Cayson put his hand in his pocket then downed the rest of his glass. "I'll catch you guys later." He turned and headed back to the bar.

"Okay...I don't care what you guys say, there's something bothering him." I chased after Cayson and caught up to him at the bar. My brother walked by me and headed straight for the blonde. I ignored him and focused on Cayson. "What's going on? Is everything okay?"

Cayson looked at me, his face guarded. "Nothing. I'm fine."

"Then why are you acting weird? You keep pushing me away and you don't even want to be around us. The last time I saw you everything was fine, but now you're...different. Did I do something?"

He sighed then rubbed the back of his neck. Conflict was in his eyes. Cayson told me everything and I wasn't sure why he was holding back now. "I'm sorry...it's not you."

"Did one of the guys do something? Trinity?"

"No," he said quickly. "It's nothing like that."

"Then what is it? You can tell me, Cayson."

"Actually, this time I can't."

What did that mean? "What?"

"I'm sorry I'm being a jerk. It's not my intention."

"Can I do something to help?"

"No." He took a deep breath and returned his hand to his pocket. "Just forget it, okay?"

"Forget what?"

"This whole thing." He grabbed a flute from a waiter then downed half of it. Then he spotted Roland talking to the blonde. "Going in for the kill, huh?"

I decided to drop it. Whatever was bugging Cayson was personal. "Yeah. I just hope she isn't married."

"I don't think it makes a difference to him. So, having a good time?" he asked.

I shrugged. "Yeah. I don't like doing work things with my family though. My dad is different. When he's at home with us, he's fun and relaxed. When he goes to work functions, he's detached and guarded."

"It comes with the territory."

"I just feel bad for him sometimes."

"Don't. It's a small price to pay for what he gets in return."

"I suppose..."

"Happy to be home?" he asked.

"Yeah. We played laser tag earlier today."

"I'm jealous," he said. "I love laser tag. Who won?"

"My parents." I rolled my eyes. "They totally ganged up on us."

"I think that's the point," he said with a laugh.

"But it's still not fair. My mom is really good."

"So are you."

I shook my head. "I'm no match for her. She's good at everything she does." I looked back over my shoulder and saw that Conrad and Trinity had left. They were probably sitting at a table. "You want to sit down?"

"Sure." He walked with me until we reached a table. Couples were slow dancing in the middle of the room. The women wore long ball gowns, and the men all wore suits. My dad was dancing with my mom in the center, his face pressed close to hers. He held her so close that there was no space in between them. Then he leaned in and pressed a kiss to the corner of her mouth before he pulled away.

"They're still in love," Cayson said.

"I know..." I rolled my eyes. "It's gross."

He smirked. "My parents are gross too."

"You want to dance?" I blurted. *Why did I just ask him that?*

"Uh...sure." He shrugged.

I got to my feet then walked with him to the dance floor. I'd never danced with Cayson before. He seemed to know exactly what to do. He grabbed one hand and held it in his own then placed the other on my hip. I wrapped my free hand around his neck then let him lead the dance.

"You know how to waltz?" I asked.

"My dad taught me." He held my hand while he gracefully moved me. The other couples were doing the same thing and we fit right in.

"You're good."

"Thanks." He looked into my eyes for a moment. Suddenly, he looked away. "You look nice."

"Thanks. My mom picked out the dress."

"She has good taste." He spun me under his arm then pulled me back.

"I don't know...she married my dad."

He laughed. "Good point."

"Are your parents here?"

"Yeah. They're mingling somewhere."

"What did you guys do today?"

"My dad and I got a few beers and watched a college football game."

"That sounds nice."

"I like spending time with my dad—even though he drives me crazy sometimes."

"Me too."

Cayson's blue eyes reflected the light from the chandelier. I could see every crystal and every light. His eyes seemed brighter, magical.

"What?" he asked.

"Nothing." I wasn't sure why I didn't tell him the truth.

The music ended and Cayson dropped his hands immediately. "Thanks for dancing with me."

"I should be thanking you. I asked."

"Well, it would be a little cocky for me to prematurely say you're welcome." He smirked.

"Well, thank you."

"You're welcome."

We walked back to the table then sat down.

Trinity and Conrad joined us.

"Hanging out with my sister on a Saturday night...fun." The sarcasm was heavy in Conrad's voice.

"It's not my fault you got rejected," Trinity snapped.

Roland joined our table then sat down. "I'm hooking up with Blondie later tonight." He patted his own shoulder.

"Does Blondie have a name?" I asked.

He shrugged. "If she does, I don't remember it."

Such a jackass.

We made conversation for the rest of the night while the benefit continued. Cayson was quieter than he normally was, and Trinity didn't mingle with any of the men. It seemed like we were all off in some way. I hardly saw my parents because they were having a great time. Uncle Mike and Aunt Cassandra were lost in the crowd, and Grandpa was too busy break dancing. Even though we were the ones in our youth, we were definitely the lamest people there.

***

We came home a little after midnight and went straight to bed. Even though my room was on the other side of the house, I could faintly hear my parents going at it. It was cute they were in love, but could they knock it off for like a minute? When I looked at the clock, I realized it was 2 a.m. God, my parents were annoying.

Unable to get back to sleep even an hour later, I went downstairs for a glass of water. I left the lights off because I knew the route through the house better than the back of my hand.

When I reached the kitchen, I saw the red light blink across every window. My dad had the finest security system for the house. He was anal about stuff like that. I headed to the refrigerator then opened the door.

189

In the refrigerator light, I saw Roland grabbing the keys from the hook. "What are you doing?" I whispered.

He shoved the keys into his pocket. "Hooking up with Blondie."

I looked at the time. "It's three in the morning."

"That was the only time she was available."

"Why?"

"Her husband is asleep."

I slammed the door shut.

"Shh! Keep it down."

"She's married?" I asked incredulously. "Roland, don't you dare."

"It's not my fault her man can't satisfy her."

"Roland, don't. What if her husband comes after you?"

He laughed. "You think I'm scared? If he even touches a hair on my head, I'll make him regret it."

"And if her husband works for the Preston Empire, you're giving Dad a bad name!"

"Calm down. She isn't going to get caught."

I eyed the key rack. The key to my SUV was still hanging. "You better not be taking Dad's car."

"Why? He let me drive it earlier."

"With his permission. He's not giving it to you now."

"Geez, calm down. You're such a tight ass."

"You need to knock it off. This is serious."

"I'm not going to be lame like you. I'm actually going to take some risks and enjoy myself."

"Of all the women in the world, why do you have to pick a married one?"

"Because she's hot," he snapped.

"Roland, I mean it. Don't do this."

"Are you going to tattle on me or something?"

I sighed. "No. You know I never would. But just listen to reason for a second."

"Nope." He headed toward the door. "I'll be back before sunrise."

"Dad gets up early so make it sooner than that."

"Thanks, sis." He winked then faced the alarm pad. He disarmed the alarm before he walked out.

I sighed then opened the refrigerator again, getting a glass of water. The fact he was screwing a married woman really got under my skin. What if she had kids? What if he was breaking up a marriage? Roland was more reckless than I was. I understood he was younger, but still. I downed the whole glass and felt the coolness moved down my throat. Then I wiped my upper lip, hoping my brother didn't get caught.

When I headed out of the kitchen, my dad rounded the corner with a gun in his hand. He held it like a cop, one hand rested underneath the other for balance. My eyes widened and I was about to scream when he quickly pointed it at the ground.

"Oh my god." I clutched my chest and breathed hard. "What the hell are you doing?"

"Sorry, pumpkin. I didn't mean to scare you."

"Why do you have a gun?"

He kept it pointed at the ground. "Did you touch the alarm pad?"

How did he know? "No."

He opened the panel and examined it. Then he turned back to me. "Are you lying to me?"

"No." *Technically, I wasn't.* "What's going on?"

"Someone disarmed it."

"How do you know?"

"There's nothing that goes on in my house that I don't know about." His voice was intense. His anger was barely below the surface. "Now I'll ask you again, Skye Preston. Did you touch the damn alarm pad?"

He never cursed at me. "No. I didn't."

He examined my face before he looked away. "Where's your brother?"

Now this was tricky...

"Uh..."

He looked to the key rack and realized his keys were gone. "He took my car." He marched to the garage then opened the door. "That brat took my car." He shut the door again and came back to me. "Where did he go?"

I eyed the gun in his hand. "Please put that away."

His eyes softened when he stared at me. "I'm sorry I scared you." He walked to the counter then dismantled the gun piece by piece. It lay in a pile on the counter, unable to be used.

When did he learn to do that?

"I take the security of my family very seriously. I never gamble with something I can't afford to lose."

What made him this way? Did something happen a long time ago?

He came back to me and stared me down. "Where did he go, Skye?"

I hated lying to my father but I couldn't rat out my brother. It was an unspoken code.

"You will answer me." The threat was in his voice.

I was glad the gun was unusable. I knew my father would never hurt me. He didn't even spank me when I was little, but that didn't mean

I wasn't scared of him sometimes. Just his words alone inflicted wounds. He was an intense man. Just a look from him could make you crumble. "I don't know...why don't you just call him?"

"Are you lying to me, Skye? You know how I feel about that."

Ugh. "I know where he is but I'm not telling you anything. I'm sorry, Dad."

He clenched his jaw. "Is he safe? Is he doing something dangerous?"

"Yes, he's safe. No, he isn't doing something dangerous. He's just hooking up with some girl."

My dad relaxed noticeably. "What girl?"

"I can't say..."

"Someone he met at the gala?" Now he started to get angry again.

"No comment."

He clenched his fists by his sides. "These are people I work with. The last thing I need is drama in my company, and a bad name from my son. He can screw around with anyone else, but this is unacceptable."

"I told him it wasn't a good idea."

"Men never listen to the wisdom of women."

"Are you going to call him?"

He thought for a moment. "No, the damage has been done. I'll let him think he got away with it until he walks back into this house. Then, I'll eat him alive."

Damn, I felt bad for my brother.

"I understand why you won't rat on him. My brother and I are the same way. But now you will do something for me. You will not warn him about this, Skye. I mean it."

"Okay."

"I have your word?"

"Yes, Dad."

"Now go to bed." He dismissed me then turned to the gun on the counter.

"Please put that away before you confront him."

He didn't look at me. "I take gun safety very seriously, Skye. I've had them since you were born but you never saw them for a reason. I don't intimidate my children with fear. I intimidate them with respect. There's a big difference."

I walked behind him and headed to the hallway. "Dad?"

"Yes, pumpkin?"

"Did something happen...to make you this way?"

He tensed at the counter but didn't turn around. A few heartbeats passed before he spoke. "A lot, actually. I've seen too much to discuss, and I've almost lost more than I could afford."

"What...?" I wasn't sure if I wanted to know.

"I'm sorry, Skye. I promised your mother I wouldn't tell you. Please don't ask me again."

My mom doesn't want me to know? What doesn't she want me to know? I wasn't stupid enough to ask my father twice. I headed upstairs to my room but couldn't sleep. Knowing Roland was about to be attacked made me anxious. I felt bad for him. He made this decision even though I tried to get him to change his mind.

***

I knew Roland was home when I heard my dad yell.

"Sorry. Did I scare you?" my father snapped.

"Shit, Dad. Why are you lurking in the dark like a troll?"

"Do I look like I'm in the mood for jokes?" His voice practically shook the house. "Where were you?"

"Uh, out..."

"In my car?"

Roland was quiet for a while. "I didn't think you would mind..."

"Then why did you tiptoe behind my back? Don't play games with me, Roland. I promise you will always lose."

"I just wanted to drive a nice car, okay?"

"Without my permission? That car doesn't belong to you. It belongs to me, your father, the man who gave you everything since the day you were born. How dare you disrespect me like this. You defied my trust just to borrow the car for an evening? If you weren't an adult, I'd let this slide. But you're a grown man, Roland. If you don't know the meaning of respect, then I obviously have failed as a parent."

Ouch...

"Dad, I'm sorry."

"Don't apologize until I'm done." His words sliced through the air. "If you think you can sneak out of my house without my knowledge, you're an idiot. I know everything that comes in this house and everything that leaves every hour of the day. Don't flatter yourself to think you can outsmart me."

"Maybe you need to chill a little bit..."

I covered my face even though no one could see me.

My father said nothing for a long time.

God, the tension was killing me.

"I've never been more disappointed in you in my life."

Ouch...

"What's the big deal?" Roland said. "I borrowed your car and took off. It's the only bad thing I've ever done. You're acting like I killed someone."

"Just because you have a clean slate doesn't mean any crime you make is vindicated. Now where did you go?"

"Just out."

"Out where?"

"And about."

"Roland, answer me."

"I was out with a girl, okay? You used to be a shithead when you were younger. I know you were with a different girl every night. I know you drove Grandpa crazy. You aren't a saint."

"I never said I was. But we aren't talking about me. We're talking about you. And your grandfather didn't go easy on me. Believe me, compared to him, I'm tame."

"I fucked some girl then I came home."

"Why did you have to do it in the middle of the night?"

Oh no. Here it comes.

"Just because..."

"Roland, answer me."

He remained silent.

"I'll either find out from you or I'll find out in a different way. If you choose the latter route, you'll be a coward. Keep that in mind. If you want me to treat you like a man, you need to act like one. Real men own up to their mistakes and look the devil in the eye as they admit them."

Roland stayed quiet for a while. Finally, he spoke. "She's married. She wanted to make sure her husband was asleep."

Minutes of silence passed.

"You bedded a married woman?" my father asked.

"Like you haven't."

"The only married woman I've ever had is your mother. You're playing with fire, Roland."

"I didn't get caught so it's okay."

"It is not okay." My father's voice grew louder. "I'm not going to tell you how to conduct your personal life. I'm not going to stick my nose in your business. What you do with your dick is none of my concern. But you need to think this through. If you have any respect for marriage, you need to rethink this. How would you feel if your wife cheated on you?"

"She would be satisfied so that would never happen."

"Roland, I'm being serious."

"Fine. I wouldn't like it."

"I taught you better than that. Tell me you'll never do this again. And mean it."

Roland sighed. "I'm sorry. It won't happen again."

"Don't bullshit with me, Roland. The fact you hooked up with one of my employees or the wife of one of my employees is a slap in the face to me. It will take time for you to earn my forgiveness for that. Of all things, I'm most hurt about that decision. I respect my workers, and I'm embarrassed that my own son, a possible future CEO, doesn't."

"I made a mistake. I was just bored at the gala and wanted something to do."

"You were bored?" My dad was even more irritated. "You're just making this worse."

"I'm sorry. I'm sorry. I learned my lesson and I won't do it again."

"Learned what lesson?"

"I'll never sleep with a married woman and I'll never steal from my father."

"And I hope you learn to respect me at some point in time."

Roland stayed quiet for a while. "Dad, I do respect you..."

"I don't believe you."

"I do...I was just being an ass."

"You really hurt me, Roland. You'll have to do better than that if you ever want to repair that damage."

My brother stayed quiet for a long time. Nothing happened. I wondered if my father had returned to his bedroom. I wondered what was happening. Did Roland walk away? Was the conversation over?

Then I heard Roland cry. "Dad, I'm sorry. I'd take it back if I could..." My brother never cried. You could beat his face with a baseball bat and he wouldn't blink an eye. Only my father could make a grown man crumble into pieces.

"It's okay, Son." His voice was gentle.

I imagined they were hugging.

"I just worry," my dad said. "I'm not going to be around forever and I need to know you can take care of yourself. And I don't mean financially. I need to know you're a strong man that is both gentle and kind. I need to know you will raise my grandchildren right. I need to know you can take care of your mother and sister if something happens to me."

"Dad, don't talk like that."

"I sugarcoat things for your mother and sister but I won't do that with you. You're my son, and you need to be prepared."

"You talk like someone is after you."

"When you're as rich as I am, someone is always after you," he said quietly. "Being a father isn't just about providing and putting food on the table. It's about the lessons you teach your children, the people you mold them into. Money means nothing to your mother and I. Family, friendship, and love is all we care about. And I want to make sure you have those same morals. Sleeping with a married woman doesn't qualify."

"I said I was sorry..."

"I know. I forgive you, Roland. Just learn from your mistakes."

Roland stopped crying. "I love you, Dad."

"I love you too, Son. Just don't piss me off again."

Roland laughed lightly. "If you're bad, I can only imagine how bad Grandpa was."

"Your grandpa is the man I respect most in this world. He was hard on my brother and I. There were times when I hated him, despised him. But he did a damn good job raising your uncle and I into fine men. And for that, I will forever be indebted to him. The day your sister was born, I promised myself I would be the same way with you—the best father I could possibly be."

"You're doing a good job, Dad."

My dad was quiet for a while. "That means a lot to me, Son."

Nothing else was said. Eventually, their footsteps were heard on the wooden staircase. Doors were shut and the house was silent once again. I didn't realize tears were coming out of my eyes until I felt a drop on my cheek.

Chapter Seven

Cayson

I didn't know what to do about Skye. Whenever I was around her, I was even more obsessed with her. The feelings only grew more prominent. I entertained the idea of us being together. Sometimes I imagined that she might feel the same way. I got in so deep that I hallucinated she was in love with me too.

Then I saw Zack push her up against a wall and it brought me back to reality.

This wasn't healthy. These feelings were not normal. I just wanted them to end, to go away. All it was doing was hurting me. So I decided to put some space between us. I avoided her whenever possible. I tried not to think about her, to pretend she didn't exist.

But then the gala came up and ruined everything.

I couldn't get away from her when we were in an enclosed vehicle. I couldn't run away from her at the benefit. The more I tried to push her away, the more I hurt her. She looked at me with pain, like I stabbed her in the chest. I hated it. I hated myself for making her feel that way.

So I stopped.

And now I was back to square one.

I went downstairs and placed my luggage by the door. Roland was about to pick me up.

My mom was distraught. "God, I'm going to miss my baby." She wrapped her arms around me and embraced me, tears in her eyes. "You're so handsome, Cayson. Just like your father."

I hugged her back. "I'm going to miss you too, Mom."

"Please move back here after college. I hate not seeing you every week."

"Of course, Mom."

She breathed a sigh of relief and pulled away. Every time I left, it was hard for her.

My dad clapped me on the shoulder. "Thanks for coming down."

"You know I wouldn't miss anything, Dad."

He pulled me in for a hug. "I love you, Son. I know I drive you crazy and I appreciate you putting up with me."

"Well, you're my dad. I have to…"

He laughed. "I see how it is. Call me when you get back."

"Dad, I'm a grown man."

My mom started crying. "He's not a little boy anymore." My mom's dark skin protected her from lines of age. She still looked beautiful, classy, despite the years that had passed. My friends always claimed she was a MILF, which always made me uncomfortable.

"Call me anyway," my dad said. "It just gives me peace of mind."

"Okay." There was no point in arguing with him.

A car horn sounded outside.

"That's my ride," I said.

My mom wiped her tears away. "I'll see you next time, honey. I love you."

"I love you too, Mom." I walked out before she could burst into tears again.

Roland rolled down the window. "Get in before they change their minds."

I laughed then threw the bags in the truck. Then I got into the backseat next to Skye.

My parents stood outside and waved as Roland pulled away from the house. I stopped staring when they were finally out of sight. "Brutal..."

"I know," Skye said. "I always cry when I leave my parents' house. I just hate saying goodbye."

"I know what you mean."

She pulled out a deck of cards. "Want to play poker?"

"Not for money," I said. "Because I feel like a jerk running you dry."

"How about we play for dinner? Loser buys."

"You're on."

We played a few rounds while Roland drove back to Boston. Skye was pretty good at the game. She knew when I was bluffing and when I wasn't. But that went both ways. I could read her pretty well too.

I really wanted to push her away so I could get over her, but she was my best friend in the world. There was no one I'd rather do anything with. I'd even rather play basketball with her than any of the guys. She was the person who made me laugh until I cried. She was the only person I could cry in front of. She was everything to me.

What the fuck do I do?

Maybe I should just tell her. It would make our relationship strained and uncomfortable but she would understand why I needed my space. We would never be the same again, but I couldn't keep going on like this. It was getting worse over time.

Skye won the winning hand. "Looks like you're buying me dinner."

"Damn."

"You know what my favorite is."

"Everyone knows what your favorite is," Trinity said as she rolled her eyes.

"I like pizza too, so we're good," I said.

She put the cards back in the box when we arrived at my apartment. "Home sweet home."

"Thanks for the lift," I said.

"No problem. My dad paid for the gas," Roland said.

"And the car," I added.

"And probably the road too," Trinity said with a laugh.

I unbuckled my safety belt then opened the door.

Skye grabbed my arm. "Dinner tomorrow?" The fear in her eyes told me she was scared I was going to ignore her again.

God, she was killing me. "How about later in the week? I have a few things to take care of."

She released my arm. "Okay."

I shut the door then got my bags out. When I was back in my apartment, I tried not to think about Skye. She looked so damn beautiful in that pink dress. It complimented her skin tone and hair color perfectly. She was a living fantasy. Slow dancing with her didn't help my attraction to her. Being so close to her, touching her, was pure torture. I was going crazy.

My phone vibrated in my pocket. I pulled it out and looked at the screen.

Whatcha doing?

It was Jasmine. *I just got home.*

Are you horny? Because I know I am.

She didn't make me work for it at all. It was probably because I made her come every time. I wasn't in the mood at all. What I really wanted was to curl up on a couch with Skye and kiss her. Just kiss her. Nothing else. I wanted to feel her smooth skin with my hand. I wanted to feel her lips with mine. I wanted the closeness, the intimacy, and the love.

Realizing that made me depressed. How was I ever supposed to get over her if I kept thinking about her all the time?

I typed a message. *Come over.* Maybe if I slept with Jasmine enough times, I'd get over Skye. She was sexy and beautiful. She was easy to get along with. And she was great in bed. Maybe it would make me want other women. So far, it made me feel less lonely, even though that feeling didn't last long. As soon as I saw Skye again, I was desperate for her.

On my way.

***

The sex was good. She was spontaneous and sexy. She did things most other girls wouldn't do. Her body had curves in the places I liked. Her legs were long and lean, and I liked the way they felt wrapped around my waist. It was a good way to release the frustration I had.

I lay in bed when we were done and stared at the ceiling. She lay beside me, her head resting on my bicep. One leg was woven around mine, and her hand rested on my chest. I didn't kick her out like I used to. She'd become a friend as well as a booty call. And she understood I wasn't emotionally available.

"How did you get so good in bed?" she whispered.

I smirked. "Practice, I guess."

"Most guys can't make me come, and when they do, it's a fluke."

"Maybe they aren't trying to."

"That's true. Guys can be dicks."

I rested one hand behind my head and sighed.

She trailed her fingers across my chest. "How was your weekend?"

"It was okay. It was nice to see my family. What did you do?"

"Worked."

"You probably made good tips."

"I did. Being pretty always helps."

I smirked. "And you're very pretty."

She nuzzled closer to me. "How was it being around Skye?"

I sighed, knowing I'd never get away from her ghost. "I tried to ignore her most of the time, but she knew something was wrong. So I abandoned that plan."

"How long have you felt this way about her?"

I shrugged. "I don't know...years."

"And she's never noticed? I find that hard to believe."

"She's blind, apparently."

"And stupid."

"Hey, don't go there." My voice became serious.

"Well, she is. She has you pining for her heart and she doesn't even care."

"In her defense, she doesn't know how I feel. And secondly, she sees me as a brother. When you grow up together, it's bound to happen."

"I'm just jealous. I wish you were in love with me. I'd be the happiest girl in the world."

That made me a little uncomfortable "You'll find a man who adores you, Jasmine. Just don't expect it to happen overnight."

"Can I ask you something?"

"You will anyway."

"If you didn't feel this way for her, would I have a chance?"

This was dangerous territory. "I made it clear I wasn't emotionally available."

"I know. It's a hypothetical question."

"I don't know. I'm not sure how I would feel toward you. I know I find you attractive and I care about you. But that's all I feel right now."

"Why don't you try to get over her with me?"

"What do you think I'm doing?"

"I mean you should give me a real chance. Take me out on a date and spend time with me.

Try to find an emotional connection to me. You know what they say; the best way to get over someone is to move onto someone else."

"That isn't fair to you, Jasmine."

"No, it isn't. But if you were someone else, I wouldn't offer this. But you're special."

"I...I don't know."

"Just think about it."

I didn't respond.

"I should probably get going. How about another round?"

"I'm pretty tired."

She moved under my sheets toward my waist then sealed her mouth around me. Instantly, I was hard and ready. I closed my eyes and enjoyed what she was doing to me. Then I wanted her again so I took her.

***

I avoided Skye all over again. I knew I owed her dinner but I was going to act like I forgot. I didn't want to sit across from her at a restaurant and have a great time. I didn't want to keep wishing she was my girlfriend. I didn't want to feel sick every time I saw her with Zack. So I just avoided her, like a coward.

I didn't visit her at Manhattan Grub on Wednesday night. It was a tradition I'd never take up again. When I wasn't in class, I was studying or spending more hours in the lab. Since

I was so determined not to think about Skye, I was doing even better in my classes. I committed myself to the task obsessively and didn't think of anything else.

When I was sitting in my apartment studying, Slade walked through the front door.

"Hey. Let's play ball." He had a basketball in his hands.

I looked up from the coffee table. "Yes, please come in," I said sarcastically.

He grabbed a beer out of the fridge then plopped down on the couch.

"You think you should drink alcohol before exercising?" I asked.

"It's not like I'm eating before I swim." He downed half of it then put it down. "How was the weekend with the family?"

"Good. My parents miss me like crazy."

"It's been three years." He rolled his eyes. "They need to get over it."

"I know...but I miss them too."

"Cry me a river." He spun the ball on his finger. "How's avoiding Skye at all costs going?"

"Okay...but she cornered me on the weekend. I really had nowhere to run."

Slade laughed. "Sometimes I wonder if she has feelings for you but she's in denial or something."

"Please don't torture me." I didn't have the heart.

"Sorry, man." He spun the ball on his finger again. "There's a party at the frat house this weekend. A lot of cute babes will be there."

"Will Skye?"

"Not that I know of. I would assume she's spending time with that jackass boyfriend of hers."

"Why is he a jackass?" I asked.

"Because he's not you."

I smirked then closed my textbooks.

"So, ball?"

"I guess."

My bedroom door opened and Jasmine stepped out only wearing my t-shirt. "Do you mind if I take a nap?"

Slade eyed her, focusing on her legs for almost a full minute.

"Sure," I said. "I'm going to play ball with Slade."

"Okay." She smiled then shut the door again.

Slade winked at me. "Nice."

"Thanks."

"So, is this becoming routine?"

"I guess."

"Do you like her?"

"I like her as a friend."

"And fuck buddy," he added.

"She knows how I feel about Skye so I don't feel like a jackass."

"Wait." He put the ball on the table. "She knows you—"

"Dude, I eat on here."

"Oh." He put the ball on the ground. "She knows you're in love with Skye and she doesn't care? At all?"

"I think she cares a little bit, but no, not really."

He stared at me with new eyes. "Dude, you're a god. You need to show me your moves. My girls are always like, 'Oh my god. I love you. Don't leave me. Let's get married.' And I'm like, 'No fucking way.'"

I laughed. "You want to know my secret?"

"Please."

"Just be honest."

He stared at me incredulously. "If I walk up to a girl and tell her I want to fuck her brains out, not talk, and never see her again, she's just supposed to be down with that?"

"Well, I would say it a little nicer than that."

"But you kinda have a relationship with this girl."

"It's more of a friendship than anything else. It's nice sleeping with the same person because it gets better every time you do it. The first time with someone is usually a little awkward. You don't know what they like and they don't know what you like."

"Not me. The ladies love it."

"Well, you're just gifted, I guess."

"Damn right." He stood up and grabbed the ball. "Now let's play some ball."

***

Slade and I walked into the frat house and took a look around. The bass was pounding in our ears, and all the girls were wearing swimsuits.

"I guess it must be a beach theme," Slade said.

"In the fall? It's almost Thanksgiving."

He shrugged then pulled off his shirt.

I did the same.

"This is better anyway," he said. "Now we can tell who really has a nice body and who stuffs their bra."

"Yeah...because I've always cared about that."

"And Victoria's Secret makes all those push-up bras so their tits look nicer than they really are. Personally, I'd like to know if a girl has real melons or cucumbers before I get down and dirty."

Seriously, I didn't know why he and I were friends sometimes. We were so different. "Sure..."

We headed to the keg and poured two cups of beer. I poured out the foam that floated at the top.

Slade inspected everyone in the room. "What do you prefer? Blondes or brunettes?"

"They aren't cattle."

"Just answer."

"Well, the girl I'm obsessed with is a brunette."

"But the woman you're fucking is a blonde."

Knowing Jasmine and I slept together regularly made me feel like an asshole. "I'm not hooking up with anyone tonight."

"Why the hell not? Because no pussy is as good as Skye's?"

I cringed. "Dude, she's your cousin. And no. It's because of Jasmine. I never said we were exclusive but maybe she thinks we are."

"So, you're in a relationship?"

"No," I said quickly. "But...I don't know. Why pick up some other girl when I have a great thing with Jasmine?"

"Because you never want to tap the same ass twice."

"Why? I think it gets old being with someone new every time."

He gave me a strange look. "I'll never understand why you're my best friend."

"Me neither."

He shrugged. "Whatever. I guess you can be my wingman for the night."

A table near the wall was knocked over and a vase shattered on the ground. Two girls in pink bikinis started laughing hysterically at the mess they caused. Their hair was in their face, but it was obvious they were totally wasted.

Slade eyed them. "Easy targets."

"They don't know their nose from their ass."

"Which is why they'll be easy."

"No, not cool."

He sighed. "Fine."

The girls continued laughing.

"Oh no, I cut myself." The blonde held up her hand and kept laughing.

I recognized that voice. I turned and looked.

Trinity wiped her hand on her leg, smearing the blood. Her bikini barely covered anything. Her flat stomach had a navel piercing, and her cleavage was pressed together in the swimsuit.

I looked at the brunette and felt my heart sink. *No.*

Skye lay on her back and laughed hard, pointing at her.

Fuck. "Slade?"

"What?" He was eyeing a girl in the corner.

"It's Trinity and Skye."

He turned back and looked. "God fucking damn it."

"Let's get them out of here."

We left our beers on a table and came close to them.

Skye stopped laughing when she saw me lean over her. "Why are you naked?" She laughed again.

I'm surprised she even recognized me.

Slade scooped Trinity into his arms. "I'm taking her home because if she does something stupid, Uncle Mike will buy the university just to burn it to the ground."

"Good thinking. I'll get Skye home." I looked around, wondering if Zack was there. If he was, I'd hate him even more.

Slade carried Trinity out the door.

"Your tattoos are so hot," Trinity said as they walked away.

"Yeah, I know," Slade said.

I focused on Skye. "We need to get you home."

"Shit, you work out a lot." She eyed my chest and stomach.

I felt my cheeks blush slightly. It was the first time she complimented my appearance like that. I ignored her words. "Come on. Up you go." I gathered her in my arms then lifted her from the ground. The swimsuit she wore hardly covered anything. I forced myself not to look out of respect for her. But I guess if she was dressed like this, she didn't want to be respected.

Once I was outside, the cold air hit us both. Slade took the car so I'd have to carry her to her apartment. I put her down for a moment then pulled my shirt over her, trying to keep her warm so she wouldn't get sick.

"It smells like you…"

I lifted her again then carried her through the grounds, the shortest way possible.

Her arms were wrapped around my neck and she rested her face against my chest.

I didn't say anything to her because I didn't see the point. Her responses would be illogical and incoherent. I tried to keep her as close to me as possible so she'd stay warm. I was so glad Uncle Sean would never know about this. He would be pissed. And Uncle Mike…I didn't even want to think about it.

I wasn't sure why Skye was even there. I expected this behavior from Trinity but not her. Maybe she got thrown into the situation like I did with Slade all the time. I had to hope that was the case. Because it would scare the shit out of me if I wasn't there to take her home. Some guy could have taken advantage of her. She could have gotten hurt. I tried not to think about it because it made me die a little bit inside.

Where the hell was Zack? Shouldn't he be taking care of her? Not me? Didn't he care that his girlfriend was going to a beach themed frat party?

When we arrived at her apartment, I used my spare key to get inside. I shut the door with my foot then carried her to her bed. When I set her down, I glanced at her legs. They were long and perfect. I sighed then started to tuck her in.

"Cayson?" she whispered.

"I'm here, Skye. I know you feel crummy right now but you'll feel better in the morning."

She sat up then ran her fingers through her hair. She stared at me, giving me a look I'd never seen before. Maybe it was because she was drunk. Maybe it was because she didn't feel good. "You always take care of me..."

I'd never seen Skye drunk like this so I didn't know what to expect. She was obviously vulnerable, emotionally real. It was a side to her I'd never seen before.

"Zack doesn't treat me the way you do. He doesn't open every door for me or put me first. He says he loves me like he's trying to get it over with. You never tell me you love me but I don't need to hear it. I know you do."

Where was this going?

"He doesn't make me laugh like you do..."

My heart was beating so fast the blood was loud in my ears. I was suddenly breathing hard, unsure where this conversation was taking us. The world was deathly silent. I could even hear the crickets outside her window. I stared at her face, seeing the moisture build up in her eyes.

Her bottom lip quivered slightly. I glanced at the freckle in the corner of her mouth, longing to kiss it like I had for the past five years. I didn't say a word, letting her do all the talking.

She fell silent, saying nothing more. A staring contest happened between us. It was dark in the room but I could still see her face. She could see mine. Then she touched my bicep, rubbing the muscle.

My heart skipped a beat.

Then her hand moved to my shoulder then the back of my neck. She gripped me tightly then moved her face close to mine.

We were so close together I could feel her breath fall on my skin. The scent of rose hips was heavy, mixed with the alcohol on her breath. I breathed hard, unable to stop the adrenaline coursing through my body. I wanted this. I'd wanted this forever.

Then she closed the gap between us and pressed her lips to mine.

I took a deep breath, caught off guard by the sudden burn on my lips. Her mouth was locked to mine, and my body shook slightly. I couldn't believe this was real, that this was really happening.

After I recovered from the initial shock, my lips moved against hers. They were soft like I imagined. I felt every inch of her mouth, wanting to savor it. She tasted so good, like cherry. I breathed into her mouth, unable to breathe through my nose because I needed so much air. My stomach hurt because the butterflies were killing me.

Knowing my greatest fantasy was becoming a reality, I cupped her cheek and deepened the kiss. A quiet moan escaped her lips, telling me she enjoyed me as much as I enjoyed her. She felt the powerful chemistry between us, the all-consuming need for each other. I always hoped that something was between us, that she didn't just see me as a friend. I wanted so much more with her, a life with her, a love with her.

She sucked my bottom lip then slipped her tongue into my mouth. When our tongues danced together, I felt my hand tremble. The kiss wasn't what I expected it to be. I imagined this moment so many times but I never expected it to be this amazing. It blew my mind.

Her hand moved to my chest, feeling the powerful muscle underneath. It slid down to my abs, feeling me. She never touched me this way, never even acknowledged my sex appeal. Now she wanted me the way I wanted her.

I gave into my darkest desire then kissed the corner of her mouth, wanting to taste the freckle even though I couldn't. "I've always wanted to do that." Then I kissed her again, not planning on stopping until we both couldn't stay awake a second longer.

Skye grabbed my shirt and pulled it off, revealing her body in the swimsuit. I glanced down, seeing her chest, and then tore my gaze away. My mouth found hers again, needing to taste her.

Her hand left my chest and moved behind her back. She untied both strings to her bikini then let the fabric fall.

My lips stopped moving, knowing what just happened. I shouldn't look. I wouldn't be a gentleman if I did. But I couldn't help it. I wanted her for longer than I could remember. I looked down at her chest, seeing the most gorgeous and cock-throbbing image of my life. She was perfect.

Unable to control myself, I leaned over her and sucked each nipple. She dug her hand into my hair, moaning while I touched her. I'd never been this turned on in my life. I'd never felt my heart bleed like this. This is what I wanted for so long.

Skye pulled her bottoms off, driving me crazy. Now she was naked beneath me, wanting me.

I lay her on the bed then moved over her, kissing her again. I pressed my chest to hers, feeling her breasts against me. My hand moved down her legs, feeling the smoothness. I couldn't believe I was touching her. I couldn't believe this was happening.

Skye reached for the top of my jeans, and that seemed to bring me back to reality.

I steadied her hand, realizing this was wrong. While I loved what was happening, never wanted it to stop, I couldn't do this. She was drunk, and I didn't want my first time with her to be like this. I wanted so much more.

"Cayson..."

Hearing her say my name made me want to keep going. But I held back. I moved off of her then pulled the sheets up, covering her beautiful body. "We'll pick this up tomorrow."

"I don't want to wait." She grabbed my neck and pulled my lips to hers.

I melted all over again. "Skye...I've wanted you for so long."

"Then take me."

God fucking damn it. I pulled my lips away. "Tomorrow." I breathed hard, trying to recover from the loss of blood to my head.

She stared at me with disappointed eyes.

"I'll come back in the morning with breakfast. We'll talk about this then."

"Stay here."

I would but I didn't trust myself.

"Just go to sleep. The sooner you fall asleep, the sooner you'll wake up."

She finally gave in. "Okay."

I leaned down and pressed my lips to her forehead, feeling joy in my heart. Skye was finally mine. She was meant to be mine and now I finally had her. My life was complete. "Good night."

"Good night." She closed her eyes and sighed.

After another long look at her, I walked out and locked the door.

***

I got no sleep that night.

All I could think about was how much my life had changed. I had to convince myself it wasn't a dream. It really happened. Skye wanted me and I wanted her. I always hoped she felt something more for me, but I always assumed it was just wishful thinking. But she did. She really did.

As soon as the sun came up, I showered and got ready for the day. I was too excited to sit still. I wanted to climb on top of my building and tell the world Skye was mine. I wanted to head to Zack's apartment then punch him in the face, just to be spiteful. I wanted to kiss Skye again. That's all I wanted to do when I got over there; lay on her couch and kiss her until her lips were chapped.

I headed to a coffee shop and got her coffee, a pumpkin spice latte with soy and no foam, and got her breakfast. I couldn't stop smiling. The clerk looked at me like I was on speed.

225

Then I headed to her apartment, my fingers drumming on the steering wheel because my excitement couldn't be contained. My life was forever changed. Everything was different. I was complete. Now I could do everything with her. I could take her to dinner and the movies and be honest with her. I could spend all my time with her and not have to hide my true feelings. I could kiss her whenever I damn well pleased.

I jogged up the stairs then opened her door with my key. After I set our breakfast on the counter, I looked for her. The bathroom door opened and she stepped out, her hair wet and her pajamas wrinkly. She still looked beautiful to me. I admit I thought about her naked body after I saw it. Honestly, I couldn't stop thinking about it. She was even sexier than I thought.

She groaned then rubbed her temple. "God, I feel terrible."

I smirked. "I got you coffee, breakfast, and aspirin."

"Thank you. You're a life saver."

"I'll get you breakfast every morning if you'd like."

"Then I'll have to start paying you. And I'm broke."

"You don't have to pay me anything." I stared at her, waiting for her to join me. "Well, you don't have to pay me in cash."

"Food?" she asked with a laugh.

"No, I was thinking of something else."

"Like what?"

She really couldn't figure it out?

She came to the counter, not looking at me. Then she grabbed her coffee. When I came around to kiss her, she walked away and sat on the couch, blowing the steam away.

What was going on?

"What happened last night?"

I suddenly felt cold. "You don't remember?"

She rubbed her temple again. "I remember going to that frat party...and drinking...a lot."

"That was the last thing you remember?" My heart started to slow down, almost not beating at all.

"Yeah...something about breaking a table. Or maybe it was a vase? I don't know."

My heart stopped for a full second. Time slowed down, crushing me, breaking me. She didn't remember what happened last night. She didn't remember anything. It was like it never happened. The first kiss I had with her never existed. The way she looked at me never came to pass. None of it was real.

I was just a drunken mistake she couldn't even remember. Maybe she didn't even know it was me. Maybe she thought I was Zack. Maybe she thought I was just some random guy she thought was hot. I was nothing. I meant nothing to her. The greatest night of my life was just a blur to her, something she couldn't even recall.

I put my heart on the line. I showed her how much I cared about her. I gave myself to her. She threw herself at me and I covered her up. I could have slept with her and she wouldn't have even known. I could have been anybody. I could have been a random stranger.

"Cayson?" She stared at me, concern in her eyes.

I remembered every single time I cried in my life after I was five. My sister flushed my favorite stuffed animal down the toilet; one that Grandpa Preston got me. My friend passed away after drunk driving. And that was it. Those were the only two times.

And now this was the third time.

"I have to go." I turned my back on her so she couldn't see my face. I got out of there as fast as I could. The tears were inevitable and my heart was breaking. I felt so stupid, so foolish, for ever thinking I meant anything to her. I was just a friend. I was nothing.

I got into my car then hit the road. I didn't drive back to my apartment. I just drove. The streets were icy but I didn't care about the risk. I felt the warm tears fall from my eyes. Feeling the moisture made me feel more pathetic. I couldn't believe a single girl had this affect on me, had the ability to manipulate me like this. I was sick of it. Skye wasted so much of my time and I wasn't going to waste any more of it. I was done with her.

Done with her.

Chapter Eight

Skye

"Have you seen Cayson?" I asked Trinity when we sat together in the library.

"Um...not since the benefit at home." She licked her finger then flipped the page of her magazine.

"Was he at that frat party we went to?"

"I don't think so. I know Slade was."

"You saw him?"

"Yeah. He took me home. He said I was being irresponsible."

"Do you remember everything?" I asked. "How did I get home? I woke up and I was in my bed—naked."

"I think Cayson took you home."

"He did?"

"I think Slade mentioned that. But I really can't remember. Don't quote me on that. Why?"

I was trying to rationalize Cayson's behavior the other day. "Cayson came over the next morning with breakfast. He was in a good mood and everything seemed fine. Then all of a sudden, he just stormed out. He didn't drink his coffee or eat his food. It was weird..."

"Maybe he had to be somewhere."

"On a Sunday? No. His behavior was odd."

I shrugged. "I don't know what to tell you. You could just ask him."

"Yeah, I guess I could. I wasn't sure if texting him would just annoy him."

"Why would it annoy him?"

"He's just been a little off lately. I think something is bothering him."

Trinity returned her focus to the magazine.

I tried to study but I kept thinking about Cayson's behavior. It was so odd. I'd known him my whole life so I always knew when he was upset. But I couldn't figure it out. It was even more peculiar that he didn't just tell me.

I forced myself to get back to work and not think about it.

"You want to have game night this weekend? Invite everyone over?" Trinity didn't look at me when she said it.

"Yeah, that would be cool. Your place?"

"Sure. I'll invite everyone."

"Just family?"

"Yeah."

Zack came to our table, placing a coffee on the counter. "I got your favorite."

"Thanks." I inhaled the scent and immediately felt more awake. Then I took a sip, immediately noticing the odd taste. "What is this?"

"Caramel macchiato."

Ugh. Zack never listened to me. I didn't bother complaining. Coffee was still coffee.

"What?" Trinity asked. She knew something was up.

"Nothing," I said.

"What?" Zack asked. "Did they mess up the order?"

"No...this just isn't what I drink. I've never had a caramel macchiato in my life."

"Isn't it your favorite?" Zack asked.

"No." Now I was getting irritated. "You must be getting me confused with one of your other girlfriends."

He rolled his eyes then sat beside me. "You know you're the only one. Want to come over tonight and watch a movie?"

"Isn't football on tonight?" I asked.

"Yeah. Same thing."

"No...watching a movie and watching sports is completely different."

"Whatever. You want to come over or what?"

I sighed. "I guess."

Trinity looked at me over her magazine, giving me a look, and then looked down again.

"What?" I asked.

"Nothing," she said.

"I'll make you dinner," Zack said.

"Frozen pizza?"

"You like pizza, right?" he asked.

"Yeah, I guess."

"I'll see you then." He kissed my cheek then left.

Trinity eyed me. "What are you doing with him?"

"What?"

"He's so annoying. That guy never listens to you."

"He told me he loved me."

She put down her magazine. "What? When?"

"He asked to come to the gala and meet my parents and I said no. Then he said he loved me and said it was time to meet my parents."

"He just blurted it out? No romantic evening or making love?"

"No, it was odd."

"Why does he want to meet your parents so much?"

I shook my head. "I have no idea."

"Did you say it back?"

"What do you think?"

"And he was just okay with that? That you rejected him?"

"He said he was." I shrugged.

"It just gets weirder and weirder..."

"I don't understand him. I feel like he's in a hurry to settle down with me. I'm not sure why."

"I guess he could be madly in love with you." She drummed her fingernails on the table. "But it doesn't seem like it. He can't remember anything about you and he cares more about football than spending time with you."

"He does love my rack."

"Well, who doesn't?" she teased.

"I tried breaking up with him but he completely refused it."

"He refused it?" she asked incredulously. "When someone wants to break up, you break up. The other person doesn't get a say in that."

"He doesn't agree. Then he kissed me and was all mushy-mushy... I crumbled again."

"So, he seduced you?"

"Pretty much."

"Honestly, I don't see this relationship lasting so maybe you should just dump him."

"Maybe..."

She grabbed my coffee and took a drink. Then she made a face. "Damn, that tastes like shit."

I laughed. "You're telling me."

***

I went to Zack's later that evening. He was wearing jeans and a tight t-shirt. He did have a nice body. I couldn't deny that.

"Hey, baby." He kissed me when I walked inside. "You look nice."

"I'm wearing a yoga pants and a sweater," I said incredulously.

"You still look hot to me." He eyed my chest then looked away.

"Oh, you were talking to my chest, not me."

He smirked. "You're finally catching on." He moved to the oven and pulled out the frozen pizza. "Dinner is served."

"Yum," I said sarcastically. Zack didn't have extra cash to take me out to dinner or nice places. I never cared about that, but a sandwich would still be better than frozen pizza.

Zack put some slices on his plate then handed me my own.

I couldn't help but compare him to my dad. My father always served my mom food before he got his own. Cayson was the same way. I really shouldn't compare Zack. I knew how he was when we got together.

We moved to the couch then sat down. Football was on so he was totally absorbed in that. I leaned back and watched the game, trying to stay entertained. I didn't mind watching sports, but Zack and I were so busy with school that I thought we should spend some time together. Instead of complaining, I ate my pizza quietly.

When the game was finally over, he turned off the TV. "Good game, huh?"

"Yeah." I tossed my paper plate on the coffee table.

He moved closer to me on the couch, his hand reaching for my thigh. "I like these yoga pants." His lips moved to my ear and he started to kiss me. I leaned my head back and gave him more space. I liked it when he kissed me and touched me. He was good at it. But the actual sex sucked.

He continued to kiss me while he slowly peeled my clothes away. My hands gripped the end of his shirt and yanked it off. Then I undid his pants, wanting to see him naked.

Zack scooped me up and carried me into his bedroom. When I was on my back, he kissed my inner thighs then slowly moved up. When he was at the apex of my thighs, I writhed on the bed and moaned. He was good with his mouth.

Then he moved further up my body.

"No, don't stop," I blurted.

He sighed, clearly not wanting to do it, and then went back down, kissing me the way I liked. It was hard for me to enjoy it when I knew he didn't want to do it, but I found my climax anyway, really needing to be satisfied. Then I let him climb on top of me and slip inside me. He always wanted me on my back so he could stare at my tits. It was an obsession with him. He rocked me hard and fast, sweating and groaning while he slammed into me over and over. In less than four minutes, he came inside me, moaning the entire time. I was glad I already got my fix otherwise I would have been unsatisfied yet again.

I immediately got up and changed.

"Why don't you sleep over tonight?" he asked.

"Because I have class in the morning."

"But you never sleep with me."

I didn't like to cuddle with people. It was too uncomfortable. "Maybe during the weekend."

He sighed then got dressed, ready to walk me to the door.

"Good night, baby." He kissed my cheek when we got to the entrance.

"Good night." I walked to my car in the dark then headed home, wanting to sleep in a bed by myself.

Chapter Nine

Cayson

Something snapped inside my head. While I was hurt, shattered into a million pieces, I was also reborn. The fact I didn't mean anything to Skye gave me the extra push to forget about her, to really accept that she would never be mine. If I stayed this way, I would be in pain forever. Now I had rage to help me move forward.

"Why are you in a bad mood?" Slade sat across from me in the student lounge, his history textbook in front of him.

"Because I'm pissed," I blurted.

He cocked an eyebrow. "Do you want me to get you a sandwich or something?"

"No. I'm not hungry."

"Are you sure? Because when I'm hungry, I act like a jackass."

"Then are you always hungry?" I snapped.

"Dude, what the hell is up with you? You're like a nuclear bomb about to go off."

"Because I am." I pushed my book away, unable to study.

"Tell me what's going on. Did Skye do something?"

"Yep, she did."

"What?" He was practically at the edge of his seat.

"You remember that night of the frat party?"

"Yeah. It was just last week."

"Well, I took Skye home. I carried her up the stairs and into her bed. I tucked her in, being the good guy that I am." The bitterness carried in my voice. "She started telling me I treated her better than Zack ever did, and that I made her laugh like he never did. Then she kissed me."

Slade's jaw was hanging. "Then why are you so mad?"

"Because we started making out. It was perfect. It was the best night of my life. She took her clothes off and wanted to sleep with me."

"Did you?" His eyes were as big as orbs.

"What do you think?" I snapped. "That I would sleep with the love of my life while she was drunk off her ass? Of course, not."

"Oh." His disappointment was evident. "Then what happened?"

"I told her I'd come back in the morning with breakfast. We could talk about our relationship then. I assumed she and I were together and she was going to dump Zack. But when I came back the next morning, she had no memory of it. It was like she blacked out."

"Are you serious? She doesn't remember anything?"

"Nothing. The last thing she recalled was knocking over that table."

"Did you tell her what happened?"

"No." My anger came out again. "Why should I? It didn't mean anything to her so why should either one of us remember it? I'm sick of the way she keeps hurting me. I'm done with her—for good."

"So...you're over her?"

"No. But I will be very soon."

Slade was quiet for a while. He stared at me, trying to find something to say. "I'm sorry, man. But maybe this is a blessing in disguise."

"Yeah..."

"Now you can really move on."

"I intend to."

Slade kept staring at me, a sad look on his face.

"What?"

He shrugged then rose from the table. He came over to my side and opened his arms. Then he awkwardly leaned down and gave me the weirdest hug I've ever had. He patted my back a little too hard then stepped back. "I'm sorry that happened to you."

"Thanks..."

The moment became tense so he walked back to his side of the table then plopped down. He coughed. "Anyway..."

"Yeah..."

"So, now you're going to be my right hand man? Getting a different girl every night?"

"No. I had something else in mind."

"What?" he asked.

"Jasmine."

"You're going to be her boyfriend?"

"Something like that."

"Well, she is pretty hot."

"And she's a sweet girl."

He sighed. "I guess everyone will officially give up on you and Skye."

I rolled my eyes. "No, everyone already gave up. And now so have I."

***

I texted Jasmine after class. *What are you doing?*

Thinking about you. What are you doing?

Wondering if you'd like to come over.

You already know the answer to that.

Half an hour later, she showed up at my door. Her blonde hair was silky and soft. Turquoise earrings hung from her lobes, bringing out her eyes. She wore skin-tight jeans and a loose sweater. A red scarf was around her neck.

"You look nice."

"Thank you." She took me in quickly. "You do too." She stepped into my apartment, desire in her eyes. "How do you want me?" Her hands

241

moved up my chest until they reached my shoulders. She stepped closer to me, our bodies touching.

I grabbed her hands and pulled them down. "Actually, I want to have dinner with you."

Confusion came into her face then her eyes softened. "Dinner?"

"Yeah. If you'd like to join me."

She understood the significance of my words. "You'd like to try?"

"If you can be patient with me."

She smiled. "I can be as patient as you like."

"Good." I took her hand and walked her out of the apartment. We headed to the sports grill then sat by the window. I ordered a beer and she ordered wine. When I felt her stare at me, I met her gaze. "Yeah?"

"Did something happen?"

"Yeah." I looked at the menu then put it down. "I picked up Skye from a party, and being drunk, she kissed me and told me I meant something to her. The next morning she didn't remember anything. It was like it never happened." I felt angry and hurt every time I said it.

"Did you tell her what happened?"

"No. I'm not going to."

"Why?"

"Because it obviously didn't mean anything to her. She probably thought I was some random guy."

She processed my words for a moment. "But didn't she actually say you meant something to her?"

"Yeah…"

"So she knew it was you. Just because she doesn't remember it doesn't mean she didn't mean it."

I guess she had a point. "She was drunk and out of her mind. Maybe she was just rambling. She even wanted to sleep with me and that's not like her. Plus, she's not a cheater. It was just a big drunken mistake that she was fortunate enough not to remember."

Sadness came into her eyes. "I'm sorry, Cayson. I know how you feel about her."

And I didn't want to feel that way anymore. "It's okay. Actually, this is the best thing that could happen to me. Now I'm ready to move on."

"With me?"

"I'd like to try."

She smirked. "Well, that works for me. I'm just sorry you didn't get what you really want."

I shrugged. "That's life. Now let's forget about Skye."

"Okay." She picked up her menu and looked at the entrees. "I'm getting the chicken fingers."

"Good choice. I'm getting the hot wings."

"We are a perfect match." She winked at me.

The waitress came to our table and we put in our order. Then we sat in comfortable silence.

Jasmine wasn't my usual type. There was nothing wrong with being a waitress but I preferred intellectuals. But Jasmine was smart, too smart to be waiting on people. She was beautiful and kind. She was empathetic toward others, and she had a carefree spirit. There were a lot of attributes about her I liked.

"How's school?" she asked.

"Good. The same, really."

"I can't even imagine all the knowledge shoved inside your brain."

I smirked. "It's like a box of cats in there. How was work?"

She shrugged. "When I bartend, it's good money, but getting hit on every night gets old."

"I can imagine."

"Which was why I liked you so much. I could tell you were a gentleman—a very rare find."

My cheeks blushed slightly.

"So, can I ask you something?"

"You can ask me anything, Jasmine."

"I'm not trying to get clingy, but what are we?"

"I don't know. I guess we're dating."

"Let me rephrase that. Are we exclusive?"

I shrugged. "Do you want to be?"

"That's a stupid question," she said with a laugh.

"Then we are."

She smiled. "I knew my patience would be rewarded."

"I'm not really the kind of guy to sleep around anyway. I prefer the same partner for a long period of time. The sex is better."

"Me too."

The waitress placed the food on the table and we dug in.

"What are you doing for Thanksgiving?" she asked. "I can't believe it's just a few weeks away."

"My family usually does something all weekend. We have game night, a laser tag competition, and then Thanksgiving dinner."

She smirked. "That's very...nontraditional."

"We've never been traditional. Other than my parents and my sister, I'm not technically related to anyone else. But I'm as good as."

"That's really sweet. How did that happen?"

"Our parents have a dysfunctional and dependent relationship with everyone else. Slade's dad and my dad are best friends. My dad is best friends with Skye's mom too. And Trinity's dad is Skye's father's brother...it's complicated."

She laughed. "I can tell."

"Basically, we're family. What are you doing?"

"Probably sleep in, and then wait until midnight to do my Black Friday shopping online. Then I'll catch up on my shows on Netflix."

Did that mean she was alone? "You don't spend it with your family?"

"No. My father left when I was young. I've never had a relationship with him. And my mom is a drunk. She and I don't speak. And I'm an only child." She said it like she was discussing the weather. There was no bitterness or anger. It was like she didn't care.

But that broke my heart. She spent every holiday by herself? No dinner? No company? "I'm sorry..."

"It's really not so bad. People always feel sorry for me, but I'd much rather spend it alone than with people who only make me miserable. So don't pity me. It's fine, really."

I just couldn't accept that. "Come over for Thanksgiving."

She looked at me like I was crazy. "To your parents?"

"Yeah. We hang out all weekend and do a bunch of fun things. You'll have a great time."

"But...wouldn't that give them the wrong idea?"

I shrugged. "I'll tell them you're my friend. It's really not a big deal."

"Have you ever brought a girl home before?"

"Well, no. But they aren't going to care. If you don't want to stay with us, you can stay with anyone else. Skye and Trinity both live in mansions. Slade's parents have an apartment in New York City. Each one of them would welcome you with open arms."

"Um...it's okay, Cayson. But I appreciate the offer."

"No." I felt the anger break through. "I'm not letting you spend it alone."

"Cayson, I don't want people to get the wrong idea about us."

"Who cares?" I said. "I don't care what anyone thinks. If I tell my dad what you are to me, he'll believe me. And maybe you and I will get there someday. We're just getting a jumpstart."

"I just don't want you to pity me."

"Well, I do. I'm sorry. No one should spend Thanksgiving alone."

"I've been doing it for years..."

"That streak is going to end."

She picked at her food then smirked slightly. "You're very sweet, Cayson."

"You're my friend and I care about you. If you were a guy friend, I'd still invite you."

She took a few bites then looked down.

"So, you'll come?"

"I'll think about it."

"Okay." I watched the game on the screen while I ate my hot wings and fries. She picked at her food across the table, eating very little.

After we were finished, I paid the tab.

"Let me get it," she offered.

I grabbed her hand across the table. "Let me make this clear. I don't let girls pay for meals. Don't bother trying. All you'll do is waste your time." I released her hand then left the tab at the end of the table.

"I've been warned..." She put her purse over her shoulder then stood up.

I walked with her out the door then drove back to my apartment. She looked out the window and kept her silence. The roads were icy from the cold as winter deepened. I was always warm despite the season but I kept the heater on for her.

When we came back to my apartment, she immediately went into my bedroom. I followed her, knowing what was coming.

"Can I sleep here?" she asked as she undid her scarf.

"You don't need to ask me that, Jasmine."

"Can I leave a few things here?"

"Sure."

"Okay." She stripped off her clothes until she was just in her cheeky panties. I was hard the moment I looked at her but I kept thinking about someone else. When Skye took off her bikini, I saw every inch of her skin. Her breasts were round and perky, cock-throbbing. Her waist curved into an hourglass figure, and her hips were wide. Her stomach was small and had an insignificant amount of flab, but I loved the sight. She had the curves of a real woman, someone I longed to have.

I realized what I was doing and I stopped myself. I closed my eyes for a second then forgot about my dream girl, the woman I would never have. I was moving on, forgetting about her forever.

I looked at Jasmine again and only saw her. Her skin was smooth and pale, reminding me of a winter morning. She had curves in all the right places. There was nothing wrong with her. She was perfect in her own right.

"Are you going to keep me waiting?" She put her hands on her hips and stared at me.

"No." I pulled my shirt off then came to her, crushing my mouth against hers. My hands moved over her naked skin, squeezing and grabbing. The last kiss I had was the best one I'd ever had, but I couldn't remember it. It was an embrace that never should have happened. And as far as I was concerned, it never did.

Chapter Ten

Skye

"I brought Operation." I tossed it on the table.

Trinity gave me that look she'd been giving me my whole life. Her eyes narrowed together and she put her hands on her hips. It was a look that clearly said, "You're stupid."

"What?"

"That game is like twenty years old. Does it even work anymore?"

"Cayson and I played it a few months ago so I'm sure it does."

"Well, that's not something all of us can play."

"You never know," I said.

"Good thing you have big boobs because your brain is small."

I glared at her. "What games do you have?"

"Twister. Clue. Uno. Guess Who."

"Ha! Guess Who is a two player game!"

She gave me that same look again. "I'm just telling you what I have."

"Too bad your boobs are average size."

She threw a pillow at my head.

I laughed. "Don't argue with my father's daughter. You will always lose."

"Don't fight my father's daughter because you'll always lose." She squeezed her bicep.

"What are you squeezing? I don't see anything."

She threw another pillow at my head.

"You definitely aren't good with the words."

She turned to grab another pillow but they were all gone.

"Oh no. It looks like Trinity is out of ammo." I grabbed the pillows and threw them at her. "Sucker!"

Conrad and Slade walked through the door, carrying cases of beer.

"The kings have arrived," Slade said.

"So bow down, ladies." Conrad placed the case on the counter then ripped it open.

Trinity and I exchanged a look then threw the pillows at them.

Slade held up his hand. "Hey, what the hell?"

"Don't mess with the queens of this house," I said.

Slade grabbed a beer then tossed it to me.

"Do you have a bottle opener?" I asked.

"No. Do you have a lighter?" he countered.

I raised an eyebrow. "What are you going to do with a lighter?"

"You've never opened a bottle with a lighter?" he asked incredulously.

"Should I have?" I asked.

Conrad dug his hand in his pocket then fished one out. "Here." He tossed it at Slade.

"Why do you have a lighter?" Trinity demanded.

"So I can see in the dark," Conrad snapped.

"It's not a flashlight," Trinity snapped. "It's an open flame. Why do you have to be an idiot?"

"Why do you have to be a whore?" Conrad countered. "That sounds like a more important problem to discuss."

She rolled her eyes. "So if I wear a slutty outfit on Halloween, I'm a whore?"

"Yep." He looked at Slade.

Slade flicked on the flame then held it under the cap for a few seconds, burning it. Then he flicked it off with his thumb. "Works like a charm."

Conrad did the same thing and popped his off.

I rolled my eyes. "Boys..."

The door opened again, and Roland came inside. "We better play poker for some serious dough because game night is lame."

"You can only throw so many parties and not get sick of it," Trinity countered.

Roland tossed a few bags of chips on the counter. "Look how polite I am." He grabbed a beer and then snatched the lighter from Conrad's hand. He did the same thing to his beer then popped off the cap.

"How did you know that?" I asked.

Roland shrugged. "Dad has taught me a few things."

We hadn't discussed the night he got in trouble, but I knew he didn't think I ratted him out. He'd done a lot of things when we were growing up and I always kept my silence. My brother and I weren't extremely close, but that was a silent agreement we honored, not to tattle on each other. It made us a united front against our parents.

Theo and Silke walked inside.

"Yo." Theo put another case of beer on the counter.

"This isn't a frat party," Trinity said.

"I drink this like water," Theo said.

Silke put a bottle of wine on the counter. "Because I have some class."

Theo laughed. "Yeah, okay."

Trinity looked at me. "Is Zack coming?"

I just wanted it to be family tonight. I invited him sometimes, but most of the time I didn't. The time I spent with my family was holy and sacred. It was a circle hard to penetrate by outsiders. I guess I didn't like sharing it with many people. "No."

"Good." She stood up then placed the games on the floor of the living room.

The door opened again, and I looked up, hoping to see Cayson. I hadn't seen him in almost two weeks. For some reason, his absence was always more profound than everyone else's. He was my best friend in the whole world. Plus, he owed me dinner and had never taken me.

He stepped inside wearing dark jeans and a gray hoodie. His eyes looked a brighter shade of blue when he wore light colors. Sometimes I saw flecks of different colors deep inside if I looked hard enough. His chest was defined even in his sweater. I never noticed that before. His shoulders were broad and thick, like he rowed often. I stared at him for several seconds, taking him in.

Then a woman walked in behind him. In her tight clothing, I could see the curves of her body. She had the hourglass figure guys loved, a great ass, and a chest that almost rivaled mine. Her blonde hair was pulled over one shoulder, but it looked like a curtain of silk. Red lips and blue eyes highlighted her face. She was very pretty.

"Hey, guys." Cayson kicked off his shoes by the door.

Everyone eyed the girl with him. He hadn't brought anyone into our circle in years, so everyone understood the significance.

Cayson put his arm around her waist. "This is my girlfriend, Jasmine."

Girlfriend? He had a girlfriend? I know he mentioned he went on a date but...I didn't think it was anything serious. How long had this been going on? Did he love her? Why hadn't he told me about her?

"Hey." Roland waved at her. "Welcome to the party."

Conrad came to her and shook her hand. "I like blondes too."

She laughed. "Good to know."

Cayson pushed him back. "Ignore him."

Slade came to her then nudged her in the side. "Please tell me you have a twin sister."

Cayson pulled her closer to him. "She's off limits, guys. Leave her alone."

"Now we have to play strip poker," Theo said. "But just with Jasmine."

Cayson rolled his eyes. "They're teasing. Just ignore them."

She smiled. "I know. I'll take it as a compliment."

She was sweet too. *Ugh.*

They came further into the room then headed to the counter.

"What can I get you to drink?" he asked her.

I stayed on the couch and stared at them, watching how gentle he was with her.

Trinity caught the look. "You're staring awfully hard..."

"What?" I said. "I was just admiring her boots."

She rolled her eyes. "Whatever, Skye."

Cayson grabbed her a beer and twisted off the cap with his bare hand. Then he grabbed himself one too.

Why was this bothering me so much? Was it because he never mentioned it to me? Was it because he kept me in the dark? I couldn't put my finger on it.

"Why don't you mind your own business over there?" Slade snapped.

I glared at him. "I'm just surprised. Cayson never mentioned her to me."

"He doesn't have to tell you shit, Skye. He doesn't owe you a fucking thing." Venom dripped from his voice.

Why was he being so hostile toward me?

Cayson and Jasmine came to our circle and sat down. He sat close to her, whispering with her and making her giggle.

Was he not going to say hi to me? I was always the first person he spoke to, the first one to share a story with. Now I didn't even exist.

"I think we should play UNO," Trinity said. "It's easy to play with a bunch of people."

"I think we should play strip poker." Theo wiggled his eyebrows.

"In case you haven't noticed, a lot of us our related to each other here," Roland snapped.

"Not my problem." Theo picked up a deck of cards and winked at him.

"UNO it is." Trinity shuffled the deck and handed out the cards.

When I was looking at Cayson, Jasmine turned her stare onto me. She watched me, studying my face. Then she turned away, not saying a word to me.

What was that about?

We got the game started, and like always, Cayson won the first round. He was good at everything he did. Sometimes it annoyed the other guys because they felt like they couldn't compete.

When we played again, Jasmine won.

That ticked me off but I wasn't sure why.

Eventually UNO got old so we just sat in a circle and talked while we drank.

"How did you guys meet?" Trinity asked Cayson.

"Well..." He tore the label off his bottle.

"I spotted him in a bar I work at and I asked him out." She said it without shame. "I knew he was a catch the second I laid eyes on him. And the rest is history."

She works in a bar? Is she a waitress?

"And I couldn't say no." Cayson smirked. "I mean, look at her."

I felt a pain in my stomach.

"So, you got some cute girlfriends?" Slade asked. "Cute, slutty, girlfriends?"

"I got all kinds of girlfriends." She said it with a smile. "It just depends on what you prefer."

"Slutty," he blurted. "Like, really slutty."

She chuckled. "I'll see what I can do."

"Can I get in on that?" Roland asked.

"Aren't you only into married women?" Conrad jabbed.

"You slept with a married woman?" Trinity's eyes practically fell out of her head.

Roland shrugged. "I may have..."

Trinity cringed. "That is so gross."

"You're gross," he snapped.

This could go on forever...

"Did you get caught?" Slade asked.

"Not by her husband," Roland said. "But my dad found out I stole his car."

"Oh shit," Conrad said. "Your dad must have been pissed."

"Like you wouldn't believe..." Roland sighed.

"If I pulled that number on my dad, I would have a broken leg," Conrad said.

"Well, our dad is a little intense," Trinity said. "I'm not sure how Mom puts up with him."

"He's a billionaire," Conrad said. "That's how she puts up with him."

"Mom doesn't care about that," Trinity said.

"Neither does mine," I said.

Jasmine eyed all of us. "I didn't realize I was mingling with that kind of crowd…"

"We're pretty quiet about it," Roland said. "But if you're into money, I got it." He winked at her. "Cayson's family is poor compared to mine."

Cayson rolled his eyes. "Thanks, man."

Roland shrugged. "I'm just saying…"

Jasmine leaned in close to him. "I'd take a poor perfect man over a rich jerk any day."

Cayson put his arm around her shoulder and smirked. "I like what I'm hearing…"

I couldn't stop watching them. He was affectionate with her all the time, touching her and holding her. I didn't like it even though I couldn't explain why.

We spent the rest of the night talking, but I didn't participate much. Seeing Cayson with a girlfriend rubbed me the wrong way. I couldn't stop staring, seeing how he held her hand and waited on her hand and foot. The love shined in her eyes, and she looked at him like he was the most amazing man in the world. Her hands touched his arm and then his thigh. The sexual attraction was evident.

I couldn't shake the feeling of sadness. It was deep in my veins and heavy in my throat. I couldn't explain why. I didn't know what was going on. It was just a feeling.

Cayson and Jasmine left early and walked out. I couldn't help but wonder what they were going to do when they got home. When I imagined him kissing her, it made me uneasy. Was it because I saw him as a brother? As family?

When he was gone, I realized he didn't speak to me once.

He didn't even look at me.

***

A week later I texted him. *Hey. How's it going?*

Cayson always responded in a heartbeat. Even if he was in class, he typed back a response. This time, three hours passed before he said anything. *Good. You?* It was short and to the point.

You still owe me dinner.

Twenty minutes went by before he responded. *Maybe next weekend. I got a lot of stuff going on.*

Something wasn't right. He was off. He'd been off for a while. *Can we meet right now?*

Like, right this second?

I need to talk to you.

This time his response was immediate. *Is everything okay?*

Yes, I'm fine. But I want to talk to you.

261

Then another fifteen minutes went by. *I'm in the library. I have a few minutes to spare—nothing more.*

A few minutes to spare? He used to have all the time in the world for me. *I'll be there in a second.*

K.

I reached the library then moved to the corner where he usually sat. He was wearing a black jacket with a gray t-shirt underneath. He didn't smile when he saw me. In fact, he looked annoyed.

"Hey." I sat across from him.

"What's up?" He flipped through the pages of his lab book. His voice sounded bored, hollow.

What was going on? It was like we weren't even friends anymore. "Can you at least look at me when you talk to me?"

He stilled for a second. Then I noticed his left hand clenched into a fist. I'd known Cayson long enough to know when he was angry, and for some reason he was. He released his hand then met my gaze. "You have my full attention."

His eyes didn't hold the same warmth they used to. It was like he loathed me, hated me. So much had changed and I had no idea what caused it. Did I offend him? Say something to hurt his feelings? I felt like I lost my best friend and I didn't even know why. I controlled my emotions so I wouldn't cry, wouldn't expose myself to him. "Cayson, did I do something to piss you off?"

"No." His voice was hollow.

"A few weeks ago you stormed out of my apartment without saying goodbye. Did I do something?"

"No." His eyes were guarded.

"You didn't even talk to me at game night last weekend."

"What are you talking about? I talked to everyone. We were sitting in a damn circle."

Damn circle? "Cayson, why are you different toward me? You keep saying I didn't piss you off but I feel like we aren't even friends anymore." I was barely holding on, about to break.

"Now that I have a girlfriend, I guess I don't have all the time in the world to spend with you."

"Why didn't you tell me about her? You tell me everything."

"My personal life isn't any of your business." The venom was heavy.

What the hell was going on? It was like he was a different person. Now I was breaking apart. My best friend wasn't even there anymore. Cayson loathed me for reasons I couldn't understand. What did I do? What the hell happened? I couldn't sit across from him a second longer. I stood up then hid my face. "I feel like I've lost my best friend." I walked away without saying another word.

When I was finally out of the library, I broke down into tears. The icy wind stung my face and burned my skin. I sniffed in the cold air, feeling my lungs hurt with every breath. Cayson was the person I relied on for everything, and he literally disappeared overnight. He didn't exist. The last time I remember him was when we went to that conference. When we came home, everything was different.

He was gone.

Chapter Eleven

Cayson

I knew I was being a dick to Skye but I couldn't help it. The only way for me to get over her was to push her away. Believe me, hurting her hurt me. But this was the only way. If I babied her like I used to, I would make no progress. If I spent all my time with her, noticing the curve of her neck and the rosiness of her cheeks, I'd be in love with her forever. This was how it had to be.

But I didn't feel good about it.

As the weeks went by, I focused on school. I didn't hang out with the gang as much as I used to because I was avoiding Skye. I hung out with Slade and Conrad, hitting the gym and playing ball with them, but other than that, I avoided everyone. Jasmine came over often, sleeping at my place then leaving late in the morning.

We'd been spending a lot of time together, and I was fond of her. But I didn't feel anything more than that. That passionate and all-consuming love I felt for Skye hadn't switched to Jasmine. I thought she was a beautiful girl and I enjoyed her company, but that was it. I didn't feel anything.

Maybe I just needed more time. Change couldn't happen overnight. It took time and hard work. We went out to dinner and to the movies, doing things normal couples did. But sometimes I worried Jasmine would fall in love with me when I couldn't reciprocate that emotion. The longer I was with her, the more I feared it would happen.

Maybe everyone was only meant to have one real love and I already had mine. I fell in love with Skye and that feeling was unshakeable. Maybe I would never feel that way for someone else ever again.

That sounded depressing.

Jasmine lay beside me in bed, trickling her fingers down my chest. "I love your body. It's so strong."

I turned and leaned over her, taking a nipple into my mouth. "I love your body. It's perfect."

She moaned quietly while she felt me kiss her.

I ran my tongue in the valley between her breasts then lay back down.

"Skye is such an idiot. But I'm so glad she is."

I didn't like talking about her, especially in bed. So I said nothing.

Jasmine cuddled into my side, wrapping her body around mine.

I wasn't a big fan of cuddling but I didn't mind doing it with her. I knew it was important to women to cuddle after sex so they didn't feel used. I would do whatever she wanted to make her feel better.

"Are you still in love with her?" she whispered. Desperation was in her voice.

"Jasmine, I think I'll always be in love with her. I wouldn't waste your time hoping that will change."

Her fingers still stroked my chest. "Okay."

"I'm sorry. I really am."

"I know." She fell silent, not saying another word.

***

I went to the library the next day and found a table in the corner. My back faced a bookshelf and I pulled out my books. I didn't like to wear headphones when I studied because it was too distracting. I preferred the echoing silence of the library. It was large enough to get lost in the sea of books. And if I were home, I'd probably watch TV or play video games and not get much schoolwork done.

I was finishing my analytical chemistry lab report when I heard voices from behind me.

"Did you ask her if you could spend Thanksgiving with her?" a guy said.

Another man sighed. "I don't see the point. She's pretty adamant about not letting me meet her family."

I recognized that voice because I hated the owner of it so much. It was Zack.

"She wouldn't take me to this gala for her dad's company even though I pretty much begged her to take me. Fucking annoying."

I wasn't sure what Zack was talking about but I didn't care. I opened my backpack and searched for my headphones. I'd rather listen to music than his voice.

"I even dropped the L word to get her to take me. That bitch wouldn't budge."

My hands stilled. *Did he just say what I think he said?*

"That's rough, man," his friend said. "It's sounds like she's not really into you."

"She's not," Zack said. "She tried breaking up with me twice but I persuaded her not to. But I'm running out of options. I just need to meet her parents and get her dad to like me. Then I can marry her then make sure there's no pre-nup. Then I'm fucking set for life."

My hands shook as I listened to him. I couldn't believe what I was hearing. Zack was using Skye for her money. That's what his game had been the entire time. He never loved her. He never cared for her. He had the most amazing girl at his fingertips and he didn't even give a damn. My hands shook.

"And then one of her guy friends was trying to steal her for awhile. The pussy finally backed off. It's just getting harder and harder to keep her tied down. Sometimes I lose sight to why I'm doing this but I have to remember to keep going. I want half of everything from her. I never want to work and she's my best way to secure that."

I couldn't believe what I was hearing. It was such a stab to the chest. My immediate instinct was to march over there and beat the shit out of him. But then reason took over.

I pulled out my phone then hit the record button. Then slowly, I turned behind me then tucked the phone between two books, catching their conversation.

"So, you don't even like Skye?" the guy asked.

"No. She's fucking annoying. I mean, she's good in bed and has amazing tits, but that's it. If she would just swoon over me and cooperate I could get this done quicker."

"I'm sure her dad isn't stupid. He would probably see right through your plan."

"No," Zack argued. "I'd tell him I want to be lawyer and politician. I'm sure he would like a man that could take his self-interest into consideration for congress."

"And I'd doubt he'd let her marry you without a pre-nup."

"I could talk her out of it. She's not bright."

It was getting harder and harder for me to listen to this.

"So, are you still seeing Vanessa?"

"Yeah. She hates this arrangement, but I keep reminding her that we'll be filthy rich when this plan works."

"Just don't get caught," his friend said with a laugh.

"Skye has no idea. She's totally oblivious. Dumb girl."

I snatched my phone and ended the recording. I had everything I needed. Skye didn't need to hear him rip her apart even more.

I stared at my phone and sighed. I didn't want to be the one to give this to her. I didn't want to be the one to hurt her. She wasn't in love with Zack, but I knew she would doubt her intelligence for not realizing what Zack was doing. Her confidence would be shaken, and she would be hurt.

Why did I have to be the one to overhear the conversation?

I sighed then grabbed my stuff. I headed the opposite way so Zack wouldn't see me. He had no idea that his infuriating plan was about to fall apart. And when Skye told her dad what happened, he would make sure Zack never had a job for the rest of his life. He would make his existence so insufferable that death would be a desirable option.

When I was outside, I sighed then texted Skye. *Hey. I need to see you.* We hadn't spoken in weeks. Our last conversation didn't end well. I was staying away from her, avoiding her at all costs. Our relationship wasn't the same and our friendship was ruined. It made me sad because I missed her like crazy, but I had to put myself first. I couldn't stand to feel this pain anymore.

I'm at home.

I was glad she didn't argue with me. I wasn't sure how she would respond based on our last conversation. *I'll be there in 5 mins.*

K.

I walked to her apartment on the other side of campus then knocked on her door. I didn't use my spare key because it felt odd. Stress was eating away at me while I stood there. I didn't want to show her this recording. I didn't want to hurt her.

She opened the door, her eyes guarded. "Hey."

"Hey." I stared at her, noticing the deep color of her blue eyes. The freckle in the corner of her mouth caught my attention. I remembered the last time I kissed it, the last time I melted.

"Did you need something?" She didn't let me inside like she used to.

"I want to talk. Can I come in?"

She stepped aside then closed the door behind me. Then she crossed her arms over her chest and faced me.

I noticed she was thinner than the last time I saw her. I didn't like that. Her body was perfect and she didn't need to change a single thing. A lump caught in my throat when I looked at her. With a sigh, I pulled my phone out of my pocket. "I have something to tell you and I really don't want to have this conversation."

"Why?"

"Because it's going to hurt you."

Her eyes flashed slightly. "Okay..."

"I was in the library when I overheard Zack talking to a friend. Apparently, he's only been dating you because he wants to marry you. And by marry, I mean secure his financial future. He's been trying to meet your parents so he can get their approval to take your hand. Then he was going to refuse to sign a pre-nup so he could take half your assets and never work again."

She didn't react as I said this.

I pressed the play button on my phone and didn't say another word.

She stared at the ground as she listened to it. When the recording ended, she still didn't react. Silence stretched for a long time. Her eyes were guarded and her lips were pressed tightly together.

I wasn't sure what to do.

Then she sighed and covered her face with her hands. "I feel so stupid…"

I put my hands in my pocket, standing across from her.

"Now I know why he dropped the L word so randomly and so quickly. Now I know why he wanted to meet my parents so much. Now I know why…now I know." She dropped her hands, revealing the coat of moisture in her eyes. "God, I'm so stupid."

"You aren't stupid. He lied to you. Just because you trust someone doesn't make you dumb. It makes him a fucking asshole."

She stepped away and turned around, walking slowly. She was wearing jeans and a purple sweater, my favorite color on her. Her long hair framed her shoulder, looking lustrous and silky.

The emotion overtaking me, I pressed my chest to her back then wrapped my arms around her waist, holding her to me. "Skye, I'm sorry."

"I know, Cayson…"

"He doesn't deserve you. He never did." I pressed my mouth close to her ear, feeling heat spark in my fingertips.

"I can't believe someone would do that…would trick me like that."

"He's a piece of shit, Skye. Don't let him tear you down."

She sighed, swallowing the lump in her throat. "He never showed any interest in me until we had a class together. When he heard my last name when the teacher took roll, that must have been when he decided to make his move." She shook her head. "I'm such a sucker."

"Don't blame yourself. Getting hurt by someone doesn't make you weak. It makes you stronger because you aren't going to let it tear you down."

She turned around, breaking my embrace. "Now I know why my father is the way he is. He never trusts anybody. He observes moments more than he participates in them. When he's in public, he's calculating and cold. Only when he's behind closed doors with a security system does he thaw."

I saw the change deep within her eyes. I grabbed her hands, feeling them in mine. "Skye, don't let him ruin you. I mean it."

"I'm not letting him ruin me. I'm letting him teach me."

I hated seeing the pain on her face. It was unbearable. "Don't change who you are. You're such a beautiful girl with a beautiful spirit. You're kind, generous, and warm. Stay that way."

She closed her eyes and sighed, letting a tear escape.

My heart stung just from watching it. I rested my hand on her cheek then wiped away the drop with the pad of my thumb. She breathed heavily when she felt me.

"I miss you so much..." Another tear fell.

The words went straight to my heart.

"I miss this...I miss you." She opened her eyes and looked at me, the coat of moisture shining in the light.

I swallowed the lump in my throat, feeling the emotion move all the way to my stomach. "I miss you too."

She moved into my chest and wrapped her arms around my neck, hugging me. My hands moved around her waist, feeling her petite frame in my arms. She cried quietly, using my body as a crutch. Listening to her cry was unbearable. I tried to tune it out so I wouldn't cry too.

She cried for an hour, mourning her loss. I eventually moved her to the couch, lying with her. Her arm was around my waist and she kept her face buried in the crook of my neck. I rubbed her back, trying to calm her down. Eventually, her sobs turned into quiet tears. And then she fell asleep altogether.

My phone vibrated in my pocket. I checked the message.

Can I come over? It was Jasmine.

I couldn't leave Skye right now. *I have plans. Maybe tomorrow.*

Okay. I miss you.

I didn't say anything back. I tossed my phone on the coffee table and returned my attention to Skye, listening to her breathe. I wished I could make this better. I wished I could do something to eliminate the pain. But in the back of my mind, I kept thinking one thing.

If she were mine, she would never know pain.

Chapter Twelve

Skye

When I woke up the next morning, Cayson was still there. His face was close to mine and he was watching me. Judging the exhaustion in his eyes, he hadn't slept all night.

His hand pulled the hair out of my face gently, touching me like he had a hundred times. "Would you like some breakfast?"

My voice came out coarse. "I'm not hungry."

"I can get you some coffee."

"No, I'm okay."

"Okay." His hand moved to the back of my neck and rubbed me gently.

"Thanks for staying with me..."

"Yeah." Pity was in his eyes.

I wanted to stay on this couch and cuddle with him all day long. The pain didn't seem so unbearable when his arms formed a cage around me. I felt safe, that nothing could hurt me. Even in my darkest hour, he made me feel strong.

"I hope you're feeling better."

Not really. "Slightly."

His hand rested on my upper back and he looked into my eyes, the pain deep within.

I wanted to ditch class and stay like this forever. I wanted Cayson to hold me, to chase away all the dark thoughts. But I knew he couldn't. He had class and other obligations. He had a girlfriend... "You should probably go..." I sat up then looked at the time. It was already after eight. "You're already missing your first class."

"I don't care about my classes, Skye." He sat up and looked at me. "I care about you."

This was the Cayson I missed, the best friend that would do anything for me. "I know. But I'm going to mope around here. There's nothing you can do."

He sat close to me and took my hand. "I can mope with you."

I rested my head on his shoulder and sighed. There's nothing I wanted more than to crawl into bed with him and forget about the world outside my apartment. I didn't want to think about what Zack did to me. I didn't want to think about the pain. "Cayson, go to class. We'll talk later." I stood up then ran my fingers through my hair.

"Are you sure you'll be okay?" He stood up and stared me down. "Because I don't mind staying. I really don't."

"Yes, Cayson. Please go."

Conflict was in his eyes. He thought for a moment before he came to me and hugged me. "I love you, Skye."

The air burned my lungs as I inhaled. "I love you too..."

"Call me if you need anything."

I felt his solid frame in my hands. He towered over me, and he was easily twice my size. His hard chest felt like concrete when he leaned against me. "I know."

Then he cupped my cheek then pressed his forehead to mine. It was something we'd never done before. He closed his eyes and just held me, breathing hard. The intimacy we shared was foreign to me. We'd cuddled and touched, but this was something new. Then he leaned away and stepped back. "Zack fucked with the wrong girl." He walked out and shut the door behind him.

When I was alone again, I sat down and felt tears flood to the surface. I wanted Cayson to stay but I wasn't so selfish to ask him to. School was important to him, and I would never intervene in that.

All my blinds were shut so I was sitting in the dark. I had class today but I wasn't in the mood to go. I was too distraught, too hurt. It wasn't just the fact Zack was cheating on me. It didn't hurt me that he said he loved me when he didn't. He hurt me when he tricked me, used me, and I had no idea. I felt like an idiot for letting a liar into my inner circle. I was ashamed of my stupidity.

The tears came again and I fought them back. Crying over a piece of shit like Zack was stupid. It was pointless. But I couldn't help it. I was hurt. The past six months was a complete lie. It was bogus.

I grabbed my phone then searched for the name I longed to see. No one else in the world would understand how I felt besides him. He may not have experienced the exact same thing, but I knew him well enough to understand that he'd experienced a lot of pain and a lot of disappointment. I hit the send button.

He answered on the first ring. "Pumpkin, how are you?"

Hearing the love in his voice made me break down. The tears fell when I tried to stop them.

Alarm came into his voice. "Skye, are you okay? Are you hurt?"

"I'm okay...I'm okay."

"Does someone have you? Is someone hurting you?" He always jumped to the worse possible conclusion.

"No, I'm safe. I'm fine." I breathed through the sobs.

"Talk to me, pumpkin."

"I just...I feel so stupid."

Even though my dad didn't know what was wrong, he was patient with me. "I'm leaving my office now. I'll be there in two hours."

"No…you don't need to do that. Don't leave work because of me."

"Work doesn't mean shit to me. I'll be there in two hours."

I knew I shouldn't argue with my dad. And honestly, I wanted him to come. "Okay…"

"I love you, pumpkin. I'll be there soon."

"I love you too, Dad."

He hung up.

I put my phone on the coffee table then curled up in a ball, trying to fall asleep.

***

My dad arrived in less than two hours. He didn't understand speed limits or basic laws. They didn't apply to him. He knocked on my door. "Pumpkin, it's me." Fear was in his voice.

Even though I looked like shit, I answered the door. "Hey…"

He stared at my tear stained face and he immediately mirrored the look. Pain flooded through his eyes, just like Cayson's, and he looked like he lost the world. Wordlessly, he shut the door behind him then embraced me, pulling me to his chest and squeezing me hard.

My dad held me and rubbed my back gently. Feeling him surround me with unconditional love made me upset all over again. Zack never loved me. He didn't care about me. He used me, took advantage of me, and I let him. I started to cry.

My dad guided me to the couch and set me down. Then he sat beside me with concern still in his eyes. He put one arm around my shoulder, tucking me into his side. "Tell me."

I didn't know where to begin. "Dad, have you ever been used...because of your money?"

His hand stilled on my back. "More times than I can count. Why?"

"Did you feel stupid?"

"Yes."

"What happened?"

"Why are you asking?"

"I'm just curious. You're so withdrawn and cold. Whenever you're in public, you're a different person. Your walls are always up and you're untouchable. You're suspicious of everyone and you don't extend any warmth. But when you're home with us...you're different. You're happy. What happened to make you that way?"

He processed my words for a long time. "I don't have enough time in the day to explain every incident that has made me so hateful toward other people. Unlike your grandfather, I've had a hard time seeing the good in others. They will use you and take you for everything you have. Very few people in the world will truly love you for you. I'm happy when I'm home because your mother loved me from the beginning. She loved me despite my wealth, and my extended family is the same way. No one else in the world treats me that way. I'm lucky I have anyone at all."

"Has a girlfriend ever used you?"

He stared at me for a moment. "Yes. My last girlfriend before your mother lied to me and tricked me into being with her. She wanted my wealth for security, and she was willing to do anything to get it. She really hurt your mother. And fortunately, your mother loved me enough to forgive me."

"You cheated on Mom?"

"No," he said quickly. "Never. But I left her for this other woman—because I thought she was pregnant."

"Was she?"

"Yes, but it wasn't mine."

"What happened to her?"

"I couldn't care less." Anger was in his voice. "Skye, why are you asking me this?"

I wiped my tears away. "My boyfriend...or my ex-boyfriend used me."

He stared me down. "How?"

I never thought I would tell my father this but I was desperate. "We've been dating for six months. He kept insisting on meeting you and Mom. I never understood why. He even told me he loved me so he could come to the gala. I didn't say it back. Then Cayson overheard him talking to a friend in the library..."

My dad's face was unreadable. He was guarded, but anger was coursing in his eyes.

"He's just with me for my wealth. He planned on marrying me and then divorcing me, taking half of my assets. He's been cheating on me the entire time. He never cared about me. He never loved me. I feel so stupid..." More tears bubbled under the surface.

My dad didn't react. He kept his arm around my shoulder, and I felt it tremble slightly. I expected him to explode, to demolish my apartment, but he didn't. He kept calm. "I'm sorry that happened to you, Skye. I always feared my wealth would sabotage your life and I'm sorry it has."

"It's not your fault, Dad."

"And I'm sorry you've learned that people are innately evil and greedy. That's a lesson I hoped to spare you from."

"I just feel stupid..."

"Don't," he said gently. "When you have everything, people will want it. And that's just how it is. Now you understand why I'm so protective of you and your...personal life."

"Yeah..."

He kissed my forehead. "You're such a beautiful girl and you're too smart for your own good. You're smarter than your mother and I put together. I know this is hard for you. It'd be hard on anyone. But don't let him bring you down. He's just one asshole, and there is a sea of great men. You will find someone who loves you for you, someone you trust implicitly. And you will be happy."

"Like you and Mom?"

"Happier than us." Moisture built up in his eyes when he looked at me. "I've been through a lot of pain, but seeing my daughter cry over a broken heart has to be the worst I've ever bared."

"I'm sorry...I didn't mean to hurt you."

"Don't apologize. If I share the load with you, you don't have to carry it all by yourself." He wiped a tear away with the pad of his thumb. "Would you like to know a story about your mother and I?"

I nodded.

"I was with a woman I was in love with. She was beautiful and perfect. I bought a ring and planned on proposing to her. Actually, your mother helped me pick it out. But then she cheated on me, dumped me, and then left me for someone else. I was devastated, heartbroken. Your mother was there for me, being the best friend I needed. And at some point, something changed. She wasn't just my friend anymore. A night of drunken sex opened my eyes and made me realize what was right in front of me. I fell in love with your mother in a way I never felt for that other woman. And in the end, that heartbreak was the best thing that ever happened to me. Because if it hadn't happened, I wouldn't be with your mother." He cupped my cheeks. "And I wouldn't have you."

His words clenched my heart painfully.

"I know this is hard for you, but you'll realize it's the best thing that ever happened to you. You will find a better man, and now you'll be able to recognize him because of this pain. You will be wiser for it, and of course, you'll be stronger for it."

Somehow he made me feel better. Even though Zack was a horrible mistake, he taught me a valuable lesson. I'm glad I learned it early in life compared to my father.

He pulled a strand of hair from my wet cheeks then rested his hand on my shoulder. "Did that help?"

I nodded. "It did." I wasn't crying anymore.

His eyes turned serious and malicious. The warmth that radiated from him a second ago was gone. "Tell me his name."

I hated Zack, but I wasn't sure he deserved what my father had in mind. "What are you going to do to him?"

"You let me worry about that." He didn't touch me, just stared me down. "Skye, his name."

"You can't kill him." I knew it was a ridiculous accusation to make, but my father could get rid of someone if he really wanted to.

"His name."

"Dad."

"Skye."

"Promise me you won't kill him."

He clenched his jaw. "I promise."

"What are you going to do?"

His eyes burned in demonic fire. "Secure his financial future—just like he was doing with you."

What did that mean?

"He will never find a job when he graduates. He will flip burgers just to make ends meet. He will put in eighty hours a week at minimum wage just to pay his rent. All he will know is the life of a poor man. Every time he turns for help, he'll never get it. His apartment will be broken into constantly, his prized possessions looted. His record will register him as a sex offender so he'll never have a date as long as he lives. He will resort to prostitution when his hand isn't doing the job. Then he will be thrown in jail for his crimes. When he gets out, the cycle will repeat. And he will loathe himself for ever fucking with Sean Preston."

My heart accelerated at his words. It was a lifelong punishment he would never escape. My father would ruin his life—literally. "That's too harsh..."

"Skye, give me his name. If you don't, I'll just get it from your brother or your cousins. This will happen."

"Dad, I know you're upset but you don't mean that."

"I don't?"

"No...I know you're protective of me but that's extreme. You know it is. I don't want that and neither do you."

He took a deep breath then held my hand. "You're right. I guess I don't know how to control my anger sometimes. People can do whatever they want to me and it doesn't bother me. But when it comes to my family...I'm harsh."

I patted the top of his hand. "I know, Dad. It's okay."

"I still want his name." The seriousness was back in his eyes.

"Why?"

"Just tell me, Skye."

I swallowed the lump in my throat. "Zack Stone."

"Thank you." He relaxed visibly then rubbed his palms together. His Rolex flashed in the light. "Have you had breakfast?"

"No." I wasn't hungry, not after that threat.

"Would you like to join me?"

"It's okay, Dad. You should get back to work."

He gave me a firm look. "Like I've said a hundred times, work means nothing to me. Businesses rise and collapse every day. Regimes grow and fall. But my family means everything to me. Now have breakfast with me."

"Okay."

We headed to a diner in town then ordered waffles. My dad ate slowly and barely touched his food. He was a health nut. His body was still thick and toned despite his age. He did boxing and martial arts after work for exercise. My mom didn't exercise as often as he did, but they would run on the beach together sometimes.

When we finished, we went back to my apartment.

"Want to watch a movie?" he asked.

It meant the world to me that he was spending all day with me. He dropped everything in a heartbeat when I needed him. I had the best parents in the world. Not just because they gave me everything financially, but they showed me how much they loved me every single day. "Sure."

I sat next to him on the couch and covered myself with a blanket. He flipped through the channels until he found something.

His phone rang. He glanced at it then took the call. I know he wouldn't have answered it if it were anyone else but my mother. "Baby?"

"Mike told me you took off from the office and you aren't answering your phone. Is everything alright?"

"Skye called and asked to see me."

Her voice changed. "Is she okay?"

"She's fine. I'll explain when I get home."

"Okay." She breathed a sigh of relief. "When will you be home?"

"Late tonight."

"Can you call me when you leave?"

He smirked. "Why don't you just check the GPS on my phone?"

"Just call me, Sean."

"You're starting to sound a lot like me." He was clearly enjoying teasing my mom.

"Whose fault is that? Now will you call me?"

"I'll think about it."

I rolled my eyes while I listened to them.

"You aren't getting any from me tonight."

He laughed. "Yeah right. I'm calling your bluff."

"I mean it."

"Please, you're worse than I am."

"Do I need to cover my ears?" I said.

"I guess you'll find out if I made good on my threat when you get home." My mom's tone was dark.

My dad quickly changed his tactic. "I'll call you, baby."

"That's what I thought."

"But you know I'll always call you."

Her voice softened. "I do."

"You guys are going to make me gag," I said.

My dad chuckled. "I love you, baby."

"I love you too."

"Bye." He waited for her to hang up first. Then he placed the phone on the coffee table.

The door opened and Cayson walked in. He was carrying a pizza and a liter of soda. He stilled when he saw my dad. "Oh. Hi, Uncle Sean."

"Hey, kid. What did you bring?" my dad asked.

"Skye's favorite is pizza," he explained.

"Just like her mom." My dad smiled.

I rose from the couch then went to him. "Thanks but we ate not too long ago."

"Save it for later." He watched me closely with concern in his eyes. "Everything okay?"

"Yeah, my dad made me feel better."

"Good." He nodded slowly. "I'm glad."

"Thanks for staying with me last night."

"You don't need to thank me, Skye."

I tucked a strand of hair behind my ear, suddenly feeling nervous.

"I'll let you get back to your dad," he said. "But you can call me if you need anything, even if you just want to talk."

"I know, Cayson."

Cayson walked over to my dad on the couch. "Hey, Uncle Sean."

My dad rose and hugged him. "Thanks for looking after my daughter."

"Of course. I always do."

He patted Cayson's shoulder. "Having a fine young man like you and the rest of your cousins gives me peace of mind when I'm not around."

"You can count on me."

"I know." He smiled at him. "And don't worry about Zack. I'll take care of him."

Cayson's face became slightly pale. "Okay. Go easy on him."

My dad had an evil look in his eye. "I know you don't mean that."

"You're right. I don't."

My dad put his hands in the pockets of his suit. "I'll tell your father I saw you and you're doing well."

"Thanks. Tell him I said hi."

"I will."

"Bye, Uncle Sean."

"Bye."

Cayson walked toward the door then gave me one final look before he left.

My dad sat back down on the couch. "Cayson is a good kid. I like him."

"I like him too." I sat back down and pulled the blanket over me.

"He could be a good influence on Roland. I wish Cayson would rub off on him."

"Roland is a good guy too."

"I know he is, pumpkin. I'm very proud of my son. His maturity level just isn't the same."

"Weren't you reckless and wild when you were young?"

He smirked. "Yeah..."

"Roland will grow out of it."

"I'm sure he will."

My dad and I watched the movie then TV for the rest of the night. When we got hungry, we devoured the pizza, leaving nothing behind. I started to grow tired but didn't want him to leave.

"I'll stay until you fall asleep."

"Okay." I lay on the couch and he tucked the blanket around me. He sat in the other chair while he waited for me to fall asleep. It was already eleven in the evening and he had a two-hour drive but he didn't seem to mind.

Because my father would do anything for me.

***

The next morning, my father was gone. But he left a gift behind.

A vase of white lilies was on my counter, and there was a note.

A father loves a daughter
Like no other love on earth.
From the day that he first meets her
Nothing can compare her worth.
Forever are they bonded
With a love that never fails.
For always he will hug her
And kiss her goodnight with fairy tales.
He will love her and protect her
With strong arms just in case
But will also hug her tenderly
With a fatherly embrace.
Eskimo kisses touch her nose
With a giggle and a squeeze
And that sparkle in her little eyes
Could bring him to his knees.
What more could any father want
Than a daughter so sweet and pure
There's nothing in this world so rare
Of that he can be sure.
A fathers love is so unique
It cannot be replaced
He will always treasure times with her
And the memories embraced.

A smile stretched my lips when I read it. Then I looked at the flowers again, remembering every time he's given them to me. They were always white lilies, the flower that reminded him of me. He always did sweet things like that, making me feel special.

In that moment, I realized how stupid it was to be upset over what Zack did to me. He didn't care about me but I had people who did. I was fortunate enough to have a family that loved me for me, not the money in my father's bank account. Zack couldn't tear me down and I refused to let him.

I showered then went to class, suddenly feeling rejuvenated. I didn't think about Zack at all. We would cross paths eventually, and I looked forward to it. He was the one who hurt me and made me feel small, but I would do the same to him at the first opportunity.

I was studying in the library when Zack made his appearance.

"Hey, baby." He leaned down to kiss me.

I turned my head. "God, your breath stinks."

He flinched. "What?"

I waved the air in front of me. "Gross."

The library was silent so everyone could hear me even though I didn't raise my voice.

People at the nearby tables glanced at us, eyeing Zack.

Zack stepped back, embarrassed at my words. "Uh, sorry." He cupped his mouth then breathed, trying to smell it.

"What do you want?" I blurted.

He cocked an eyebrow. "What do you want? Just to say hi to my girlfriend." He lowered his voice to a whisper.

I didn't lower my voice. "I'm not your girlfriend anymore. I'm dumping you."

"What?" Fear moved into his eyes. "Why?"

"Because you're shitty in bed."

His eyes widened and he looked around, hoping no one heard that.

"You should study the female anatomy because you obviously don't know how to make a girl come."

The girls at the nearby table giggled.

Zack's face turned red. "Why are you being a bitch right now?" His voice was still a whisper.

"Why am *I* being a bitch?" I asked incredulously. "It's not my fault you have a small ship and you don't know how to rock the boat."

Now other tables were laughing at my cruelty.

Zack was starting to get angry. "Why are you acting like this?"

"Sorry, did I hurt your feelings?" I packed my bag and put it over my shoulder. "Maybe your pathetic moves and horrible lies work on Vanessa but they won't work on me."

His eyes widened at the mention of her name.

"I'm done with you, Zack. I'm going to find someone else to share my zillions of dollars with. Someone who actually knows what a clitoris is."

The girls next to us burst out laughing.

Then I grabbed him by the throat, catching him off guard. I got close to his face, making the fear move into his eyes. "Come near me again, and I will emasculate you further." I gave him a long glare before I walked away, shaking my hips and holding my head up high.

It didn't erase the months I wasted, but at least the end of our relationship went out with a bang.

Chapter Thirteen

Cayson

"Why the hell are we meeting at ten o'clock at night wearing all black?" Conrad asked.

"Yeah?" Theo asked. "What's this about?"

I leaned against the counter and crossed my arms over my chest. "Because we're going to beat the shit out of someone tonight. And we're going to enjoy it."

"What?" Slade asked. "Who? Dude, you're scaring me. You're the Buddha of this group. Why would you initiate something like this?"

"You're about to find out," I said darkly.

Roland walked in, wearing jeans and a sweater. "This better be good because I have an exam tomorrow."

"Like you studied anyway," Slade jabbed.

"Actually, I did," Roland snapped.

"Quiet down," I said. "We need to talk."

"What's this about?" Roland asked.

"Zack." I hated saying his name.

"My sister's boyfriend?" Roland asked. "What happened?"

"I overheard him in the library talking to a friend. He admitted he was only with Skye for her money. He planned on seducing her into marriage so he could take everything from her. Allow my recording to explain the rest." I hit the play button and set it on the counter. It played out the entire conversation. When it was over. I shoved the phone back into my pocket.

Roland's back straightened and he had a crazed look in his eye. "He fucked with my sister like that?"

I nodded.

Roland and Skye weren't extremely close. They hung out in the same circle but they didn't confide everything to each other, or anything at all. But I knew he was protective of her, and if someone messed with her, he was livid. "He used her that whole time? I'm ripping this fucker's head off."

Everyone else was equally pissed.

"I say we kill him." Slade had a serious look on his face. "I'm not kidding. We dump his body into the ocean—in pieces."

"I say we beat him so bad he's in the hospital for a week," Theo said.

"Wait until my father hears about this." Roland rubbed one knuckle with his palm.

"He already knows," I said. "And he told me he would take care of him. But I'm not sure what that means."

"I do," Roland said. "My dad is going to ruin his life. Believe me, that fucker will regret messing with my sister."

"I'm sure he will. But I want to get a few hits in myself." No one used the girl I loved and got away with it.

"That makes two of us," Slade said. "What's the plan?"

"I know he has basketball practice for the alumni group tonight. It usually gets out at ten." I clenched my fists. "I say we wait outside his apartment for him to come home then beat him senseless."

Roland smirked. "I like that idea. A lot."

"Then let's go."

***

We parked down the street then headed to his apartment building. Students were always out and about this close to campus. When he came home, there would be a crowd to witness it. And it would only humiliate him.

"Hoods," I said.

Everyone pulled theirs up, concealing their faces.

When we rounded the corner, we were too late. A group of people were on the sidewalk, watching Zack get slammed into his Volvo.

"What the fuck?" Roland said.

A man wearing a black hoodie and dark jeans gripped Zack by the throat and threw him across the hood of the car. The man's hood was up, concealing his face. We were all there so I had no idea who it was. Perhaps it was just a coincidence.

Zack fell to the ground, blood oozing from his face. He gripped his stomach, coughing.

The man grabbed him then slammed him back on the car with a strength that made me flinch.

"Oh shit!" The crowd stepped back, too afraid to do anything but watch.

"Stop!" Zack started to scream. "What the hell did I do?"

The guy dragged him back then threw him on the concrete. Zack's face was so bloody he couldn't be distinguished. He groaned and tried to crawl away, but his body was unresponsive.

The man gripped him by the throat then leaned over him. He said something undecipherable, something only Zack could hear. Whatever it was must have been frightening because Zack's eyes were wide. Then the guy kicked him in the side, making Zack turn over.

The man stood up then spit on Zack's face. The light from the street lamp penetrated his hood slightly, and I could see his blue eyes. I caught a glimpse of his face. He looked in our direction like he recognized us.

"It's Uncle—"

I covered his mouth so he wouldn't give away Sean's name.

Skye's father jogged away, leaving Zack on the pavement. A moment later, we heard the sound of a helicopter taking off. It was too dark to see anything but we could hear the blades spinning.

Roland nodded. "Damn. My dad is a fucking badass."

I pulled my hood down. "Let's get out of here before we attract unwanted attention."

"Yeah," Conrad said.

We headed to the car then took off, not wanting to be seen by the ambulance or the cops. When we were back in the apartment, we relaxed and spoke freely.

"Holy shit," Slade said. "Uncle Sean almost killed him."

"Don't fuck with my dad," Roland said. "That guy will fucking kill you."

I still couldn't believe that happened but I guess I wasn't surprised. "Don't tell the girls what we saw—especially Skye."

"Why?" Roland asked.

"I doubt Uncle Sean would want her to know," I said.

"She's stupid if she thinks our dad would do nothing," Roland said.

"She knows he would use his wealth and power to sabotage his life, but I doubt she thinks her own father would almost kill him," I argued. "I think it's better left unsaid."

"Fine," Roland said. "I'll keep his secret."

Slade shook his head. "Maybe it's a good thing you and Skye never worked out. Could you imagine what he would do if you hurt her?"

That didn't scare me in the least. "No. Because I never would."

***

I went by her apartment the next day. I needed to stay away from her for my own safety but I also needed to know if she was okay. How could I turn my back on her right now when she needed a friend? I would never be so selfish.

I used my key to walk inside.

She was sitting at her kitchen table doing homework. She was wearing dark jeans and a red cardigan. A golden necklace hung around her throat. I spotted the vase of white lilies on her coffee table. I knew whom they were from without asking. "How's it going?"

"Good. Just finishing a paper for my business ethics class."

"I'm sure it's good with all your experience." I walked to the table and sat across from her.

"My father refuses to do business outside the United States. Not because he hates foreign relations, but he refuses to employ slave labor just to keep the costs low. All his employees are Americans, including his buyers for parts and production. And I have the same viewpoint, which is what I wrote about."

I nodded. "Very cool."

She smiled then tucked her hair behind her ear. She seemed a lot better. She was in a good mood again. Her windows were open and a good vibe echoed in the walls of her apartment.

"I'm glad to see you're doing better."

"Me too. My dad put everything in perspective."

"He's a smart guy."

"He is. He made me realize that this experience is actually a good one. Not only did I learn from my mistakes, but now I know how to find the right guy next time. I won't be so easily fooled."

Then why didn't she realize I was the right guy? "Have you spoken to Zack?"

"Yes. I dumped his ass in front of everyone in the library. And I made sure every girl knew he wasn't good in bed."

I smirked. "That's pretty embarrassing."

"I hope it was."

"Did you tell him you knew?"

"In a way. I didn't give him any satisfaction or tell him how upset I was. I just dumped him and warned him not to come near me again."

"Good. That's the best way to go."

She flipped her notebook over and looked back at her computer. "Zack was just a waste of time and I'm ready to move on and forget about it."

I was glad she was doing so much better. Her father could comfort her in a way I never could and I'm glad he was there for her. My best wasn't always enough. But then again, I hadn't raised her.

If she was better, that meant I needed to distance myself again...which I wasn't looking forward to. After I spent the night with her, I got hooked all over again. I watched her sleep, staring at her exquisite face and wishing I could kiss her again. I wished Zack never existed and that I was the man she deemed worthy of her heart. She never would have been hurt or betrayed. We'd both be happy.

But that wasn't reality. Jasmine was my girlfriend, the woman I was fucking. Skye didn't see me that way and she never would. "Well, I should go and work on some homework."

"Do it here," she said. "We used to do that all the time."

That was a bad idea. "I'm taking Jasmine to dinner in a few hours." That was a lie but I needed an excuse.

"Oh." Disappointment came into her eyes. "Do you love this girl?"

I wasn't expecting such a personal question. "No."

She nodded slowly. "I was surprised when you didn't mention her to me."

I shrugged. "I was just busy."

"So, you really like her?"

Why was she asking me this? "I enjoy her company. We have fun together." What more did she want to know? I couldn't tell her I was just fucking her to forget the person I was really in love with.

"Well, I'm happy for you, then."

Actually, she sounded sad. "Thanks…"

She stared at me, waiting for me to leave.

"Well, I'll see you later."

"Yeah."

"Let me know if you need anything."

"Cayson, I'll be fine." She said it with confidence.

"Okay. Bye."

"Bye."

I shut the door and sighed, missing her the moment she was gone.

***

Jasmine was at my door when I arrived. And she looked pissed.

"What?" I asked.

"You've been blowing me off for the past week. If you don't want to be with me anymore,

306

just say it to my face. Don't drag me along like this. It's mean and cruel." Emotion was heavy in her voice. Her eyes were teary. She was really shaken up about it.

"I haven't been blowing you off. I—"

"Don't lie to me. I'm a big girl and I can take it."

I tried not to snap at her. "I'm not a liar. I thought I already proved that to you by bluntly telling you I was in love with someone I couldn't have." I clenched my jaw while I spoke. "If I want to end this relationship, I'll tell you. I won't cheat on you and I won't just drop you without a word. We've known each other for a while now, and I assumed you already knew all that."

She crossed her arms over her chest and sighed. Shame was on her face. "I'm sorry."

I stared at her, waiting for more.

"I've just been burned in the past. I admit I have trust issues."

Pity rose in my heart. "I'm sorry to hear that."

"I didn't mean to make assumptions. I know you're a good guy, Cayson."

I opened my door then pulled her inside, not wanting to have this conversation in the hallway. "What happened to you?"

She wouldn't look at me when she said it. "I was in a relationship for a long time but he was cheating on me on and off with his ex. On our two-year anniversary, he left me and went back to her. They were married three months later."

That was a depressing story. "You didn't deserve that."

She shrugged and said nothing.

I cupped her face and looked her in the eye. "I can't give you love. I probably never will. But I can give you my complete and utter honesty. I can give you my friendship. And I can give you my fidelity."

Her hands moved to my arms. "I know…"

"Don't worry about that stuff with me. I know that's hard and I get that. But you'll just waste your time."

She nodded. "Okay."

"Now let me explain what I've been up to this week."

She waited for me to speak.

"Skye's boyfriend was basically a con artist. He was with her just to steal her wealth. I caught him in the act and told her about it. The whole week has been a little crazy with that."

She gasped. "He was using her the whole time?"

I nodded.

"What a fucking jackass."

"I know." I was glad Uncle Sean beat the shit out of him and put him in the hospital.

"That poor girl."

"I know. She's doing better. Her dad came down and made her feel better. And I spent the night."

"You slept with her?" She raised an eyebrow.

"On the couch," I said. "Nothing more."

She didn't question me further.

"I was doing a good job avoiding her until this happened. Now I have to start over. Seeing her cry and sleeping with her just put me back in that place. It's so easy for me to fall for her again and again. I'm doomed."

She rubbed my arms. "No, you aren't. You will get over her eventually. It'll just take some time."

"Yeah." I found that hard to believe.

"Cayson, there's one thing I want from you."

"Name it."

She seemed flustered. "When you're with me…I don't want you to think about her."

That was a reasonable request. "I don't, Jasmine. I admit she comes into my head sometimes but I push her away."

"You promise?"

I nodded. "I promise. I respect you too much to do that to you. But I admit I think about her in that way at random times. Sometimes I'm in class and I'll imagine kissing her. Sometimes

I'll be eating dinner and I'll have a sexy daydream. But that's it."

"Okay." She didn't seem pleased with the response but she wasn't angry either.

"Can I take you to dinner?" I pulled a few strands of hair off her neck.

"Sure."

"Then let's go. I'm starving."

"And let's get dessert—and bring it home."

I smirked. "I like your thinking."

"Moments of brilliance come every now and then."

"I'll keep an eye out for them." I smirked then pulled her out of the apartment.

***

We headed to the sports bar to watch the football game on Thursday night. I brought Jasmine along because we spent a lot of time together. Plus, if Skye was going to be there, I needed a distraction.

We slid into the booth.

"Hey." Slade winked at me.

I nodded then put my arm around Jasmine.

Conrad slid me a glass then poured beer from the pitcher. "Would you like a beer, Jasmine?"

"No, thank you," she said.

"Can I get you some wine?" I asked.

"No, I just want water for now," she said.

"Okay."

Roland had his eye on the screen. "My dad and I have a bet going."

"How much?" I asked.

"The loser has to do the dishes after Thanksgiving dinner."

Slade cringed. "Man, that would suck to lose."

"You're telling me," Roland said. "So I have to win. Plus, it's my dad. I have to beat him anyway."

"He probably paid the NFL to win in his favor," Conrad said with a laugh.

Roland sighed. "I sincerely hope not."

The girls came to our table. Trinity and Silke were in the front, and Skye was in the rear. I noticed all the heads that turned in their direction. They were all pretty girls, but Skye was exquisite. She looked at me and saw my arm around Jasmine. Then she dropped her look, watching the TV in the corner.

Roland slid out of his seat and went to her. "Hey, sis. How's it going?" Roland had been particularly attentive to his sister for the past week. He normally acted like he didn't care about her existence at all, but he obviously did.

"Good. You?"

He put his arms around her and held her. "You know you can talk to me, right?"

"Yeah..." She leaned her head against his chest.

Everyone watched their affection but nobody teased Roland for it.

"I really am better, Ro. Don't worry about me." She pulled away and gave him a smile.

"Okay. Can I get you a beer? Maybe some mozzarella sticks?"

"Yes. And yes." She laughed slightly.

"Coming right up." He guided her to the booth then headed to the bar.

Trinity smiled. "That was so cute."

Skye shrugged. "I guess Roland does like me—sometimes."

"I would never do that for my sister—because she's ugly," Conrad said.

Trinity hit his shoulder. "Yes, you would. You're protective of me every single day."

"Just because I don't want Dad to get mad at me." He drank half his beer.

She rolled her eyes. "Sure. Whatever."

Roland came back and put the beer and cheese sticks in front of Skye. "Can I get you anything else?"

Slade leaned close to Skye's ear. "Milk this."

She smirked. "No, thank you. That was very sweet, Roland."

He sat beside her then stole a cheese stick. "I know you would do it for me."

I kept my hand on Jasmine and sighed. Skye and I were so close but we were still so far away. Just being around her was hard. I couldn't help but feel awkward and out of place. If we were together, the group dynamic would be so different. If anything, it would be better.

Slade looked at Jasmine. "So...how about those cute girlfriends?"

"Are you going to sleep with them and never call them again?" she asked.

"Naturally." He smirked.

"Then I don't have any girlfriends." She sipped her water.

Slade sighed. "Come on. Share the wealth."

"I'm not going to throw one of my girls under the bus," she said.

"Throw them under me." Slade laughed at his own comment.

Roland squared his shoulders. "I'm a good guy. Hook me up."

"Didn't you sleep with a married woman?" she questioned.

Roland sighed. "Damn it. I'm never going to live that down."

"Well, it was pretty bad," Conrad said.

"Don't act like you wouldn't do the same thing," Roland snapped.

"Actually, I wouldn't," Conrad said. "I would never hook up with one of my dad's employees. That's a big no-no. He would take away my car, my money, and my Rolex. And my mom would throw a fit. Sometimes she's worse than he is."

Jasmine touched my arm. "Cayson is the only guy I'd hook up a girlfriend with, but he's already mine." She gave me a seductive grin.

I kissed her gently then pulled away. When I looked at Skye, she was staring at her cheese sticks like they were the most interesting things in the world.

"So, what's the craziest sex the two of you have had?" Slade asked. "Behind a dumpster? Against a tree on the school grounds? At the foot of the bed?"

I glared at him. "Slade, this isn't up for discussion." I shared my personal life with my friends regularly, but I did keep certain aspects private out of respect for my partner. Most girls didn't want their sex lives to be public knowledge.

"On the dryer in the laundry room." Jasmine smirked. "While it was on and drying someone else's clothes."

Everyone fell silent. Slade's jaw was almost touching the table. Roland looked at me like I was a god. Conrad held his beer halfway to his lips, staying still like someone hit pause during a movie. I blushed slightly, realizing what they were thinking.

Slade finally closed his mouth. "Shit. Cayson, you're the man." He held up his hand to high-five me.

I stared at it and did nothing.

Jasmine took my hand then did it for me. "It is worthy of an acknowledgment."

Conrad clapped me on the shoulder. "You. Are. A. God."

When I looked at Trinity, she had a bored look on her face. Then I noticed the full plate of cheese sticks. Skye wasn't sitting in her spot anymore. She was gone. When I looked across the room, I saw her disappear into the bathroom.

Was that just a coincidence?

Chapter Fourteen

Skye

I spent the next few weeks getting back in my groove. I still felt a twinge of anger for the way Zack played me, but I pushed it away. Being upset was just a waste of time. I needed to move on and forget about it. I didn't love him anyway so he really didn't hurt me as much as he could have. I'm just glad my heart was strong enough not to let him in.

My dad kept in touch. He would text me every day and say a few quick words.

Did you see the game last night? My dad was a sports fan like I was.

Yeah. That interception was brutal.

If the QB gets three interceptions for a game, you know he needs to be benched.

He didn't ask me how I was doing or if I was okay. He always stayed clear of the topic of Zack, discussing completely different issues. But it was nice not to talk about it. He was checking on me but being discreet about it.

He texted me on a different day. *How did you do on that business ethics paper?*

I got an A.

Typical.

You made me that way.

No. You get it from your mother. I slacked off in school.

Then how did you get a BA and MBA from Harvard?

I slept with a few professors.

Dad!

I'm teasing, pumpkin. No, I was a very hard worker. But my intelligence will never rival your mother's. You get both your brains and beauty from her. Thankfully.

No wonder Roland is an idiot. He gets that from you.

LOL. No, he has your mother's intelligence too. But he is a younger version of me. I'm lucky she gave me two beautiful children.

She deserves a medal.

You've seen that rock on her finger.

I smirked then put my phone away. My dad was a nice distraction. He reminded me I was loved even if he didn't actually say the words. The conversation with him was natural and unforced. I was close with my mom, but the relationships between my two parents were completely different. The humor was different and so was the tone.

I didn't see Cayson for the next few weeks. Honestly, I was avoiding him a little bit. Seeing him with Jasmine just rubbed me the wrong way. I couldn't figure out why. She was a nice girl. She was pretty and smart, and it was obvious she was head-over-heels for him. But...I just didn't want to be around them.

I never saw Zack. I expected him to corner me somewhere on campus and beg for another chance. When he did, I planned to knee him in the groin. I warned him not to come near me and he never did. I guess he wasn't quite as stupid as I thought.

By the end of the second week, I came down with a terrible cold. I was coughing constantly and my eyes were red. I was exhausted and didn't even want to get out of bed.

My brother noticed my absence from school and texted me. *Why aren't you in class?*

I'm surprised you noticed. I coughed into a tissue then lay back on the couch.

Don't be a brat. Is everything okay?

I'm sicker than a dog. I'm not sure if I'll be coming to Thanksgiving.

What? You have to. Mom's stuffing is the best.

It's not going to be good when I blow mucous all over it.

Eww...yeah. Nevermind. Stay home.

That changed pretty quickly.

Do you need anything?

No, I'm good. I put the phone down then snuggled with a blanket on the couch. I couldn't keep anything down because I kept throwing it up. I was so plugged up, I couldn't breathe. I was too tired to get up for water or food. I was just a mess. And my lungs hurt every time I breathed.

My phone vibrated again. *Your brother tells me you're sick.* It was my dad.

I have a cold.

Do you need anything? Only my dad would drive two hours to bring me cough medicine.

No. I'm fine. Roland will get me something if I need it.

Will you be missing Thanksgiving?

At this rate, yes.

Okay. Get better so that can change.

I'll try. I put my phone down and tried to go to sleep. The only time I didn't feel like crap was when I was unconscious.

My front door opened and I cracked an eye. Only one person came into my apartment unannounced. Everyone had a key to my place but he was the only one who used it.

Cayson came to the couch. "I heard you were sick."

"Man, word gets around fast." I had a coughing attack and covered my mouth.

Concern came into his eyes. "You look terrible, Skye."

"Thanks," I said sarcastically.

He put his hand on my forehead. "You're scorching hot."

"I *am* sick..." I coughed again.

He went to my counter then sorted out the bags he brought. "I got cough medicine, crackers, soda pop, Nyquil, and everything else you could possibly need."

"Thanks. Now go before you get sick."

He came back to me then felt my forehead again. "No. You're too unwell. I can't leave you."

"What? Don't be ridiculous, Cayson. You have class."

"Class is important, but not as important as you."

Cayson was always there for me, no matter what. He seemed like he cared about me more than himself. "You're so sweet..."

"Only to you," he whispered.

"What?"

He spoke up. "Only to those I care about."

"Oh. But you really should get to class."

"Don't waste your energy arguing with me. I'm not leaving." Firmness was in his voice. He rested his hand on my neck. "Open your mouth."

"What? Why?"

"Let me look at the back of your throat."

Oh. Sometimes I forgot Cayson was pre-med. I opened my mouth and he stared inside.

"You're definitely sick."

"Wow, you're smart," I said sarcastically.

He felt my forehead again. "You're so hot, Skye."

320

"What?"

"Your forehead—you're hot."

"Oh…yeah."

He sighed. "Does it hurt when you cough?"

"Yeah. A lot."

"Have you been able to keep anything down?"

"No…"

He looked at my skin then pinched it.

"Ow!"

"I was checking to see if you're dehydrated."

"Obviously, I am."

He laughed slightly. "Skye, I think we should go to the hospital."

"Don't be ridiculous. It's just a cold." I coughed again, feeling it deep in my lungs.

"I think you have pneumonia."

"What? No. I've never been to the hospital for anything."

"And that means you never will? What kind of reasoning is that?"

"I just don't need to go. I'll stay home and feel better in a few days."

"I really think you have pneumonia." He put his hand on my chest and felt it rise and fall.

"Are you a doctor?"

"No, but I'm not stupid."

"Cayson, just go to class."

"No." He stood up then disappeared into my bedroom.

"What are you doing?" I yelled. A coughing attack struck me and I gripped my chest while I tried to get through it.

"Sorry, I can't hear you when your lungs are trying to get rid of the bacteria living in them," he snapped. He came back with an outfit. "Change into this and we'll go."

"I'm not going."

He grabbed my forearm and gave me the death stare. "You. Are. Going." He wasn't usually this aggressive with me. I tended to always get my way but Cayson wasn't letting me. "Get dressed." He pulled the blanket down, exposing me in my sweats and t-shirt. I wasn't wearing a bra but Cayson didn't look at my chest once. "Do you need help getting changed?"

"I think I can do it."

"Okay." He walked into the kitchen then turned around, playing with his phone.

I took a deep breath then stood up, trying to get my pants off. Somehow I stumbled and fell on the ground.

"Skye, are you okay?"

"Yeah...I'm just so weak." My sweatpants were around my ankle. I knew I looked absolutely hideous and pathetic. I'd never been so embarrassed in my life.

"Let me help you." Cayson came beside me then pulled my bottoms off. Then he helped me get my jeans on. He didn't seem uncomfortable by my nearly naked body. It was like he'd seen it before. He didn't make me feel on display or ugly.

When his hands reached my shirt, he closed his eyes then pulled it off. Then he felt for the new shirt then helped me get it on. When I was covered, he opened his eyes and handed me my jacket. "Put this on and stay warm."

I tried to pull it onto my arms but my body wouldn't respond. Cayson finished the work then pulled me back to the couch. "If you're just sick, you shouldn't be this weak."

Maybe he was right. Maybe there really was something wrong with me.

He grabbed my purse then put it over his shoulder. Then he lifted me from the couch.

"I can walk…"

"You couldn't even change. I'm not letting you walk downstairs."

We left my apartment then he got me into the passenger seat of his car. He buckled me in and checked the safety belt before we drove to the hospital. He stayed calm for the drive, acting like everything was fine.

I was a little scared.

Cayson, reading my mind like always, grabbed my hand. "You'll be okay, Skye. All you need is antibiotics and you'll be good as new."

"I hope so."

"I know so."

Cayson checked me in at the front desk then I was given a room in the emergency department. I changed into a gown then tried to get comfortable. I kept coughing and it wouldn't stop. There wasn't a tickle in the back of my throat. It was like an explosion every time.

Cayson sat at my bedside then pulled out his phone.

"What are you doing?" I demanded.

He eyed me. "Texting your dad."

"Don't you dare."

He raised an eyebrow. "Why? You're in the hospital and I know he'd want to know."

"He went to Paris with my mom for a business meeting. If you call him, he'll abandon everything he's doing and take the first flight home. By the time he gets here, I'll be discharged. And since he can't get here right away, he'll ask Uncle Mike to come instead. Then he'll tell my grandparents and everyone else. Everyone will come for no reason and it'll just be embarrassing."

Cayson smirked. "You know our family pretty well."

"So please don't call him."

"I feel irresponsible if I don't."

"You brought me down here and you're taking care of me. You aren't irresponsible. You can tell him when he gets back from Paris."

"When will that be?"

"In a few days."

"What if it's something more serious?"

"Then you can tell him."

"Deal." He put his phone away.

I sighed in relief, grateful that crisis had been averted.

The nurse came in and took my blood sample. Then I was given a chest x-ray. I hated hospitals. They said they were clean but I knew they weren't. I just hated lying in a bed that so many other people had laid in before me. It made my skin itch.

"I want to go home..."

Cayson scooted his chair closer to my bed and held my hand. "You'll be out of here soon." His thumb moved over my knuckles gently, soothing me.

I moved to the edge of the bed, as close to him as I could get. An IV was in my arm and I kept coughing. But I wanted to be as close to him as possible. He made me feel better.

Cayson stared at me, his hand still caressing mine. "Is there anything I can do?"

"Just having you here is enough." I held his hand close to my chest, snuggling with it.

"Do you want me to call the others? Your brother?"

"No. Just you." I closed my eyes and tried to breathe without hurting my chest.

His other hand lightly touched my head. Then he moved his fingers through my strands of hair, soothing me quietly.

Feeling him touch me was what I needed. Cayson always made me feel better even when I felt absolutely horrible. He calmed me enough to let me fall into a deep sleep. The blackness filled my vision, and I couldn't remember anything else.

Cayson whispered in my ear. "Skye, the doctor is here."

I moaned then opened my eyes, seeing Cayson's face close to mine. "Okay..."

He pulled away but continued to hold my hand.

"Ms. Preston?" The doctor sat in the stool at my bedside.

"Yes?" My voice was raspy.

"The x-ray and blood work confirms you have pneumonia. I'm giving you antibiotics and it should clear it up quickly."

"Can I go home?" I blurted.

"We're going to keep you overnight for observation. You can go in the morning."

Ugh... "Thank you."

He nodded then left the room.

"Look who was right." Cayson gave me a cocky smirk.

"It was just a lucky guess."

"Guess? No, I made that decision based on evidence. It was pretty obvious you didn't just have a cold."

"Does it really matter who was right or wrong?"

"Yes." He stayed at my bedside and held my hand. "Because I was right."

"Damn… Well, thank you for bringing me here."

"You're welcome."

"I guess you can leave now." I didn't want him to go. I wanted him to stay with me, to hold my hand. Whenever he was near, everything was better.

"I'm not leaving, Skye. I'll be here all night. Then I'll take you home in the morning."

I couldn't help but feel relieved. "Thank you."

"Sure." He rubbed my knuckles then massaged the muscle of my hand. "Now get some sleep."

"You're going to sit in that chair all night?"

"I'll be fine. Don't worry about me."

"It can't be comfortable…"

"It is."

I moved over to the side of the bed. "Lay with me."

327

"I'm pretty sure that's not allowed."

"The night shift is coming on. They'll probably hardly check on me until the morning. Come on."

"I don't want to squish you. That bed is pretty small."

"You won't. Besides, I'll sleep better."

Conflict was in his eyes.

I pulled the sheets back. "Come on. It's too cold in here anyway."

He sighed then kicked off his shoes. Then he lay beside me, pulling the covers over both of us. I snuggled into his side and rested my head on his chest. We fit together perfectly, like we were made for each other. His hand moved through the strands of my hair, relaxing me with every touch. I had to move my arm a certain way because of my IV, but other than that, I was comfy.

I inhaled his scent while we lay together, enjoying the sound of his breathing. I was freezing before he joined me under the covers, but now I was baking. He was a personal heater, keeping me warm despite the chill.

I fell asleep quickly, losing track of my thoughts. I was thankful Cayson brought me to the hospital. If he hadn't, my pneumonia would have become worse. And I was even more thankful he didn't call my dad. That would have been a nightmare.

***

When I woke up the next morning, Cayson was staring at my face.

"Did you sleep okay?"

"Yeah," he whispered. "I woke up a few minutes ago."

"I told you we wouldn't get in trouble."

"Yeah." His arm was around my waist and we were close together, practically a single person. "How do you feel?"

"A little better...about the same."

"Give it time."

The nurse came into the room. "You lovebirds are so cute. You can't stand to be apart. Adorable."

I felt my cheeks blush. If I told her we were just friends, she wouldn't believe me.

"You're all ready to go. Just change into your clothes and pick up your prescription on the way out." She pulled out my IV then walked out and gave me some privacy.

Cayson left the bed then handed me my clothes. "Do you need help?"

"I think I can handle it."

"Okay." He turned around and closed his eyes.

I untied my gown then pulled it off. Slowly, I put everything back on. The exhaustion would creep into my veins and I would have to take a break, but piece-by-piece, I got everything on.

"Are you decent?"

"Yeah."

He turned around and helped me out of bed. "Can you walk?"

"Yeah...it just hurts to breathe."

He grabbed my hand and helped me stand up. Then he put his arm around my waist, supporting me. "Let's head to the car."

He drove me home then carried me up the stairs to my apartment. After he placed me on the bed, he opened my drawer and pulled out a pair of pajamas. "You need to stay in bed and get better." He pulled out my prescription then left it on the nightstand.

"I can't believe I have to miss class..."

"I'll get all your assignments and your notes."

"How?"

"I'll just talk to your professors."

"You would do that?" It amazed me how sweet he was.

"Yeah, of course." He grabbed the covers and pulled them back. "Now get in bed."

I sighed. "I don't want to go to sleep."

"How about we play poker while you relax?"

I would love that. "Cayson, I know you must have other things to do."

"Don't worry about that. Now get in bed and I'll get the cards."

"Okay."

He left my bedroom so I could change. Then he returned with the deck of cards. "What are we playing for this time?"

"You still owe me dinner, if I recall."

"Then how about double or nothing?"

"Ooh...two dinners?"

"Yep." He shuffled the cards then handed them out.

We played for a few hours, and in the end, I was the victor. "Hmm...where do I want to eat?"

"That's not fair. Uncle Mike taught you how to play."

"And how to count cards."

"Cheater." He smirked at me.

"Maybe you just suck."

"Maybe I let you win. Did you think of that?"

No... "Do you?"

He shrugged. "I'll never tell."

"Tell me." I hit his arm playfully.

"Nope."

"Jerk."

He laughed and put the cards away. "I guess I should head out...is there anything you need before I go?"

I didn't want him to leave... *What was wrong with me?*

He caught the sadness in my eyes. "Unless you prefer me to stick around."

"No, it's okay. You should go."

Cayson kept staring at me. "I'll sleep on the couch, then."

I didn't want him to sleep there. "Could you sleep with me instead?" I didn't realize how desperate I sounded. He just made me feel good, made me feel warm. With him, I got a good night's rest despite all the aches and sores.

Conflict was in his eyes. "Sure."

"You don't have to…"

"No, I don't mind. Just let me shower first."

"Okay."

He headed into my bathroom then turned on the water. I could hear it run through the walls. He came back with damp hair. His jeans and t-shirt were back on. And he slid into bed beside me. When his arms wrapped around me, I felt relaxed again. Even though I was sick, I felt good. My throat wasn't so painful and my stomach didn't hurt. His hand moved through my hair again, lulling me to sleep.

***

"Are you feeling better?" Trinity walked inside and put the pizza on the counter.

"Yes, much." I stayed on the couch, painting my nails.

"I hear through the grapevine you had pneumonia." She put a slice on the plate then sat at the counter.

Oh no. That meant my dad would know very shortly. "Who told you that?"

"Cayson."

I guess it was bound to get out.

"Yeah. I'm better now."

"Is it...contagious?" She eyed me with a concerned look.

I smirked. "No. You're safe."

"Phew." She munched on her pizza. "I also heard that Cayson stayed with you for three days..."

"Yeah. He took me to the hospital on the first day then helped me get better the second day. Then he went to class the following day but still slept over here."

"In your bed?" She gave me a pointed look.

I was sick of this accusation. "We didn't sleep together."

"Who the hell sleeps with a guy but isn't into them?" She stared at me like a bat just flew out of my nose. "You seriously can look me in the eye and tell me Cayson isn't more than a friend?"

"Yes..." I felt pain in my heart the moment I said it. It was the anxiety I felt when I lied. My body tensed up and I felt sick. I hated lying and I was horrible at it. My father taught me at a very young age that lying was unacceptable. Honestly,

I wasn't sure what I felt anymore. Whenever I saw him with Jasmine, my heart hurt. Whenever I didn't see him or speak to him for days at a time, I missed him. When he didn't show up at Manhattan Grub like he used to, I didn't like it. Did that mean something?

"Then answer this. You aren't related to Theo at all and you've known him for just as long. Would you sleep with him?"

"We aren't as close," I argued.

"He's a great guy just like Cayson. What's the difference? They are both equally attractive."

"There's more to it than that..."

"Yeah, I bet there is. I think you love Cayson and you never fell in love with Zack because your heart was already taken. I don't know why your head is shoved so far up your ass but it needs to come down. Why won't you just admit it?" Her features softened. "Skye, it's me. You can tell me anything."

I was so confused...was it possible I had feelings for Cayson? Could that even happen? What if I was but my mind was in denial? What if my heart really felt that way but it wouldn't admit it to my brain?

"Skye, come on. What are you afraid of?"

A lot of things. "This conversation doesn't matter because he has a girlfriend."

She rolled her eyes. "She's a fuck buddy."

"It seems like she means a lot more. If she didn't, he wouldn't bring her around."

She studied my face. "Are you telling me the only reason you haven't told him you have feelings for him is because he's seeing someone?"

This was getting dangerous. "I don't feel that way about him. Back off."

"Whoa..." She held up her hands. "Geez, calm down. Every action you take tells me you're into Cayson. I'm sorry if I just wanted to know. We tell each other everything so I didn't think it was a big deal." She tossed her paper plate in the garbage then headed to the door. "I'll see you around—when your head is out of your ass." She walked out, leaving me alone.

I sighed then sunk into the couch, trying to organize my feelings. When I was with Cayson, I loved his touch. I was always comfortable around him, telling him exactly what I was thinking and feeling. We had a great time together. Of all the people in our group, he was by far my favorite. Maybe I did feel something...

But he had a girlfriend. Wouldn't it be wrong to feel something for him? If he was seeing her, he obviously didn't feel anything for me. I was just his friend, a sister he wasn't related to. He'd watched me eat dirt and stick a pencil in my nose. He watched me grow up, making mistake after mistake. He'd seen me without make up more often than my own mirror. How could he

335

even see me in a different way? What if I opened up and told him about these...mixed feelings? Would it make him uncomfortable? Would it push him away? Would it hurt our friendship? And if he did feel the same way and something came of it, what would that lead to? What if we did get together then broke up? Would one of us be ostracized from the group? What would happen?

All of these thoughts kept circling in my mind. Did I feel something for Cayson? I wanted to say no, but I felt a pain deep in my stomach. In the back of my mind, I knew something was there. Trinity was my best friend but I only told her a smidge of the things I revealed to Cayson. He was different than everyone else, special. Why?

Maybe I should just talk to him, tell him what I'm thinking. That would be the responsible thing to do. If he didn't feel anything, he wouldn't push me away. It wouldn't end our friendship. It might be awkward for a while, but it would get back to normal eventually.

But what if I was wrong?

My phone rang and I glanced at the screen. It was my dad. Without answering it, I knew why he was calling. I sighed then took the call. "Hey, Dad."

"Hey." The tone in his voice suggested hostility. He didn't call me by my nickname, which told me everything I needed to know. "So, I hear you were in the hospital." He could even intimidate me over the phone he was so good at it.

"I knew you were out of the country with Mom and I didn't want to worry you."

"You let me make that decision." His anger was palpable.

"I just had pneumonia—nothing serious."

"I don't give a damn what you have. I'm your father and you should have called me."

"If you were in the country, I would have."

"Skye, I could have arranged for you to see a better doctor. I could have gotten you a better room. Leaving me in ignorance makes me absolutely useless to you."

"I didn't need any of those things. Everything worked out fine."

"You still should have called me."

"If I did, you would have sent Uncle Mike and everyone else to my bedside, causing a panic over nothing. It was just a small infection. Cayson took care of me the entire time. He never left my side."

"And I'm grateful." There was a small growl in his voice.

"Dad, you're overreacting."

"No, I'm not. I'm upset you didn't tell your mother and I you were unwell. I don't care if you're a legal adult. You're still our

337

responsibility. Do not leave us in the dark—ever again."

"I only did because you weren't around. By the time you got back from Paris, I would have been home. You would have wasted your time leaving your meeting early. That's all."

"Like I said, you let me worry about that. I have ways of traveling that average people don't."

"I'm sorry, okay? I won't do it again."

"Promise me."

"I promise."

He breathed into the phone. "How are you feeling?"

"Fine. The antibiotics worked and I can breathe easy."

"Is there something I can get you? Do you need me to speak to your professors?"

"No, Cayson took care of it."

"He's a good kid."

"Yeah..."

"Has that piece of shit bothered you?"

I knew whom he was referring to. "No."

"Good."

We sat on the phone for a while. The silence stretched between us. He had nothing left to say and neither did I.

"Pumpkin, I'll let you go. It's getting late."

"Dad?"

"Yes?"

"When you and Mom got together...who had feelings for who first?"

He said nothing for a long time. Silence echoed around the line. "Why do you ask?"

"I'm just wondering."

"Your mother realized her feelings for me first. At the time, I didn't feel the same way. It was just a huge misunderstanding. That conflict turned into a huge fight and she left, moved as far away from me as she possibly could. But in her absence, I realized she wasn't just my best friend.

"Every Saturday night, I went out alone. I went to bars and tried to move on with my life. But the only person I really wanted to be with was her. When I jogged in the park, I wanted to call her and meet her for ice cream. When I was alone in my apartment, I imagined I heard her voice. It quickly dawned on me that she was everything to me. And, simply put, I couldn't live without her. So, I chased her down and refused to let her go.

"Your mother claims she always felt that way for me but she didn't realize it. And after our reunion, I realized I felt the same way. When I initially met her in college, I thought she was breathtaking. I didn't want to be just her friend the moment I laid eyes on her. But I quickly sabotaged that with my own stupidity. In a weird and twisted way, she was always my soul mate. It just took us a very, very long time to figure that out."

His words echoed in my mind long after he said them. I processed everything, dissecting every meaning and every phrase. My parents were the most devoted couple on the planet, and they weren't that way just because they were in love. It was because they were friends—best friends.

"Did that answer your question?"

I nodded even though he couldn't see me. "It did."

***

Even though it was past nine, I drove to Cayson's apartment. My heart was beating faster than it ever had. Despite the light sleet on the road, my hands were sweaty. The steering wheel was ice cold and it felt good against my palm. I didn't turn on the radio because I knew nothing could calm me down.

I was really doing this.

When I pulled into the parking lot, I spotted his car. A light layer of snow was on top of it, telling me he hadn't left his apartment all day. I stayed in the car, trying to gather my bearings before I went to his door and confessed every feeling in my heart.

God, I was nervous.

If he didn't feel the same way, it would crush me. But what if he did? What if he felt something, no matter how small and insignificant? What if he and I were meant to have what my parents had? What if our story was similar if not the same? Zack and every other boyfriend I had were completely wrong for me. The only constant men in my life were my father and Cayson.

Cayson was everything I wanted in another person. He was my best friend, the person I shared everything with. With him, I was never afraid to whisper my darkest secret. When our hands touched, I felt more than just the heat from his body. When I stared into his eyes, I saw the stars of the universe. I knew this predicament was tricky. Going from friends to lovers wasn't a simple walk in the park. It took ten years for my parents to get it right. Would it be so hard for us? Or would it be simple? Would I walk to his front door and pour my heart out to him and he would take it? Or would he reject it?

I couldn't stay in the car anymore even though I wished I could. While I dreaded what I was about to do, I felt compelled to do it. Otherwise, I would just go back to what I was doing before, watching Cayson from a distance, living every moment with him but not really diving headfirst. I couldn't be a coward. My parents weren't and I refused to be one.

The walk up his steps was the longest I've ever taken. The complex was deathly quiet. Everyone was inside to escape the winter chill. I was immune to the frost. My heart was releasing so much heat that I was sweating.

When I arrived at his door, I stared at it for a long time. I had no idea how our conversation would go once I walked inside. But that didn't mean I should turn around. I closed my eyes and steeled my nerves. Then I opened them again and knocked.

Shit, there was no going back.

I knocked and I know he heard it. Footsteps sounded behind the door. He was coming closer.

You can do this, Skye. Cayson loved me no matter what. If he didn't feel the same way, he wouldn't sacrifice our friendship. He was a good man and I knew he would never do that.

I slowed my breathing, trying to appear calm. But damn, that was hard.

The door finally opened, and my insides spilled onto the floor.

"Skye?" Jasmine cocked an eyebrow while she looked at me. "What are you doing here?"

I looked at her outfit and felt nauseated.

She was wearing one of Cayson's t-shirts. I recognized it because I bought it for his birthday years ago. It was loose on her, trailing to her thighs.

I couldn't speak. My mouth suddenly felt dry. I hated picturing him with her, with anyone. Her blonde hair was perfect and shiny. She had flawless skin and perfect facial features. It didn't surprise me that he wanted her. Who wouldn't? She had long legs that were toned and defined. She barely had any fat on her. She was skinny, much skinnier than I was. I had flab on my stomach and an ass that would barely fit into my jeans. She was supermodel status. I was...I was plain in comparison.

"Skye...are you okay?"

I hadn't spoken once. No wonder why she was giving me that look of concern. "Sorry...I just came by to talk to Cayson. Is he here?"

"He's in the shower. Do you want to wait?"

All the courage I had was gone. Jasmine was the girl in his life. She wasn't just a fuck buddy. She obviously slept over and spent most of her time with him. It was clear she adored him, even loved him. Maybe he felt the same way for her. "No...I should I go." I turned away.

"Do you want me to tell him you stopped by?"

"No," I blurted. "I'll just talk to him later." I turned away from the door and headed down the hallway. The door closed when I reached the stairs.

Once I was in the stairwell and hidden from view, I sat down and pulled my knees to my chest. Intense heat burned under my eyes then gave way to moisture. My eyes fluttered slightly and tears dripped down. I didn't bother to wipe them away. When they reached my lips, I tasted the salt.

I covered my face with my hands and controlled my breathing. The pain was excruciating, unbearable. I wasn't sure what my feelings for Cayson were when I drove to his place tonight. But now I knew beyond a doubt how I felt.

I tried to push the thoughts away. I pretended they didn't exist for as long as possible. But now the truth was hitting me right in the face like a slab of bricks. I had nowhere to hide and nowhere to run.

I was in love with Cayson.

But it didn't matter anymore. He was with someone he cared about, a girl he spent most of his time with. She meant something to him. They had a relationship. They cared about each other. My feelings were irrelevant.

I missed my chance.

Chapter Fifteen

Cayson

"Two more." Slade stood over me with his hands under the bar, ready to catch it if I needed help.

I bent my elbows and let the weight fall to my chest. Then I pushed the bar out again.

"One more, dude."

"I can count," I said through gritted teeth.

"Then shut up and finish it."

I did the last rep then let him help me stack the bar. My arms were shaking and I took a deep breath. My face was red and sweat formed at my temples.

"You did good, man." He patted my shoulder.

I wiped my face with a towel. "Thanks."

Slade glanced over his shoulder and spotted two girls near the free weights. They were eyeing both of us, not being discreet about it. "Looks like they're into tattoos."

"Or maybe into muscle."

"I think it's a mixture of both. I got the blonde. You get the brunette."

I rolled my eyes. "For the hundredth time, I have a girlfriend."

"She's not your girlfriend," he snapped. "She's your very clingy fuck buddy."

"She's not clingy." I sat up and rested my elbows on my knees.

"Are you joking? Didn't she throw a hissy fit when you were spending time with Skye because of what that fucker did to her?"

"She was just concerned."

"No, she's clingy. I hate that shit." He rubbed his bicep while he stared at the girls. "Now you take the brunette."

"Slade, no."

"Fine. Take the blonde. I don't give a damn."

"Slade." I gave him a firm look. "I'm not available."

"So, let me get this straight. You're committed to this girl but you're in love with Skye? Is it just me or does that sound insanely fucked up?"

"It is fucked up. But Jasmine is aware of the situation."

"And she knows you spent every waking hour with Skye this week? Wiping her ass and feeding her with a spoon?"

"In so many words..."

Slade rolled is eyes. "I've fucked a lot of chicks with ridiculously low self-esteem, but I have to say she is by far the worse."

"You haven't fucked her."

He glared at me. "You know what I mean."

"Well, she's a really cool girl and I hope I can get over Skye and give her what she deserves."

"How's that going for you?" he said sarcastically.

"Stop riding my ass, Slade. I know it's a terrible situation—especially for Jasmine."

"This is what I don't get..."

I rolled my eyes. "Here we go."

"Skye sleeps with you every night and holds your hand like you're her Prince Charming. Last time I checked, she and Theo weren't related and they don't snuggle like bunnies in winter."

"Well...we're just different."

"No, she has to have feelings for you. Either that, or she's just a conniving bitch that needs all your attention."

I gave him the death stare. "Don't call her that."

"She's my cousin. I can call her what I want. You know how many times she's called me an asshole?"

"But you *are* an asshole."

"And she's being a bitch. There's no possible way that she's blind to your feelings. She totally knows it and she just uses you, preys on your feelings for her so she can feel better about herself. If that doesn't make her a bitch, I don't know what does."

I pointed at a fifty-pound weight plate on the ground. "You see that?"

"Yeah. What's your point?"

"I'm going to smash your skull in if you don't stop calling her that."

"Whatever. Fine. I'll call her a...dragon from now on."

Slade said some odds things, but that was a top contender. "What?"

"I can't call her the B word so I'll call her a dragon. She breathes fire and torches your heart. She's greedy and hoards all her gold so she doesn't have to share it with anyone. And she's cold-blooded—like a lizard."

I couldn't think of a response to that. "You shouldn't say anything mean about her at all. She's your family."

"And family tells each other the truth. And being related doesn't automatically make you liked. You aren't my family but you're more of a sibling to me than my own twin. Bloodlines don't mean jack shit."

I didn't respond because I didn't want to encourage this conversation. I knew Slade loved his cousin, but when it came to this topic, he was vicious with her. I understood he was protective of me, but sometimes he got too emotional about it.

Slade looked at the girls again. "I can tell the blonde wouldn't mind it if I did the slippery dolphin on her."

"The slippery what?"

"Dolphin." He nudged my side. "You know what I mean?"

"No. I really don't."

"You know, when you pull your cock out of her pussy then slip it up her ass?"

Slade still amazed me with some of the things he said. "I still don't understand how we're best friends."

He smirked at me. "Don't act all innocent. I know you've done it."

I was very quiet about my personal life. Not because I cared what people thought of me, but because I wanted to respect the women I'd been with. I wasn't the type of guy to gossip or spread rumors about a girl.

"You don't fuck a girl in the laundry room then pretend you've never done the slippery dolphin."

I looked at the time and ignored him.

"I can tell what kind of girl Jasmine is. And she's not against anal."

"Can we stop talking about my girlfriend now?"

"Fine. Whatever. If you really haven't done it, you should give it a try."

I drank out of my water bottle and kept my mouth shut.

"Are you ready for Thanksgiving?"

"Like you wouldn't believe. I'm just not looking forward to having a magical weekend with Skye. At least Jasmine will be there."

Slade's eyes were about to fall out of his head. "Hold up. You're taking Jasmine with you?"

"Yeah."

"To a holiday?"

I nodded.

"With your whole family?"

"Why is this so hard for you to follow?"

"Are you guys dropping the L word or what?"

"No. She doesn't have any family so I invited her."

"The first girl you bring to your parents is some girl you're banging to get over Skye? Seriously, this is getting twisted."

"She's coming as a friend."

"Your parents aren't going to think that."

"Yes, they will. I've never lied to my father so he believes everything I say."

He rolled his eyes. "Kiss ass."

I hit his arm and pushed him off the bench.

The two girls snickered from their corner.

Slade glared at me. "You're lucky I'm going to let that go."

"Don't disappoint your girlfriend."

He came back to the bench and eyed them. "Fine. If you don't want one, I'll take both."

"Both?"

"I'll give them both the slippery dolphin." He winked at me then walked to them, giving them his best moves.

Not wanting to give one of the girls an opportunity, I went home.

***

I called my dad and he answered on the third ring.

"Hey, it's nice to hear from you," he said. "I feel like I'm always calling you."

"Because you are."

"To what do I owe the pleasure?"

"I just wanted to let you know I'm bringing someone to Thanksgiving this weekend."

Silence ensued. My dad spoke up thirty seconds later. "You're bringing a girl?" He couldn't hide the excitement in his voice.

"No. She's just a friend. She has no family and nowhere to go this weekend so I invited her. I hope you don't mind."

"Of course we don't. The more, the merrier. But I'm having a hard time believing she's just a friend…"

I decided to go with the truth. "I'm sleeping with her but it's nothing serious."

"That sounds complicated."

"It's not. She's okay with the arrangement but she's my friend and I do care about her. I don't want her to be alone on Thanksgiving."

"Is there a reason why she doesn't mean more to you?"

I wanted to tell him but he was Skye's mom's best friend. It was too risky. "I just don't feel anything for her."

"Maybe you will..."

"I doubt it," I said honestly. "I really don't want you guys to read into this. The last thing I want is for Mom to treat her like a daughter when you aren't going to see her again down the road. Don't get attached to her. She isn't the woman I'm going to marry."

"Wow...that's harsh," he said with a laugh.

"I just want you to understand what this relationship really is. So, do you understand?"

My dad sighed. "Okay. Thanks for telling me."

"And tell Mom."

"I'll give her a...nicer version of what you told me. I don't think she'd be proud of you for sleeping around like Slade."

"It's not like that. And frankly, what I do in my personal life is none of your business. I only told you so you would be prepared."

"Okay. Your mother has been waiting for you to bring home someone special...I guess she'll have to wait a little longer."

Or a lot longer. "I'll see you soon."

"Alright, Son. I love you."

"I love you too, Dad." I ended the call then sighed, hoping my dad took me seriously.

***

Roland pulled up to the curb then rolled down the window. "Throw your shit in the back and let's go."

"Hello to you too." I grabbed my bags and threw them in the back. Then I went inside and retrieved Jasmine's.

Roland cocked an eyebrow. "Dude, how much crap did you pack?"

"Jasmine is coming."

"Oh." He scratched his forehead. "Thanks for the heads up."

Jasmine came out with her bag over her shoulder. I could tell she was nervous.

"You'll have a great time. I promise."

She relaxed. "Okay."

I opened the back door and let her get inside. Then I walked back around and took the other seat.

Skye was sitting in the passenger seat but she didn't look at me. She didn't say hi to me.

"Hey, Skye. Are you feeling better?"

She still didn't turn around. "Yeah..."

Roland eyed her. "Why are you in such a bad mood all of a sudden?"

"I'm not," she argued. She looked out the window, ignoring her brother.

Roland turned in his seat and looked at me. "Does everyone know you're bringing her?"

"I called my parents yesterday," I said.

"Okay." He turned around and put the car in gear. "But like I said, some notice would have been nice."

"Just drive," I said irritably.

"Am I intruding?" Jasmine asked.

"No," I said immediately. "Roland is just being a dick."

Roland looked at me in the rearview mirror. "You want to walk?"

"You want me to slap you upside the head while you're driving?"

"You want me to crash?" Roland snapped.

"Just drive." Skye's voice came out quiet. "And fast."

What was her problem? The last time I saw her, she was cheerful and upbeat. She slept with me in her bed and cuddled with me. Now she was back to being indifferent. Her mood swings were starting to annoy me.

We drove in silence on the freeway, watching the snow on the road. Jasmine reached for my hand and held it, rubbing her thumb across my knuckles. The touch reminded me of the way I held Skye's hand, and for that, I felt guilty.

Skye touched the radio and turned up the music, drowning out all other sound in the car. Roland eyed her from the driver's seat but didn't comment on it. Then he kept his eyes on the road, driving carefully over the frosty streets.

Normally, we would play a game on the drive. Sometimes we would play cards and sometimes we would play a license plate game. The time spent traveling usually sped by because we had so much fun. But now the car was full of hostility and awkwardness. Was this just because I brought Jasmine? I was certain everyone liked her. No one ever had a problem with her when I brought her around.

Jasmine pressed her lips to my ear. "Is it always tense like this?"

"No...something is off."

"Is it me?" she asked fearfully.

"No." I pressed my lips to hers and gave her a gentle kiss. When I pulled away, I spotted Skye looking at us in the rearview mirror. Her gaze flickered away like she hadn't been staring at us. *This trip was getting weirder...*

Two hours later, we finally arrived at my house in Connecticut. The lawn was covered in snow and so was our apple tree in the front lawn.

Smoke rose from the chimney near the back of the house. Jasmine eyed it with trepidation.

"Thanks for the ride," I said to Roland.

"No problem. You need help with the bags?" he asked.

"No. I got it." I looked at Skye but she was staring out the window, ignoring me. I got out then popped the trunk. Once I pulled everything out, I turned to Jasmine. "Stay here, please."

"Okay." She stood by the bags.

I walked to the passenger window then tapped on the glass.

Skye tried not to look at me as she rolled down the window.

"Is everything okay?" I asked.

"Yeah, I'm fine."

She didn't sound fine. "Why are you lying to me?"

Her cheeks reddened slightly. "I said I was fine. Now go."

Her hostility wasn't appreciated. "Do you have a problem with Jasmine?"

"No...I guess I'm just surprised that you're bringing her to Thanksgiving."

"Why?"

She pressed her lips together and said nothing.

Skye had never acted this way before. "It was common knowledge that I hated Zack—we all did—but we put up with him because you wanted us to. You could at least try to make Jasmine feel welcome. This time of year isn't exactly easy for her." It was the first time I snapped at Skye like that. I guess I was a little resentful that I skipped class two days in a row just to take care of her. That I gave her every single piece of me and she didn't care. She made me suffer more than any man ever should and she didn't blink an eye over it.

I grabbed our bags then carried them to the front door, not looking back.

"What did she say?" Jasmine asked.

"She's just not feeling well," I lied.

"Oh."

We got to the front door and I rang the bell.

The door burst open and my German Sheppard practically tackled me, almost knocking me over.

"Whoa, boy." I laughed then scratched him behind the ears.

His tongue hung out while he pawed my legs.

Jasmine petted his head. "What's his name?"

"Pop-Eye."

"The sailor man?" she asked with a laugh.

I shrugged. "My sister and I named him when we were little."

She smiled at my dog. "It's nice to meet you, Pop-Eye."

Pop-Eye barked then put all his paws on the ground.

My dad came out then gripped my shoulder. "I'm glad you're home."

"Me too."

He hugged me tightly, practically breaking my back and then pulled away. Then he looked at Jasmine. "It's nice to meet you. I'm Cortland, Cayson's father."

She shook his hand. "It's nice to meet you. I'm Jasmine."

"Very pretty name." He dropped his hand and stepped aside.

Teary-eyed like usual, my mom embraced me hard. She was a foot shorter than me so her head always moved to my chest. "You're so handsome, honey."

"Thanks to you."

She pulled away and smiled at me. "Actually, you can thank your father for that."

My dad flexed his arm. "I still got it."

"Maybe flab," I teased.

"Hey, I'm still a stud. I hit the gym every day with your Uncle Mike."

"You should hit it harder," I said.

My mom walked to Jasmine and immediately hugged her. "Welcome to our home, dear."

Jasmine was caught off guard by the warmth my mother showed. "Thank you..."

My mom pulled away and smiled at her. "My name is Monnique."

"It's nice to meet you, Mrs. Thompson."

"That's my mother-in-law's name. Call me Monnique."

"Okay." Jasmine didn't seem as nervous.

My sister came out, looking just like my mom. She had darker skin than I did, and her brown eyes were bright and dark at the same time. "I was hoping you'd get snowed in and wouldn't be able to come."

"I was hoping you slipped on some ice and were in the hospital," I snapped.

She stuck her tongue out at me. "Jerk."

"Brat."

"Hey, enough of that," my dad said. "It's Thanksgiving."

"Don't remind me." My sister rolled her eyes.

I turned to Jasmine. "This is my annoying sister, Clementine."

Jasmine shook her hand. "It's nice to meet you."

"Yeah..." Clementine dropped her hand quickly.

"Ignore her," I said.

We walked inside and placed our bags in the doorway.

"I cleaned your old bedroom so you guys should be comfortable there," my mom said.

"Thanks." I grabbed our bags and carried them to the bedroom.

Jasmine came behind me. "They are going to let us sleep together?"

"Why wouldn't they?" I asked.

"Well...isn't that awkward?"

"They know we have sex."

Her eyes widened. "You told them?"

I shrugged. "My parents aren't stupid. They know I'm not a blushing virgin."

Her cheeks reddened slightly.

"It's nothing to be embarrassed about. My parents are cool. They lived together before they got married."

"It's still...awkward. I assumed your mother would be really anal because you brought me home for Thanksgiving."

"Well, they know about our relationship."

She sat on the bed. "What do you mean?"

"They know we aren't serious. I told them you were my friend and I didn't want you to be alone on Thanksgiving."

"So...they think I don't mean anything to you?"

"No, that's not what I said. I just said you aren't the girl I'm going to marry so they don't need to freak out."

She flinched at my words then her breathing changed. She blinked her eyes a few times before she stood up and headed to my door. "I need to use the restroom..." She walked out then disappeared down the hallway.

A second later, I realized my mistake. "Fuck." I rubbed my temples while I sat on the bed. That was a stupid thing to say and I felt like an asshole. Could I be more insensitive? I made it clear this wouldn't turn into anything, at least it was incredibly unlikely, but I didn't have to blurt that on a holiday. I wanted to build a time machine just so I could redo those last few minutes. God, I was an idiot.

I stayed in my bedroom and gave her a minute to compose herself. I'd have to work hard to fix the mess I made. She knew the parameters of this relationship so my words shouldn't be so shocking, but blurting it like that was still really stupid.

After I gave her enough time to recover, I walked to the bathroom down the hall and knocked lightly. "Jasmine?"

"I'm just freshening up. Give me a second." Her voice was full of tears.

I rested my head against the door and sighed. "Please let me in." I heard the sound of plates from the kitchen. My mom was finishing dinner and my dad was setting the table. I wanted to make this right before we sat down to eat.

"Leave me alone, Cayson." Her voice was weak.

"Jasmine, come on. I'm not going to talk to you through a door."

A few seconds later, she unlocked the door.

I went inside then shut it behind me. Her makeup was fixed and the tears were gone but I still saw redness in her eyes. They were moist, about to overflow with water.

I sat down on the lid of the toilet then pulled her into my lap, sitting her on me. She didn't fight. "That was a stupid thing to say and I shouldn't have said it. I'd take it back if I could."

She rested her hands on my shoulders, gripping me.

"I'm sorry." I cupped her cheek and directed her look on me. "I didn't mean to be insensitive."

"It's okay. I'm overreacting anyway. I guess I just..." She trailed off.

"What, Jasmine?"

She rested her face against mine and closed her eyes. "Nothing."

I moved my hands through her hair and held her close to me. Her breathing was decreasing and she was calming down. If I gave her a few moments of peace, she'd be back to normal in time for dinner. "You're beautiful, Jasmine. Every time I look at you, I think it."

She pressed her lips to mine and gave me a deep kiss. It was passionate and slow. The distinct taste of salt was on her tongue. My hand fisted her hair and gripped it tightly.

Then she pulled away, feeling better. "We should get out of here before anyone notices..."

"Yeah. I would hate to find an explanation of why we're in here."

She smirked. "Bathrooms turn us on."

I laughed. "We have some weird fetishes."

We left the bathroom and sat at the kitchen table. My mom laid out all the food before she sat down. Clementine sat across from me, wearing a red sweater and purple scarf. She was a pretty girl but with a dangerous attitude.

My dad poured wine for my mom and himself. "Jasmine, do you like wine?"

"I love it."

He poured her a glass then put the bottle on the table.

"Thanks for offering me a glass." I shot him a glare.

"Are you a girl?" he countered.

I rolled my eyes then poured my own wine.

Jasmine ate the potatoes off her plate. "These are really good, Mrs. Thom—I mean, Monnique."

"Thank you, dear." She smiled then cut into her chicken. A foot tapped me under the table and I realized my mom was trying to play footsies with my dad. *Gross.*

My dad turned to Jasmine. "Do you know Cayson from school?"

"Actually, I'm a waitress. He came in with his friends and that's how we met." She kept her elbows off the table and ate with grace.

"You're a waitress?" Clementine said with disdain. "That's it?"

I glared at her. "Knock it off or I'll pour gasoline in your hair in the middle of the night." Why was my sister being such a bitch?

My dad glared at me. "Don't talk to your sister like that."

"But she—"

He raised his hand. "I'll handle her."

I sighed then shut my mouth.

My dad turned to Clementine. "Don't be rude to our guest. If you're going to act this way, please leave. And I don't mean the table. I mean the house."

Damn...Dad laid down the law.

Clementine sipped her water then fell silent.

"Apologize to Jasmine," my dad commanded.

Clementine ignored him.

"Apologize or grab your keys and leave."

"Are you five years old?" I snapped. "Sometimes I can't believe you're an adult."

"I'm sorry," she blurted. "There."

I sighed then turned to Jasmine. "I'm sorry about her. She's normally not this bad."

"It's okay." Jasmine acted like she wasn't hurt.

"Anyway," my father said. "What restaurant do you work at?"

"The sports bar near campus," she said.

My mom nodded. "You must know a lot about sports."

"Too much," she said with a laugh. "But it's nice having a common interest with Cayson."

"We usually watch football together on Monday nights," I said.

"Do you have a favorite team?" my dad asked.

"The Chargers," she answered.

I rolled my eyes. "I don't know why because they suck."

"They're the underdogs," she argued. "Someone has to root for them."

"That's the dumbest reasoning I've ever heard," I said with a laugh.

She shrugged. "Well, I like them."

Clementine focused on her food and remained silent, not participating in the conversation.

"Do you have any hobbies?" my dad asked. "Skiing?"

"I want to go to cosmetology school," she answered. "I like hair and nails."

Clementine grinned but didn't say anything.

"Very cool," my mom said. "I like to do my own hair but I wouldn't say I'm a professional at it."

"I would," my dad blurted. He tried to touch her foot under the table but only touched mine.

Gross.

"How's school?" my dad asked.

"Good," I said. "Nothing new to report."

"I heard Skye got pneumonia and you took care of her." My dad sipped his wine.

"Do you old people do anything else besides get together and gossip about us?" I asked.

He shook his head. "Actually, no."

At least he was honest about it.

"That was really sweet of you," Clementine said. "I'm sure Skye appreciated it."

Okay...what the hell? It was the biggest mood swing I've ever seen.

My dad ignored her out of place comment. "Sean wasn't too happy to be the last to know."

"Well, he's psycho." I remembered the way he beat the shit out of Zack in front of a group of students.

My dad smirked. "He's not normal, that's for sure."

"What's going on with you guys?" I asked. "What do you do all day since Clementine and I don't live here?"

My dad shrugged. "The same thing we did before you were born."

Clementine and I both made a face.

My mom laughed. "We have sex like all other humans."

"But it's gross," Clementine said. "You shouldn't be allowed to do that."

My dad smirked. "That would just make the sex hotter."

Clementine and I made a face again.

"I'm sorry my parents are disgusting," I said to Jasmine.

She laughed. "It's okay. They're cute."

"No, they aren't," Clementine said firmly.

We finished dinner then Jasmine headed to the sink. "Let me help you with the dishes, Monnique."

Clementine rolled her eyes. "That girl is trying way too hard." She said it loudly and without shame.

I kicked her under the table. "Don't be a bitch," I hissed.

My dad kicked me. "Don't call your sister that."

I growled. "Then control her mouth."

My dad sighed then leaned toward her. "Clementine, what is your problem?"

"Nothing." She got up from the table then walked away.

"It would be nice if my own daughter offered to help," my mom said loudly, making sure Clementine could hear.

I touched Jasmine on the shoulder. "I'll be right back."

"Okay." She kept washing the dishes.

I walked into my sister's room then grabbed her by the arm. "Why are you acting like a shithead?"

She twisted out of my grasp. "Because you brought a stupid tramp here."

My sister was totally out of whack. She annoyed me all the time but she'd never been vicious and mean before. "She's not stupid and she's not a tramp."

"I don't like her. Why would you bring her here?"

"She doesn't have a family for Thanksgiving. Can't you be nice and just make her feel welcome?"

She crossed her arms over her chest. "Are you stupid? I just told you why. I. Don't. Like. Her."

"Why? You don't even know her." I was having a hard time keeping my voice down.

"What happened to Skye?" She stared me down.

Ugh, I was sick of talking about the damn girl I couldn't have. "What about her?"

"I thought you loved her?"

"I do but she doesn't love me. This isn't news. I need to move on and get on with my life."

"So you pick up trash? I know she's a rebound but you can do better than that."

"She's not trash! She's a sweet girl."

"And she's a waitress? Why the hell would you be interested in someone like her?"

"*Someone like her*? What the hell is that supposed to mean? There's nothing wrong with being a waitress. Mom doesn't work. She stays home all day. Isn't that worse?"

"Mom used to be a nurse and actually went to college."

"And what the hell are you doing with your life?" I snapped. "Where's your college degree?"

Her eyes narrowed. "I'm a violinist. I actually have grace and talent."

"No, it sounds like all you are is a damn hypocrite."

"It's different. I'm not dating you."

I cocked an eyebrow. "What's that supposed to mean?"

"She's not good enough for you. Cayson, you're so smart, funny, generous, and handsome. You shouldn't be with a loser."

"First of all, did you just give me a compliment?"

She rolled her eyes.

"And secondly, she's not a loser. You didn't like her the moment she walked through that door and you haven't even gotten to know her."

"I don't care. I don't like her. I don't want you to marry her."

"Who said anything about marriage?"

"You wouldn't have brought her here unless she was the one." She stared me down.

I sighed. "Clementine, I only brought her here because she doesn't have any family. She was going to spend the holiday all by herself in her small apartment. I invited her here as a friend. She and I are dating, but I certainly don't love her and I doubt I ever will. She's aware of all of this."

My sister relaxed. "So, there's still hope for you and Skye?"

Just forming the answer in my mind was painful. "She and I will never be together. She sees me as a friend and nothing more. I know you wanted us to be together. Shit, everyone did, but it's not going to happen. I'm trying to move on and Jasmine is my first attempt. Please be nice to her. I may not love her and I don't see a long-term future for us, but I care about her very much. "

My sister sighed. "Okay. I'll try."

"Thank you. But if I do move on and you treat the woman I love with anything but respect, I won't hesitate to pour syrup in your hair and destroy it."

She smirked. "Okay. That's fair."

"Please apologize to her—and actually mean it—and try to make her feel welcome."

"Fine. I'll do it for you."

I smirked. "And thanks for all those flattering comments. I always knew you liked me."

"Don't let it go to your head." She rolled her eyes.

Jasmine came to the door. "Sorry, am I interrupting?"

"No," I said. "Come in."

She stepped close to me then eyed Clementine with fear.

I stared at my sister, silently telling her to speak up.

"I'm sorry I was rude to you." She said it with more conviction. "I'm just protective of my big brother. I only want the best for him."

"I accept your apology," Jasmine said. "And I'm glad you got your brother's back."

"To the end of time."

I pulled Jasmine out of the room. "Movie time?"

"Sure."

We sat on the couch with my parents. Clementine came in the room a second later, taking the recliner.

"Who wants to watch a chick flick?" My mom raised her hand.

Clementine raised hers and so did Jasmine.

My dad sighed. "Damn it."

"Chick flick it is." My mom smirked then picked out a movie.

I pulled Jasmine close to me, showing affection in front of my parents. I didn't care if they saw and I didn't care what they thought. Jasmine was hesitant at first but she eventually reciprocated.

While we snuggled on the couch, snow fell lightly outside. The fire burned in the hearth, keeping us warm. Fall and winter were my favorite seasons. There was something beautiful about the cold. The powder outside made wonderful parts for snowmen. The feel of warm soup in your stomach after shoveling the driveway made the chore more bearable. And spending time with my family during the holidays made me feel lucky.

But I couldn't deny what was missing. I wished Skye were sitting on the couch with me, cuddled under a blanket. I would hold her hand and rub her knuckles with the pad of my thumb. When my parents went to sleep, I'd make love to her in my bed. Of course, Skye would resist but I wouldn't care.

But that wasn't real. And it would never be real.

Chapter Sixteen

Skye

I didn't want to wake up the next morning. This was the worst Thanksgiving ever. It already hurt knowing Cayson had a girlfriend but knowing he actually brought her to meet his parents was just nauseating. She meant even more to him than I originally thought. I was so stupid for showing up at his doorstep about to confess the feeling in my heart. *So stupid.*

A knock sounded on my door. "Skye, are you alright?" It was my mom.

"I'm okay. Just getting a late start."

"Breakfast is downstairs and it's getting cold."

"I'm not hungry." I was never not hungry so that sent out an alarm.

"Honey, I'm coming in." She cracked the door then came to my bedside.

I didn't stir or move. The curtains in my room were still closed, blocking out all possible light.

My mom sat at the edge of my bed then stared at me. "Is something on your mind?"

I didn't want to talk about Cayson. She was best friends with his father so I couldn't trust her this time. "I guess I'm still under the weather from the pneumonia." It was cruel to lie to my mom but I didn't have an alternative.

She pressed the back of her hand to my forehead. "You don't have a fever."

"It's nothing serious. I'm just a little sluggish."

"Is that all that's bothering you?"

How did parents know when you were lying? Every time? "Yes, Mom. I'll be up in a little bit."

"Everyone is coming at three so be ready by then."

"I will."

"Want me to save you some breakfast? I made your favorite; orange French toast."

"No, it's okay. I'll save room for dinner."

"Alright, honey." She moved her hand through my hair then kissed my forehead.

When she left my bedroom, I felt empty and alone.

***

At three o'clock, the door burst open.

"I got wine. I got beer. I got eggnog with rum. I got it all." Uncle Ryan held up the bags.

"And I brought something more appropriate..." Aunt Janice stepped inside with a platter of sweet potato yams.

My mom smirked when she stared at her brother. "You know, we're not twenty-one anymore."

"But our kids are." Ryan wiggled his eyebrows.

"You're a horrible role model," she teased.

"Shut up," Uncle Ryan snapped. "You're just mad my kids actually like me. I know your two brats despise you."

"They do not despise me." She crossed her arms over her chest and scowled.

"I have an idea," Aunt Janice said. "How about we hug and get along since it's Thanksgiving?"

"You mean the day when the pilgrims came to America and gave the generous Indians syphilis?" Uncle Ryan shook his head. "Yes, what a wonderful day to celebrate."

"Just hug your sister and be nice," Aunt Janice snapped.

Ryan rolled his eyes and put down the booze. Then he hugged my mom. Despite the way he just teased her, he held her for a long time, saying something inaudible. They were two peas in a pod. When she wasn't with my dad, she was usually with him. Even though they bickered like two hens in a cage, that was how they related to one another.

Uncle Ryan ended the embrace. "You look nice today."

My mom smiled. "Thank you. You do too."

My dad came from the kitchen then hugged Uncle Ryan. "Long time, no see."

"I know," Uncle Ryan said. "We haven't played poker in almost three days."

"I want a rematch," my dad said.

"Double or nothing?"

"How about triple or nothing?"

Uncle Ryan smirked. "You got a deal. I just hope the bank will give you a loan to help with your children's tuition."

"We'll see," my dad said vaguely.

Slade walked in after him, Silke beside him. "Dad, where's the booze?"

"After dinner." Uncle Ryan didn't look at him.

"Come on, just a little spiked eggnog." Slade winked at him.

"Okay. Fine." Uncle Ryan handed him the bag.

"I don't think so." Aunt Janice stared down her husband, the fire burning in her glare. "I said no booze until later."

Slade rolled his eyes. "Mom, you're such a party pooper."

"Put the bag down," she snapped.

He sighed. "Fine. Geez, loosen up a bit."

"Grow a pair," she snapped back.

Slade laughed then walked away.

Uncle Ryan came to me. His eyes always lit up when he looked at me. There was a distant affection in his eyes, and it always came to the surface when he took me in. "Hey, Skye."

"Hey, Uncle Ryan."

He pulled me into his arms and gave me a big hug. "You're such a pretty girl. Sometimes I can't believe my sister made you."

I laughed then pulled away. "Well, my dad helped. I think."

He wiggled his eyebrows. "I guess we'll never really know, right?"

"I'm not deaf, Ryan." My dad's voice echoed from behind him.

Uncle Ryan rolled his eyes. "I could take him—with one hand."

"He's actually pretty strong," I said.

"Honey, you haven't seen anything." He patted my shoulder and looked at me again. "Let me hug you again."

I giggled. "Why?"

"Because I love you so damn much." He pulled me in for another hug then lifted me off the ground.

I laughed while he held me to his chest.

"My dad loves his nieces and nephews more than he loves his own kids," Slade snapped.

"Gee, I wonder why..." Aunt Janice shot Slade a glare.

"Whatever, Mom. You love me." He nudged her in the side. "I'm your first born."

"We were born at the same time, idiot." Silke flipped her hair over one shoulder.

"I'm still a minute older."

Uncle Ryan put me back on the ground. "Now where's that stud of a nephew of mine?"

"Over here." Roland fist bumped his uncle. "You're looking good, man."

"Well, your aunt is insatiable in the bedroom so I got to keep up my stamina." He flexed his arms.

"TMI, man."

Ryan laughed then hugged him. "I'm glad you don't look like your mom because you would have been one ugly boy."

Roland laughed. "My sister looks like my mom and she's still an ugly girl."

Ryan laughed and pulled away. "Good one, kid." He fist pounded him again. "So, when am I going to put some ink on ya?"

My dad gave my uncle a firm look. "Don't even think about it."

"What?" Ryan asked. "They are both adults. How about a tramp stamp for Skye?"

My dad's eyes widened. "If you weren't my brother, I'd fill a vial of your blood and put it right in the entrance way."

Ryan cocked an eyebrow. "That was oddly specific...have you given this a lot of thought?"

Roland and I both laughed.

"Just don't touch my kids," my dad said.

Ryan poked Roland in the shoulder. "Ooh...I'm touching him."

My dad rolled his eyes and walked away.

Roland gave him a high-five. "Only you can get under my dad's skin."

Ryan smirked. "Only because he lets me. And he only does that to very few people."

Uncle Mike and Aunt Cassandra walked in, Trinity and Conrad with them. Trinity was holding a flower vase, and Conrad held a pan with a lid on top.

"I know it's not Christmas but we don't see our nieces and nephews that often so we brought gifts," Uncle Mike said.

"Ooh....I like gifts." Roland rubbed his hands together greedily.

My dad hugged Uncle Mike first. "Thanks for coming."

"I would have come even if you didn't invite me." Uncle Mike smirked.

"But I would have invited you." My mom hugged him next. My mom had a special bond with everyone. She seemed to be the glue that held everyone together. It even seemed like my dad's own brother preferred my mom over his flesh and blood.

Conrad scowled. "Mom, can I put this down now?"

"In the kitchen," she said.

He headed to the left and through the door.

Trinity went to my mom with the vase of winter flowers. "A gift for the hostess from the Prestons—the other Prestons."

My mom smiled as she took it. "Thank you. I know exactly where these will go."

Uncle Mike carried a sack full of gifts. "Alright, let me start handing these out..."

Uncle Ryan came to him, smirking. "Hey Santa." He grabbed his red sweater and felt the fabric in his fingertips.

Uncle Mike glared at him. "I'm not Santa. Cassandra says she likes it when I wear red."

"And bring a sack full of gifts?" Uncle Ryan was always a smartass.

"I don't have the gut so I can't be Santa," Uncle Mike argued.

Ryan smirked. "I know you're into girdles..."

Uncle Mike looked at my mom. "Get him away from me before I embarrass him in front of his kids."

Ryan looked at Trinity. "Hey, you want to get a free tattoo?"

Uncle Mike's eyes were bigger than I'd ever seen them. "I'm going to stab your eyes with needles."

"What a joyous holiday..." My dad rolled his eyes.

"Get on with the gifts," Roland said.

Uncle Mike pulled out a gift, which was wrapped in Christmas paper.

Uncle Ryan stared at him with a smirk on his face.

"Don't even say it." Uncle Mike gave him the death stare.

Roland ripped the wrapping off. "Whoa...an electronic drone with a camera? No way!"

"Now you can get aerial views down a girl's shirt." Uncle Mike winked.

My dad didn't look happy. "And how would you feel if someone did that to your daughter?"

Mike shook his head. "They wouldn't. Because they know they'd be tortured in a Chinese prison."

"Oddly specific..." Ryan rubbed his chin. "He's given this some thought."

"I can't wait to fly this thing. Thank you, Uncle Mike." Roland stared at the box.

"You're welcome, kid. But I want a hug as payment."

"Sure." Roland hugged him hard then stepped back. "I wonder if I can get a view of the ocean with this."

"It can fly up to ten miles."

"Wow!" Roland came to me and showed me the box. "Nice, right?"

I rolled my eyes. Boys and their toys...

"Skye, come here." Uncle Mike pulled out a small box for me. "For the lady."

I smiled then ripped the wrapping off. It was a black velvet box. Then I opened it, seeing the plain white gold band inside. I took it out and examined it. On the outside were engraved names. *Sean. Mike. Ryan. Cortland. Flynn. Grandpa Andrew.* I didn't understand the significance.

"Next time a guy messes with you, just show him that. He'll know what he's up against." He gave me a slight smile.

I was moved. "Thank you, Uncle Mike."

"You're welcome, kid." He hugged me tightly before he pulled away.

My dad came close to him. "That was thoughtful."

"What can I say? I'm a thoughtful guy."

My dad smirked then patted his shoulder. "Thank you."

"What did you bring me?" Slade asked. He was impatient, like always.

Uncle Mike pulled out a gift shaped like a bottle. "Here you go. I think you'll like it."

He ripped off the wrapping paper. "Wow...this brandy is a hundred years old."

"And I'm sure it'll be amazing," Uncle Mike said.

"Alcohol?" my mom asked. "Really?"

Uncle Ryan grabbed the bottle and examined it. "You're sharing this with me."

"Alright, Dad." Slade hugged Uncle Mike then stepped away, staring at the bottle.

Uncle Flynn and Aunt Hazel came inside, their two sons with them. Theo had his hands in his pocket, and Thomas stood beside his father.

"Now the party can get started," Uncle Flynn said. He started to dance.

Hazels sighed. "He drank on the way here."

Uncle Ryan nodded. "I always knew I liked that guy."

Uncle Mike waved the guys over. "Get your gifts."

"Gifts?" Theo asked.

"Yep." He handed them two boxes.

When they opened them, they took out sunglasses.

"They are the unbreakable and unable to be lost kind," Uncle Mike explained.

"The kind that can get run over by a car and nothing happens?" Theo asked.

"Yep." Uncle Mike nodded.

"So cool." Thomas put on his pair.

Uncle Mike hugged them both before Flynn and Hazel came closer.

Flynn cocked an eyebrow. "Were we supposed to dress up?"

"No." Uncle Ryan smirked. "Why?"

"Isn't Mike Santa?" Flynn asked.

Mike glared at him. "Shut your mouth or we'll see if you can get run over by a car and have nothing happen."

"Whoa...Santa is cranky." Flynn rolled his eyes.

Uncle Ryan laughed at the pissed look on Mike's face.

Uncle Cortland and Aunt Monnique came inside next, the people I was dreading to see. I loved my aunt and uncle but I knew that meant I would have to see Cayson...and his girlfriend.

"My wife made that cranberry sauce you love," Cortland said when he reached my mom.

"Good. I love it." My mom smiled then hugged him.

"Happy Thanksgiving, Scar."

"Happy Thanksgiving," my mom said back.

"Thanksgiving is the dumbest holiday in the world," Flynn said. "It's when the Englishman basically wiped out a whole race of people. Nothing worth celebrating."

"Anything that involves food and booze is worth celebrating," Uncle Mike said.

Uncle Flynn and Aunt Hazel hugged me then Uncle Cortland and Aunt Monnique moved toward me. Good thing my parents had a huge house to fit all of us. Otherwise, it would be tight.

Cayson walked inside, holding hands with Jasmine.

I felt sick to my stomach.

"Hey." Uncle Mike pulled him in for a hug. "I got you a gift."

"For what?" Cayson asked.

"Because you're my nephew—that's why." He handed Cayson the gift.

Cayson tore the wrapping off. Then he opened the box and revealed a gray stethoscope. His eyes lit up when he looked at it.

"This was made in 1816 by Rene Laennec—"

"The inventor of the stethoscope?" Cayson's eyes were about to fall out of his head.

"I don't expect you to actually use it but I thought you might like to have it."

Cayson's hands shook while he held it. "I don't even know what to say..."

"Don't say anything at all." Uncle Mike pulled him in for a hug.

For a moment in time, I forgot about Jasmine standing close to him. I just saw Cayson, the humble and appreciative man I'd known all my life. He didn't care about flashy gifts or expensive things. He cared about the things that really mattered. He treasured people and history.

"Thank you, Uncle Mike." He stepped away and put the stethoscope back in the box.

"Hey, beautiful." Uncle Mike looked at Jasmine. "I got you something too."

"Me?" She pointed at her chest, confused.

"Come over here." He pulled out a box and handed it to her. "I know you aren't my niece, but if you're important to one of my kids, you're important to me."

Her hand shook while she took the box.

Cayson put his hand on her hip and gave her a reassuring tap. "Open it."

She opened the lid and saw a necklace inside. It had the Boston Red Sox symbol on it.

"I know you're a sport fan," Uncle Mike explained.

"I don't even know what to say…" She felt the chain in her hands.

"Nothing. Just accept it."

"Thank you," she blurted. "No one has ever given me jewelry before…"

Everyone in the room tensed in sadness. It was a heartbreaking thing to hear.

Jasmine's eyes burned with tears. "Thank you."

"You're very welcome." He patted her shoulder.

Cayson led her away then put the necklace on her.

Ugh…now it was harder for me to hate her.

"And last but not least..." He pulled out the last box. "For Miss Clementine."

She smiled and stepped in front of him.

"I'm going to be honest and say I didn't pick this out..." He handed her the box.

She opened it and saw the heels inside. "Oh my god! These are Swank and Sharks!"

He smirked. "You can thank your Aunt Janice for those."

She jumped into his arms and hugged him. "Thank you."

"You're welcome, kid."

She stepped away then immediately tried them on.

Grandma and Grandpa came through the door with smiles on their faces. "Happy Thanksgiving!" my grandpa said.

"Happy Thanksgiving," we said back.

My grandpa walked past Uncle Mike and stopped. "Ho Ho Ho. Merry Christmas!"

Uncle Mike scowled at him. "Go to hell, old man."

***

The holidays were always a big celebration at the house. Just like on Christmas day when we spent three hours opening gifts. On Thanksgiving, we had too much food to eat and stomachs too small to stuff it into.

We sat at the table and scooped the food onto our plates. I tried to sit at the opposite end of the table so I wouldn't have to look at Cayson or be anywhere near him. I was isolating myself from my cousins and friends, but I just wanted my space. I sat between Uncle Mike and Uncle Ryan with my dad across from me.

I kept my eyes glued to my own plate, but against my will, I snuck a few glances at Cayson and Jasmine. His hand was resting on the back of her chair and he engaged her in conversation. I couldn't hear what she was saying because the conversations were too loud. But she was laughing, hanging on every word he said.

When I felt someone stare at me, I looked across the way and saw my mother watching me. She wasn't eating, just staring. I quickly looked down and pretended I wasn't crying over the man I couldn't have.

When we were finished, my mom sighed. "I really don't want to do the dishes."

"I'll help you, baby." My dad patted her thigh.

"He's still pussy-whipped after all these years," Uncle Ryan said.

I cringed. "Gross."

"Tone down the language around the kids, alright?" my dad said.

"They are all adults. You think they don't talk like that already?" Uncle Ryan asked.

"I'm pussy-whipped," Slade said. "But not by any pussy in particular." He laughed at his own joke.

Aunt Janice smacked his arm. "Watch your language at the table."

"But I can say it anywhere else?" he questioned.

"Just stop talking," Aunt Janice said. "Be silent."

"Maybe if I had some eggnog I would be..."

"If we all pitch in and do the dishes, it'll be over quick," Uncle Cortland said.

"You know what I say?" Grandpa said. "Paper plates next year."

"Dad, that's tacky," my mom said.

"Who cares?" Grandpa said. "My grandson just said he's in love with pussy. You can't get tackier than that."

Uncle Ryan laughed. "That's my boy..."

"I'll help," I volunteered. It was better than watching Cayson suck Jasmine's neck all night.

My mom gave me that look she had since I was little. She knew I was up to something.

We cleared the table and started stacking the dishes.

"Can I say something first?" Jasmine said.

Everyone stilled, not clanking their silverware and plates. It was silent.

"I really appreciate you letting me spend the holiday with you. You've all been so wonderful to me and I really appreciate it." Jasmine smiled slightly then looked down.

Ugh. It was getting harder to hate this bitch.

My mom smiled. "You're always welcome, honey."

"I'll drink to that." Uncle Ryan raised his glass then clanked it against Cortland's.

We stacked the dishes then my dad started washing them in the sink.

"I can wash them, Sean. Don't worry about it." My mom rubbed his back gently.

"I got it, baby. You can stack them in the dishwasher."

She gave him a firm look. "You work all week. Let me do it."

He turned off the water and faced her. "You think making a home and raising my kids isn't work?"

"Well, our kids are out of the house. I can't take credit for that anymore."

"Just stack the dishes, baby."

"Why don't I—"

He crushed his mouth against hers and silenced her with a kiss. He held it for a moment before he broke away. My mom saw stars in her eyes. "Now shut up and stack the dishes."

She blushed. "Yes, sir."

He smirked then turned on the water.

Ugh. No matter where I went, I couldn't get away from love. Why couldn't someone else be miserable like I was? I wanted to go in the living room with everyone else, but I knew Jasmine would be sitting on Cayson's lap like a damn cowgirl. But I couldn't stay there because I was about to get run over by all my aunts and uncles.

I decided to go into the living room and join everyone on the couch. I sat in the corner, as far away from Cayson as I possibly could. Jasmine was sitting close to him, her hand on his knee.

Did it make me a bitch that I wanted to yank her hair out of her skull?

Slade was drinking his brandy right out of the bottle. "Shit, that is good."

"You're going to be wasted before the night is over," Silke said.

"That's the point." Slade took another drink.

Theo had his glasses over his head, and Thomas did the same.

Trinity kept staring at Slade, glaring at him.

"What?" Slade barked.

"Nothing. You're just annoying," Trinity said.

"I'm always annoying to you." He rolled his eyes then looked away.

Cayson moved his hand to the back of Jasmine's neck and rubbed her gently. "I told you it would be fun."

"You were right." She smiled at him, the love in her eyes.

His hand pulled a few strands of hair out of her face, just the way he did to me. I remembered the last night we slept together. He touched me just like that, lulling me to sleep. Now his hands were on her, touching and caressing her. It was making me light-headed.

"You know what I'm thankful for?" she whispered.

"What?" He lowered his voice.

"Finding you."

I looked away, unable to bear it a second longer. I needed fresh hair. I need to breathe. I couldn't sit there and watch them love each other. Why did it take me so long to realize how I felt? Cayson hadn't had a girlfriend in years. Why did he have to get one when I finally realized how amazing he was? But even if he didn't have a girlfriend, he still may have rejected me. Perhaps I was doomed either way.

Without saying a word, I left my spot on the couch then walked into the backyard. Snow was on the patio and the grass. It was so cold, I instantly saw my breath. But it was dark. Shadows covered me, making me feel calm. I could distantly hear the sound of voices coming

393

from the house. When I turned and looked through the window, I saw everyone gathered in the living room, not even noticing my absence. The only person Cayson noticed was Jasmine. I was just a friend, a sister.

"Skye?"

I recognized my mother's voice. I'd know it anywhere. Even if I couldn't see her, I could feel her. Her warmth was a beacon like the sun, touching everything even if it didn't want to be touched. "Mom?"

She came closer to me, her feet crunching on the snow. When she was close enough, I could see the features of her face in the dim lighting from the house. "Why are you out here alone?"

I tightened my arms across my chest, fighting the cold. "Just to get some fresh air."

"In the snow?" she asked incredulously.

"It was a little warm in there."

"I see…"

I turned my body, looking at the ocean even though I could hear it.

"Skye?"

"Hmm?"

"Tell him how you feel."

I stilled at her words. *She knew. How?* "What?"

"Cayson. Tell him how you feel. It would be a lot more productive than standing outside in the cold."

I didn't see the point in denying it. She clearly knew. "How did you know?"

"I see the way you look at him. You've been doing it for a while now. But the look you gave him tonight really showed it. If you don't want him to be with anyone, why don't you just tell him that?"

"In case you haven't noticed, he already has a girlfriend," I said bitterly.

"They aren't serious."

"He brings her to Thanksgiving just because?" I asked incredulously.

"Cortland told me Cayson brought her along because her parents abandoned her and she has no living family. And he also said Jasmine isn't the woman he's going to marry."

Now I felt like a bitch for thinking so many horrible things. "He said that?"

"Yeah," she whispered. "I'm not sure how much she means to him, but he's not in love with her. If you're going to say something, do it now. Before his feelings change."

I sighed. "I'm not going to intervene. They're in a relationship and I would hate myself if I broke that up just to be selfish."

"It's okay to be selfish once in a while— and for a very good reason. Skye, are you in love with him? Or do I even need to ask?"

"I...I've never felt this way before. Every time I see him with her, I want to die..."

"Then that answered my question. You should tell him."

"When I went to his apartment to tell him the truth...she answered the door wearing his clothes. I got too upset so I just left."

"Try again."

"Mom, I don't think he feels the same way anyway. All I'll do is ruin our friendship and make him awkward."

"Isn't your friendship ruined anyway—in a twisted way?" Her voice was gentle. Somehow, her presence kept me warm enough to survive the cold.

"I can't do it. Jasmine seems really nice and sweet...and it's obvious she's in love with him."

"But he isn't in love with her. What if he does feel the same way about you but you aren't saying anything?"

"If he was in love with me, he would have told me by now."

"Or maybe he didn't because of the same reasons you're giving. Skye, I know you're scared. I get that. But if this is the man you want, you have to do something. Let me tell you, relationships aren't easy. What your father and I have is a product of twenty years of marriage and ten years of friendship before that. We didn't get here overnight. There was trial and error—over and over."

"But that's different. You guys are meant for each other."

"And what makes you think you and Cayson aren't? You've always had a very special relationship. We all know it."

I stepped away. "Mom, I'm done talking about this. I appreciate you trying to help but there's nothing you can do."

"Skye—"

"Mom, I said no."

She fell silent, moving close beside me. "Just think about what I said." She turned around and headed back to the house, leaving me standing in the cold alone.

Chapter Seventeen

Cayson

"Thank you for bringing me to Thanksgiving," Jasmine said as she sat on the couch. "It was nice not to be alone this year."

"You're welcome. I told you my family would love you." I sat beside her in my apartment. The magical weekend was over and now we were back to reality. I enjoyed school, but whenever I was home, I never wanted to come back. "You're welcome to come for Christmas."

"I can only imagine how over-the-top that holiday is." She smirked at me.

"It is pretty ridiculous. The adults buy all of the kids gifts and they usually can't fit in the car."

"You're so lucky." A twinkle was in her eyes.

"I know." I always knew that. In a complicated way, I had ten different parents. Jasmine didn't even have one.

She held my hand while we snuggled on the couch. "Everything okay with Skye?"

I shrugged. "She was acting very peculiar, wasn't she?"

"It just seems like she hates me."

"She doesn't," I said quickly. "I'm not sure what her problem was but it wasn't that."

Jasmine sat in thought for a long time. "The other day, she…"

I turned to her, listening.

She suddenly ended the sentence. "Nevermind."

I let the subject drop.

"I'm glad your sister came around."

I rolled my eyes. "Clementine is a diva. I hate her but I love her at the same time."

"I think it's cute. She's just protective of her older brother."

"And I think it's annoying."

"Why did she dislike me so much in the beginning?" she asked.

I didn't have the heart to tell her. I already made her cry once and I didn't want to do it again. "You're prettier than she is."

"I am not. She looks just like your mom."

"My mom is pretty but Clementine is hideous. I've seen her first thing in the morning and at night when she puts this weird paste on her face."

Jasmine laughed. "I'm sure you're exaggerating."

"Nope. It was like Halloween every night."

She shook her head slightly. "I know I spent all weekend with you, but do you mind if I sleep with you?"

"No. You're always welcome to stay with me."

"Good. Because my heater is crappy and you do a much better job keeping me warm."

"Oh, now I see how it is." I smiled.

"And because I think you're hot—no pun intended."

I scooped her up in my arms and carried her to my bedroom. "I better get started on that."

She giggled while I carried her. "I'm looking forward to it."

Once we were in bed, we stripped our clothes off then combined our bodies. We hadn't had sex over the weekend because it was too awkward being down the hall from my parents' room. But now I was eager to be inside her.

She lay under me while I rocked into her slowly. She was always excited for me, gripping me and biting her lip while she stared at me. Even though I didn't love her, she was definitely a good lay. I leaned over her and tapped my headboard against the wall repeatedly. I felt bad for my neighbors.

"I love you..." It was so quiet, it was barely a whisper.

I wasn't sure if I heard it at all. Was that just my imagination? When I looked down at her, her face wasn't any different. Maybe I conjured the entire thing in my mind. I kept going, pulling her close to me while I made her feel as good as she made me feel.

***

The following week was pure torture. After having a holiday break, I was eager for the semester to end entirely. But that wasn't until Christmas break. I missed sleeping in every morning. Now I was back in class, learning about chemicals and making sure my lab book didn't get stained with liquid bromine.

I didn't see Skye on campus. She was usually in the library with Trinity or with one of the others. But we never crossed paths. As much as I wanted her out of my head, she would never leave. I remembered her odd behavior and couldn't help but wonder what her problem was. The last time we were together, the closeness between us was paramount. She didn't want me to leave her side and she slept with me three nights in a row. Now she was indifferent to me. Her unpredictable nature and ability to just disregard me hurt and angered me at the same time. What could I have possibly done to piss her off?

On Friday night, Roland had everyone over for poker night. Skye and Silke usually played with us while Trinity took care of the food. But when I showed up with a case of beer under my arm, Skye wasn't there.

The guys were gathered around the table, the cards and shots on the surface.

"So, did you give her the slippery dolphin?" Slade asked. He winked at me.

I rolled my eyes. "If I did, I wouldn't tell you."

"So, that's a yes," Roland said with a nod. "Good job, man."

I didn't bother arguing with them. "Where's your sister?"

He shrugged. "Off in her own world."

"Why didn't she want to come tonight?" I asked.

"She said she had plans," Roland said.

"With who?" I asked.

He glared at me. "Are you a detective or something? What's with the third degree?"

I rolled my eyes then sat down, getting the game started.

"Everyone liked Jasmine," Theo said. "I know my parents did."

"She's a sweet girl," I said. "What's not to like?"

"She doesn't have any family?" Roland asked.

I shook my head. "Her parents took off and she doesn't have any living relatives."

"Geez...that's brutal." Slade dealt the cards.

Trinity put chips and salsa on the table. "Does that mean Skye is history?"

Everyone stared at me, wondering what my response was.

I shrugged. "I don't want to be in pain anymore. I just want to move on and forget about her."

Silke sighed. "You've been saying that for years."

"I know..." That knowledge just made me more depressed.

"Maybe you shouldn't sleep with her three nights in a row," Roland said sarcastically.

"I couldn't say no, alright?" I felt my shoulders tense. "She asked me to."

"Forget about her," Slade said. "She just likes the attention since Zack isn't around anymore. I don't know what you see in her. She's just a self-absorbed—"

I gave him a threatening look.

"Dragon," Slade finished.

Everyone looked at Slade, confusion on their faces.

He threw his cards down. "It's a long story. We don't have enough time tonight."

Everyone threw their cards down and took new ones. A somber tint filled the atmosphere, or maybe that was just me. I wasn't sure. I tried not to think about Skye for the rest of the game. But of course, that never worked.

***

Another week went by and she and I didn't speak. We didn't cross paths. Every time an event was going on, she wasn't there. She always mysteriously had other plans. But I didn't know who with since the group pretty much stuck together.

I started to wonder why she was absent. Was something bothering her? Was something wrong? Did I do something? She told me everything and now I was trash to her. What was her problem? I did everything for her and this is the thanks I got?

I headed to the library but didn't see Skye in our usual spot. She was never there. But I knew she had a break between classes so she had to be studying somewhere. The library was massive so I walked past the bookshelves, checking the other tables. By chance, I finally spotted her sitting alone, reading a textbook. If she was isolated like this, she was obviously avoiding all of us.

I threw my bag down then sat across from her.

She flinched at my unexpected appearance. Her eyes widened slightly before they dilated again. Within a second, she retained her composure.

"Why are you avoiding me?" I blurted.

"I'm not..." She tucked a strand of hair behind her ear then looked down.

"You just prefer sitting alone in a corner with cobwebs?"

"I study better without any distractions."

"Is that what you've been doing for the past two weeks?" I barked. "Studying?"

"Yes..." Her voice betrayed her nervousness.

"Skye, what's your problem? I take you to the hospital and look after you. Then I sleep with you for three nights, and now you're acting like we aren't even friends."

"I've just been busy."

"You didn't speak to me once at Thanksgiving. And every time we get together, you're never there. Did I do something to piss you off?"

"No, of course not."

"Then what's your problem? We used to be best friends and now you act like you can't stand me."

"It's not you..."

"And what's that supposed to mean?" I hated being harsh with her, but her childish behavior was really getting on my nerves. I isolated myself from her before, but I had a good reason. And I wasn't rude to her. I still spoke to her and acknowledged her.

"I'm just busy...okay?"

"You've always been a terrible liar." I stared her down, feeling my annoyance bubble.

She sighed then closed her textbook. "I have to go."

"That's convenient."

She didn't look at me as she packed her stuff. An indifferent look was on her face, like I meant nothing to her. She shouldered her bag then turned around.

"You used to tell me everything. Now I don't even know you..."

She stilled but didn't turn around. Then she walked away.

Chapter Eighteen

Skye

It was too hard to be around Cayson. Every time I looked at him, I thought about Jasmine. He was in a relationship and he was happy. There was no possibility I would ever be with him. I needed to move on but I was quickly realizing how hard that was.

I hated hurting him. The pissed look on his face went straight to my heart. I wanted to confess and just tell him the truth, hoping it would bring us closer together. But I knew the knowledge would just push him further away. So I kept it to myself, bottling it deep inside.

Any time the gang got together, I never joined them. I stayed in my apartment and entertained myself. I didn't want to see Cayson and pretend everything was normal. And I couldn't stand to see him with Jasmine. I hated watching him kiss her, touch her. The tenderness they shared made me want to gag. She was a very nice girl, someone I could probably be friends with, but I just couldn't stop hating her. She didn't deserve my hostility but I couldn't help it.

Roland invited me over for movie night. *We're watching the old Godzilla movie and we're going to make fun of it. Come over.*

I have homework. Maybe next time.

How much homework could you possibly have? That's all you ever do.

I didn't respond. Hopefully, he would just leave me alone. When he didn't send a message back, I knew I was in the clear. I curled up on the couch and watched TV, trying to find something to distract my mind. If I went to my brother's, Cayson would be there. And he would probably bring his girlfriend along too.

Thirty minutes later, my lock turned and the front door opened.

"Doing homework my ass." Roland came to the couch, glaring at me.

"I was just taking a break. And don't just barge into my apartment."

"Dad gave me a key for a reason."

"Not to come over whenever the hell you want," I snapped.

"That's at my discretion." He eyed my pajamas and unkempt hair. "Skye, what's going on?"

"I'm just tired, okay?"

He sat on the couch beside me. "I'm starting to get worried..."

"Just because I don't want to hang out with you doesn't mean there's something wrong."

"For three weeks straight?" he asked incredulously. "Come on. Something is up."

"No, there isn't."

"Do you want me to call Dad?" he threatened. "Because I will."

I glared at him. "That's not funny."

"Then tell me what's up? You've been weird since Thanksgiving."

"Roland, just leave me alone." I was starting to grow frustrated. "I don't want to hang out. I don't want to do anything. Just go." I sighed then leaned against the couch.

"Skye...what's wrong?"

I ran my fingers through my hair in frustration. "Roland, I asked you to leave."

"How can I go when you're like this? I'm worried about you."

"Well, don't be."

"I know we aren't extremely close but...I really wish you would tell me. I care about you. I love you..."

Now I felt like a bitch. My brother was being sweet to me for the first time and I was pushing him away. "I love you too, Roland. But I just want to be alone right now. It's nothing personal."

"Are you depressed over Zack?"

I tried not to laugh. "No."

"Is it something else?"

"Roland, just go." My voice sliced through the air. "Tell everyone I said hi and enjoy your movie."

He sighed, finally giving up. "Okay. I hope you change your mind."

I watched him, waiting for him to leave.

He finally left my couch and headed to the door. "I guess I'll see you around..."

"Yeah."

He walked out and locked the door behind him.

I stayed on the couch, basking in my own misery.

***

The next few days were spent in solitude. I avoided everyone as much as possible. I didn't even go to work just because I didn't feel like talking to anyone. Maybe if I stayed this way long enough, my feelings for Cayson would go away. If I never saw him, it was bound to happen.

Right?

I picked a quiet spot in the library then put my things down. Just when I opened my textbook, I had visitors.

"Alright." Roland came from behind the bookshelf, followed by everyone else except Cayson. "It's time for an intervention."

Slade smirked at me. "You're going to tell us what the hell is up your ass."

"You better be dying or something," Trinity said.

They boxed me in so I couldn't get out. Damn it.

Slade sat across from me. "So...what's your problem?"

"I don't have a problem," I said quietly.

"Bullshit," Roland said. "You've lost like ten pounds in the past month. And we all know you didn't do it on purpose."

"Why won't you just talk to us?" Trinity said. "We're family."

I hated myself for hurting them. "It's not you guys..."

"Then what is it?" Roland said. "We're really worried about you, Skye. If this intervention doesn't work, I'm calling Dad."

That was a frightening threat.

"Come on," Slade said. "Talk to us. You think we're going to judge you or something? You got a bun in the oven?"

I glared at him. "No."

"Then tell us," Trinity said. "You're seriously scaring us."

I ran my fingers through my hair, knowing I was backed into a wall. They knew something was up and I couldn't keep hiding it. And it would be nice to talk to someone about it, especially the closest people to me. There were no secrets between us, and it felt odd to hoard one now. "Okay...you have to promise me you won't say a word."

411

"Done," Slade blurted.

"I mean it. You can't say anything to Cayson."

Trinity's eyes widened. "Why?"

"I don't want him to know," I said simply. "So you can't tell him."

Roland was practically at the edge of his seat. "What is it?"

I couldn't believe I was going to admit this out loud.

"You're killing us, Skye." Trinity hit her fist on the table. "Just tell us."

I felt like a horrible person for saying it out loud. "I...lately I've been...it's just—"

"You got into to Harvard," Slade snapped. "You can make better sentences than that."

"I'm in love with Cayson," I blurted. *God, it felt good to get that off my chest.*

Trinity covered her face and gasped.

Roland broke out in a smile.

Slade jumped on the table and started dancing. "Yes! Finally! Yes!"

Everyone in the library looked over at us, watching Slade.

Trinity pulled on his jeans. "Get down! You're going to get us in trouble."

Slade jumped back down. "Hallelujah. I thought this day would never come."

"And I almost gave up," Roland said.

What the hell were they talking about? "Sorry?"

"You seriously don't know that Cayson has been in love with you since...forever?" Trinity said. "He's been hooked on you for years."

"Pretty much since he saw you in a swimsuit after your tits came in," Slade said.

"You think he just waits on you hand and foot because he's bored?" Roland asked. "I'm your brother and I don't even look after you like that."

I couldn't process this. "What?"

Trinity shook her head. "Lady, I've told you this at least a hundred times. This shouldn't be surprising."

Slade laughed. "She really had no idea. That's hilarious."

"Cayson was in love with me?" I asked.

"No. He *is* in love with you," Slade said. "Now go find him and tell him what's up."

I couldn't do that. "He has a girlfriend."

"No," Slade said. "She's a glorified fuck buddy. She doesn't mean shit to him."

"He took her to Thanksgiving," I argued.

"Because she had nowhere else to go," Roland snapped.

"It's the truth," Slade said. "Go talk to him."

"Maybe she was just someone to spend time with but it's clear their relationship is different now." My hand shook slightly, unable to

413

believe that Cayson felt the same way I did...at one point in time. "It's pretty obvious they care a lot about each other. I can't intervene."

"Maybe they do but that doesn't matter," Trinity said. "He's been in love with you forever. He'd dump her in a heartbeat."

"And that would be wrong," I said. "She's totally hung up on him."

"Too bad, so sad," Slade barked. "Cayson made it clear he was just dating her to get over you. It's not like it'll catch her by surprise."

I know what I saw. Cayson treated her with tenderness and respect. It was more than just a fling, more than just a friends-with-benefits relationship. "I don't think he feels the same way anymore..." I remembered our last conversation and how angry he was.

"Yes, he does," Slade said. "I promise you. Just talk to him."

"No." I packed up my things. "I love Cayson but I'm not going to break up his relationship with Jasmine. I'm not selfish. I'll have to wait until it ends and hope for the best or...just move on."

Roland groaned. "You're killing me here."

"Don't say a word to him," I said firmly. "You guys promised."

Slade looked like he might hit me in the face. "You're so close. You're just going to give up now?"

I turned away. "I'm not giving up. Maybe one day our timing will be better. Jasmine is a nice girl and I feel horrible declaring my love for him when he already belongs to her. I feel like an adulteress."

"We get that," Roland said. "And if this were any other relationship, we would agree. But we all know for a fact Jasmine doesn't mean anything to him."

"I might believe you if he didn't take her to Thanksgiving…" I couldn't erase the sight of them together from my mind.

Trinity growled. "I'm about to smack some sense into your thick skull, Skye. This is stupid. He loves you and you love him. There's absolutely no reason for you two not to be together."

"I wish things were different…but they aren't." I gave them a sad look before I walked off. "And I accept that."

***

When I got home, I climbed under my covers and lay in bed. I thought about what my family had told me. Cayson used to be in love with me. When I thought about our past, how well we clicked and how he did everything for me, I couldn't fathom how I never noticed it. His eyes always lit up when I walked into a room. He listened to every word I said and remembered it.

He knew how to make me laugh, make me feel alive.

How did I not notice? If I had, he would be mine right now. I felt so stupid. I wasted all that time when I could have been with him. Now he was with Jasmine, a pretty girl with a perfect body. I could never compete with that.

Overcome with grief, I pulled the blankets over my head and tried to disappear.

Chapter Nineteen

Cayson

I sat on the couch and typed up my lab report. My notebook was covered in acid and god knew what else. Turning in a fresh piece of paper was necessary. When my door burst open, I was distracted.

"Dude, we need to talk." Slade slammed the door and walked inside.

"Yes, just come right in," I said sarcastically. I put my computer down then stood up.

"If you care that much, just lock your door."

"Or just knock."

He walked into my bedroom and took a look around.

"What the hell are you doing?"

He came back. "Is Jasmine here?"

"No."

"Is she coming over?"

"No. What's this about?"

He was squirmy, barely able to stand in one spot. "I need to tell you something but I can't actually tell you."

"Goodie..."

"So you need to guess."

"Why can't you just tell me?"

"Because I promised not to. Now focus, man. This is important."

"But not important enough for you to actually tell me?"

"Don't be a smartass. Now is not the time."

I crossed my arms over my chest and sighed. This should be good.

"Okay..." He rubbed his hands together. "Let me think."

"That's a first," I said sarcastically.

"Okay." He clapped his hands. "I got it."

I stared him down.

"Okay, so...you and Jasmine are doing it, right?"

"Yes..."

"Who else would you like to do it with?" His eyes were wide and about to fall out of his head.

"Like a threesome?"

He growled. "No. Who else do you have a thing for?"

"Um...Skye."

"Yes! Good!"

I was so confused.

He rubbed his chin. "Okay...so you know how Jasmine is head-over-heels for you?"

I couldn't follow his thought process. "I guess..."

"Okay, maybe that other person we mentioned feels the same way." He wiggled his eyebrows at me.

"What?"

He made a circle with his fingers then shoved his other fingers through it, making a very crude gesture. "What if the other person wanted to do this with you?"

I gripped my skull. "What the fuck are you talking about?"

"You know how Uncle Sean and Aunt Scarlet are like soul mates and shit?"

Seriously, I'm going to hit him.

"What if that's you and Skye?"

"But it's not..."

"But what if it is." He was hopping on his feet.

I had enough of this. "Slade, just get out."

"No! You're so close."

"I'm seriously going to strangle you."

"Skye is in love with you!"

I flinched. "What?"

He sighed. "I promised her I wouldn't tell you but fuck it. You need to know."

"Wait...what?"

"She just told us few hours ago."

"She actually said those words?" My heart was racing. Suddenly, my palms were sweaty.

"Yes! That's what I've been trying to tell you."

"No...you've been making crude gestures and talking about threesomes."

"Whatever. Now you know. Go to Skye and talk to her."

"You're sure you heard her right?" I found it hard to believe.

"Yes, Trinity and Roland heard it too. That's why she's been acting weird lately. It's because she can't stand to see you with Jasmine."

That would explain a lot...but was it too good to be true? "Slade, are you sure you didn't just misinterpret what she said?"

"No! I know I'm not the smartest guy in the world but give me some credit."

I couldn't process this. It was my greatest dream. Could it actually be true? "I...I just find it hard to believe."

"I heard it with my own eyes."

"You mean ears?"

"Whatever! Go to her, dude."

I gripped my skull then paced the room. Could this really be happening? She was the woman of my dreams, the person I wanted since I could remember. She finally felt the same way? What had changed? "How long?"

"I don't know. But she felt this way before Thanksgiving."

"Slade, you have to be absolutely sure. Because if I go over there and talk to her, I'm going to make an idiot out of myself if you're wrong."

"Dude, I'm not." He looked me straight in the eye.

I paced the room again, feeling the panic.

"Dude, what are you waiting around for?"

I grabbed my phone and my keys.

Slade smiled. "Go get her and fuck her brains out!"

That was the furthest thing from my mind. "I have to take care of something first."

"What? Do you really need to go to the store right now?" He fished his hand in his pocket. "You need condoms? I got plenty." He tossed them at me.

"No. I'm going to break up with Jasmine."

"Right this second? Can't it wait? You've been in love with this girl for like five years and now you can actually have her."

"But I can't do anything if I have a girlfriend. I may not love Jasmine but I respect her. I'm not talking to Skye until I break it off."

Slade rolled his eyes. "Well, hurry up and get it over with."

I walked out the door then looked at him. "Are you coming?"

"You want me to be there when you break up with Jasmine?"

"No. I want you to get out of my damn apartment."

"Oh." He walked into my kitchen then grabbed a beer. "Alright. I'm out."

I shut the door then locked it.

"Good luck, man."

"Yeah, thanks." Without waiting for him, I ran to my car and took off.

***

"What a nice surprise." Jasmine opened the door, the sparkle in her eyes.

"Hey." I was dreading this. I hated breaking up with people. It sucked. If I weren't such a coward, I would just text her.

She caught the sadness in my eyes. "Everything okay?"

"Can I come in?"

"Yeah, sure." She stepped aside and let me walk in.

I looked at her, steeling my nerve. I didn't want to hurt her but I had to.

"What is it, Cayson?"

I took a deep breath before I started. "Jasmine, I'm not going to sugarcoat this. I promised I would always be honest with you and I'm upholding that vow."

"Okay..."

"Our time together has come to an end."

Her breathing increased slightly and moisture built up in her eyes. "Why?"

"I just found out that Skye has feelings for me. And you know how I feel about her... If there's any chance I can make it work, I have to take it. I know being with her ends my time with you, but...that's what my heart wants."

She nodded slowly then blinked her tears away. "Well, I'm happy for you."

I didn't believe her but I didn't say it. "I'm sorry, Jasmine. I think you're a beautiful girl with a lot to offer. We had a lot of great times together. But my heart is meant for someone else."

"I know." She blinked her eyes again, holding back the flood of tears.

"I'm sorry."

"So, she told you this? You already spoke to her?"

"No. Slade told me. I haven't seen her yet. I wanted to talk to you first."

"Oh..."

I pulled a strand of hair from her face then tucked it behind her ear. "I wish things were different."

"Me too."

I pulled her close to me and looked her in the eye. "You'll find someone much better than me."

"I doubt that." Her voice came out as a whisper.

I didn't have a response to that. "I guess I should go..."

"Cayson?"

"Yeah?"

"Can I have one more thing?"

"Anything."

"Could you...hold me for a moment before you go?"

Her request went straight to my heart. "Of course." I pulled her into my arms and held her close to me. She rested her head against my chest, her hair covering her face. She was breathing hard, trying not to cry. Her arms circled my waist, holding me close. I let her have her moment, knowing this was hard for her. I never meant for her to get so attached to me. She understood the parameters of this relationship but that didn't mean she didn't get too close to the fire.

When she pulled away, she wiped the tears from her face, unable to hold them back. "If it doesn't work out...and you find yourself alone in the world...please call me."

Even after what I was doing to her, she still wanted me. I couldn't believe it.

"Because the way you feel about Skye...is the way I feel about you." She gave me one final look before she walked into her bedroom and shut the door.

I stood there, feeling hollow and empty. I was an asshole for doing this to her, for making her fall in love with me when I knew I could never return that emotion. I hated myself for it.

I left her apartment then walked down the stairs. When I reached the end, I stopped. The girl of my dreams was sitting at her apartment, not knowing I was about to head over there and confess my every thought and feeling. But that felt wrong.

I was with Jasmine for months. I may not have loved her, but she was important to me. It felt wrong to rush to the girl I really wanted, abandoning the first one. It was like she didn't matter even though that wasn't true.

I sat on the last stair and thought about my time with Jasmine. I grieved for the end of our relationship, cherishing the laughs and good times. There was nothing wrong with her. She had a body that caught the attention of every guy. She had a smile that would make most men weak at the knees. She was a joy to be around, making me smile even when I thought it wasn't possible.

Snow started to fall outside, drifting quietly to the ground. My breath came out as vapor, and I felt the coldness every time I inhaled. But I stayed there, sitting in the darkness and listening to the silence of the world. I didn't want to forget about Jasmine and the relationship we had. I knew in my heart I could have fallen in love with her if I wasn't already in love with someone else.

When an hour passed, I rose and headed to my car. I was ready to seize the moment, to take what I'd wanted all my life. I was ready to be with the girl I'd wanted for years. No longer would I just be her friend, her family. I would be something more.

Something I was meant to be.

***

After I knocked on the door, she didn't answer. I knocked on it again but there was no response. Snow had settled on my shoulders and it was melting into the fabric. Her car was in the lot, buried under a foot of snow. I knew she hadn't come or gone for several hours.

I took out my key and walked inside. She was probably avoiding me, but I wasn't going to let her.

When I walked in, she was sitting on the couch. She looked at me with pain in her eyes. She stood up and let the blanket fall to the ground. She wore a t-shirt and sweatpants. Her face was free of make up, but I preferred the look. She was beautiful no matter what she wore or how she painted her face.

I went further into her apartment, my hands by my side. I didn't say anything, waiting for her to acknowledge me, to speak.

She walked around the couch, her arms crossed over her chest. She was cut off from me, keeping her distance. "Can I help you with something?" Her voice was lifeless, like she didn't care I was there.

"I just wanted to talk."

She leaned against the back of the couch, hardly looking at me. "About what?"

I stared her down, examining her face and the darkness in her eyes. I waited for her to look at me, to see the emotion in my face. I waited until she finally turned. When she met my gaze, she looked away again.

"Look at me."

She flinched at my words then turned back to me, her eyes guarded.

"You know why I'm here."

Her eyes widened slightly then her pupils dilated. Now she was tenser, more guarded. "I really don't."

I took another step toward her, my shoulders square and my hands clenched. My heart was beating dangerously fast, and my palms were sweating. I hid the unease in my heart. I wanted her so much that I wanted to grab her and never let go. I was holding back, not letting my heart take over. There was still a possibility that Slade was wrong. "I broke up with Jasmine."

Her chest suddenly rose at my words, expanding. A small explosion happened in her eyes. It disappeared as quickly as it happened. "Why?"

I came closer to her, invading her personal space. When I reached her, I noticed her breathing increased. Her arms tightened across her chest. She looked away, like she was nervous or scared. I never had this affect on her before. "You know why, Skye."

She took another deep breath then squirmed under my gaze. "I do?"

I stepped in front of her, my face closer to hers. Then my hands moved to the couch on either side of her, boxing her in. "Yeah."

Unable to move, she stared up at me. She lowered her hands to her sides but she was still distant with me.

"Do you love me, Skye?" I stared into her eyes while I said it, caring more about her reaction than her actual response.

"Do you love me?"

"I've loved you my whole life."

She took a deep breath then her eyes developed a coat of moisture. Her eyelids fluttered, trying to hide her emotion.

"It's always been you. I never thought you would feel the same way. I assumed I was just your brother, your friend. Every time I looked at you, you looked back at me with a friendly expression. I dreamed one day that would change. Because I honestly believe you and I are destined for something more, that we are amazing friends but we would be much greater lovers."

She breathed hard while she stared at me. "Did you love her?"

"Never. I told Jasmine how I felt about you from the beginning. She understood the relationship was only temporary. I was desperately trying to get over you. Every time I saw you with Zack, I wanted to die. I hated it. Not only did I think he was a jerk, but I hated knowing you preferred him over me. With me, you'll never know pain. With me, you'll only know joy."

She blinked several times but the tears couldn't be denied. "I'm sorry it took me so long to realize how I feel. I guess I've always felt this way...I just never realized it until now."

"That was what I always hoped for."

"So...would you be willing to try...with me?"

I smirked slightly. "I'll do more than try. This is the end of the road for me. I don't need to date you to know you're the only woman for me. I don't need to spend a lifetime with you to know I'm going to grow old with you." Courage filled my veins and I rested my hand on her cheek. "You're mine forever, Skye. I'm not letting you go."

"I don't want you to."

"I can't believe this is happening. I have to remind myself it isn't a dream."

"Me too…"

I wanted to kiss her, to feel my lips against hers and know she was mine. "There's something I need to tell you."

"What?"

"When you were at that frat party months ago, I carried you home. After I tucked you into your bed, you told me I was a better man than Zack was, that I made you happy in a way he never did. And then you kissed me."

Her eyes widened. "I did?"

"You kissed me for a long time. Then you took off your clothes and pulled me to you. Do you remember any of it?"

Her eyes became lost as she tried to recall the memory. "I guess vaguely…did we sleep together?"

"No. But that was our first kiss."

"Is that why you were so distant with me afterwards?"

I nodded. "I thought that was the beginning of our relationship. When you didn't remember it, I felt hurt."

Her eyes softened. "I'm so sorry, Cayson. I never meant to hurt you."

"I know you didn't. But I guess I should have known that you loved me—even then."

"I think I did."

"You don't remember our first kiss, but I'll make sure you remember this one." I cupped her face and closed the distance between us. When my mouth touched hers, I felt alive. My entire body burned in flames. My lips ached from the overwhelming touch. She sighed and moaned into my mouth, feeling the same chemistry I did. She was drunk last time so it could have been a fluke. But this time was even better.

She gripped my shoulders while she deepened the kiss, wanting more of me than I could give. She sucked my bottom lip then let it go free. Then she crushed her mouth against mine again, barely letting me breathe.

My hands gripped her waist and I clung to her, holding her tightly. She was so small in my hands. I felt like a giant in comparison. I couldn't believe I was actually kissing her...and she was kissing me back.

"I love you." She said it while she breathed into my mouth, clutching me.

"And I love you, Skye." I pushed her against the couch and pressed my chest against hers. Warm tears moved down her face and to our lips. I could taste the salt, feel her emotion. I couldn't believe she loved me in the way I loved her, with the same intensity and longing.

I grabbed her then lifted her from the ground, carrying her to her bedroom down the hall. She kept kissing me, not breaking her stride. When I lay her on the bed, I moved over her.

She looked up at me with emotion in her eyes. Her hands moved up my chest and to my shoulders. She dug her fingers into the muscle, feeling me for the first time. The look in her eyes was different. She didn't look at me like I was her friend. Her longing was evident, and so was the love. My hands trembled just from looking at her.

I couldn't believe this was real.

"Stay with me this weekend," she whispered, running her fingers through my hair.

"I was going to whether you invited me or not."

"Good." She pressed her lips back to mine and kissed me. "Because I'm never letting you go."

I spent the evening fulfilling my greatest fantasy. I kissed her on her bed, touching her and feeling her touch me. Our hearts beat as one, and for the first time, I felt whole, complete. She was what I'd been missing. She was what I needed. She was my soul mate, my other half. And now I was hers.

***

"Don't leave." She pulled me back from the door. "Stay with me." She wrapped her arms around my neck and kissed me.

It was hard not to melt into a puddle on the ground. "Skye, I have to go."

"No..." She grabbed my bottom lip and sucked.

"I'll be back in a few hours."

"Where are you going?"

"I'll tell you when I get back."

She growled then kissed me again. "Then please hurry."

"Believe me, I will."

She wrapped her arms around my waist and held me close. "I guess I could take a nap. We haven't been sleeping much."

I smirked. "Good idea, baby."

"Will you sleep here tonight?"

"I'll be here every night—as long as I'm welcome."

"You have a key, don't you?"

"I do." I cupped her face and kissed the corner of her mouth, tasting her freckle. "Get some sleep."

"Okay. Hurry home."

"I will." I kissed her forehead. "I'll be back before you know it." With one more look at her, I walked out then got into my car. Then I hit the road, driving in the snow.

Two hours later, I pulled up to the house. The sky was overcast so it was dark. The lights from the windows were bright. I knew they were home because I could see light from the TV through the window.

I sighed then walked to the door and knocked.

A second later, Uncle Sean opened it. "Cayson? What are you doing here?"

"I wanted to speak to you."

Concern came into his eyes. "Is everything okay?"

"Yes. Everything is fine."

Aunt Scarlet came to the door. "Hello, Cayson. Would you like to come in?"

"Sure." I stepped inside and they both stared at me.

"What's this about?" Uncle Sean asked.

I looked at Aunt Scarlet. "Can I have a moment alone with my uncle, please?"

"Sure. I'll be upstairs." She patted her husband's shoulder before she disappeared.

Uncle Sean stared me down, waiting for me to speak. He was always warm around me, but now he was on his guard. I didn't blame him. I knew he didn't like surprises. Everything needed to be under his control. I sincerely hoped this would go over well because his approval was important to me.

"I've been in love with your daughter for longer than I can remember. Her smile is something I live for and her warmth keeps the cold away. She's my best friend in the world. I respect her and love her fiercely. I came here today to ask for your permission to date her. I promise to take care of her and treat her with nothing but respect. I won't let you down. Your blessing would mean a great deal to me."

His eyes softened while he stared at me. He pressed his lips together tightly before he loosened them. "Cayson, you're like a son to me. There's no one I'd rather have for my daughter. And you honor me by asking for my permission. That means a lot to me."

I released the air I was holding in my lungs.

"But I have to ask one thing."

"Okay."

"Are you still with that girl?"

"No. I broke up with her before I told Skye how I felt. She's the only one for me, sir."

His eyes softened again. "It's Uncle Sean. Don't ever call me anything else."

"My apologies."

He gripped my shoulder then pulled me in for a hug. "You're too young to understand this, but when you become a father someday, you will. Making sure your daughter is with the right man is something that will consume you and terrify you. All I want is the best for my baby girl. The fact that she chooses you makes my life a million times easier." He pulled away and smiled at me. "Please marry her."

I was speechless. I knew my uncle loved me, but I didn't realize how much he respected me. He was practically giving me his daughter without any fear. He trusted me with someone he loved more than anything. "I intend to."

Uncle Sean turned toward the stairs. "Baby, come here."

Aunt Scarlet came down the stairs. "The men are finished?"

Uncle Sean put his arm around her. "Cayson asked for my permission to date Skye."

Aunt Scarlet's face broke out in a smile. "That's absolutely wonderful." She came to me and hugged me. "I always hoped my daughter would find a man good enough for her father."

"I don't know about that," I said with a laugh. "But I'll do my best."

She cupped my cheek. "You are the best, honey."

My cheeks blushed at their wonderful praise. "Thank you. I should probably get going before it gets too dark."

Uncle Sean patted my shoulder. "Good idea. Drive safe."

"I will."

Aunt Scarlet kissed my cheek. "We'll see you soon."

I left the house then got into my car. They stood on the porch and stared at me until I left their driveway. Then I hit the road and tried to get back to Skye as quickly as possible.

***

When I walked in the door, she jumped into my arms. "You're home."

I laughed when I caught her. "You missed me?"

"Like crazy."

I rubbed my nose against hers. "I missed you like crazy too."

"Now will you tell me what you were up to?"

"I will. I went to see your father."

She flinched. "Why?"

"To ask his permission to be with you."

"What did he say?"

"That he couldn't have picked a better guy."

Her eyes softened. "My father loves you, Cayson."

"I know. I just didn't realize how much until now."

She held me close. "I can't believe you drove all the way there just to ask him."

"You aren't just some girl, Skye. You're the one. And I want to do this right."

She pressed her forehead to mine. "You did."

I held her in the doorway, feeling her petite size in my arms. It was hard for me to understand she was real. I'd dreamed of this intimacy, dreamed of her touch, and now I finally had it. She was mine.

And I wasn't going to let her go.

Chapter Twenty

Cayson

The sun rose and distant rays of light flickered through the curtains. The warmth was appreciated. Snow covered the ground and the earth wouldn't thaw until spring. The joy from the holidays still lingered, but I couldn't care less about it. I already had everything I wanted.

Skye was still asleep. Her lips were relaxed, and the freckle in the corner of her mouth caught my attention, like it usually did. She wore one of my t-shirts and my boxers. We were cuddled under the blanket, keeping warm against the winter chill outside.

I stared at her face, unable to look away. I'd been getting less sleep since we got together. Instead of drifting off, I preferred to stay awake and enjoy every second of her. She was mine—finally. It was hard not to appreciate her, to soak her up every minute we were together.

My hand moved around her waist, feeling her petite frame. She was small in comparison, dwarfed by my large size. It took me a moment to understand this was real, that she was really by my side. We stayed up late talking about nothing in particular. And now I was still here—but not as her friend.

I brushed a loose strand of hair from her face, feeling its softness. Everything about her was perfect. Her thin legs touched mine under the blankets. I was only in my boxers, and I liked feeling our skin touch.

It was hard not to press my lips to hers. I wanted her to wake up, to stare into those beautiful eyes I adored. But I held back, letting her enjoy her slumber. Another hour passed before her eyes fluttered open.

She took a deep breath and released it as a sigh. Her eyes took a moment before they focused on my face. Then a grin spread on her lips, making my heart melt. "Morning." Her voice was hoarse and cracked.

"Morning." I took a deep breath, feeling the happiness flood my body.

Her hand moved to my chin, feeling the thick stubble that formed over the week. I'd been staying at her place every night so I forgot to shave. "You're hairy." The smirk was still on her face.

"Do you want me to shave?" My hand moved slightly up her shirt, feeling the skin of her ribs.

"I'm not sure...I like it."

"You like hairy men?" I teased.

"No. But I like you." She moved the back of her hand along my chin, feeling the resistance.

"I'll leave it then."

"Just don't let it grow into a beard. I don't like those." She cringed slightly.

"Maybe I will anyway."

"Fine. Then I won't shave my legs," she threatened.

It was my turn to cringe. "You win."

She smirked. "I always win."

My fingers trailed along her ribs. "Because I let you."

Fondness shined in her eyes. "I guess chivalry isn't dead after all."

"Not for you, no." I cupped her face then leaned in, the excitement coursing through my veins. Every time I leaned in to kiss her, my heart wanted to give out. My lips longed for hers, needing a taste. I pressed my mouth to hers and gave her a gentle embrace. Her lips were slightly dry from the night before but she still tasted delicious. When I pulled away, I looked at her face.

She had a dreamy look in her eyes, like she was light-headed and confused. "You're a really good kisser…"

I grinned. "No. I think you make me that way."

"I really don't think so. Because every other guy I've kissed slobbered like a dog."

I laughed. "That's gross."

"You're telling me..." She snuggled closer to me, her hand moving across my stomach. "I don't want to go to class."

"Neither do I." My hand trailed through her hair and to her neck.

"Let's just stay here—forever."

"You won't get much of an argument from me. But knowing you, you'll get hungry at some point."

Right at that moment, her stomach growled. "Ugh. You know me so well."

"I do." I pressed my lips to her forehead, loving the touch.

She sighed then sat up. "I guess I should get ready then. Why does the weekend have to go by so fast?"

"I wish I knew."

She leaned over and gave me another quick kiss on the lips.

I melted, like always.

"I'll see you at school." She crawled off me then stood up.

I grabbed her arm then yanked her back to me. "One more."

"Cayson, no. You know what will happen."

I gave her a mischievous grin. "I don't care." I pulled her to the bed then moved on top of her.

"I haven't even brushed my teeth."

"Don't care about that either." I pressed my lips to hers then felt her legs wrap around my waist.

Skye turned into mush below me. Her lips sought mine, the passion deep within.

I was going to be late to my first class.

Oh well. I couldn't care less.

***

Slade spotted me down the hallway. He shielded his eyes with his hand, like he was trying to spot something across a desert. "No...it couldn't be."

I rolled my eyes, knowing what was coming.

"Could that be Cayson...my old best friend that I haven't seen in three weeks?"

I closed the gap between us. "You know I've been busy."

He narrowed his eyes while he stared at my face. "What the hell is this?" He slapped his hand against the side of my face. "Are you a lumberjack?"

"I haven't had time to shave."

"You can't be having sex every second of the day. You got to shower sometime."

I felt the hair on my face then lowered my hand. "It's not that. I've just forgotten about a lot of things since we got together."

"I hope a condom isn't one of them."

I never talked about my personal life, and now it was even weirder because Skye was the woman I was dating.

"Because Uncle Sean would kill you if you knocked up his daughter. I mean, like actually kill you." His eyes widened then he acted like he pointed a pistol at his head then pulled the trigger. "Boom."

"Thanks for the demonstration," I said sarcastically.

"I always wondered if theatre was my calling." He gave me the same cocky smirk he constantly wore.

"Skye and I aren't having sex, not that it's any of your business, so we have nothing to worry about."

Slade's jaw almost hit the floor. "Then what the hell have you been doing? Painting each other's nails?"

"We've been spending time together...talking."

He gripped his skull. "You've been talking since we were two. What more could you possibly have to say?"

"I don't know...it's different now that we're together."

"Seriously, you guys are the lamest couple I've ever heard of."

"I'm not in a hurry. I've got the rest of my life to make love to her."

"Make love?" His face contorted like he might vomit. "What are you? A girl?"

"Well, I'm not fucking her."

"You should be," he snapped. "Have you at least fooled around?"

"I'm not having this conversation with you." I turned on my heel and walked down the hall.

"Come on, spill it." Slade walked beside me. "I'm your best friend."

"Skye is different. I don't want you gossiping about her to other people."

He sighed and rolled his eyes at the same time. "You know I would never do that, man."

"You've done it with every other girl I've told you about."

"Because they were fuck buddies. I know Skye is different. Shit, everyone knows she's different."

"And she's your cousin...why would you want to know anyway?"

"Not in detail," he hissed. "Just in general. Come on, I tell you everything."

I sighed, knowing I was going to regret this. "We haven't done anything."

Slade froze on the spot. "I...I hope I didn't hear you right."

"We've kissed—a lot. But we—"

"Please tell me this is a damn joke."

"We're taking it slow."

"Like the 1800s?" he snapped. "Why don't you sit for an oil painting too?"

"I just don't want to mess it up. She's not just some other girl."

"I get that. But she's not your friend anymore. She's your girlfriend. By definition, you should be tit-fucking her."

I glared at him. "Could you be more PG?"

"No. Sorry, man. Grow a pair."

I should have expected this from him.

"All kidding aside, did Skye say she wanted to take it slow?"

"No..."

"Then I'm confused. She probably is too."

"I don't see what the big deal is." I shook my head.

"Because you've been in love with her for five years and now she's finally yours...I just assumed you'd want to fuck her."

I gave him a threatening look.

"I mean, make love. Whatever."

"I think about it...among other things. But I'm not in a hurry."

"Clearly..." He started walking down the hallway again. "Want to play ball tonight?"

"Skye is coming over."

"Aren't you sick of her by now....and all the *talking*?"

I smirked. "I love talking to her."

"You've been blowing me off for three weeks, man. I gave you a grace period because I thought you were getting laid, but that extension is over."

I had been neglecting Slade lately. Now I felt like a horrible friend. "Tomorrow night."

"No. Tonight. I'll be at your place at seven."

"Slade—"

He walked away before I could get another word in.

I sighed then walked to class, knowing I needed to concentrate.

Chapter Twenty-One

Skye

I wore leggings and a loose sweater. Gold earrings my mom gave me hung from my lobes. Light make up gave my face some color. The winter chill made my cheeks paler than the snow on the ground. When I deemed myself to look as nice as possible, I drove to Cayson's house.

Being with him was indescribable. He was a boyfriend that was also a best friend. I could tell him anything and I knew exactly what to say to make him laugh. He stared at me with affection in his eyes, making me feel beautiful without the use of words. It was more than I could ever have hoped for.

But I was scared.

What if it didn't work out? What if we walked our separate ways? What would that do to our friendship? I feared getting in too deep. Because in a short amount of time, he became air and water to me. I couldn't imagine my life without him. It was an existence I feared.

I came to his door and knocked.

He opened it in a flash, like he'd been waiting for my arrival. His eyes were bright with emotion. They were blue and icy, reminding me of a winter storm by the sea. His broad shoulders could carry the weight of the world, and his chest was strong enough to lift a mountain.

My eyes moved to his chin, seeing the lack of stubble. "You shaved."

His arm hooked around my waist and pulled me inside. "Do you like it?"

"I think you look handsome either way."

He rubbed the fresh skin then smirked. "Slade called me a lumberjack today."

"Oooh...I'd like to watch you chop down a tree shirtless any day."

He smirked then cornered me into the door, pressing my body flat against it. Then his face moved close to mine. His eyes suddenly turned dark, serious. I recognized the look because he'd given it to me countless times. "You look beautiful."

"Thank you."

His hand moved up my neck and into my hair. He fisted it before pressing his lips to mine, giving me a hot and aggressive embrace.

I melted at his touch. I couldn't get over how well he kissed. He knew exactly how to brush his lips against me. His tongue danced with mine, always lighting me on fire just enough before he pulled away. Every kiss was purposeful and precise. Sometimes he would pull away altogether, his lips moving past mine in a devilish tease. Then he kissed me, knocking the wind out of me.

His hands moved to my hips under my shirt. That was where he always touched me, never going higher or lower. I knew Cayson respected me and didn't want to rush a physical relationship, but I couldn't deny how anxious I was. If he was already an amazing kisser, what else was he amazing at?

He finally broke the kiss then rubbed his nose against mine. "I could do that all night. But I suspect you're hungry and thirsty."

"For you."

His eyes softened then his hand trailed to my neck. "I can't believe you're mine."

"I can't either…"

"I've waited so long for you…but you were worth all the heartache."

I hated thinking about the way I hurt Cayson all these years. My ignorance and naivety was ludicrous. Everyone told me how he felt but I never listened. It was hard to understand. "I'll make it up to you."

"Please do." He gave me another kiss before he stepped away. "I made chicken and rice pilaf."

"That sounds good."

"The chicken just needs a few more minutes. Can I get you something to drink?"

"I'm okay."

He grabbed my hand then led me into his living room. He had a small apartment with a single bedroom. But it was enough space for one person and a friend. He sat on the couch then pulled me into his lap. We faced one another and he leaned his head back, just staring at me.

Cayson usually touched me at all times. His embraces were innocent, massaging the back of my neck or my legs. But desire burned in his eyes. And I could feel his arousal against my hips, legs, and ass whenever we cuddled. From what I felt, it was impressive.

"Skye?" He pulled down one side of my loose sweater, exposing my shoulder. Then he leaned in and gave me a slow and torturous kiss. He knew how to ignite me without trying.

How was I oblivious to him for so long? Cayson was hot—like really hot. "Cayson?" I bit my lip while I felt his warm mouth against my shoulder.

He pulled away then sat up, his face just below mine. "I see you every day, but when we're apart, I still miss you." He kissed the freckle in the corner of my mouth, making me yearn for him more than I already did. "I miss you like crazy."

"I miss you too…" I felt my nipples harden and the area between my legs burn. I wanted more than just the heated kisses we shared. His perfection and mind-blowing touch, even in the most innocent places, were driving me wild, making me want him more than I already did. Passion and heat burned between us, but neither one of us had acted on it—yet. I knew Cayson was waiting until I was ready. And I already knew he was wondering when that would be. "You must be wondering why we haven't done anything more than kiss..."

He leaned back and stared into my eyes. "I can't deny how much I want you. You're the sexiest woman I've ever seen. Every curve of your body excites me in a way I can't explain. I want you more than any other woman I've had in my life. But, Skye, I'm not in a hurry. And I'm not going anywhere." His hands gripped my waist, his fingers spanning my back. "I'm a very patient man, and I will wait as long as you want me to. There's no pressure. So please don't worry about it."

"That's the thing...I don't want to wait."

Fire leapt to life in his eyes. It cracked and sizzled, turning into slow burning embers. His hands dug into my skin slightly.

"But...I'm scared."

The desire evaporated. "Scared of what, baby?"

I didn't know how to verbalize it, at least in a way that wouldn't offend him. But he must be thinking the same thing...or at least thought it at one point. "There's no turning back if things don't work out or something bad happens in our relationship. Our friendship will be ruined—forever."

He processed my words for a second, his eyes conveying his thoughts. "I never want to be just your friend again, Skye. And I don't plan on it."

"I don't either," I said immediately. I cupped his face, looking into his eyes. "You mean the world to me, Cayson. And you've made me happier than I've ever been. This is where I belong."

"Then there's nothing to be scared of."

"But...what if something happens?"

He grabbed my wrists then brought them together in his hands. "Don't think like that, Skye."

"But what if it does? What will happen to us? I just feel better talking about it...just in case."

He sighed then kissed one of my wrists gently. "No matter what we promise, no matter what we say, it won't change what's already come to pass. We'll never be what we used to be—even if we broke up now."

"But down the road..."

He looked me in the eye. "No matter what happens between us, I'll never stop loving you and I'll never stop caring. If you were another girl, it would be different. But you're special to me. You've always been special. And I never want to lose you from my life. Even if you cheated on me and broke my heart, I still wouldn't turn my back on you. I wouldn't leave the group and I wouldn't avoid you. I'll always be around—forever."

"Me too..."

He kissed the other wrist. "Most ex's can't be friends. But we're different, Skye. We are far more mature than anyone else our age. And I know our love is strong. Nothing will keep us apart."

I nodded.

"Do you feel better now?"

"Yeah...we're family. And we'll always be."

"Exactly." He leaned back and rested his hands on my thighs, rubbing me gently. He stared at my face, never looking away.

I leaned forward, my head pressed to his. Then I closed my eyes, enjoying the silence. Cayson moved his hands to my waist, gripping me. I leaned down and found his lips, feeling their softness.

His hands tightened around me slightly, conveying the pleasure my mouth was giving him. They moved up my sweater, feeling my bare skin.

My hair fell around his face, blocking him in. I deepened our kiss, feeling his lips with my small mouth. His tongue found mine, dancing slowly. He breathed hard into my mouth, showing his excitement.

Finally giving into what I wanted, I broke our kiss then grabbed the end of my sweater.

Slowly, I pulled it off then dropped it on the couch. I wore my black lacy bra. It pushed my breasts together and made them look bigger than they already were. Cayson stared at them for a moment with desire burning in his eyes. Then he looked back at me, his lips desperate for my touch. He pulled me toward him, kissing me again.

I felt his chest beneath his shirt. Every groove and line was hard. He worked out and was in great shape, but I didn't realize just how strong he was. How was I immune to him for so long? Now I couldn't stop picturing him shirtless. I couldn't stop imagining how he would feel inside me. My lips were constantly desperate for his. I needed him—all the time.

I lifted his shirt then yanked it off. I tossed it aside then stared down at his body. His chest was wide and strong. His stomach was lined with hard abs. He was thick like a slab of wood and strong like a concrete wall. My hands moved down, feeling every inch of his perfection. "Damn, you're so hot," I blurted.

Cayson stared into my eyes while I touched him. It didn't seem like he heard me. His hands fingered the waistline of my leggings but he didn't pull them down. Then he gripped me and pulled me closer, his lips finding mine. He sat up, holding me close to him.

My chest pressed against his. Our stomachs almost touched. I moved my arms around his neck, my mouth devouring his like I couldn't get enough. Cayson moved his hands up my back, feeling the small muscles underneath. He moved past my bra clasp to my shoulders. Then he came down again and back to my waist.

I knew he didn't want to push me. He wanted me to make it clear what I wanted. I doubted he was always this sensitive when he was fooling around, but since our relationship was different, he was cautious. While I continued to kiss him, I reached behind me and unclasped the strap. My bra was immediately loose on me and it started to fall.

I broke our kiss and stared at him, wanting to see his reaction to me.

Cayson felt a strap in his hand but he didn't pull it down. His breathing was hard and he didn't stare at my chest. His eyes were glued to mine, like he was afraid to look. I grabbed the hand that held the strap then pulled it down. His breath hitched. The rest of the bra came with it.

I hated my chest. Guys constantly stared at it instead of my face. It was hard to tell if a guy was really into me because of my personality or just my appearance. It seemed like they were immediately smitten with my rack. But with Cayson, it was different. I already knew he loved me for me, that my chest had nothing to do with it. And I wanted him to enjoy my body.

Cayson still wouldn't look. His eyes were locked to mine.

I grabbed his large hands then placed them over my breasts, making him squeeze them. He swallowed the lump in his throat then moaned quietly. "Touch me."

That seemed to unwind him. His hands moved back to my waist and he pulled me closer to him, his mouth closing around a nipple. He kissed it then sucked it hard, taking it into his mouth.

Seeing the passionate way he took me only made me more aroused. I loved feeling him suck my skin, tasting me. He kissed my entire chest, exploring each breast while he dug his fingers into my skin, trembling slightly.

My head rolled back and I closed my eyes while I enjoyed how good it felt. It never felt this way before, this amazing. With every other guy, I felt used and tarnished. Cayson made me feel loved and sexy at the same time.

"God, you're beautiful." He licked the valley between my breasts. His mouth moved all the way to my throat, tasting me. He stopped when he reached my chin, placing a gentle kiss there.

My hands moved to the button of his jeans and undid them. Then I tried to yank them down.

Cayson hooked one arm around my waist then stood up, still kissing my neck. He pulled his jeans down with one hand then kicked them off, not breaking his focus on me. Then he sat back down, in his briefs.

His hands moved to the top of my leggings then he yanked them down. He got them over my ass before he rolled me to the couch then pulled them the rest of the way off. I wore a matching black thong. I wasn't sure what would happen tonight, but I wanted to be prepared.

Cayson stared at me for a moment, taking me in. His eyes lingered on my legs before he grabbed them and adjusted me on the couch. Then he pulled one over his shoulder and kissed the inner thigh.

My body had never been worshipped like this. My hands fisted his hair, feeling the soft strands.

His mouth moved to the opposite thigh, kissing it in the same way.

My head rolled back, loving the way he was making me feel. He was already an amazing lover.

Then he moved up my stomach, kissing the skin around my bellybutton. He kissed the area of my ribs then moved back down to my hips. He pulled down my thong slightly and he kissed the now exposed area, lighting me on fire.

"Cayson..."

He immediately moved up my body and crushed his lips against mine, like he needed the embrace in order to survive.

My hands glided down his strong back, feeling every muscle. When I reached his briefs, I gripped the brim then slowly pulled them down, exposing him. I didn't look because our lips were engaged but I felt every inch of him as he was revealed. His length lay against my stomach, and I didn't need to look at it to know how large it was. He definitely put Zack to shame. I pulled the fabric down to his knees and he kicked them off the rest of the way.

When he was naked, he ended our embrace and stared at me, waiting for me to look.

I gripped his biceps and glanced down. Instinctively, I licked my lips, liking what I saw.

Cayson moaned while he watched me, the excitement in his eyes.

I wrapped my hand around his shaft and rubbed him gently, massaging the tip with my thumb.

He breathed hard while he felt me. Then he grabbed my thong and slid it off. When it was gone, he stared at me for a moment before his eyes moved to mine again.

I didn't kiss him. Instead, I felt his naked body against mine. We'd been friends my entire life and I never thought of him this way before. But now we're together. And it felt right. It made me wonder why we hadn't done this a long time ago. "You're beautiful."

"Not as beautiful as you," he whispered. He hooked his arm around my waist then pulled me to him as he stood up. My legs instinctively wrapped around his waist, and he carried me into his bedroom.

He carefully laid me on his bed, my head hitting his pillow. Then he pressed his head to mine. "I want to taste you."

I knew what he meant. "I do too."

He kissed my chest and stomach as he moved down. When he reached the area between my legs, he gently kissed me.

And I went wild.

He rubbed his tongue against my clitoris, making a circular motion. Then he slipped his tongue inside me, applying the right amount of pleasure in all the right places.

I writhed on the bed, gripping his hair with one hand and the sheets with the other. "Cayson..."

His thumb moved to my clitoris, applying the same circular motion.

My head was spinning. My heart was racing. I couldn't control my breathing. He was making me feel so good, better than I've ever felt. His mouth was warm and inviting, sending me to a climax so strong I almost didn't recognize it. "Oh my god..."

Cayson continued to please me, making it last as long as possible.

When the sensation passed, I was out of breath. My hand moved through my hair, unsure what else to do. I was disoriented, caught off guard by how good it felt.

Cayson moved back up my body slowly, my moisture still on his lips.

"Why the hell did we wait so long?" I blurted.

He smirked slightly. "You tell me."

"God, you're good at that. You're fucking hot."

His cheeks blushed slightly. "I'm glad you think so."

"Like, really hot. Wow."

He kissed my chest, probably trying to hide his face. "I'm glad I can please you. I've never gotten so much pleasure out of it."

"Until now." I pushed him to his back then climbed on top of him.

His head hit the pillow and he looked up at me with desire in his eyes.

I moved down his body until I met his cock. It was thick and long, and it twitched when I came near. I grabbed his shaft then put his tip in my mouth, moaning as I did it. I hated giving head. It was the worst. But with Cayson, I enjoyed it, despite his large size.

Cayson breathed hard while he lay back on the pillow. His hands moved to my hair, pulling it from my face. Then he gripped it with one hand, fisting it.

I took him deep in my throat, as far as I could go.

"Skye..."

I moved up and down, doing my best to give him the most amazing blowjob of his life. He certainly gave me the best head I'd ever received.

His other hand rested on the back of my neck, guiding me slightly when he got really into it. "Fuck, that feels good."

I sucked his tip then ran my tongue across it before I took him deep again.

He breathed hard, his chest rising and falling. "Skye...I'm going to come." He cupped my neck, getting ready.

I didn't pull him out. I kept going, wanting to taste him.

He continued to breathe hard. "If you don't want me to come in your mouth, pull me out."

I deep-throated him again.

He took a few more breaths before he suddenly tensed. A deep moan from the back of his throat escaped his lips. He gripped my neck, holding on. "Mmm..." He filled me, releasing into me.

I swallowed it as it came, noting how much it was. When I was certain he was finished, I licked his tip then pulled him out.

He was still catching his breath, winded.

I crawled up his chest then leaned over him.

"You're really good at that..."

"Only because I enjoyed it."

He cupped my face and kissed me gently. The kiss lasted for several seconds, the connection passing between us. Then he pulled away, affection in his eyes. "You blew my mind."

"I think I blew your load."

He chuckled then smirked at me. "That too, definitely."

I lay next to him, getting comfortable on his bed.

Cayson pulled the sheets over him then snuggled close to me. His hand moved through my hair while he stared at me, his eyes boring into mine. "I've never seen or shared anything so beautiful in my life."

My heart convulsed at his words. I never expected Cayson to be such a gentle lover. Nor did I expect him to be so romantic and tender. He was thoughtful, passionate, and sexy. "Nor have I."

He continued to move his hand through my hair, his eyes never leaving my face. He stared at me like I was a work of art, a piece on the wall of a great museum. I realized then that I recognized that look. He'd given it to me hundreds of times. I just didn't recognize it before. "I can't believe I didn't notice..."

"I wasn't very discreet about it."

"And everyone told me...but I thought they were just joking."

"No, definitely not." His hand moved to my shoulder, touching the skin lightly. "But it's okay. It took us awhile to get here, but it happened. And that's all that matters."

"Yeah..." I grabbed his hand then brushed a kiss across his knuckles.

His eyes softened when he looked at me.

"Is that why you never wanted to talk about your personal life?" I whispered.

"Yeah."

"I feel so stupid now."

"Don't," he said gently.

"Is that why you hated Zack?"

He chuckled slightly. "No. That guy was a dick. I hated him regardless. But more so because you noticed him and not me."

"I wasn't thinking clearly..." Zack would always be one of my biggest regrets.

"It's in the past. Let it go."

My hand moved to his chest, feeling the mound of muscle underneath. "Can I ask you something?"

"Skye, you can ask me anything. You know that."

"It's about your personal life."

"You can ask about that too."

"How many girls have you been with?" I was just curious. Since he never talked about his rendezvous, I really had no idea.

He thought for a moment. "I'm not sure. More than fifteen but less than twenty."

That was more than I expected. "Were they ever serious?"

"No. A lot of them were similar arrangements to the one I had with Jasmine."

"Oh." I didn't like thinking about her. I got jealous all over again. "On the plane, you told me you were in love with a girl. Who was it?"

He smirked. "Seriously? You haven't figured that out yet?"

"I just wanted to make sure..."

"I guess you *are* stupid," he said with a laugh.

I hit his arm gently. "Hey. Don't be mean."

He pulled me closer and kissed my forehead. "You're the only one, Skye. It's always been you."

My heart melted at his words. I felt special, cherished. Cayson was the perfect guy and he only wanted me. "I can't believe I was immune to your charms for so long. Now, I can't stop thinking about kissing you when I'm in class.

At night, I think about you in ways I never did before."

"I like what I'm hearing."

I smiled. "I just can't believe it took me so long to open my eyes."

"Tell me more about these fantasies." His hand moved to my waist.

"I just...think about us."

"Doing what?" He rubbed his nose against mine.

"Making love."

"I've been thinking about it for five years. And I'm looking forward to the real thing."

"I am too..."

He kissed my forehead again.

"When did these feelings start?"

He shrugged. "A long time ago. I can't recall the exact moment. It wasn't something you did or said. It just happened. I started to notice the sound of your laugh, the way your hair shined in the sun. I hung on to every word you said. I didn't think about other girls, only you. And it hit me one day; I was in love with you. And the fact those feelings never went away only solidified that."

"Well, I'm glad you're mine now, Cayson. I never want to be without you." I clutched him tightly.

"Neither do I, baby." Emotion filled his voice as he said it. His hand moved through my hair again, being gentle like always.

I rested my head on his chest and listened to the beating of his heart. It was slow and steady. His chest rose and fell with every breath of his lungs. It felt like the rising tide on the shore. I listened to him breathe, treasuring the quiet companionship. Feeling his body wrapped around mine in his sheets felt right, felt perfect. It was what I'd been missing my whole life. He was the guy for me, the one I had all along. I just never noticed.

The front door opened and closed. "It's time to play ball. Cay, get your ass out here!" It was Slade.

Cayson sighed. "Damn."

"What's Slade doing here?"

"He said I've been ditching him for weeks. He wants to hang out. I told him you were coming over tonight but he obviously doesn't care."

"How did he get in?"

"I have no idea." He pulled the blanket off then pulled on his sweatpants. "I'll be right back." He walked out and shut the door, leaving it cracked.

I heard their conversation.

"Can you stop barging into my apartment?" Cayson demanded.

"Could you stop being a dick and actually hang out with your best bro?"

"I said tomorrow."

"I want to play today." Slade bounced a basketball on the hardwood floor.

"Thanks for getting my floor dirty," Cayson said sarcastically.

"If we were at the courts, it wouldn't matter."

"How did you get in anyway?"

"Through the front door, idiot." Slade bounced the ball again. "I'm starting to think Uncle Sean paid your way into this school too."

"But it was locked."

"It's called a lighter."

"What?" Cayson asked. "How did you get in with a lighter?"

"I'll show you."

"I don't want you to show me," Cayson said immediately. "I just want to know how you broke into my apartment."

I left the bed and pulled on one of Cayson's shirts.

"I'm not breaking in. Do you see me stealing anything?" Slade asked.

"That's looting," Cayson corrected. "What you are doing now is breaking in."

"Potato-potato."

"Slade, I think it's time for you to leave."

468

"What are you guys doing in the bedroom anyway?" Slade dropped the ball then moved to the kitchen. "What smells good?" He opened the oven door. "Ooh...chicken."

I opened the door then stepped out. "Cayson, go play ball with him."

"Listen to your woman." Slade came to the living room then spotted me only wearing Cayson's shirt. Then he glanced at Cayson's naked chest. A wide smirk spread on his face. "About time you guys started to get it on. Shit, I thought you were waiting until marriage for a second. I was about to call a psychiatrist."

Cayson didn't bother commenting to that. "Baby, it's okay. I made plans with you first."

"No, you should spend time with Slade. I've been hoarding you."

"Damn right you have," Slade said.

"Can I have a private conversation with my girlfriend?" Cayson asked, giving him a glare.

"I don't know," Slade said. "Can you have a girlfriend and keep your best friend at the same time?"

"Conrad, Theo, and Roland haven't complained once," Cayson argued.

"Because they're rubbing their dicks together. They're fine," Slade said.

Cayson rolled his eyes.

"Babe, just go," I said. "I'll see you later."

Cayson's eyes lost their light. It was obvious he didn't want our time together to end. "Okay."

"Thank god," Slade said. "Let's go. Then we're hitting the bar after that. I need a wingman to pick up chicks with."

"Having a girlfriend means I can't pick up girls anymore," Cayson reminded him.

"But you can help me. You know, distract the fat ugly ones so I can go for their cute friends," Slade said.

"That doesn't sound fun at all," Cayson said.

"Then dump Skye," Slade said.

I laughed then looked at Cayson. "Just go and have a good time."

Cayson sighed then joined me in the bedroom. "I'll be out in a second, Slade."

"'Ight. Hurry up," Slade said. "No quickie before we go."

Cayson shut the door and sighed. "I'm sorry."

"Don't be sorry. I've been neglecting Trinity and Silke too. We've both been bad friends."

"Yeah..."

I changed back into my clothes then fixed my hair.

Cayson put on his gym shorts and a t-shirt. Even in that, he still looked hot. "What?" He caught my look.

"You're just...really hot."

He smirked. "I'm always uncomfortable when girls say that, but I really like hearing it from you."

"I'll say it more often then." I grabbed my purse then walked out.

Cayson grabbed his wallet and keys. "Alright, Slade. I'm coming. But don't light your way into my apartment again."

"Don't be pussy-whipped and it won't be a problem." Slade dribbled the ball as we walked out.

Cayson walked with me to my car. Slade was beside him, spinning the ball on one finger.

"I'll see you tomorrow." Cayson cupped my face and kissed me.

"Okay. Have fun."

"Thanks." He kissed me again before he stepped back and watched me get into my car. Then, like a perfect gentleman, he watched me drive away.

As soon as I got back to my apartment, the longing hit me. I missed him like crazy, needing him desperately. I thought about when my mom talked to my dad on the phone when she visited. She would always say she missed him even though she saw him just a few hours earlier.

471

Now I knew exactly how that felt.

Chapter Twenty-Two

Slade

The house was crowded with people. One side of the wall was stuffed with kegs, and every one held red Solo cups while they mingled. A haze of smoke filled the air. The scent of cigarettes and marijuana came into my nose.

I took a deep breath. "Man, I love that smell."

Cayson cocked an eyebrow. "Of pollution and body odor?"

"It's the smell of a party."

He shook his head and sighed.

I practically had to drag Cayson here. "Loosen up, man."

"I just feel weird coming since I'm not single."

"Please don't tell me you're going to be one of those guys that stops living his life because he has a girlfriend." I gave him a firm look.

"No. But I don't want to pick up girls with you either."

"Just calm down. Skye trusts you. And she knows you're whipped hard. She hasn't got anything to worry about."

Cayson sipped his cup then looked bored.

I rubbed my hands together. "Now...who should I ruin tonight?"

"Why do you have to *ruin* anyone?" Cayson asked.

"It's not fun otherwise." I eyed the girls in the room, noting their curves in their sweaters and jeans. "There's a lot of talent here tonight."

Cayson glanced at his watch. "The sooner you get laid, the sooner I get to leave."

"You're no fun anymore."

"I was never any fun before."

"True."

"Where are the other guys?" Cayson asked.

"I don't know. They said they were coming." I glanced at my phone to see if I missed any messages.

A loud commotion happened in the center of the room. Girls were pulling down their pants and having a thong contest. They were shaking their asses, making their bright underwear turn heads.

Cayson turned away, more interested in a picture on the wall.

"Now this is my kind of party."

"Why don't you try to meet a nice girl? I'm telling you, the sex is so much better if you're with the same partner."

"How would you know?" I snapped. "You aren't even having sex with your girlfriend."

He didn't bother to respond.

474

"Besides, we both know I'm not the girlfriend type."

"I think you could be if you wanted to—for the right person."

"Nope." I crossed my arms over my chest and tried to pick someone to take back to my place. I narrowed my eyes on a cute brunette. "She's cute."

"Yeah..." Cayson didn't seem impressed.

"But her thighs are too big." I scanned the crowd again.

Cayson laughed. "You're such a jackass."

"You act like you didn't know that already." I continued to look, my eyes searching for the perfect girl to hit my sheets.

"Cayson!" A geeky guy with glasses came over. "Isn't this party awesome?"

He had 'loser' written all over him. "First-timer?" I teased.

The guy didn't catch on. "Did you finish that lab report?"

"No." Cayson sighed. "I'll probably do it Sunday night...or Monday morning, actually."

"I never considered you to be the procrastinator type."

"He's pussy-whipped now," I explained.

Cayson rolled his eyes. "I have a girlfriend so I've been distracted..."

"Oh." The guy nodded. "Cool. I got a lot of girls hanging around but I can't make up my mind."

I tried not to laugh. "I'm going to go for the kill." I patted Cayson on the shoulder then walked away.

Cayson continued to talk to his geek twin.

When I came closer to the other brunette I was looking at, I realized she wasn't as pretty as I thought. Distance and darkness had that effect. I continued to move through the crowd, looking for something worth my time. The house was packed and it was difficult to scan my options. Then I spotted a blonde on the other side of the room. She had long thin legs that stretched for days. Brown heeled boots were on her feet and skin-tight black jeans clung to her form. Her ass was toned and prominent. Her waist was petite, and her hour-glass figure was noticeable. I couldn't see her face, just her back. But I liked what I saw. Her long blonde hair trailed down her back in slight curls. "Bingo."

"Just drop it in. It will dissolve in seconds." The guy standing nearby held the red cup out.

He dropped the pill inside and stared at it. "Alright. You're good."

The hair stood up on the back of my neck. I knew what they were doing. And I didn't like it one bit. If you had to use date rape drugs to get laid, you were lower than dirt.

"I'm going for it." The guy with the cup walked across the room. And he headed right to the girl I had my eye on. He reached her and engaged her in conversation. When she turned slightly, my heart fell.

The beautiful girl I targeted was someone I knew. *Trinity.*

Her deep green sweater clung to her curves tightly, showing off her flat stomach and boobalicious chest. For a moment, I felt awkward. She was annoying as hell yet I was stalking her like prey.

Then she took the cup from his hand, accepting his offer.

Fuck. No.

Anger exploded inside me like a lit stick of dynamite. I was livid, seeing red. My hands were shaking, and I couldn't see straight. My head was about to ignite because I couldn't hold the blood rage.

I marched through the crowd, time suddenly slowing down. Every one moved like a snail. The music stopped. Trinity slowly brought the cup to her lips, about to take a drink. That sped me forward.

I slapped the cup to the ground, watching it spray across the girls' boots and jeans.

"Slade, what the hell?" Trinity snapped.

My fury was focused on the piece of shit. Without thinking or speaking, I slammed my fist against his jaw so hard he flew to the ground. "Fucking asshole."

The entire crowd backed up, knowing a serious fight just broke out.

"Slade?" Trinity's eyes widened. "What the hell are you doing?"

I grabbed her arm and pulled her behind me. "Stay out of the way. Now."

The guy rubbed his jaw then came back to his feet. He squared his shoulders and stared me down. Then he rushed me. Using my Krav Maga training, I spun him around then threw him to the ground. He groaned when his bare back hit the tile.

"Slade, behind you!" Trinity's voice came to me.

I figured his boys would come to his aid. I turned around then grabbed the first one by the neck. I choked him hard then threw him on top of his buddy. A third guy came after me and I took care of him too. Taking on three guys at once was no problem for me. I kicked their ass, making everyone in the vicinity gasp and step back.

"Slade, knock it off." Cayson grabbed my arm. "You're going to kill them."

I jerked away. "You think I care?"

Roland came out of the crowd. "Knock it off. Seriously. You made your point."

"What the hell did they do?" Conrad asked.

The guys were lying on the ground, gripping their bloody noses and choking.

I spit on them. "If anyone else thinks about using roofies around me, they'll meet the same fate as these guys."

The crowd was deadly silent, hanging onto my words.

I turned around and grabbed Trinity by the arm. "Come on. Let's go."

"But—"

"Don't argue with me," I snapped. I dragged her out, parting through the crowd and pushing people aside. When we were outside, our feet crunched against the hard snow. Trinity was struggling to keep up. She was wobbling on her heels, clearly drunk off her ass.

"What the hell is going on, Slade?" She tried to turn me around but only managed to fall over.

She was going to break her ankle at this rate. I pulled her back into my arms. "What the hell is going on?" I yelled in her face. "You were about to take a date rape drug. The only thing I should be hearing from you is your gratitude."

"How do you know?" Her words were slurred.

"I saw them. Now what the fuck is wrong with you? You don't take an open drink from a random dude! How many times have I told you that?"

"I...he was nice."

"You just put out for any guy?"

"You're one to talk," she snapped.

"I'm a dude. I don't need to worry about being raped. It's not the same thing at all, Trin."

She pushed me away. "Just leave me alone."

"To do what?"

She tried to walk back to the house but she was struggling through the snow.

I grabbed her arm and pulled her in the opposite direction. "We're heading home."

She twisted her arm away. "You don't care about me anyway. What does it matter to you?"

"I don't care?" I asked incredulously. "I just beat the shit out of three guys for trying to fuck with you."

"Whatever."

"No. Not whatever. Now come on."

"Just leave me alone, Slade." Her voice was becoming quiet. "You hate me."

"I don't hate you!" I picked her up and pulled her to my chest. "Now stop talking. You're fucking annoying."

"See?"

"See what? Like you aren't a brat to me every other second."

She tried to squirm out of my grasp. "I'm just going to drive."

"You're drunk, Trinity."

"Fine. Then you drive."

"Didn't bring my car." I carried her across the snow toward my apartment. My place was much closer than hers, at least by a mile.

"I can walk!"

"No, you can't. And you can't take off your shoes." She was light in my arms. Weighing a little more than a hundred pounds, she was like an easy day at the gym.

She finally shut up and rested her head against my chest. Her hand grabbed my shoulder then loosened.

Silence finally fell. My feet crunched against the snow while I walked. Small flakes fell from the dark sky, landing on my nose. My phone kept vibrating in my pocket, telling me everyone was calling me to ask what the hell happened. I ignored it and kept walking, hoping Trinity would fall asleep so I wouldn't have to hear her bitching about how I beat up that 'nice' guy.

I finally ascended the stairs to my apartment then got the door open.

She stirred when she realized where we were. "I thought you were going to take me home?" Her voice was hoarse.

"I'm not walking a mile in the snow. You'll have to stay here." I put her down on the ground, but she wobbled. "God, you look like Bambi."

"You look like a douchebag."

"Good one," I said sarcastically.

481

I moved into the hallway then grabbed an extra blanket. My apartment was packed with shit. My guitar leaned against the TV in the corner and my *Playboys* sat on the coffee table.

Trinity walked to the kitchen table and cringed. "Why do you have a hundred condoms sitting there?"

"That's a stupid question," I snapped.

"But a hundred?" she asked incredulously. "*A hundred*? That's ludicrous."

"Stop talking. You're more annoying when you're drunk."

"You're a bigger dick when you're drunk."

"I'm sober. So, I'm just a dick in general." I tossed the blanket and pillow on the couch. "Now shut up and go to bed."

She stared at the couch. "I'm not sleeping there."

"Then have fun sleeping on the floor."

"No." She stumbled as she headed to my room.

"I don't think so..." I chased after her.

She lay on the bed and tried to kick off her shoes.

"I'm not sleeping on the damn couch," I said with a growl.

"Neither am I. The cushions are going to make me break out."

"You think my bed is any cleaner?" I snapped.

"I'm sure even a disgusting pig like you washes his sheets."

"You'd be surprised."

She finally got one shoe off then tried to catch her breath.

"God, you're pathetic. Why do you always need to get so drunk that you don't know your nose from your ass?"

"I could ask you the same thing."

"No, you couldn't. Now go to the couch. I'm sleeping in my bed."

"Take me home or I'm sleeping here." She got her other boot off then lay back on the bed.

I growled. "I take it back. I do hate you."

"The feeling is mutual, asshole."

"Yeah, I'm such an asshole," I said sarcastically. "I saved your ass from getting raped."

She lay on the pillow and said nothing.

"Whatever." I pulled my shirt off then kicked off my shoes.

She glanced at me, seeing the tattoos along my ribs. Then she looked away.

I pulled my jeans down and stood in my boxers.

"Um…do you mind?"

"Don't act like you don't like it." I pulled the covers back and got between the sheets.

"Why are you always so cocky?"

"Because I have a lot to be cocky about."

"Anyone can get a tattoo. That doesn't make you a bigger man."

God, she was annoying. "How about we play a game?"

"A game?"

"Yeah. Who can shut up and stay that way the longest."

She sighed then pulled her shirt off. Then she took off her pants.

I didn't look at her once.

She got under the covers and stayed on her side of the bed.

My phone rang again. It vibrated on the floor where it sat in the pocket of my jeans. I groaned then fished it out before I answered it. "What?"

"Dude, what the hell happened?" Conrad snapped. "Where's my sister? Is she okay?"

"I thought you hated her?"

"I do. Now is she okay?"

"She's fine. She's staying with me tonight. We're both too drunk to drive."

He breathed a sigh into the phone. "Did those guys really try to...do what you said?"

"Yeah." It pissed me off just thinking about it.

"I'm glad you were there."

"Yeah...I just wish I had killed them."

"I'm going to have a big talk with my sister when I see her next."

"I don't think you need to. I'll give her a good speech when she wakes up tomorrow."

"Don't mention this to my dad, okay?"

"You think I'm crazy?" I asked.

"I'm glad we're on the same page."

"Yeah..."

"Well, I'll talk to you later."

"Yeah." I hung up and tossed the phone on the nightstand. I ran my fingers through my hair then closed my eyes, trying to find sleep. But it was a struggle. My heart wouldn't stop racing. I kept thinking about what would have happened to Trinity if I wasn't there. It was something that made my stomach clench in pain. It was a fate I couldn't even stand to consider. She drove me crazy, made me want to slap her, but I couldn't deny what she meant to me. She was my family, someone I'd known my whole life. I would die if that happened to her, to any of the girls in my inner circle. I knew I was a jackass that treated people like shit, but there were a few people I really cared about—even if I never showed it.

***

When I woke up the next morning, the sun was beating on my face. I forgot to close my curtains the night before. I took a deep breath before my eyes fluttered open. What I saw caused me to do a double take.

Trinity was cuddled into my side, her arm around my torso. Her face was rested in my neck, her warm breath falling on me. My arm was around her waist and I could feel the dip in her back.

What the fuck?

I immediately moved away, trying to untangle our bodies. I didn't do that cuddling shit.

She stirred when she felt me move. "God, my head…"

I opened my nightstand, riffled through all my handcuffs, bondage, and condoms until I found the bottle of aspirin. "Here." I tossed it at her.

She fumbled with the cap until she got it off. "How do you expect me to swallow this?"

"With your throat," I snapped.

"I need water."

"God, you're high maintenance." I got out of bed then retrieved a glass of water. I practically threw it at her.

She swallowed the pill then rubbed her head. She was only wearing a pink bra. Her breasts were pushed together, and her skin was pale, like winter morning. Her lips were red from her make up from the night before. Her eyeliner and eye shadow were smeared.

"You should wash your face. You look like shit."

She grabbed the pillow then slammed it hard into my face. "Go to hell, Slade."

"I will—one day." I walked into the bathroom then took a whiz.

She came in behind me and turned on the sink.

My back was to her but I was mid-stream. "Um…do you mind?" I snapped.

She ignored me and washed her face.

I growled then finished.

She wiped her face with toilet paper and dried her skin. Then she tossed it in the garbage, where she saw a pile of used condoms. "You're so disgusting."

"I'm disgusting?" I barked. "At least guys don't come inside me. Now that shit is gross." I walked out and headed into the hallway.

"Aren't you going to wash your hands?"

"Not when your fat ass is in the way."

She grabbed the towel then chucked it at me.

"This is me caring." I walked into my room then changed.

She followed me a moment later, wearing just her bra and matching thong.

As much as I knew I shouldn't look, I did anyway. I'd seen her in a swimsuit so I knew what her body looked like but I still took a peek. Her stomach was flat and her navel was pierced. Her breasts curved out, being perfectly proportioned to her size. Her legs were long and thin, and her ass was toned and lifted. I knew she hardly ate and worked out like crazy. It showed.

She pulled her clothes on and got dressed, not looking at me. "What time is it?"

"Noon."

She adjusted her top then fixed her hair. "Are you going to take me home?"

"Yeah, sure."

She walked to the front door and waited for me.

I grabbed my keys and we walked out together. We got into my truck then headed toward her house. She rested her face against the window, her eyes closed.

I turned on the radio.

"Turn that off," she snapped. "I have a headache."

"It's my car. I can do what I want."

She hit the button and turned it off. "You can not listen to music for a few minutes."

I didn't want to argue with her so I let it go.

When we arrived at her house, she jumped out then slammed the door. She didn't say bye or even look at me.

I don't think so.

I killed the engine to my truck then went after her. "Why are you being a bitch right now?"

"A bitch?" She got her keys in the door. "I didn't do anything."

"Are you at least going to thank me?" I snapped. "I saved your ass."

"You don't need me to stroke your ego. It's already big enough as it is." She got the door opened and stepped inside.

I chased after her. "This is serious, Trinity. You shouldn't go to parties alone and get that drunk. And don't take drinks from strangers. Ever."

She crossed her arms over her chest and said nothing.

Was I missing something? "Why isn't this a big deal to you? Do you understand you could have been raped? By multiple guys? They would have taken you—"

"Stop." She held up her hand. And finally, the emotion was in her eyes. "I get it. I learned my lesson. I'm sorry."

At least she admitted it. "Don't say you're sorry. Be smart and take care of yourself. What if I weren't there, Trinity?"

"I get it, okay? Stop repeating yourself."

"I just want to make sure you understand how serious this is."

"I do. Now go." She turned away, hiding her face.

I sighed, not knowing what to do. I knew she was upset but I wasn't sure what to do to fix it. I wasn't good with the whole emotional thing.

I didn't know how to comfort someone, especially a girl.

She sniffed then breathed hard.

I knew she was crying.

Ugh, this was awkward.

I sighed then came close to her. I put my hands on her shoulders and rubbed her gently.

"Thank you, Slade. I do appreciate it."

My hands stilled. "You're welcome, Trin."

She turned back around, the tears gone. "You can go now."

Something was keeping me there. "I need to know you'll be smarter about this. No more taking drinks from random guys, okay? If something happened to you…I couldn't bear it."

Her eyes softened. "I will. I promise."

That was what I needed to hear. "Okay."

Tension stretched between us.

"Well, I'll see you around…" I turned and walked away.

"Okay."

I walked out the front door then closed it behind me, not looking at her again.

Chapter Twenty-Three

Trinity

I knew I made a stupid decision. And it frightened me that the consequences of that stupidity could have been dire. What was wrong with me? What if Slade hadn't been there? It freaked me out so much that I forced myself not to think about it.

When I went to the library on Monday, Skye was there.

"Hey." She studied me for a moment with concern in her eyes.

Being in a tight group meant everyone knew everything the moment it happened. "I'm okay," I said proactively.

"I'm glad Slade taught those guys a lesson." She highlighted a few sentences in her textbook.

"That Krav Maga should be illegal," I said.

"Good thing he knew it." She adjusted her glasses over the bridge of her nose.

I sat there, not in the mood to read or do anything.

"Do you want to talk about it?"

"Not really." I looked out the window, trying to think of other things.

"Maybe you and Slade will get along better now..."

I tried not to laugh. "I doubt it." I didn't want to talk about Slade or that horrible night anymore. "How's it going with Cayson? I haven't seen you to ask."

She couldn't hide the smile on her face. "Wonderful."

"He's the whole package?" I gave her a playful grin.

"Ooooh yeah."

I chuckled. "Lucky you. Have you been humping like rabbits?"

"No...we haven't done it yet."

"What? Why?"

She shrugged. "Just taking it slow. But we fooled around the other night. That was fun. Mucho fun."

I laughed. "I bet it was. Cayson is a good-looking guy."

"I'm not sure why I was immune to him for so long."

"Because you're stupid," I blurted.

"Apparently."

"This is when I get to say, told you so. Every time I said Cayson was in love with you, you never believed me."

"I know...I'm not sure why I was in denial."

"Like I said, you're stupid."

She glared at me through her spectacles.

"I'm just saying..."

Cayson entered the library then spotted us at our table.

"Your boyfriend is coming."

Skye immediately pulled her glasses off like she was embarrassed.

"He's seen you wear them before," I said.

"But now he's my boyfriend."

"I really don't think he cares."

"Hey." Cayson only had eyes for her. He leaned down and kissed her. "I missed you."

"I missed you too." She couldn't wipe away the grin on her face.

He put his backpack down and sat beside her. "Why aren't you wearing your glasses?"

I grinned. "Because she's embarrassed."

Skye gave me that look that clearly said, "Shut your mouth."

"Embarrassed of what?" he asked. He leaned toward her. "I think you look cute when you wear them."

"You don't think I look like a nerd?" she asked hesitantly.

"Well, since I'm a nerd, I find that attractive." He grabbed the glasses then slipped them over her nose. "That's better." He kissed her forehead before he pulled away.

"You guys are ridiculously cute," I said.

"I know," Skye said with a sigh.

Cayson rested his hand on her thigh while he opened his textbook. "Anything new?"

"No," I said immediately.

Cayson looked at me with concern in his eyes. But he didn't say anything. He probably picked up on the tension.

Slade stepped into the library with an energy drink in his hand. He found our table and made his way over. For some reason, when I saw him, my heart rate increased slightly. He wore a gray t-shirt and dark jeans. The colors of his sleeves brought out his blue eyes. He walked past the table with an air of indifference. Then he slid into the seat beside me, downing his energy drink.

I eyed it. "Those are so bad for you."

"Taking drinks from random guys is bad for you," he snapped.

I would never live that down. "I'm just trying to help you."

"Thanks, Mom."

Seriously, I wanted to slap him sometimes.

"She's right," Cayson said. "The epinephrine in that can really mess up your heart, especially over a long period of time."

"Well, I choose to live my life how I want. Did you know stress can really mess up your heart?" Slade countered.

Cayson shrugged. "I tried."

"You want to head to the bar to watch the game tonight?" Slade asked. "The Steelers are playing."

"Um..." He eyed Skye.

Slade rolled his eyes. "You're so lame, man."

"I'm not asking her for permission," Cayson said immediately. "I just had plans with Skye tonight."

"Change them. She can come too." Slade finished his drink then crushed the can with his hand. "Invite everyone. I don't care."

Cayson looked at Skye. "What do you think?"

"Yeah, let's watch the game," Skye said. "I want fries and hot wings anyway."

Cayson gave her a fond look. "I should have known food would be the deciding factor."

Skye shrugged. "I like food."

"You coming?" Slade asked. He looked at his can when he said it.

Who was he talking to? "Sorry, are you talking to me?"

"Who else would I be asking?" he snapped.

"Well, look at me when you talk to me."

He rolled his eyes. "Okay, Princess."

"Do you even want me to go?"

"Would I have asked you if I didn't?" He finally looked at me.

Cayson sighed. "Peace—just for a few minutes."

"Please," Skye said.

Slade rolled his eyes then crushed the can into a thin strip with his bare hands. "I'll see you guys there at six." He stood up and left his trash on the table.

"I hope you don't expect us to throw that away," I noted.

He growled then grabbed the can. On his way out, he tossed it in the recycling bin.

"You guys are so weird..." Skye stared at me as she said it. "He beats up three guys to protect you but then you argue like hyenas fighting over a dead carcass."

"He and I will never get along." I leaned back in my chair, trying to forget about how pissed off Slade made me.

"Yeah...we're figuring that out." Cayson smirked.

***

As soon as I got home, there was a knock on the door.

I put down my bag then looked through the peephole. My brother was standing on my doorstep. I sighed then opened it, knowing I'd have to get this over with sooner or later.

He walked inside then looked at me. His eyes were dark and focused, like he was furious or on the verge of tears.

I decided to speak first. "Look, I know what you're going to say and I don't want to deal with this right now. I made a mistake and I learned my lesson. I'll be smarter from now on. Get off my ass." I turned around then opened the refrigerator, looking for a bottle of Evian.

Conrad stayed behind me and said nothing.

I grabbed the bottle then took a drink. I set it on the counter and waited for him to scream at me and call me a stupid whore.

Conrad stepped closer to me. He wore a gray hoodie and his hair was slightly messy. He had dark hair like my father. We hardly looked anything alike. Only our eyes seemed to be similar. "I'm not here to yell at you."

That was a first.

"I just wanted to see if you were okay." He rested his hand on the counter next to me and put the other in his pocket.

"Nothing happened, Conrad. I'm fine."

"But...I'm sure you were shaken up about it."

"Not really. I was drunk so everything was numb. And Slade dragged me out before I could really think about anything."

He sighed. "I'm so glad he was there."

"I'm not sure how he knew what was going on. But he did."

He stared at me, concern in his eyes. "Are you sure you're okay?"

"I'm fine. Really."

"Please be more careful. Most of the time I can't stand you and I think you're annoying as hell...but...I do love you."

Warmth flooded my heart. "I love you too."

He coughed into his hand then shifted his weight. "Should we hug or something?"

"I guess we could."

He closed the gap between us and hugged me quickly. Then he pulled away.

"You aren't going to mention anything to Dad, right?"

"No. You never tattle on me and I'll never tattle on you."

"Thanks. I'm not worried about how he would treat me. Honestly, I'm terrified of how he would react to those three guys."

"I know, right?" He chuckled slightly. He put both hands in his pockets. "Are you watching the game tonight?"

"Yeah, I'll be there."

"Cool." He ran his fingers through his hair. "I know you and Slade argue a lot...but maybe you should try to be nice to him since he...you know...obviously cares about you."

"He's the one that's an asshole every second of the day. It's hard to be nice to him."

"It's just some friendly advice." He walked out and shut the door behind him.

I didn't need any advice when it came to Slade. He was the definition of an asshole. And just because he saved me didn't mean I'd let him treat me like dirt. No way.

***

We got a booth in the corner and faced the large screen TV.

"Come on!" Conrad shouted. "Score, goddamn it!"

"Go...go...go!" Roland thumped his hand against the wood of the table.

Slade leaned forward on his elbows. "I'm about to be a thousand bucks richer."

The player made it to the end zone.

"Yeah, baby!" Slade clapped his hands. "Alright."

"Who did you bet a thousand bucks with?" I asked.

"Online sport betting," he answered.

"Isn't that illegal?" I asked.

"Anything worth doing is illegal." He spoke without looking at me then drank his beer. His arm was covered in various tattoos. A black squid moved up his forearm and a grizzly bear was on his bicep. His body was a canvas of random images. But he used color in every single one. Instead of traditional black ink, he was covered in bright hues, like red, green, blue, and orange.

"Does your dad know?" I asked.

"Duh. He bets too." He finished his second beer but didn't seem affected by it.

Cayson had his arm around Skye while his free hand held his beer.

Roland watched them. "This is so strange…"

"What?" Conrad asked.

"Seeing them together," Roland said. "I thought it would never happen, and now that it finally has, it's hard to understand."

"Get used to it." Skye leaned in and kissed Cayson on the cheek.

Cayson smirked then gave her a fond look.

Roland cringed. "Just keep it PG, alright?"

"You talked about fucking that married woman countless times," Skye countered.

"Totally different." Roland drank his beer then wiped his lips.

"No, it isn't," Skye snapped.

"You're my sister," Roland said. "It is different."

"Sexist pig," she mumbled.

"Annoying brat," Roland mumbled back.

Slade stared at the screen like it was the most fascinating thing in the world. "If they win with a score of 28 to 22, I win ten grand."

"Shut up," Conrad said. "How?"

"The odds are slim but it could happen," Slade said. "I did a lot of research."

"Imagine how well you would do in school if you used all the time you spent on gambling, doodling, and playing your guitar toward your classes," Cayson said.

Slade didn't seem to care. "Nah."

I sipped my wine but couldn't drink most of it. I was sick of alcohol from the previous weekend. My body needed a break.

"Do you want some more hot wings or fries?" Cayson asked Skye.

She shrugged. "I guess some fries wouldn't hurt."

"We just ate," Roland snapped. "How can you possibly be hungry?"

"Because I am," Skye argued.

Roland rolled his eyes. "I hope you like fat girls, Cayson. Because Skye is going to be huge."

"I like it when a girl knows how to eat." Cayson leaned toward her. "I'll be right back. Keep my seat warm."

"Or I could just sit in your lap," she whispered.

"Don't make me gag," Roland said.

Cayson left and headed to the bar.

I sighed in sadness. I couldn't deny how envious I was. I wished I had a great guy that loved me the way Cayson loved her. All I had were a string of guys that meant nothing. And I meant even less to them. Good guys were hard to find, nearly impossible. I'd given up at this point.

Cayson retrieved the basket of fries and placed them in front of Skye. "Eat up."

"Thank you." She gave him a bright smile before she started to munch.

I glanced at Slade. His eyes were glued to the screen. "Fucking refs. It seems like none of them are even qualified."

"Maybe they paid their way through school," Cayson said.

"They have referee school?" Slade asked with a raised eyebrow.

"Yeah, it's in Australia." Cayson drank his beer and avoided Slade's look.

I didn't know anything about football but I knew that was totally off.

"Australia?" Slade asked. "But they don't even have football over there."

Roland tried not to laugh.

Conrad was struggling too.

Cayson shrugged. "They want the refs to have absolutely no distractions during their training."

Slade's eyes narrowed. "But how would they practice if there're no football games?"

"They have all virtual testing," Roland said.

Slade stared at them suspiciously. "Wait a second..."

Cayson smirked.

"You're fucking with me, aren't you?" Slade asked.

Roland laughed. "I can't believe you bought that."

"Idiot," I murmured.

"You're one to talk," he snapped.

I sipped my wine and ignored his look.

"I'll get you back, Cayson," Slade threatened.

"Oooh…I'm so scared." Cayson laughed.

"You should be." Slade returned his eyes to the TV.

We watched the rest of the game then squared the tab. Cayson and Skye immediately paired off then headed home together. Roland and Conrad were inseparable so they drove together. I was the only one who drove on my own.

"See you later." Slade headed down the sidewalk, his hands in his pockets.

"Did you walk?" I asked.

"Yes, genius."

"You want a ride?" I asked. "It's cold."

"And sit with you in a car? I'm good." He kept walking.

I knew he was a dick but I was getting sick of his attitude. "Do you ever get tired of being a jackass?"

He didn't turn around. "No."

***

I got a text message from my father a few days later.

Breakfast on Sunday? He usually came down every other week. It was a routine we established a long time ago. It was unspoken but always acknowledged.

Sure.

I'll pick you up at 9.

Okay.

My father never brought my mom. It was always something only he and I did. I loved my mom but we weren't nearly as close as my father and I. I still remember going to work with him when I was younger. He'd let me play with my toys in his office, and he even took me to meetings with him. When he finished his workday, we would go by McDonald's and never tell my mom. He and I were always rule breakers.

On Sunday morning, he knocked on my door.

I wore my black leggings with boots and a thick sweater. A gold bracelet hung on my wrist and my hair was pulled over one shoulder. When I opened the door, I saw him wearing his usual attire. He wore dark jeans and a t-shirt. A dark blue blazer covered him, keeping him warm. My dad was at least a foot taller than me, if not more.

"Hey, Trin."

"Hey, Dad."

He stepped across the threshold and gave me a warm hug. He held me for a long moment before he pulled away. "Hungry?"

"Do you know me at all?"

He smirked then walked out. "Then let's get our grub on."

I walked out then locked the door behind me.

"The usual?" he asked.

"Yes, please."

He walked to his Porsche then opened the passenger door, letting me get inside. Then he walked around the car and got into the driver's seat. My dad was the only guy I knew who treated me like a lady. Every other guy couldn't care less about chivalry. My brother wasn't even nice to me.

My dad pulled onto the road and headed to the diner we always went to. It was a tradition that we never broke. When we arrived, he opened the door for me and even pulled out my chair.

"How's school?" He sat with his back perfectly straight then looked at the menu.

"Good. Nothing too interesting." I looked at the menu even though I already knew what I would order. It was the same thing I always got. "How's work?"

"Good. Nothing too interesting." He smirked while he read through the menu. "Are you getting the strawberry waffle with bacon and eggs?"

"When do I ever order anything else?" I said with a smile.

"Well, you always look at your menu so I know you consider it." He put the menu down. "New York steak and eggs for me."

"A very hearty meal."

He nodded. "I'm a big guy."

My dad wasn't fat. He was thick with muscle and strength. His eyes were blue, but most of the time they looked gray. He had an intimidating look about him. He looked like his brother but he had his own distinct features. I knew my father boxed for exercise and trained in martial arts. He was an intense person sometimes. "How's Mom?"

"Good. She's doing Cross Fit now."

"That doesn't surprise me. She's always been super fit."

"She's a fit chick. A hot one." A grin was on his face.

My mom was still pretty, even after all these years. "She could outrun you."

"Now let's not get carried away..."

The waitress approached our table. "I already know what you want, Trinity." She smiled then turned to my dad. "What can I get you, sir?"

"Mike," he answered. "Steak and eggs. Medium well, please."

"You got it." She took the menus.

"And some coffee, please," I blurted.

"Make that two," my dad added.

"Of course." She walked away.

My dad stared at my neck. "That's a nice scarf."

I felt the purple fabric. "Thanks. I got it on sale."

"It's a good color on you. Brings out your eyes."

"Thanks, Dad."

"Anything new?" he asked. He leaned back in his chair then rested his hands in his lap.

I thought about the party I went to last weekend and what almost happened. No, I couldn't bring that up. What could I talk about? "Cayson and Skye are cute together."

He nodded. "Your uncle Sean is very happy about that. I am too."

"Yeah...I can't believe it took them so long to figure out their feelings."

He shrugged. "Sean took longer."

"So I've heard from Skye." I crossed my arms over my chest and leaned back.

"Your brother behaving himself?"

"As far as I know. But if he wasn't, he wouldn't mention it to me."

"Like you would tell me anyway." He had a playful look in his eyes.

I shrugged. "I've never been a tattle-tell."

"Good. Those are annoying."

I chuckled. "Yeah, they are."

"Juggling any guys?" he asked.

My dad always asked this question in a calm way, almost like he didn't care. But I knew how protective he was of me. The last time I had a boyfriend, he insisted on meeting him and his entire family. It was an ordeal... "No."

He nodded. "Seeing just a single guy?"

"No guys at all," I answered. I hadn't dated in a while. I was getting tired of it. Most guys were jerks, boring, and horrible kissers. I wanted a guy to sweep me off my feet but I was quickly realizing that would never happen. I shouldn't bother waiting.

"Any reason why?" he asked.

"No...I just haven't met anyone who's worth my time."

"Good. I'm glad you're picky. You deserve nothing but the best, honey."

I smiled slightly then dropped it.

"You have the rest of your life anyway. And I don't want to have a heart attack anytime soon."

"Then you probably shouldn't order a steak," I noted.

He smirked. "I'm a man. I order what I want."

"You sound like a caveman," I said with a laugh.

"Me like meat," he said in a deep voice.

I laughed again.

"So, how are your classes?"

"You already asked me that."

"And you didn't give me a sufficient answer." He stared me down, suddenly becoming serious.

I shrugged. "Classes are alright."

"Conrad made it sound like you don't like school much."

"He did?" *When did he say that?*

He nodded. "He said you were more interested in fashion." He stared at me like he was waiting for a response. When I didn't say anything, he kept going. "Trinity, is that true?"

"Well, I do like fashion…"

"More than business?" he asked.

I guess I should just be honest. I could tell my dad almost anything. Sometimes I feared I would disappoint him for not wanting the company, something he spent his life doing. "I guess I'm not that into it…"

He nodded slowly. "Do you have any desire to take over the company with Skye?"

Not really. What should I say?

My dad leaned over the table. "Honey, you can tell me anything."

I looked down. "I guess I don't want to disappoint you."

"You could never disappoint me." Thick emotion was in his eyes. "Honey, I want you to be happy. Don't do something you don't want to do. Talk to me."

"I guess...no, I don't really want to do that. I think it's amazing that you and Uncle Sean have done such a great job growing the company into the empire it has become but...my heart isn't into it."

He stared at me for a long time, taking in my words. "Okay."

Okay? That's it? "What?"

"Trin, it's your life. I want you to do what makes you happy. If you don't want the company, you don't have to take it."

"But I know how important it is to you..."

He shrugged. "What does it matter? You need to live your life for yourself, not other people. No matter what you do or how aware you are of other people's feelings, you aren't going to make everyone happy. So don't bother. My dad started that company out of his garage when he was eighteen. When I graduated college, he wanted Sean and I to take over. But neither one of us wanted it. I did my own thing for years. I didn't come to it until I was ready and knew I really wanted it. Sean did the same. Do what you want, Trin. You have my support no matter what."

My dad made it so easy. "Thanks…"

"But you should really think about it before you make any hasty decisions. That's all I ask."

"You're right."

"So…what would you like to do?"

I never entertained the idea before. "Well, I like fashion."

"You could do modeling. Are you interested in that?"

I rolled my eyes. Of course my dad thought I was model material. He was blinded by his love. "Maybe design. I really like putting outfits together."

He nodded. "I know a lot of people in the city. I can set you up with something or even a designer. Or we could launch your own clothing line. Whatever you want, Trin."

Sometimes I forgot all the power my father had. "Thanks. I'll think about it."

"Okay."

The waitress returned with the food. "Plates are hot. Be careful." She set everything down then walked away.

I picked up my fork and started to eat. "What do you and Mom do now that Conrad and I are out of the house? Are you guys bored?"

He laughed. "Bored? Definitely not. It's nice having time to ourselves again. And the peace and quiet..." He shook his head. "There's nothing like it."

"We weren't that loud," I argued.

"Maybe not in high school but you certainly were growing up."

"You said I was a cute baby."

"Oh, you were. You were adorable, still are. But that doesn't mean you weren't a pain in the ass."

I glared at my dad and kept eating. "Conrad was the terror, not me."

He laughed. "You have some odd perceptions of yourself. You guys both drove your mother and I up the walls. You both had your golden moments, but also times of pure terror."

"How sweet," I said sarcastically.

He smirked. "Your mother and I miss you guys—sometimes."

"I miss being home sometimes," I said with a sigh, feeling the emotion come out.

He caught the look. "Is everything okay, Trin?"

"Yeah...I guess I miss living in a fairy tale."

He studied me for a moment. "I don't understand your meaning."

I took a deep breath. "I just expected being an adult would be awesome. It would be all fun and games. All I would do is enjoy my freedom. Life would be good, it would be great. But..."

"But what?" he pressed.

"I guess it's a lot harder than I thought."

His eyes softened when he looked at me. They turned blue for a moment, showing his vulnerability.

"I feel like I don't know where I belong. I keep making mistakes. I just want to fast-forward to the next stage. I want to find the perfect guy and marry him. I want to be married with kids. I just want to find the place where I belong..." I realized this conversation became too serious. "I'm sorry. I'm just rambling."

He processed my words for a long time. "When I first became an adult, I struggled. I was a much different man before your mother came into my life. I was a jerk, frankly. I wanted to be a bachelor all my life. All I cared about was racing fast cars and picking up different girls every night. I went through the motions, just having fun. But in reality, I was sad. When your uncle Sean got married, I realized how empty and meaningless my life was. All I did was waste time and break hearts. I had nothing to show for it. The depression hit me hard. I was a single guy, alone and broken. But then your mother came into my life, bringing the light with her."

His words echoed in my mind long after he said them.

"My point is, even though I went through a hard time, I wouldn't change it for anything. Because when you do finally find where you belong and the person you belong with, you realize you wouldn't have appreciated it so much unless you struggled to begin with." He rested his hand on mine. "You will find the place where you belong and the guy you belong with. But never speed up time. Because we really don't have long on this earth. Appreciate what you have. Because before you know it, it's gone."

My father pulled his hand away then sipped his coffee. Silence stretched between us. My dad and I always had serious conversations, but we never went as deep as this. He was a friend as well as a parent. It felt good to get that off my chest. Because, like always, he made me feel better.

Chapter Twenty-Four
Cayson

I sat down at our usual table in the library but Skye wasn't there. It was only Trinity and Slade.

"All I'm saying is, you're stupid and annoying." Slade ate his burrito while he spoke, forgetting his manners. "So just shut the hell up."

"You aren't supposed to eat in the library," she hissed.

"And you aren't supposed to talk," he snapped. "Do the world a favor and become mute."

"Ugh." Trinity looked like she might slam her textbook into his head.

I eyed them both. "Best friends, I see..."

"I wouldn't be her friend if you paid me," Slade said, still eating his burrito.

"I'm so close to smashing my book into your skull," she threatened.

"You would never hit your target." He crammed the rest of the burrito, nearly half of it, into his wide open mouth. He could barely close his lips around it.

"Gross...just take a bite and chew," Trinity said. "Why do you have to shove it down your throat like a seagull?"

"At least I eat. You're a twig."

"At least I'm not disgusting."

I couldn't stand this much longer. "Kids, knock it off. Or time-out for both of you."

Slade rolled his eyes. "I'm about to wipe a booger on her."

"Gross..." She crossed her arms over her chest and sighed.

"Have you seen Skye?" I asked. "She's usually here about now."

"No. I haven't seen her all day," Trinity said.

She usually came to the library for her two-hour break. I couldn't recall a time when she skipped it. "That's odd."

"Just text her and ask where she is, genius." Slade balled up his foil then threw it right at Trinity's face.

"Jackass." She swatted it away and it fell on the floor.

I typed the message. *Babe, I'm in the library. Where are you?*

"Excuse me." The librarian stood at our table, looking pissed. Her glasses made her eyes look three times as big. She looked like a bug under a magnifying glass.

Trinity stiffened.

"No food in the library." She was staring at Trinity, annoyance and disapproval heavy in her eyes. "You know the school rules. Now pick up that trash and throw it away."

Trinity turned to Slade, glaring at him.

Slade covered his mouth and tried not to laugh.

"I'm waiting..." The librarian crossed her arms over her chest. "You think just because you're a rich kid that you don't have to follow the rules?"

The librarian was being awfully harsh but none of us told her off.

Trinity sighed then picked up the foil from the ground. Then she threw it away.

"Now was that so hard?" The librarian gave her one final glare before she walked off.

Trinity turned her rage to Slade. "You dick!"

Slade laughed hard, hitting his hand against the table. "Oh man, that was hilarious."

"It was not," Trinity hissed.

"Dude, that book nerd hates you." Slade couldn't stop laughing. "That was priceless."

"Go to hell, Slade." She grabbed her bag and marched off.

Slade kept laughing even after she was gone. "She had it coming."

I didn't comment on it. I never understood their odd relationship. Slade treated her like dirt but he was willing to stick out his neck to protect her. He tried to act like a macho and careless guy on the outside, but he had a heart of gold underneath. That was the reason why he was my best friend. There was a lot of good to him—he just never showed it.

I turned my attention back to my phone. Skye never texted me back.

"Dude, leave her alone," Slade said. "Don't be one of those obsessive and stalker type boyfriends."

"I'm not," I said immediately. "It's just out of the ordinary for her. And the fact she isn't messaging me back is worrying me."

"Chill, man. Girls hate clingy guys."

"I'm not clingy," I said firmly. "I'm just concerned."

"She's probably taking a dump," Slade reasoned. "No reason to get upset."

I ignored his comment and called her. It rang several times then went to voicemail. What was she doing? Did she go home? If she did, why? And why wasn't she texting me back? "I'm going to look for her."

"Overreacting..." He shook his head slightly.

"When you fall in love with someone, you'll overreact too."

"Fall in love?" He leaned his head back and laughed. "Stop with the jokes. My stomach hurts."

I left the library to search for her. I walked past the classes she already had and hoped to find her there. She was nowhere to be found. I headed to her apartment but she wasn't there either. I was starting to get uneasy. The situation wasn't adding up. Where was she?

***

I headed through the school grounds toward the main building. I still couldn't find Skye so I was backtracking. The fact no one knew where she was and she wasn't answering her phone was making me panic. I wasn't sure if I should call the police or her dad. I tried to stay calm and remain logical. There was obviously an explanation for her disappearance.

When I reached the path, I heard voices.

"No, you aren't running away from me. I want to talk about this!" a man yelled, sounding threatening.

"Leave me alone!" It was the voice of a woman. And I recognized it immediately.

I turned the corner and saw Zack gripping Skye by the elbow. He was holding her phone in the opposite hand, keeping it out of her reach.

"Give it back to me," she hissed. She tried to knee him in the groin but he moved out of the way.

I suspected Zack would make a reappearance at some point, but not like this. Seeing him grip her arm sent me to the brink. If it were any girl, I'd be pissed. But since it was Skye, I was livid.

"No," he snapped. "How do you think I felt when I was stuck in the hospital for two weeks?"

"I didn't put you there!" She hit him in the stomach and tried to grab the phone.

He pushed her back. "Don't act innocent. I know it was your dad. You—"

I grabbed him by the neck and viciously slammed him into the concrete.

Skye stepped back then looked at me, relief written all over her face.

Without thinking, I raised my foot over his face and stomped down, making his nose crack and blood spew out.

"Fuck!" He clutched his face and rolled over.

"You think that hurt?" I savagely kicked him in the side, right where his ribs were. "Since you miss the hospital so much, I'll put you back there." I kicked him again. "Fucking dick."

He curled into a ball and moaned, trying to protect himself.

"Let's get this straight. Come near Skye again and I'll make it a million times more painful." I stomped on his hand, snapping two fingers.

"Fuck!"

"Cayson, that's enough." Skye's words washed over me.

Only her voice could hold me back. Like a scabbard, she could sheath my anger like no one else. The blood lust was suddenly gone. I turned away from Zack and looked at her. "Are you okay?"

"I'm fine." She walked around Zack then yanked her phone out of his grasp. "I'll be needing that." No sympathy was on her face. She came back around, joining me.

I was so relieved she wasn't hurt. I immediately pulled her into me and formed a steel cage around her with my arms. "You're safe now. Don't be scared."

"I wasn't scared. He was just being a dick."

"Well, I won't let him be one anymore." My hand moved through her hair, treasuring her.

She rested her face against my chest then sighed.

Zack climbed to his feet slowly then wiped the blood from his nose. One hand was pulled to his chest and his fingers were bent in an odd way.

I stared him down, not feeling any remorse. "She's mine now. And I won't hesitate to kill you if you give me a reason to."

He gave me a final glare before walking away.

Skye sighed then pulled away. "Please don't mention this to my father."

I would do whatever she asked. "Okay."

She looked at her phone and saw all the messages and missed calls. "I'm sorry, Cayson. You must have been worried."

"Don't apologize," I said immediately. "I'm just sorry he had you cornered like that."

"It's okay. I'm not scared of him."

That didn't mean I wasn't. I'd have to keep a better eye on her. "Is there anything I can do?"

"No. I just want to go home and eat something."

"Okay." I pulled her close to me and kissed her forehead.

"Thanks for getting rid of him. I was so relieved when I saw you."

"I'll always take care of you." I never meant anything more in my life.

She grabbed her bag off the ground and shouldered it. "Let's go."

***

Two empty pizza boxes were left on the coffee table. Skye could down a whole one by herself. Her brother teased her for it, but I thought it was hot. She had curves in all the right places, and she wouldn't have them unless she ate like a normal person.

"Poker?" she asked as she pulled out a deck of cards. A mischievous grin was on her face.

It was past nine. Since it was a Friday night, I didn't care about the time. I'd probably stay with her all weekend, and before I knew it, it would be Monday again. Time flew by with her. I never had enough of her. "Sure. But I'm not playing for money."

"Because you know I'll win."

I smirked. "No. Because I'm a gentleman."

"I don't want a gentleman. I want you."

When she said things like that, my heart fluttered. It was hard to understand that she wanted me the way I wanted her. So many years had gone by when she didn't notice me. Now everything was different. "Well, that's what you're going to get."

She pouted her lips. "You don't have to be perfect all the time, Cayson. I wouldn't mind a darker side to you."

My eyes narrowed when I looked at her.

She pulled out the cards and started to shuffle them. "Can I ask you something personal?"

"Like I said, you can ask me anything."

"Were you like this with your other girls?"

"Like what?"

"Sweet,   considerate, compassionate...stuff like that."

When I remembered my time with Jasmine, I knew the answer. "No. I was a dick most of the time."

"I can't picture it..." She shuffled the cards again and started to deal.

"I'm only sweet to you, Skye. Honestly, I'm not that great of a guy. I have a lot of regrets."

"Like what?" She placed the deck on the table and looked at me.

This was a new realm for her and I. "Jasmine is one of them."

She stared at me, waiting for me to go on.

"I told her we were just…" It was hard to find an appropriate description. I watched my language around Skye, being a gentleman. "Someone to pass the time with. Our relationship was only physical but she always wanted something more. I told her I couldn't give it to her. But then she told me she loved me…and that I was the one to her."

Emotion flashed in her eyes but she said nothing.

"I wish I'd never gotten involved with her. I know firsthand what it's like to love someone you can't have. I never wanted that to happen to her…but it did."

She stared at the cards in front of us, considering my words. "It's hard not to fall in love with you, Cayson. I'm not surprised. I'm sure it happens more often than you think."

Did that mean she was in love with me? I knew she loved me but…was it the same? "Do you have any regrets?"

She smirked. "I think it's pretty obvious what my biggest regret is."

Zack. She didn't need to say it. "Any others?"

She pulled her hair over one shoulder, revealing her slender neck. It caught my eye immediately. "You."

"Me?" *What did she mean?*

"I wish I had realized how I felt before...all the time we wasted."

"We have the rest of our lives, Skye. Don't beat yourself up over it."

She gave me a slight smile before she dropped it. "There are a few things here and there but nothing major. I never really had a serious boyfriend when I was younger because my dad would have shot them."

I chuckled. "Yeah...I could see that happening."

She rolled her eyes. "I'm glad you aren't scared of my dad."

"Who said I wasn't?" I teased.

"He loves you."

"Yeah. But that could change if I crossed a line."

She stared at me across the table. "But you never would."

Snow was falling lightly outside. The windowpanes were starting to frost. She and I were alone in winter bliss. I treasured the silence, feeling like we were secluded from the world. She was mine—and mine alone. "I'm glad you realize that."

"I trust you more than anyone, Cayson. There's no room for doubt."

"I'm glad you feel that way." Because I worked hard for that trust. I stared at the skin of her neck, wanting to press my lips against it. Her flesh would feel warm against my mouth. But there would be time for that later.

She grabbed her deck and looked at the cards. "How about we make it interesting?"

"What are you thinking?" I picked up my cards and looked through them. Uncle Mike taught me how to play and I was pretty good at it, definitely better than Skye. But I always let her win.

"Strip poker?" She gave me a seductive grin.

That caught my attention. I wanted to see Skye naked all the time—ever since I hit puberty. "I'm game if you are."

"I am too. But I'm going to be fully clothed while you're naked."

Not this time. "We'll see."

We started the round. I had a good hand and all I needed was to trade a single card. Skye thought she had a clever poker face, and maybe she fooled everyone else, but she couldn't fool me. I'd studied her face for too many years, saw it in every dream, to not understand all of its secrets. She gave a quick smile, a fake one, and then traded a card.

She was bluffing.

"You ready?" she asked.

"Yeah."

"Are you sure you don't want to fold?"

"No." I kept a stoic face, hiding everything.

"Alright...what item of clothing is this for?"

I immediately wanted to blurt "shirt" but I didn't want Skye to know that, like every other guy, I was obsessed with her chest. "Shoes."

"Okay...your feet are about to get cold." She put down her cards. She had two pairs.

I smirked then put mine down. I had a full house.

She narrowed her eyes. "Lucky hand."

"Yeah." She was going down. "Now take off those boots."

She yanked them off then tossed them aside.

"Those socks will be next."

"Don't get cocky," she warned.

Too late.

We played another round. Skye pulled her typical tricks on me but I didn't let them slide. My hand beat hers—easily.

"Now take those socks off." I stared at her, waiting for her to comply.

She sighed then pulled them off.

I smirked. *I was loving this.*

"Your luck has run out." She dealt the cards again and we picked up our piles. I had a bad hand but I knew how to play it cool. I only traded one card instead of all five.

Skye watched me, studying my face. Then she looked back at her hand.

"For the pants?" I asked.

She seemed unsure. Then she put her cards down. "I fold."

I smirked. "Someone is dropping the ball."

"Shut up. It was just a bad hand."

"Someone's touchy..."

She kicked me playfully under the table then dealt the new hand. Now she was watching me closely, trying to gauge my features like she never had. She studied her cards for a long time before she swapped them. I did the same.

"Ladies first," I said.

She gave me a cocky smirk before she put them down. "Flush. I want to see some drawers."

I put my cards down. "Royal flush."

Her smile dropped.

"I want to see some knickers."

She growled then rolled her eyes.

"Come on." I snapped my fingers. "We don't have all day."

"Why are you winning all of a sudden?"

I shrugged. "Stop talking and start undressing."

She stood up then unbuttoned her jeans.

My eyes were focused on her hands, watching everything she did. I tried to seem indifferent but I couldn't. My cock grew in anticipation. Then she lowered her jeans and kicked them away. She wore a purple thong that barely covered anything. My cock twitched in my pants. Then she sat down and was hidden from view.

Now I was even more motivated to win the next hand.

Skye dealt the cards. "I'm winning this round."

So she thinks...

We put down our cards. Skye's face fell when she saw mine. "You have two aces and two kings?"

"Yep." She only had pairs of twos and fours. "Now the top."

She growled at me then yanked it off. Her bra pushed her breasts together and made her cleavage more prominent. Her pale skin was perfect and unblemished. She was a vision, she was a muse. Nothing had ever turned me on as much as she did. My cock twitched again. And again.

Now I just had to get that bra off.

"Are you cheating?" she demanded.

"How would I cheat?" I looked at my cards and tried not to gawk at her.

"Well, you always lose. All of a sudden, you're the best poker player I've ever seen."

"I guess I'm extremely motivated." I arranged my cards then swapped them.

She eyed me suspiciously before she continued with the game.

To no one's surprise, I won the next round. I held out my hand. "I'll take those."

"You want my panties?" she asked incredulously.

"I won them."

She stood up then pulled them off.

I blatantly stared at her, unable to control myself. Her legs were toned and smooth, and my eyes went to the nub between her legs. I wanted to taste her again, to feel her dig her fingers into my hair because I made her feel so good.

She sat down again, hiding her waist from my sight. "I'll offer you another deal."

I smirked. "You can't stand losing."

"It's not that."

"Whatever you say..."

"It's not."

"Sure." I nodded my head slowly.

"You want to listen to my offer or not?"

"I'm all ears."

"Winner takes all. If I win, you have to do something...sexual to me. If I win...then I do something sexual to you. The victor gets to choose."

It sounded like I won in either case. "Sounds good. I guess I should start brainstorming now."

"I wouldn't waste your time." She shuffled the cards then passed them out.

I glanced at mine and realized I had a good hand. I wouldn't even need to try. Skye stared at her cards for a long time, biting her nails. That was a dead giveaway that she was stressed. I pretended not to notice and swapped my cards. I had two pairs. Not amazing, but I had a feeling it would beat hers. "Ready?" I asked.

"Yeah..." She placed her cards on the table. She had a pair of aces.

I smirked then put mine down.

She sighed when she looked at it.

I held out my hand. "Now the bra..."

She unclasped it in the back then let it fall. The second I saw her nipples, I was practically on the edge of my seat. She pulled it off then threw it at me. "There. Congratulations."

I grabbed the panties off the table and stuffed them into my pocket. I held her bra in the other hand. Completely clothed, I stared at her chest, liking what I saw. I was excited for what was next.

She stood up, showing me a full view. "I'll be in the bedroom." She walked away, her ass shaking.

I adjusted myself in my jeans then followed her. My heart was beating fast and I felt hot all over. The last thing I felt like doing was being a gentleman. Skye drove me wild and I wanted to be inside her.

I walked in and saw her sitting on the bed.

"What do you want to do?" she asked.

"Anything?" I asked.

"Yep." She crossed her legs and stared me down.

I came closer to her, wanting to crush my mouth against hers.

She held me back. "Nope. You have to choose one thing. If it's kissing, that's all you get."

"You have a strict set of rules."

"Yep."

"Have you played this before?" I asked suspiciously.

"Nope. Just you. Now what do you want to do, Cayson?"

We already did other things so I was eager to try something new. But I felt like a jerk for even thinking about saying it. Skye was already sensitive about it and I didn't want to irritate her. But I couldn't deny what I wanted.

"Cayson, spit it out."

I guided her on her back. "I want to kiss you."

She tried not to laugh. "Be real, Cayson. That can't be what's on your mind."

"I love kissing you."

"Come on. What do you really want?"

I said nothing, just staring at her.

"Why won't you tell me?"

"I don't want to make you uncomfortable."

"I wouldn't have made this bet if I were uncomfortable."

I glanced at her chest and looked away.

She caught the look. "You want to tit-fuck me."

Was I that obvious? I didn't respond. She didn't ask me a question so I wasn't obligated to say anything.

"Why are you ashamed to admit that?" She smirked while she ran her fingers through my hair.

"Skye, I know you hate it when men are obsessed with your chest. I don't want to remind you of them."

She cupped my face and kissed me. "You're so sweet, Cayson."

My lips burned the moment I touched hers.

"But that doesn't apply to you."

"It doesn't?"

"No. You're different. I want you to enjoy my body."

"You hated it when Zack did it."

"But I didn't love him," she blurted. "I love you."

My heart fluttered at her words. "I love hearing you say that."

"Well, you better get used to it." She kissed me again, slipping her tongue inside.

I melted at her touch, feeling vindicated for my perverse thoughts. She grabbed my arm then turned me on my back, making me hit the sheets. Then she moved off me, standing at the foot of the bed.

I'd tit-fucked a few girls but I never was excited for it before. Skye was my ultimate fantasy, the woman I used to jerk off to when I was growing up. But my desire never died out.

She unbuttoned my jeans then yanked them off, pulling my briefs with them. She left my socks on and didn't think twice about them before she pulled off my shirt. "I want to see all of you." She kissed my chest then moved down toward my waist. My cock was twitching, yearning for her. When she reached me, she took me into her mouth, shoving me far into the back of her throat.

"Fuck..." Now that she said she was okay with my lustful obsession with her, I was more open about it. I was strongly sexually attracted to her and I wasn't afraid to hide it.

Once I was wet, she kneeled at the bed, her chest level with my waist. Then she wrapped her tits around my cock and pushed them together.

Oh my fucking god.

Then she moved up and down.

I raised myself on my elbows and watched her slide up and down my shaft. I couldn't tell what felt better. Her tits sliding past my cock or watching her do it. She gave me a dark look while she did it, driving me wild. I already wanted to explode. Unable to control myself, I grabbed her tits on either side and smashed them together, thrusting my hips up and down. "Shit, that feels good."

She bounced up and down my dick, keeping her breasts together.

I was about to crumble. She was the most beautiful woman in the world and we were playing out my dirtiest fantasy. I squeezed her tits as I came, moaning as I did it. I squirted on her chest and the area below her chin. I rested my head against the mattress while I recovered from the pleasurable sensation in my groin.

Skye wiped off then climbed up my chest until her face was close to mine. "Did you like that?"

"That's the dumbest question I've ever heard."

She smirked then kissed the hair on my chin. "I'm glad you liked it."

"Shit, I loved it."

"Did Cayson Thompson just curse?" she teased.

I chuckled then rolled her onto her back. Then I showered her breasts with kisses. "I love your rack, Skye. I think it's sexy as hell and I'm not going to hide it anymore. If that makes me a pervert, so be it. I love you for a lot more, but I won't deny how these things get me going."

She ran her fingers through my hair, amusement in her eyes. "That doesn't bother me in the least. You're the only man I've ever wanted to look at them in that way."

"Well, mission accomplished." I gave her a gentle kiss before I slid down her stomach. "Now, how about your turn?"

She fisted my hair. "I thought you'd never ask."

***

"Did you see that play?" Slade put his feet on his coffee table and kept his eyes on the TV. We were watching the game at his place but I wasn't sure why. There were usually women hanging around, used condoms in places where they shouldn't be, and it was usually a mess.

"How do you fumble the ball when you're the quarterback?" I asked.

Slade rolled his eyes. "You would think the pros would have their shit together by now."

I adjusted myself in my seat but felt a lump. Unable to get comfortable, I pulled aside the cushion and looked behind it. A pink bra was lodged inside. "Gross." I pulled it out and tossed it on the floor.

Slade didn't blink an eye over it. "Oh yeah. I remember that one girl was wondering what happened to it."

"Why don't we just watch the game at my place?" Who knows what else was hidden in the crevasses of his couch.

"Because my place is better."

I eyed his closed bedroom door. "There better not be a girl in there." I couldn't count the number of times that happened. They stepped out, totally naked, and didn't even care if I saw.

"No. Calm down."

I settled back into my seat.

"What happened with Skye the other day?" He rested his beer on his thigh.

"Oh..." I hated thinking about it. "Zack cornered her and was giving her a hard time."

Anger moved into his eyes. "Kick his ass?"

"And his ribs...and his face. I got it covered."

"Fucker." Slade clenched his jaw and shook his head. "She's okay, right?"

"She's fine. She didn't seem upset about it—just annoyed."

"What did you guys do this weekend?"

"We stayed at her place and hung out."

"Hung out?" he asked.

"Played poker."

"Are you guys twelve?"

"When you're in a relationship, you do more than have sex all the time."

He shook his head. "That's why I'm going to be a terminal bachelor. So, how's her rack?"

I cocked an eyebrow. "She's your cousin..."

"I'm not asking for a description," he snapped. "Are they as good as everyone makes them out to be?"

"Definitely." I got red in the face from thinking about our last rendezvous.

He grinned then nudged me in the side. "You dog."

I wasn't going to deny it.

"What did you guys do now?"

I didn't see the harm in telling him. "I tit-fucked her."

He raised his hand to give me a high-five. "Man, those are the best. They come in a close second to blow jobs."

"For me, it comes in first."

"Skye gives horrible head?"

"No," I said immediately. "I just...really liked it."

"I tit-fucked this one girl who insisted on it even though she was flat." He shook his ahead. "It was awkward and didn't feel good. So I just fucked her ass instead."

"TMI, Slade."

"What?" He shrugged. "I'm an open guy."

"I've noticed."

"You've done anal, right?"

"Not with Skye."

"I'm sure that will be fun." He wiggled his eyebrows.

Slade was all about getting to home base. He lacked the understanding that running around the bases was the best part. Cultivating a relationship and adoring your partner made it a million times better. I hadn't had sex with Skye yet, but everything we'd done up to that point was way better than anything I ever did with someone else. "Slade, when is this going to end?"

"At seven. The Simpsons come on after that."

"No, I meant your lifestyle. This can't be as satisfying as you claim."

"But it is." He stared at the game while he said it, half listening to me.

For as long as I'd known Slade, he never had a girlfriend. He didn't even have a junior high love. Ever since he hit puberty, all he cared about was getting girls in the sack. "It's going to get old after awhile."

"Maybe when I'm forty. Then I'll reconsider some stuff. Until then, I'm very happy with my life."

"Don't you want someone that you like to be around for longer than five minutes?"

"Five minutes?" He raised an eyebrow. "Sorry, man. If you only last five minutes, I feel bad for Skye."

I gave him a hard look. "Slade, I'm being serious."

He sighed then put down his beer. "Look, it's cool that you've finally found the one girl you can settle down with. But aren't you forgetting all the years before this? How many girls did you sleep with that meant nothing to you? How many one night stands did you have?"

"Not nearly as many as you. And I was depressed the entire time."

"You enjoyed it and you know you did."

"At the time, yes. But I was definitely lonely."

"This is how it is." He talked with his hands, which he usually did when he was being serious. "You're the type of guy who's going to be rich and successful. And not just any rich, but respectable rich. You're going to be loved by your community. Everyone already adores you as it is. You'll have a wife with a house and a picket fence. You'll pop out three kids and save money for their tuitions. That's you, Cayson. Not me. I can't see any of that happening for me."

"And what do you see, Slade?"

He thought for a moment. "Living out of a bag. Inking in different parts of the world. Playing in a band for a few tours. Getting so drunk in a country I don't recognize that I can't even tell where I am. Picking up girls in various places. Just living my life."

"What about when you turn thirty? Then forty? What will you have then?"

"Why would anything change?"

"Not a lot of chicks dig old guys."

"That's not old. And I'm good-looking. You should see my dad at the shop. The girls still throw themselves at him. I'm surprised he doesn't cheat on my mom. She's so annoying that I wouldn't blame him." He laughed then drank his beer.

"I know you don't mean that."

He didn't comment.

"You're one of the greatest guys I know and I just want...the best for you." Awkwardness filled the room. I stared at the TV, feeling the tension. I wasn't an emotional guy and neither was Slade. All we did was joke around and never took anything seriously.

Slade was quiet. The silence stretched for so long that I didn't think he would say anything at all. "I know, man. I want the same for you too."

"Just think about what I said, alright?"

He shrugged. "I might."

We returned our attention back to the TV. The game continued on until it ended at seven. A rerun of the Simpsons came on.

"I love this show," Slade said.

"Me too." I put my empty beer bottle on the coffee table. "I guess I'll see you later."

"'Ight. Tell Skye I said hi."

I stared at him.

"Like you aren't going over there," he teased.

I didn't see the point in denying it. "It was nice coming over here without a naked chick walking around."

"That's a sentence no man should ever say."

I chuckled. "And make sure you throw that bra away."

"I'll probably rub one out on it."

I cringed. "TMI, Slade."

The door to his bedroom suddenly opened. A blonde with a sheet wrapped around her body came out with her eyes squinted. "Where am I?"

I glared at Slade. "I thought you said there wasn't a girl in there?"

He grinned. "Wait for it..."

Then another blonde appeared. "Please tell me you have aspirin and a beer."

Slade stood up then squeezed my shoulder. "I said there wasn't a girl in there—not *girls.*"

Chapter Twenty-Five

Skye

Trinity sat across from me in the library.

"How's your dad?" I asked.

"Good. Pretty much the same."

"Did you go to the same diner?"

"Always," Trinity said with a smile. "I told him I want to do fashion instead."

My heart stopped. "Seriously?"

She nodded.

"What did he say?"

"He supports it. He says I should do whatever I want to do. He gave grandpa the bird when he became an adult and I should do the same."

"That's really cool. So what now?"

She shrugged. "He said he wants me to think about it first. I mean, I'm almost done with college. It would be a waste to just drop out now."

"Did he say that?"

"No, but I know he's thinking it. He offered to get me in contact with designers in the city. And he even offered to fund my own clothing line."

"Uncle Mike is a good guy," I said. "I knew he would be supportive."

"He said the doors are always open if I want to change my mind. I guess it's not a big deal."

I smiled then patted her on the hand. "I'm excited for you. I know how much you want this."

"Thanks...I feel better about it now that I got it off my chest."

"Did you...get anything else off your chest?" I asked hesitantly.

"No," she said immediately. "I would never tell him that."

"A wise decision," I said with a laugh.

She closed her textbook and rested her chin on her hand. "How's it going with Cayson?"

I felt my cheeks lift with a smile. "Absolutely amazing and fantastic."

She smirked. "I can tell. How's he in bed?"

"I don't know yet."

She rolled her eyes. "Fuck his brains out already."

"I know. I want to."

"Then do it."

"I just don't want to rush anything. And he's good at everything else so I'm okay."

"How's he look down below?" she asked with a mischievous grin.

"Trinity!" I swatted her hand.

"What? It was just a question."

My cheeks blushed.

"He's big, huh?"

I covered my face because I was beet red.

"Bigger than Zack?"

"Much, much bigger."

"Oooh...lucky you."

I tried not to giggle. "He's definitely a lot to take in..."

"Did you gag when you went down on him?"

"I'm only answering your questions because you're my best friend."

"You think I'd ask you this if I weren't your best friend?"

She had a good point. "No. But I don't put the whole thing in there."

She rubbed her chin. "Maybe I should have gone for Cayson first..."

"Hey, he's mine."

She laughed. "Whoa...I'll back off."

"You better."

"But I can tell you won't be able to handle him at your back entrance."

I scanned the tables around us, making sure no one heard. "Shh!"

"I'm just saying...if you've never done it before, trying it out with a huge dick isn't the best idea."

"Okay...enough of this conversation."

"I haven't had sex in forever... I miss it."

That surprised me. "Trinity, you're gorgeous. Just go pick up some guy."

She shrugged. "I haven't really found anyone worth my time."

"Maybe you haven't looked hard enough."

"I've been to all the parties. Believe me, I've seen everyone," she said.

"Maybe you're looking in the wrong place," I said. "A party isn't the best location. Maybe you should try an online dating site."

"Is that a joke?" she snapped. "I'm not doing that. Only weird serial killers do that."

"It was just a suggestion." I backed off.

"Why can't Cayson have a brother?" she demanded.

"How about Theo? He's cute."

She shook her head. "No chemistry."

"Well, you have a lot of chemistry with Slade. Every time you're around him it's like the bomb dropping on Hiroshima."

"Don't even get me started with him. He makes my head want to explode."

"I think that's a universal feeling," I said with a laugh.

Cayson and Slade entered the library and headed for our table.

"Ugh. Just looking at him makes me want to hit him in the face." Trinity rolled her eyes.

"I hope you're talking about Slade."

"Obviously, I'm not talking about your boyfriend and his huge dick."

My eyes widened. "Shh!"

The guys reached our table just as I finished hushing her.

"Hey, baby." Cayson leaned down and kissed me.

"Hey." My spine shivered as soon as I inhaled his scent. His powerful arms made me feel safe, and I couldn't stop picturing him naked. It was such a beautiful image.

He sat beside me then kept his arm over the back of my chair. "Hey, Trin."

"Hey, Cayson." She batted her eyelashes at him then waved.

I kicked her under the table.

She giggled then looked away.

Slade sat next to her. "Let me clear the air right now." He pulled out a sandwich from his bag. "This is my lunch. And I'm going to eat it—right here and right now. I suggest you keep your trap closed if you don't want to pick up my trash."

Trinity took a deep breath, controlling her anger, and then said nothing.

"Good, she finally gets it." Slade bit into his sandwich.

I needed to change the subject. "How was the game last night?"

"Good," Cayson said. "Slade won five hundred bucks."

"Online sport betting. It's pretty awesome." Slade kept eating.

"Do you gamble too?" I asked him.

Cayson shook his head. "Not my thing. Besides, I got to take out my girlfriend."

"You know we can trade off paying."

He laughed. "That's a good one, baby." He rubbed the back of my neck while he continued to laugh.

Trinity shrugged, not bothering to say anything.

Slade finished his sandwich then crumpled his trash into a ball. "Zack hasn't been bothering you, right?"

Of course Cayson told him. "No. If he does, I'll handle him."

"No." Cayson's voice was cold. "I'll take care of it."

I didn't want to challenge him in front of our friends so I said nothing.

"I hear through the grapevine that your tits are great for fucking," Slade blurted.

Cayson flinched beside me, clearly not expecting him to say that.

I guess I wasn't surprised Cayson told Slade what happened. They were best friends. I told Trinity everything.

"Personally, I like big tits but they got to be proportional." He rolled the ball of trash between his hands on the desk.

Cayson cleared his throat. "Thanks for that info." The irritation was clear in his voice.

"No problem." Slade obviously hadn't caught on to the tension.

Cayson turned toward me like he might say something but then he changed his mind.

Trinity caught the interaction. "Skye just told me Cayson's dick is huge so now you're even."

Slade's eyes widened. "Um...gross."

I glared at her viciously. "You're the worst secret-keeper ever."

"Hey, I just saved you guys from your first fight," Trinity said. "You're welcome."

Cayson smirked at me. "You like my package?"

I hoped my face wasn't red. "Why wouldn't I?"

He chuckled then kissed my cheek. "And yes, I do like your rack—a lot."

"How romantic," Slade said sarcastically.

"I'll be right back." Trinity stood up and walked to the rear of the library in my line of sight.

Slade stared straight ahead, still playing with his foil. Crumbs from his sandwich scattered across the table. Pieces of lettuce and tomato were sprinkled everywhere.

Cayson leaned in and pressed a gentle kiss to my neck. "I love kissing you there." His lips were near my ear, his voice coming out as a whisper.

"I like it too."

"I'll do it a lot more—tonight."

That reminded me of something. "My parents are coming to town tonight and want to have dinner. I'm sorry. I totally forgot to tell you."

"As in, I'm included?" he asked.

"Yeah."

Slade smirked. "Oh no. Cayson is officially meeting the parents."

"I already know them, idiot," Cayson said.

"As her friend—not her boyfriend." Slade winked. "Good luck with that."

I rolled my eyes. "My parents already love you, Cayson. They just want to spend some time with us."

"I would love to go," he said. "A little further notice would have been appreciated…but of course I'll be there."

"We can fool around later."

"Yippie."

"And you can tit-fuck me since you like it so much." I gave him a seductive grin.

His eyes darkened in desire.

"Gross…I can hear you," Slade snapped.

"Then don't listen," Cayson said.

"It's kinda hard when I'm a foot away from you," Slade said sarcastically.

Trinity came back to the table but she wasn't alone.

"No eating in the library!" The librarian shrieked then pointed at the mess Slade made. He was caught red-handed, the trash balled up in his hands.

"Oh shit," he whispered.

"You're going to clean this up right now and you're going to serve one hour of clean up as punishment." She put her hands on her hips and glared at him.

"Can you even do that?" Slade snapped. "This isn't kindergarten."

"You bet your ass I can," she hissed. "Do you want me to call the dean and double check?"

I tried not to laugh. This was hilarious.

"Do it," Slade said. "Like I care."

"Then I'll call your mother."

That changed Slade's attitude immediately. Aunt Janice wasn't someone that just let things slide. She was strict and controlling, definitely the alpha of the house. She even kept her husband in check. "Fine. I'll do it."

"I'll see you when the library closes." She stormed off, her anger obvious in the movement of her limbs.

Slade gave Trinity the most hateful stare I've ever seen. "You fucking—"

"Payback's a bitch, huh?" She put her bag over her shoulder and strutted off, her nose held high.

Cayson and I tried not to laugh. Hearing them constantly bicker and argue was annoying, but moments like these reminded me why I put up with it.

***

Cayson arrived at my door wearing a suit.

I stared at his broad shoulders and long legs. His blue eyes stood out against the dark colors, and his chin was cleanly shaved. "Wow...you look yummy."

He smirked. "I was going to say the same thing about you." He stepped inside then moved his hands around my waist, gripping me. He kissed me long and hard. His hands moved downward to my ass. Then he squeezed it. Cayson had been a lot more forward in our relationship since I made it clear it was okay. Now he was aggressive and forward, just the way I liked. "I like this dress."

I wore a champagne pink dress that was tight on my body. This color looked good on my fair skin so I tried to wear it whenever I got a chance. A gold bracelet was around my wrist and it matched my earrings.

Cayson took a long look at me. "You look so lovely." His hand tucked a loose strand behind my ear.

My face flushed. "Thanks."

He moved closer then placed a gentle kiss on my neck, making me hot. "I could eat you," he whispered.

"Please do."

When he pulled away, his eyes were dark. "I'd love to. But it'll have to wait, unfortunately. I couldn't look your father in the eye if I saw him right after...doing that."

I smirked. "That would be awkward, wouldn't it?"

"Slightly." He reached into his pocket and pulled out a thong. "I forgot to return these the other day."

I snatched them away then tossed them in my room. "You're such a pervert."

"What? I like your underwear."

"Exactly something a pervert would say."

He shrugged. "I guess I am—at least for you."

"As long as it's only for me, I'm okay with that."

"Definitely only for you." He came to me again then pulled me against his chest. He looked down at me, his eyes lingering on my lips. "Every day feels like a dream. I just can't believe when I look at you, you're looking back at me. I can't believe this is real, that these lips are only mine to enjoy." His thumb moved across my lower lip, making my breath hitch.

Cayson was sexy without even trying. "You're confused. I'm the lucky one out of the two of us. Every girl knows it. And I'll never forget it."

His eyes twinkled in amusement. "You couldn't be more wrong, Skye. But there aren't enough hours in the day to argue with you." He leaned in and kissed me, his lips conveying everything his voice didn't. He gripped my lower back, crinkling my dress, and deepened the kiss. I wanted to drag him into my bedroom so the kiss would escalate but I knew that wasn't the best idea.

A knock sounded on the door.

Cayson pulled away, reluctantly.

"That would be my parents."

He stepped away and put his hands in his pockets.

"You don't have to not touch me just because they're around."

He sighed. "This is going to take me a while to get used to. Your father will watch me like a hawk, with the eyes in the back of his head and the cameras he has everywhere."

"That's so creepy it's not even funny." I walked to the door and opened it.

My mom was wearing a dark blue dress with matching heels. Her wedding ring sparkled in the light, and her bracelet did the same. "Hey, honey. You look beautiful."

"Thanks, Mom. You do too." I hugged her tightly. Even when I was happy, she somehow made me happier.

My dad stepped inside, wearing a black suit just like all his others. Each one was created by the top designers in the world and not a single wrinkle existed in the fabric. A Rolex shined from his wrist, and his wedding band was still in place, the one he never removed. "Hey, pumpkin." He pulled me in for a long embrace. "You look lovely—as always."

"Thanks, Dad. You look stiff—as always."

He laughed then pulled away. He studied my face for a moment. "It's nice to see you smile."

"I always smile."

"But not quite like this." He gave me a knowing look then walked to Cayson.

"Hello, sir. How are you?" Cayson stuck out his hand to shake my father's.

My dad smirked. "Just because you're dating my daughter doesn't mean you have to behave differently around me. Loosen up." He patted his shoulder then pulled him in for a hug. "You're a son to me, Cayson."

"Thanks, Uncle Sean." He patted his back then stepped away.

"Cayson." My mom opened her arms and hugged him. "You're more handsome every time I see you."

"Thank you, Aunt Scarlet."

"You look so much like your father." She pulled away and stared at his face. "It's remarkable."

"I'm not sure if that's an insult," he said with a laugh.

"It is," my dad said.

My mom glared at my dad then turned back to Cayson. "It's a very, very big compliment."

My dad gave her a hard look. "Don't forget the man you married..."

"The most handsome man in the world. Yes, dear. I know." She came to his side and hooked her arm through his. "Like you would let me forget."

"I remind you every night." He gave her a dark look.

"Okay...let's go before I throw up." I headed for the door.

Cayson opened it for me then walked out behind me.

"They're gross, huh?" I whispered.

He shrugged. "I think it's cute."

"Of course you would. You're brown-nosing."

"Am not," he argued. He put his arm around my waist and walked with me to the car.

My mom's car was in the driveway. Cayson opened the backseat for me to get inside then he sat beside me. My parents joined us.

"How about French?" my father asked from the front seat.

"Sounds good to me," Cayson said.

"I eat anything," I said.

"I know that too well," my dad said. "And my wife will eat anything, even if it's been expired for a few days."

My mom shrugged. "I don't like to waste food."

"Menton's?" my dad asked. It was a restaurant we went to a few times in Boston.

"Let's do it," I said.

He put the address in the GPS then eyed my mom's safety belt, making sure it was on. Then he looked in the rearview mirror. "Everyone buckled in?"

"Yes," I said. "But we aren't five."

"Sometimes you act like it so I have to double check," my dad said.

Cayson chuckled.

"Don't laugh at him," I whispered. "You'll just egg him on."

"He's going to tease you either way." He rested his hand on my thigh then looked out the window.

My dad drove to the restaurant, holding my mom's hand the entire time. They were so affectionate that I didn't even notice it anymore. If my dad needed both hands for the wheel, my mom rested her hand on his thigh.

When we arrived at the restaurant, the valet took the car then we walked inside.

"Reservation?" the host asked.

"No," my dad said. "But I have a party of four—for Preston."

The guy studied my dad's face and seemed to recognize him and his name. "Right this way, sir."

Cayson leaned toward my ear. "See that—power."

"No. The guy just knows my dad is loaded," I whispered.

"Same thing." He kept his hand around my waist as we walked to the table. Like always, Cayson pulled out the chair for me and let me sit down first. My dad did the same for my mother. I noticed my dad glanced at Cayson, watching him. But he didn't say anything.

My dad grabbed the wine list. "How about a bottle for the table?"

"Sure." My mom sat with perfect posture and looked like a queen.

"What are you in the mood for, baby?" my father asked.

"Anything. You have better taste than I do," she said.

"That's debatable..." He scanned the list then put it down. "Chardonnay it is." His hand moved to her thigh.

Cayson rested his ankle on his knee and placed his hand on my thigh, acting normal.

My father turned his look on Cayson. "How's school?"

"The same," he responded. "But I'm just eager to be done at this point."

"You're almost there," my mom said. "Don't get senioritis."

"I'll try," Cayson said with a laugh. "I have a few interviews coming up for medical school. I'm a little nervous."

"Congratulations," my father said with a nod. "I'm sure you'll do well."

He had interviews? He didn't mention that to me. I decided to bring it up later.

Humble as always, Cayson didn't say anything else.

My dad noticed his arms. "Your arms look like trees. Are you hitting the gym as often as you're studying?" Amusement was in his voice.

"It's the one thing Slade and I can do together that doesn't get us in trouble," he said with a smirk.

My mom laughed. "Slade is something else, but he has so much life in him—just like his father."

"I like Slade too," my dad said.

"You mean you love him," my mom pressed.

"Obviously, baby." He rolled his eyes. "I'm just glad Roland isn't so extreme."

"Why didn't you invite Roland?" I asked.

"Of course we did," my mom said immediately. "He said he had to study."

"And he didn't want to," my dad started to use air quotes, "attend our lame tea party double date."

I smirked. "That sounds like Roland."

"Has he been staying out of trouble?" my father asked.

"Even if he wasn't, I wouldn't tell you," I said.

My dad nodded. "Sounds about right."

The waitress came over and took our order. My dad ordered for both himself and my mom.

"What are you getting, baby?" Cayson asked.

"The French brie," I said.

"Okay." He took our menus and put them to the side. Then he ordered for both of us.

This was the first time I ever went out with my parents and my boyfriend at the same time. And it was really nice. My dad was calm and normal. He wasn't watching Cayson's every move. It was clear he loved Cayson, and not just because he had to. He genuinely loved him—especially for me. My mom felt the same way. It was something I never expected to happen.

"So, is my daughter driving you crazy yet?" my dad asked Cayson.

"No, surprisingly," Cayson answered.

I hit his arm playfully. "I would never drive you crazy."

"You drive my wallet crazy with how much you eat," Cayson said.

I rolled my eyes. "I don't eat that much."

Cayson chuckled. "Sure, baby."

My mom smiled while she watched us together. "How did this happen? How did you two get together?"

Cayson and I looked at each other, unsure who should tell the story.

Cayson took the lead. "Well...I've had a thing for Skye for a very long time."

"You fooled us," my mom said.

"Good," Cayson said with a laugh. "That's what I was going for. Anyway, I kept hoping something would happen between us, but it was pretty clear Skye didn't feel the same way about me. So I moved on..."

Then I took over. "When I saw him with Jasmine at Thanksgiving it just hit me. I missed him and I couldn't stop thinking about him. Everyone kept telling me he was in love with me but I never listened...I should have. And, well, you guys influenced it too. I want what you guys have, and...Cayson is my best friend."

My dad nodded his head in approval. "I'm glad it didn't take you ten years like it did with your mother and I."

"Me too," I said with a smile.

Cayson gave me a playful look then rubbed his nose against mine.

The waiter returned with the dishes and wine. We immediately dug in. I was starving so I practically inhaled my food.

Cayson smirked while he watched me.

"What?" I said.

He used his napkin to wipe my chin. "I always know when you're really hungry because you get food all over your face."

"Whoops." I shrugged and kept eating.

Cayson ate with perfect manners and acted like himself. "How's work, Uncle Sean?"

"A big snooze fest," my dad said. "Nothing worth mentioning."

"I'm so excited to work there..." I said sarcastically.

My dad sipped his wine then smirked. "Well, I've been working there for twenty years. It gets old after a while. Plus, it keeps me away from your mother."

"Don't you get tired of her anyway?" I asked.

"Do you get tired of Cayson?" my dad countered.

No...definitely not.

My dad drank his wine again. "Your mom comes to work with me sometimes but I never get anything done that way..."

"TMI, Dad." I cut into my food and kept eating.

"Your father tends to share too much sometimes." My mom gave my dad a flirtatious smile.

"When you have a hot wife, it's hard to resist her," my dad said, wiping his lip with a napkin.

Cayson looked at me. "I hope you don't distract me at work or I might kill someone."

Did he mean if we were married? "Just make sure I'm fed and that won't be a problem."

My mom looked at me. "How's Trinity?"

"She's good," I said. "She wants to go into fashion."

"That's what your uncle Mike was telling us." She sipped her wine.

"I'm happy for her," my dad said. "Life is too short to live someone else's dream."

"Did you work for the company right after college?" I asked.

"No. I worked for a stockbroker for a few years then I worked for a recycling company. Then I took over the company with Uncle Mike."

"Did Uncle Mike do anything else first?" Cayson asked.

"He worked on Wall Street," my dad answered.

My mom rolled her eyes. "The Preston boys are very accomplished."

"So are the Siscos," my dad countered, mentioning my mother's maiden name, the one Uncle Ryan shared.

"Is Slade still intent on being a tattoo artist?" my mom asked.

Cayson nodded his head immediately. "I don't think he'll ever change his mind. He's not very interested in school."

My mom shrugged. "I told my brother to let his son make his own decisions but he didn't take my advice."

"He just wants to make sure Slade keeps his options open," my dad said. "You can't blame him for that."

"Of course not," my mom said. "How's Clementine?" she asked Cayson.

"Good. We don't talk much during the school year, but I think she's good," Cayson said. "She's still a violinist with the New York Symphony as far as I know."

"She's very talented," my dad said. "Every time I tried to get Roland to learn to play the violin, he kept trying to play it like a guitar." He rolled his eyes.

I laughed, recalling the memory.

"Maybe our son is destined to be a rock star," my mom said.

"He would give his grandmother a heart attack," my dad said.

"But Grandpa would be on the tour bus," Cayson said.

I laughed, thinking about Grandpa as a roadie. "I can see it."

"So can I," my mom said with a laugh.

I wiped my plate clean then pushed it away. "I'm stuffed."

"It's a miracle," Cayson teased.

I hit his arm again. "Don't make fun of me."

"Baby, I'll always make fun of you. Sorry." He winked at me.

"Good," my dad said. "I want her to have a man who treats her like a princess but keeps her down to earth at the same time."

"Then I'm your man," Cayson said.

"I can tell," my dad said.

The waiter came over with the tab.

Cayson immediately grabbed it then slipped his credit card inside. "Dinner is on me."

"I don't think so, Cay." My dad snatched it away then switched their cards.

My mom rolled her eyes. "Here we go..."

"Then at least let me pay for Skye's dinner as well as mine," Cayson said.

"No." My dad handed the waiter the tab. "We're done with this."

"Of course, sir." The waiter walked away.

Cayson sighed in defeat.

"I'm sure feeding my daughter is already enough of a financial burden," my dad said with a smile.

"Why is everyone picking on me tonight?" I asked.

"You're an easy target," Cayson said. He turned back to my dad. "Well, thank you for dinner, Uncle Sean."

"You're very welcome, Cayson," my dad said gracefully.

The waiter returned with the receipt then we headed back to my apartment. The drive home was spent in silence. Since I was full and warm, I was sleepy. I leaned my head on Cayson's shoulder while he held my hand. Whenever I opened my eyes, I caught my dad glancing at us in the rearview mirror.

When we arrived at my apartment, my parents got out and hugged me.

"Until next time," my mom said. She never said goodbye. She always made her departure as easy as possible. I've always clung to her since I could remember and it was hard to let her go.

"Okay, Mom. I love you."

"I love you too, honey." She kissed my forehead before she pulled away.

My father hugged me hard. "I hate saying goodbye."

"I do too."

"I love you so much, pumpkin. I miss you every day."

"I miss you too."

He continued to hug me. "I could stand here all night..." He finally dropped his embrace. "Call me if you need anything."

"I know, Dad."

He hugged Cayson before he headed back to the car.

Cayson put his arm around my waist, and together, we watched my parents drive away.

When their taillights were gone, I felt sadness in my chest. "Do you feel sad when you say goodbye to your parents?"

He kissed my forehead. "I do."

"Good...it's not just me."

"Of course not."

"Cayson, can I ask you for a favor?"

"Anything, baby."

"When we settle down...can we live in Connecticut?"

He dropped his arm and looked at me with emotion in his eyes. He said nothing for a long time, just staring at me. His blue eyes faded to gray slightly, and the depth of his eyes seemed to travel indefinitely. He cupped my face then brushed his thumb over my cheek. "Of course."

Chapter Twenty-Six

Slade

If I didn't refuse to hit girls, I'd slap the shit out of Trinity.

I spent an hour cleaning the library with the librarian watching me. There was dust everywhere and I had to empty the garbage cans. It wasn't flattering work and I clenched my jaw the entire time. I couldn't believe Trinity threw me under the bus like that. She got me good.

Cayson texted me as soon as I stepped out of the building. *Roland is having everyone over for poker.*

I could use some relaxation. When?

In an hour.

K. I'll be there.

I went home and showered, getting the grime and garbage off my hands, before I changed and walked to Roland's apartment a few blocks over. Normally, I would have driven since it was freezing cold but I planned on drinking. Driving wasn't a good idea.

I walked inside without knocking and placed the six-pack on the counter. "Blue Moon— the good stuff."

"Good." Roland grabbed it and shoved the beers into the refrigerator.

A circular poker table was set in the center of the room along with chips and cards. I grabbed a beer then sat down.

Conrad sat across from me. "How's the janitor life?" He had a smirk on his lips.

"Fuck you," I snapped.

"Did you have to clean the toilets too?" Roland sat down then shuffled the cards.

"I'm about to shove this bottle up your ass." I pointed my beer at him.

Roland laughed. "I wish I could have gotten a picture of that."

I sighed then sipped my beer, wishing no one knew about my afternoon cleaning the library.

"Slade in all his glory..." Conrad chuckled. "I'm sure the girls would have loved that."

"I can still land more pussy than you," I snapped. "Whether I'm cleaning the library or not."

"Whatever, man," Conrad said. "My sister got you good."

"Brat," I mumbled.

The door opened and Skye and Cayson walked inside, holding hands.

"I thought this was a guy's night?" I demanded.

Roland shrugged. "Skye is pretty good at poker."

"Not as good as Cayson." Skye gave Cayson a flirtatious look.

Roland ignored her words. "Anyway...it's more money in the pot."

I decided not to argue. Skye was already there.

Cayson sat beside me with Skye on his other side. He grabbed her a beer and a plate of pretzels, waiting on her hand and foot.

I rolled my eyes but didn't comment. "Let's get this game started."

The door opened again and my sister walked inside. "Hey, janitor."

You've got to be kidding me...

She held out a broom. "I got this for you. I figured you'd appreciate it."

Everyone laughed.

"I'm about to shove it through your gut," I threatened.

She laughed then leaned the broom against the wall. "My brother is the messiest guy I know. Who knew he would be a professional cleaner."

"Look, I just tidied up the library for like an hour," I said. "Let's move on."

"Slade can dish it out but he can't take it." Roland laughed then sipped his beer.

"Just shut up, alright?" I peeled the paper off my bottle because I didn't know what else to do.

"Mom and Dad will be so proud," Silke said.

"That I killed you?" I snapped.

She messed up my hair with her hand then sat on the couch. "Whatever, Brother."

I flattened my hair then leaned back in my chair. "If we're done with that, let's—"

Trinity walked through the door. "I brought Heineken."

Son of a bitch.

She put the six-pack down then gave me a smirk. "I was wondering why it smelled like garbage in here. Just got off work?"

Everyone laughed.

I glared at her, wanting to pull out that pretty blonde hair.

Cayson seemed to know I reached my limit. "Okay, guys. He's had enough. Just drop it."

Trinity sat across from me, a gloating smile on her face.

I gave her another threatening glare before I dropped it.

"Let's get this game started." Roland passed out the cards. After everyone scanned their hands, they tossed their chips in. I did the same.

Trinity kept watching me, a victorious look on her face.

She was going down.

We put all our cards down, and Conrad was the winner of the hand.

"Looks like I'm going to run you guys dry tonight." Conrad pulled the pile toward him.

"It's just the first round, man." Roland dealt the cards again.

Trinity finished her first beer and moved onto her second one like she was drinking water.

"Did you not learn anything?" I snapped.

She understood my meaning. She lifted up her bottle. "Sealed bottle. And I don't think anyone here has any interest in raping me."

Roland shook his head immediately. "Definitely not."

I downed my beer then grabbed a second one.

"Slade is just insecure that I can best him in every way possible," Trinity said. "If it's not in intelligence, it's in drinking."

I tightened my grip on my bottle. "No one can match me." I chugged the bottle in seconds then left the empty glass on the table.

She did the same. "That was easy."

"At least they'll be easy to beat in the game," Roland said.

We played a few more rounds. Cayson won a few times then I took the pot. Trinity surprised everyone with a full house and we all took a huge hit. I kept drinking and she kept up with me.

She poured herself a seven and seven. Then she downed it without blinking an eye.

"Beer then liquor, never been sicker. Liquor then beer, have no fear." I stared her down, putting her on the spot.

She poured another. "If you can't handle it, that's fine. I know you probably have to work tomorrow scrubbing some toilets."

God, she was a bitch. I made myself a brandy. "Go to hell, Trinity."

We finished the poker game then settled down on the couch to watch TV. Roland and Conrad were still drinking beer. Skye hadn't had another since her first one, and Cayson stopped after his second beer. Trinity and I, however, were fighting to the death.

She had another seven and seven. Her eyes were heavy and she seemed a little tired. Her words were slurred, but she seemed fine in every other way. I was already drunk and wasn't hiding it very well. I tried to play it cool but it was becoming more difficult.

Conrad snatched a glass out of Trinity's hand. "I'm cutting you off."

"I'm cutting *you* off." She tried to hit his arm and missed. Instead she hit Skye's thigh.

"Yeah...she's drunk." Conrad returned the empty glass to the kitchen.

"You've had enough, Slade." Cayson took my glass away.

"Come on," I snapped. "Don't be a girl."

"Too bad." Cayson took the liquor away.

I lay back on the couch then turned to Roland. "You have a weird ass name."

He was buzzed too. "What kind of name is Slade? It's like blade but not really..."

"But Roland sounds...stupid."

"You're stupid."

"And don't get me started on Conrad," I said. "He sounds like a park ranger."

"What kind of name is Skye?" Roland said. "It makes my parents sound like hippies."

"Because they are," I said.

Silke sat on the other couch and quickly fell asleep. She couldn't hold her liquor like the rest of us.

"Cayson, let's go home and have sex," Skye blurted.

Cayson did a double take.

"Gross!" Roland said. He covered his eyes. "I don't want to listen to that."

Conrad moved his hands to his ears. "There you go."

Cayson's face flushed red. "All it takes is three beers and a whiskey, huh?"

"Come on," Skye said. "Why haven't we done it yet? Your dick is huge!"

Cayson's face was beet red.

"Just go do it," Trinity said with slurred words. "Ride him like there's no tomorrow."

"You're right, Trin," Skye said while laughing. "You're right about everything."

"I know." Trinity gave a victorious smile. Her cheeks were reddening from the alcohol.

Cayson was thoroughly embarrassed. "Baby, it's time for us to go home."

"What? It's just getting fun." Skye pouted.

"Come on." He pulled her up and hooked one arm around her waist. "Say goodnight."

"Nighty-night." She waved then laughed.

Once they were gone, Conrad put his feet on the couch. "Dude, these couches are so comfy."

"I know," Roland said. "And they are perfect for fucking."

"Eww." Conrad cringed then rolled onto the hardwood floor. Then he laughed. "Shit, the ground is hard."

Silke started to snore.

"You guys are lame." Trinity flipped her hair then stood up. "I'm heading home."

"You aren't driving," Conrad blurted. He tried to get up but he fell again.

"I walked, idiot." She marched to the door.

My mind was becoming hazy. I had a strong urge to sleep but I didn't want to sleep there, on the couches Roland did god knows what on. "I'm out of here too."

"Good," Conrad said. "Walk with my sister."

"I don't give a shit about your sister." I walked out and slammed the door a lot harder than I meant to.

I tightened my jacket around me then headed down the stairs. It was cold and icy outside. Piles of snow were on the ground everywhere. I loved the winter even though I preferred the summer. Girls wore short dresses with flowers in their hair. It was easy to tell who had rocking bodies and who didn't. And girls were always a little heavier during the holidays.

When I turned the corner, I saw Trinity picking up her phone from the ground. "Damn it." She wiped it off on her coat.

I laughed, watching her wipe the snow from her screen.

She looked up when she heard my voice. "Following me?"

"Why would I follow you? I'd prefer to run from you."

She checked her phone and the screen lit up. "Phew, it's not broken."

"Phew, I don't care." I walked down the path through the trees.

Trinity came up behind me and caught up to me.

"Why are you walking with me?" I snapped.

"I live this way, jackass."

I shook my head and kept my hands in my pockets. "Of all the people in the world, I can stand you the least. I can't believe you threw me under the bus like that!"

"You did it to me first! The librarian thought it was me and you never told her otherwise. Coward." She gave me a look of disgust.

"But I didn't tattle on you like a four-year-old."

"You act like a four-year-old."

"You look like a four-year-old."

She hit my arm. "So, you like to fuck four-year-olds?"

"Excuse me?" I hissed. I stopped in my tracks.

"Don't act like you don't stare at me. I've caught you so many times."

"Because you were parading around my room in a bra and thong. If you were a fat ugly cow, I still would have looked."

"Whatever." She crossed her arms over her chest and kept walking. "You have the hots for me and I know it."

I laughed because it was so absurd. "You sure think highly of yourself, don't you?"

"I know you do."

"Fuck no. I hate you. I absolutely despise you."

"Then why did you save me?" she demanded. "You could have looked the other way, picked up some girl, and went on with your life. If you despise me so much, are so indifferent toward me, you wouldn't have done a damn thing."

God, I wanted to slap her. "I would have done it for any girl. Men who take advantage of women like that should be killed."

She kept walking, keeping her jacket close around her. "All you ever do is treat me like shit. I'm sick of it. And when I stand up for myself, you throw a hissy fit like a damn girl."

"I don't treat you like shit," I argued. "I treat everyone exactly the same way. I'm not sure why you think you're special. Because, Princess, you aren't."

"Shut up, Slade."

We reached my apartment building. "Thank god."

"You aren't going to walk me home? Or invite me inside?"

"Why the hell would I do that? You walked all this way. You can make it the rest of the way." I moved to the side of the building and headed to the staircase.

She came up behind me and pushed me. "What is your problem? You act like you care about me one second then you're a dick a second later."

I stumbled forward then caught myself by my hands. The road was freezing cold. I got back to my feet and wiped my palms on my jeans. "Don't push me!"

She used all her strength and pushed me again. "It wouldn't kill you to just try and be nice to me. I'm never going to go away. We can be frenemies for the rest of time, or you can actually try to be my friend."

I stumbled back, disoriented from the alcohol and the cold. I stopped myself from falling but I couldn't stop my rage. Unable to control myself, I shoved her into the wall, making her back collide with the wood. "Push me again and I'll break your neck." I gripped her wrists then pinned them against the wall. "Got it?"

She breathed hard, staring into my face. The snow was falling lightly around us. I didn't know what time it was, but judging by the temperature and lack of people, I would guess it was past midnight. She stared into my eyes, her chest rising and falling with every full breath she took. Her blonde hair framed her face, and the dark green eye shadow around her eyes made them look big and beautiful. Black eyeliner marked the edges, making them pop. Her lips were ruby red despite the cold. Her pale skin was a reflection of the winter bite. It was fair and light, reminding me of a snowflake.

I didn't know what the hell was going on. The alcohol made me confused and bipolar. One moment, I wanted to rip her throat out, and the next, I wanted to feel her warm breath in my mouth. She stared at me then looked at my lips, thinking the same thing.

At exactly the same moment, she crushed her mouth against mine while I ravaged hers.

My mouth aggressively took hers. I caressed her, tasting her. Her lips reciprocated, brushing past mine before her tongue slipped into my mouth, lightly touching mine. I crushed my body against hers, feeling her chest push against me.

Her hands moved into my hair, messing up the strands. Then she moved under my shirt and felt the muscles of my back. Her hands were cold but it felt good. Her nails lightly dragged across my skin, applying just the right pressure.

I ripped open her coat then shoved my hands under her shirt, groping her breasts over her bra. She moaned into my mouth while she felt me take her, squeezing her.

Her hand snaked into my pants and grabbed my cock. She stroked it like she'd done it a thousand times. Her touched relayed her experience. She was making me pant, making me hot.

I moved to her jeans then unbuttoned them, still kissing her. Our tongues danced together, making me forget about the cold. I breathed hard, my cock throbbing every few seconds.

When her jeans were loose, I yanked them down and helped her kick them off. She was probably freezing but it didn't seem like she cared. She undid my fly then pulled my jeans down with my boxers, revealing my cock.

My lips moved to her neck and I sucked the skin while my hand moved beneath her underwear. I found her clit immediately and rubbed it. Then I slipped two fingers inside, feeling how wet she was.

She licked her hand then rubbed me hard, doing it exactly as I did it when I beat off. She was a pro and it was making me hornier than I already was.

I didn't want to wait any longer. I wanted to be inside her and forget the foreplay. My hand gripped her thong and pulled it off. I tossed it aside, leaving it in the snow. Then I grabbed her ass and lifted her, pinning her against the wall. Her legs automatically wrapped around my waist.

Neither one of us cared that someone could walk by at any second. My jeans were low, showing my ass, and her legs were spread to me. Like a magnet, my cock found her entrance and felt the moisture pool between her legs.

"Fuck. Do you have a condom?" I blurted.

"No. I'm on the pill." She wrapped her arms around my neck and kissed me again, her mouth touching me the way I liked.

That was all I needed to hear. I gripped her ass and tilted her hips slightly. Then I slid inside with little resistance. "Holy fucking shit." She felt so damn good. I'd never fucked a girl without a rubber and now I knew what I was missing.

She moaned then gripped me, trying to hold on.

After I took a moment to recover, I thrust my hips and moved inside her. There was no way to describe how good it felt. It was heaven, pure heaven. She was so wet and smooth. Her tightness was perfect for my big dick. I could do this all night.

"Slade...yeah." She used her arms to move up and down slightly, rocking with me.

I started to move faster, wanting as much of her as I could get.

"Fuck me." Her head rolled back while she enjoyed what I was doing to her. "Fuck me, Slade..."

I went as fast as I could, loving the feel of her skin against my shaft. My tip pierced her over and over, throbbing from how good it felt. I was breathing hard and moaning, wanting to go even faster.

Minutes passed and we clung to each other while we moved together. Trinity made noises in my ear, exciting me more. She pressed her lips to my ear and kept whispering dirty things, making me crumble. I fucked her hard and good, and I knew when I hit her in the right spot. She practically screamed when I made her come.

"God...yes."

Even though it was freezing out, I started to sweat. I'd never worked this hard during sex. I was giving her everything I had, loving the way her bare pussy felt against my dick.

When I felt the warmth pool in my stomach, stretching to every nerve in my body, I knew the orgasm was coming. Like a ball of raging fire, it burned every single part of me. It hadn't even hit me yet and it was the best sensation I ever felt. I was spiraling, plummeting hard. Then it hit me.

"Fuck yeah." I held her against the wall while I tensed up and released. I never came inside a girl before and it felt a million times better than anything else. I filled her, squirting hard. I kept my body against hers, clinging to her warmth.

When I was finished, I stayed that way, suddenly feeling exhausted. She breathed hard underneath me, trying to catch her breath. The world started to spin, and the cold suddenly hit me.

Still holding her, I grabbed her clothes off the ground and carried her to my apartment. I was still inside her. She lay her head over my shoulder and wrapped her arms around my neck.

When we entered my bedroom, I tossed her on my bed then lay beside her. It only took a few seconds for me to pass out. I didn't know if Trinity was asleep but I was too drunk and tired to care.

Chapter Twenty-Seven
Trinity

A massive migraine was thudding behind my eyes. It slammed into the front of my skull, putting me in a horrible mood before I even started my day. Last night was a blur. I remembered drinking—a lot. Everyone was there. And Slade...he...

Oh shit.

It all came flooding back to me. We fought like we were across a battlefield, and then suddenly, we were going at it against the wall of his apartment. I remembered the cold air moving into my lungs, burning me, with every desperate breath I took. I remembered the concrete wall against my back. I remembered our kiss, our tongues dancing. And I remember him inside me.

Holy fucking shit. I slept with Slade.

My eyes flashed open and I stared at a ceiling I didn't recognize. Where was I? I looked at the nightstand and spotted two pills and a glass of water. Was that for me? Then I realized I was in Slade's bed. It must have been where we passed out. I turned to my other side, expecting to see him passed out next to me.

He wasn't there.

I sat up and felt my tangled hair move around my shoulders. I still wore my jacket and shirt, but I didn't wear any bottoms. My jeans and underwear were on the floor, forgotten. Slade's side of the bed was wrinkled like he slept there the night before. But he wasn't around now.

"Slade?"

No response.

I moved to the end of the bed and felt my head pound harder. I was disoriented for a moment. I breathed through the nausea then focused my thoughts. My hand immediately grabbed the pills and shoved them into my mouth. I downed them with the glass of water.

Oh god, this was bad.

I took a few moments before I rose to my feet. My head hurt again but I pushed forward and got dressed. My phone was still in my coat pocket and so were my keys.

"Slade?"

He still didn't respond.

I walked through the house and didn't spot him anywhere. The TV was off and there weren't any dirty dishes. It was pretty clear he already took off. Did he take off because of me? Wanting to head home and get into the shower, I left his apartment.

***

I still couldn't believe what happened. Slade had been my enemy for as long as I could remember. We fought and bickered like two people who despised each other. I hated him and he hated me.

So what the hell happened?

I knew alcohol lowered inhibitions but I had to stoop pretty low to sleep with Slade, the biggest manwhore I'd ever met. My fingers moved through my hair anxiously as I processed what happened. I couldn't believe we fucked outside in the cold like that, like animals.

Even though it was Sunday, I didn't go to Skye's. She was having people over for the football game but I wasn't going to set foot in that place. What if Slade was there? God, that would be so awkward. What would I say? What would he say?

My phone lit up with a message.

Please don't be Slade. Please don't be Slade.

It wasn't. It was Skye. *Are you coming over or what?*

I couldn't ask if Slade was there. *I'm going to stay in today.*

Are you okay?

Why was she asking? *Yeah, totally. Why wouldn't I be? I'm awesome. I'm fantastic.* Okay...that was a little over the top...

I just wanted to make sure everything was okay. Slade didn't come over today so I thought something was up.

Nope. I'm peachy.

Have you talked to Slade?

Why would I have talked to Slade? I haven't seen him. No. Geez, I sounded defensive.

Well, if you see him, tell him Cayson wants to talk to him.

Since I won't be seeing him, don't depend on me.

Are you okay, Trin?

I'm peachy. I needed to stop using that word.

Skye stopped texting me so I assumed I was in the clear. I tossed my phone aside then lay in bed, wondering why I was so damn stupid and made such idiotic decisions.

***

I avoided Slade all week. Anywhere I thought he might turn up, I skipped. I didn't go to the library during my break for classes, and I steered clear of everyone in the gang. Seeing him would be the most awkward thing in the world. I wondered if he told Cayson what happened? It was my biggest fear. Nothing happened in the group that everyone didn't know about. But if he did tell Cayson, he would have told Skye...who would have confronted me. Since she hadn't, I assumed Slade kept the truth to himself.

Thank god.

The week went smooth. I didn't see him anywhere. Maybe we could just keep avoiding

589

each other and pretend it never happened. But, of course, Skye knew something was up.

Trinity, where have you been?

God, was she a detective? *I've just been busy. Did you and Cayson do the deed yet?* I didn't really care at the moment but I tried to sound normal.

Doing what?

Homework. I knew that was a bad response the moment I sent it.

You never do homework.

Ugh. *I'm sick.*

Which is it? You're busy or you're sick?

I dug myself into a hole. I stopped texting her altogether. That was probably the best idea.

A few days later, I was walking across campus through the trees when I spotted Slade just a few feet away. His hands were in his pockets and he stared at the ground. His black blazer kept his body warm from the cold.

Oh shit. I needed to hightail it out of there.

Right at that moment, he looked up. His eyes met mine and panic moved into them. Suddenly, he turned around on his heel then walked away. I did the same, trying to pretend that didn't just happen.

The next week went better than the last. Slade and I did a better job of avoiding each other. But everyone else in the group had caught on.

Did something happen with you and Slade?
Skye texted me.

Fuck. Fuck. Fuck. *No.*

Then why has no one seen either of you?

At least Slade kept our secret. I'd take it to the grave. But I needed to spit out an excuse. *We got into a fight.*

What's new? That doesn't explain why you guys are avoiding us as well as each other.

I'll see you soon, alright? You got Cayson to entertain you.

I don't care about that. I just want to make sure you're okay.

Having a best friend sucked sometimes. *I'm fine. Don't worry about me. I'll talk to you later.*

I'm always here, Trin. Don't forget that.

Like you would ever let me.

***

By the end of the second week, I knew this couldn't go on any longer. By avoiding each other, we were avoiding all the people we cared about. I wasn't looking forward to the conversation, but we needed to have it. I decided to be the bigger man.

I don't want to talk about this any more than you do but we need to.

Slade didn't respond for hours. *There's nothing to say.*

Can we just talk? We can't avoid each other forever.

591

Another hour passed before he responded. *Fine. Where do you want to meet?*

I don't care. I'm home right now.

I'll be there in an hour.

I spent the next hour dreading his arrival. I was nervous to see him and I wasn't sure why. Flashbacks of our night came to me as time passed, becoming more vivid with every passing minute. Our tongues moved together like we were desperate and our bodies were starving for one another. Even though it was outside in the middle of winter with my back against the wall, I had to admit the sex was pretty good...damn good. But that was beside the point. It was with Slade.

And that was a big no-no.

Slade arrived at my door an hour later.

I answered it, trying to remain calm.

His hands were in his pockets and he wouldn't make eye contact with me. He stared across the lawn then at my doorbell, finding it more interesting than my face.

"Come in." I left the door open and headed to the living room.

He followed me then sat on the opposite couch, as far away from me as possible.

"You think I'm going to rape you or something?"

He finally looked at me, annoyance etched onto his face. "Let's just get this over with."

"Did you tell anybody?"

"Fuck no. You think I'm crazy?" He looked at me with wide eyes. "If your dad found out, he would kill me. And I don't mean figuratively. Literally. He would stab me in the gut and watch me bleed to death."

My dad had this reputation as an overprotective father but he really wasn't that bad. It could be worse. "He wouldn't do that."

"Either way, I don't want him to find out." He ran his fingers through his hair in frustration. "Did you tell anybody?"

"No."

He breathed a sigh of relief. "Not even Skye?"

"No."

"Good. She's got a big mouth."

I crossed my legs and tried to think of something else to say. "Are we going to be weird around each other forever?"

He was quiet for a long time. "I hope not."

"Then why have you been avoiding me?"

"I figured you were in love with me and wanted a relationship or some shit like that."

I cringed. "No. I despise you as much as I did before."

He leaned his head back on the couch. "Thank god. I despise you too."

"So we really shouldn't have trouble returning to normal, right?"

"I guess not." He looked at me, a thoughtful expression on his face. "As long as we don't tell anybody."

"Believe me, I don't want anyone to know." I shook my head. "I'd never live that down."

"Like you're much better," he snapped.

"I am, actually. You're a manwhore."

"Like you aren't. Believe me, I can tell you've been around."

"What's that supposed to mean?" I demanded.

He said nothing.

"You think I'm good in bed?" I cornered him into a wall.

He still kept his mouth shut.

"You don't need to confirm it. I already know I am."

"Well, now you know I'm good too."

I refused to feed his ego so I didn't compliment him. "So, we're friends, right?"

"Yeah. Let's just never speak of it again."

"That sounds great."

"Alright." He stood up. "Um...I guess I'll see you around."

"Yeah." I walked him to the door.

"Bye." He walked out without looking back.

I shut the door, trying to forget him the second he was gone.

Chapter Twenty-Eight
Cayson

Slade had been weird for weeks. He was unusually quiet around me, not making jokes like he normally did. His eyes showed a depth they never had before. It seemed like he was lost in thought most of the time, even in the middle of a conversation.

"Skye asked me if we could live in Connecticut when we settle down. You think that means when we get married? That's what she was implying?"

Slade sipped his beer and stared at the table. A whole minute went by without a response. He didn't even blink.

"Slade?"

"Hmm?" He came back around. "What?"

"Dude...what's up with you?"

"Nothing. I was just thinking....about a paper that's due."

"You never think about schoolwork—ever."

"What was the question again?" He tried to change the subject.

"Skye asked me if we could live in Connecticut when we 'settle' down. What do you think that means?"

He kept his hand on his beer. "She's probably referring to marriage. What else would she mean?"

That's what I was hoping for. When she said those words, my heart grew wings and took flight. It was something I constantly thought about, coming home from work and seeing her every day. I wanted her to be the mother of my kids, the woman I made love to every night. It was my dream since I could remember. The fact it was a real possibility made my hands shake. "That's what I was hoping for."

"Why are you surprised?" He stared at the TV, a bored look on his face.

I shrugged. "She dated Zack for a long time but never considered marriage. And we haven't been together very long and she's already talking about it."

"It's pretty obvious how much she loves you, man. And I don't see why she would date you unless she thought it would go somewhere. Why ruin a friendship for nothing?"

"Yeah..."

"Just be happy. Don't overthink it."

"You're right." Wait a second...Slade was never right. Where were all the jokes? All the comments? "We still haven't had sex." He should take the bait.

He stared at the foam in his cup. "It'll happen when it happens."

What the hell was wrong with him? "Okay, you're really freaking me out."

"What?" He looked offended.

"What's up with you? You're all quiet and serious and stuff."

He shrugged. "I'm just tired."

I wasn't buying it. "What happened with you and Trinity?"

"She's hideous," he blurted. "I would never sleep with her."

Okay... "I didn't say you would."

"We just had a fight and we're cool now. What's the big deal?" He drank his beer and spilled a little on his shirt.

"Well, what did you fight about?"

"The usual stuff..."

"But you've never avoided each other before." What was he hiding?

"She was just being annoying and I didn't want to talk to her anymore. End of story. Shit, get off my back. Are you a detective or something? Calm the hell down. Who cares if she and I weren't talking for a while? Why don't you..." He rambled on for a full minute about me getting off his case.

I wasn't buying his bullshit. I knew something more happened but he obviously wasn't going to spill. I decided to drop it. "Got it. I'm sorry."

"You should be sorry, dick face."

"Damn, you're defensive today...."

"I just don't appreciate being called a liar!"

I raised my hands. "I never called you a liar."

"Yeah, you did. Now stop asking me about her. I told you she was ugly."

"What does her appearance matter?"

"Just...this conversation is over." He downed half of his beer then wiped his lips. His eyes were glued to the TV, pretending I wasn't there.

Geez, he was being weird.

Roland and Conrad slid into the booth, their beers in hand.

"Have you seen Trinity?" Conrad asked. He looked at me when he said it.

"Why would I know where she is?" Slade blurted. "I don't fucking know. I don't even like her. She's disgusting." He was breathing hard, practically having a panic attack.

Roland raised an eyebrow. "You okay, man?"

"I'm groovy," Slade said without looking at him.

Conrad raised an eyebrow and looked at me. He gave me a look that clearly said, "What's his deal?"

I shrugged in response.

Slade ordered another beer and downed it like water. He was clearly on edge.

Skye stepped into the bar, looking like a vision. She wore black pants that were skin-tight and a maroon sweater that went well with her skin tone. A pink scarf was around her neck and a gold bracelet was on her wrist. She looked beautiful, like always. I hardly noticed Trinity behind her. She was just a blur to me.

I got out of the booth, eager to reach Skye.

Skye gave me a breathtaking smile when she came near. Her eyes lit up like Christmas morning, and they sparkled with their own inner light. I've never seen her give this look to anyone before—just me. "Hey." She moved into my chest and hooked her arms around my waist. "I saw a really good-looking guy when I walked in, but then I realized it was you."

"I'm glad I'm the only one who catches your eye." My hand automatically moved to her neck, the place I loved to touch her most. I placed a gentle kiss on the corner of her mouth, treasuring the moment as it happened.

A quiet moan escaped her lips while I touched her. Her small hand clenched my side, holding on during the embrace. When I pulled away, she gave me a look full of love. "I love kissing you."

"I love kissing you." I gave her another kiss.

"If you don't mind moving your fat asses, we're trying to watch the game," Roland barked.

I sighed then broke the kiss. "Can I get you something to drink?"

"Can I just sip some of yours? I'm not really craving anything."

"Whatever you want, baby." I guided her to the booth and sat next to her. Trinity sat on the end, directly across from Slade.

We all watched their interaction, wondering what they would do or say. They ignored each other, like always.

"Did you have a lame time with Mom and Dad last weekend?" Roland asked.

"No, it was fun," Skye said. "You should have come."

"Ha. Yeah right." He rested his elbows on the table and watched TV.

"Mom and Dad said they wished you were there," Skye said.

"Of course," he said. "I could only imagine how boring you and Cayson were."

"Could you not be a dick for like a second?" Skye demanded.

"Nope." He drank his beer then turned his attention on Trinity and Slade. "So what happened between you guys?"

Both of them flinched.

"We just got into a fight," Slade barked.

"Why is everyone so interested in us?" Trinity stammered.

Roland raised his hands. "Sorry, I was just curious…"

"Well, don't be." Slade watched the TV again.

I finished my beer. "You sure you don't want anything?" I asked Skye.

"No, thank you."

I left the booth and headed to the bar. The bartender was busy taking drink orders so I patiently waited for him to notice me. If I were a girl who looked like Skye, I wouldn't have to wait for anything.

"Cayson?"

I recognized that voice. I turned to see the blonde hair I fisted more times than I could recall. She smelled the same way, like vanilla. Her hair was silky like I remembered. It framed her face. It was a little shorter than the last time I saw her. She must have gotten a haircut. "Hey, Jasmine." I knew I would run into her eventually.

She wore a smile but it was clearly forced. "How's it going?"

"Good. You?"

"Good." Sadness was in her eyes.

The last words she said to me on the night we broke up came back to me. She said she loved me the way I loved Skye. And I felt like a damn asshole. It was clear she still felt that way.

"I know this is awkward...but I figured it would be better just to say hi rather than pretend I didn't see you."

"I'm glad you said hi. It's nice to see you."

She nodded, loosening up a bit. "How's school?"

"Lame, like always."

She chuckled. "I can imagine. And Skye...?"

I felt the guilt in my stomach.

"She was going to come up eventually, right?"

"Yeah. She and I are great. I'm very happy." I didn't want to downplay my feelings for Skye. The last thing I wanted to do was give Jasmine the impression she had a chance with me.

She nodded slowly. "Good. I'm glad to hear it."

No, she wasn't. "Are you seeing anyone?"

"I date here and there...I'm actually on a date now." She didn't seem too thrilled about it.

"Is he weird?"

She shrugged. "He's just clingy and brags a lot. I like a guy who's humble." She gave me an affectionate look.

"You'll find the right guy. Just keep looking." There was hope. I didn't want her to lose it.

"Yeah...hopefully." She tucked a strand of hair behind her ear, something she used to do when she was nervous. "You look good."

I felt awkward. What should I say in response? "Thanks..."

"You're still working out all the time?"

"Every day with Slade."

She nodded. "It shows."

I couldn't compliment her appearance. It would feel like I was cheating on Skye in a complicated way. "Well...it was nice seeing you."

"Yeah..." She played with her hair again.

An arm moved around my waist and rose hips came into my nose. Skye moved into my side, hugging me like a teddy bear. "Where's that beer?" she asked with a playful look. She pressed her breasts into my side and practically smothered me.

Jasmine looked at the ground, clearly uncomfortable.

"Uh...I'm getting it now." This was weird. "I'll be back in a second."

"I'll wait." Skye didn't move.

Jasmine didn't look at us. "I'll see you around..." She drifted away and returned to her table.

When she was gone, I gave Skye an incredulous look. "What was that?"

"What do you mean?" She raised an eyebrow.

"You didn't have to scare her off like that." It was already difficult for me to get mad at her as a friend, but it was even harder since she was my girlfriend. But I couldn't deny how upset it made me.

"I didn't scare her off," she said, offended. "You're my boyfriend and I can touch you whenever I want."

I turned to her, trying to keep my voice down. "Don't bullshit with me, Skye. I know exactly what you were doing."

She flinched when I cursed. She was used to me treating her like a princess.

"You already won, Skye. You don't need to rub your victory in her face. Honestly, I never thought you'd be one of those girls."

"I wasn't rubbing anything in her face," she argued.

"Seriously, just stop. She already knows I love you. You don't need to come over here and claim me. You either trust me or you don't."

"I never said I—"

I walked off, not letting her finish her sentence. I stormed out of the bar then headed home. Anger consumed me, making my hands shake. I couldn't believe I turned my back on Skye like that. But just because I loved her didn't mean I'd let her get away with whatever she wanted.

Not gonna happen.

***

A few hours later, there was a knock on my door. It was almost midnight and only one person would come over at this hour. Skye and I usually slept over at each other's houses. I was so used to it by now that I knew I wouldn't be able to sleep without her.

I looked through the peephole and saw her standing on the other side. She was bundled up in a jacket and scarf. Her arms were crossed over her chest.

I sighed then opened the door, keeping an indifferent façade. I stood in the doorway so she couldn't walk in. I kept my silence, waiting for her to speak first.

She stared at me for a while, the fear in her eyes. "Can I come in?"

"No. I may be in love with you but I'm not going to let you walk all over me. Say what you came to say and leave."

Skye flinched at my aggression. "I just wanted to say I'm sorry…"

I waited for her to elaborate.

"I…I shouldn't have acted like that. You're right."

"Then why did you?"

She kept her arms across her chest. "I guess I just love you so much."

"That's not an excuse," I said darkly.

"I was jealous," she blurted. "I admit it. Seeing her talk to you with that look on her face hurt my stomach. You're mine and I...just wanted to make sure she knew that."

"Skye, she knows. I made it pretty clear when I dumped her for you."

She pressed her lips tightly together.

"I've known you my entire life, Skye, and you've never pulled this number before. You've always been trusting and calm. You've never gloated to other people and you've certainly never intentionally tried to hurt another person. And that's why I fell in love with you. I don't want that to change."

"I know...I was being a bitch."

I didn't deny it. "And it hurts me that you don't trust me."

"It's not that," she said immediately. "It was all jealousy—on my part."

I studied her face under the light from my porch. Her hair was over one shoulder and her lips were ruby red.

"It's not going to happen again, right?"

She shook her head. "No."

"Good. That's what I wanted to hear."

She stared at me, the longing in her eyes. "Do you still want me to go?"

I grabbed her arm and pulled her inside. "No. I want you to make it up to me."

Her eyes lit up. "I can do that."

Chapter Twenty-Nine

Skye

I messed things up with Cayson and I knew it. When I saw Jasmine talking to him, I don't know what came over me. And everyone at the table wasn't helping.

"Oooh...she's after your man." Slade watched them by the bar.

"She wants him to stick it to her good," Roland said. "Break up sex, you know."

"Shut up," I said.

"And she's down for anal," Conrad said. "So you have a lot to compete with."

The idea of Cayson having sex with her, any kind of sex, made me sick. "Knock it off."

"Someone's getting jealous." Roland nudged me in the side.

"If my boyfriend's ex was all over him, I'd strut over there and make it clear she'd have to go through me first," Trinity said.

"But you don't have a boyfriend," Slade noted. "You aren't sleeping with anyone..."

She gave him an irritated look.

"If you don't claim him, she's going to snatch him up," Conrad said. "And I wouldn't blame Cayson for having his cake and eating it too. You being the cake and Jasmine being the too."

They were getting under my skin even though I tried to act like they didn't. It was pretty clear Jasmine was in love with him. It was obvious every time she looked at him. I gave into the jealousy and made a stupid decision.

And now I felt guilty about it.

I knew Cayson wouldn't leave me over something like that, but I didn't like upsetting him. Our relationship was perfect. He was perfect. I didn't want to ruin it over something stupid. Honestly, I've never been jealous before. Cayson was the only one who instilled that emotion in me. I guess it's because I was head-over-heels in love with him and I've felt that way for years—even if I didn't realize it at the time.

Whatever the reason, it wasn't right. Jasmine was a very nice girl and what I did was very uncool. I admit it, and I didn't feel good about it. Luckily, Cayson let it go the moment I apologized. I learned my lesson.

Trinity sat across from me in the library and placed her magazines on the table. "I just got *Vogue* in the mail yesterday."

"Anything cute?" I asked.

"A lot of cute things." She pulled out a sketchpad and handed it to me. "I was inspired by a gown I found in this magazine. But I think mine is better."

I examined the picture, immediately impressed. "Trinity...this is really good."

"Really? You aren't just saying that?"

"No..." I was being genuine. "Do you have any others?"

She laughed. "I have hundreds. They are at home in my office."

"You should show your dad. He would open up your clothing line in a heartbeat."

She sighed. "I think I'm going to finish my bachelor's first."

"Really?"

She nodded. "I'm almost done and my dad already paid a lot of money...I may as well finish."

I agreed. "I'll support whatever you decide, Trin."

"Thanks." She gave me a smile. "So...you and Cayson okay?"

I rolled my eyes. "Yeah. I was just being childish."

"Are you still fighting?"

"No. He forgave me the moment I apologized."

"That's a relief. Knowing Cayson, he couldn't stay mad at you for long."

"I don't know...he was pretty mad."

"It all worked out, right?"

I nodded. "It did."

"And I'm sure Jasmine will keep her paws off him."

The idea of Jasmine touching him still got my heart racing. "Yeah..."

Trinity returned her attention to her magazine and flipped through the pages.

I opened my textbooks and began to study.

An hour of silence passed until I heard the chair move beside me. I turned, hoping to see Cayson. It wasn't him.

Zack was staring me down. His face was back to normal and no bruises lingered behind. Judging by the anger in his eyes, he wasn't here to discuss ponies and rainbows. "So, you and lover boy, huh? I shouldn't be surprised."

"Zack, go away."

He grabbed my wrist. "No. I'm going to talk and you're going to listen."

Trinity glared at him. "Let go or I'll break your dick."

He ignored her, still staring at me. "So, first your dad beats the shit out of me, then I find out you're fucking the guy you spent all your time with when we were together. I'm not happy, Skye. You claim I played you but it's the other way around."

"I said let her go," Trinity threatened.

I wasn't scared of Zack and I refused to act like it. "I suggest you let go of me. Otherwise, you're going to get your ass kicked by two girls."

He dropped his hand but didn't move away. "You owe me."

What? "Owe you what?"

"An apology. You totally played me."

I rolled my eyes. "You're so pathetic."

"Apologize to me or I'll make your boyfriend pay for it." His eyes held his mirth.

"Did you just threaten Cayson?" Now I was pissed. Zack could do and say whatever he wanted to me and it didn't make me blink twice. But threatening someone I cared about was another story.

Trinity left her chair and came around the table, coming behind him. Then she grabbed him by the hair and yanked him to the ground.

"Fucking bitch," Zack mumbled.

We were the only ones in the corner so no one noticed the disturbance. The Harvard library was enormous. We were practically alone.

Trinity kicked him hard in the balls. "You think that makes me a bitch? I'm not even done." She kicked him again.

He curled in a ball and moaned.

"Nobody threatens Cayson and gets away with it." She kicked him again but Zack caught her leg. Then he pulled her foot out from under her, making her fall down.

"Shut the hell up." Zack moved on top of her and held her down. "As I was saying..."

I stood up and kicked him hard in the arm.

He pressed his lips together and took the hit. "If you don't want me to hurt your friend, I suggest you knock it off."

"You're psycho. I can't believe I ever dated you," I said.

"Maybe I wasn't so bad in bed, after all."

Trinity tried to wiggle free. "Get off of me, jackass!"

The sound of approaching feet caught my attention. And Zack's. I turned and grabbed my ethics textbook, preparing to slam it on Zack's head.

"What the fuck?" It was Slade. He took one look at Zack on top of Trinity and snapped. "Fucking piece of shit!" He rushed Zack then yanked him off, thrusting his head into the carpet while he did it. "You want to die? Because it seems like it." Slade punched him hard in the jaw then rushed to Trinity. "Trin, are you okay?" He pulled her up so she was sitting. He kept his arm around her then grabbed her chin, examining her face.

"I'm fine," she said immediately. "He didn't hurt me."

Relief filled his eyes.

"But you better bust out that Krav Maga and kick his ass."

"You got it." He stood, but Zack was gone. We were both concerned for Trinity and forgot him for a moment. Slade searched the aisles then came back when he couldn't find him. "I'll see him again. And when I do, he'll have no teeth." He came back to Trinity and helped her stand up. Then he looked at me. "Skye, are you okay?"

"I'm fine," I answered.

Slade pulled out a chair for Trinity and helped her sit down. "What the hell happened?"

"Zack wanted to talk but Trinity tried to kick his ass instead," I explained.

"I kicked him in the balls a few times. I would have done more damage if it wasn't so cramped," Trinity said.

Slade rested his hand on her back and rubbed her gently. "You sure you're alright?" Concern was in his eyes.

"He didn't do anything except pin me down," she said.

I'd never seen Slade be so affectionate with Trinity—or any girl.

He breathed a sigh of relief. "I'm glad you girls are alright."

"We aren't scared of him," Trinity said. "He's a fucking pussy."

"Yeah," I agreed.

Slade gave me a firm look. "I think it's time to tell your dad, Skye."

"No." That wasn't an option.

"He's obviously not going to leave you alone," Slade pressed.

"I got myself into this mess and I'll get myself out," I said. "Zack isn't dangerous. He's annoying but not dangerous."

Slade wasn't so sure. "What does he want?"

"He keeps saying my dad put him in the hospital, which he didn't."

Emotion moved into Slade's eyes but he didn't react in any other way.

"And he thinks I had a thing with Cayson while we were together. He wants an apology."

"Weirdo," Slade said.

"He is," Trinity said. "I can't believe you were fucking him."

"Don't remind me," I said miserably.

"Cayson isn't going to be pleased when he finds out." Slade shook his head.

"I know..." I didn't want to tell him.

"He'll be hovering around you every second of the day," Slade said.

That didn't sound so bad.

Slade continued to rub Trinity's shoulder. "Can I get you something to eat?"

"We aren't supposed to eat in the library. Remember?" she teased.

He smirked. "How could I forget?"

What was going on? "I thought you hated each other?"

Slade dropped his hand immediately. "We do. I just wanted to make sure she was okay...not that I care or anything."

They were the weirdest people I knew...

***

614

Cayson came over that night with a vase of flowers. Green stems left the glass and erupted into beautiful red roses. There were a dozen and they smelled wonderful.

I studied them for a moment before I grabbed them. "They are beautiful."

His eyes shined in adoration. He stepped inside then placed a gentle kiss on my lips. "I know your favorite flower is the lily, but I also know that's your dad's territory."

I smirked. "It is a tradition."

"Roses are more romantic anyway."

"They are." I filled the vase with water then set it on the table. "But you shouldn't be getting me anything. I should be the one kissing your ass."

He grinned. "It's water under the bridge, Skye. Just forget about it."

"You let me off the hook so easily."

"Well...you gave me an incredible apology." He came close to me and hooked his arms around my waist. His nose rubbed against mine gently.

I felt redness move into my cheeks. "I guess I know what to do in the future."

He chuckled. "It looks like you do."

I rested my face against his chest, feeling it rise and fall. His scent came into my nose and I felt relaxed, comfortable. The cotton of his t-shirt felt good against my cheek.

"How was your day?" he whispered.

I immediately thought about Zack. I really didn't want to get into it until after dinner. "Fine. How about yours?"

"Pretty lame. But, then again, my life is always lame when you aren't around." His hand moved up my back and rested between my shoulder blades.

"Mine too." I felt warmth move through my body.

He pressed his forehead against mine. "Where did you want to eat?"

I shrugged. "Pizza is good."

He laughed. "You always want pizza."

"It's good," I argued.

"Whatever you want, baby." He grabbed my hand and pulled me toward the door. His phone vibrated in his pocket so he pulled it out and checked it. Then he shoved it back inside.

I grabbed my coat then we walked down the stairs.

He sighed then pulled out his phone when it vibrated again. He looked at it with a sigh then put it back in his pocket. As soon as he returned it, it vibrated again.

"Someone is popular."

He rolled his eyes. "Slade has called me five times in a row."

My heart skipped a beat. I knew why he was calling.

"Damn, what does he want?" He pulled the phone out again.

I snatched it away. "He probably wants you to head to a strip club with him or something."

He cocked an eyebrow. "There're no strip clubs around here."

"That we know of. But Slade would." It kept vibrating in my hand.

"I'll just tell him to stop calling." He held out his hand and waited for me to pass it to him.

Uh...I took the call instead. "Cayson's busy. Stop calling."

"You didn't tell him, did you?" Annoyance was in his voice.

Cayson stared at me with a suspicious look on his face.

"He'll call you later," I said.

"You had all day to tell him and it's obvious you aren't going to. Now hand him the damn phone."

"Okay, talk to you later." I hung up and put the phone in my pocket.

Cayson eyed me with a raised eyebrow. "What's going on, Skye?"

"I'm just making sure you don't get a headache." I walked to his car, feeling the phone vibrate in my pocket again and again.

Cayson knew something was up. "Is there something you need to tell me?" He walked behind me then cornered me into the door of his car. He put his hands on either side of me, caging me in. A dark look came into his eyes.

I stared up at him, seeing his breath escape as vapor. "No..."

"We've known each other for a long time, Skye. I know when you're lying. You can fool everyone else but you can't fool me." He brushed his lips passed mine, his mouth warm in the freezing night.

I cupped his face and gave him a warm kiss. "I want to wait until after dinner."

"Why?" He stepped closer to me, pinning me against the car door.

"I'm hungry."

"You're always hungry." His teasing nature was gone, replaced by seriousness.

"Well, I'm really hungry."

"And I'm really curious."

I sighed, knowing he wouldn't let up. "I'm not telling you until after dinner. And it's not even that big of a deal. So drop it."

He studied my face, seeing the determination in my eyes. He lowered his hands. "Fine."

"Thank you."

He stepped back. "You better make this worth my while."

"I always do."

Cayson opened the door for me then helped me inside before he got into the driver's seat. He was about to start the car when a vehicle slammed to a stop behind us and blocked us in.

"What the...?" Cayson looked in the rearview mirror.

I looked in the side mirror and my heart fell. Slade's car had boxed us in. *God, he was annoying.*

"What the hell is he doing?" Cayson got out and slammed the door.

I rolled my eyes then left the car, joining Cayson in the rear.

Slade left his car, the engine still on.

Cayson's eyes were wide. "Dude, what's going on?"

Slade gave me a long glare before he looked at Cayson again. "Your precious girlfriend refrained from telling you an important piece of information. And since she isn't going to admit it, I have to say something."

"Slade, stay out of our relationship," I snapped.

"You had all day to tell him but you never did. He has the right to know! And not tomorrow or a week from now. He needs to know right this second."

"I was going to tell him after dinner," I hissed.

"Sure..." Slade wasn't buying it. He looked back at Cayson. "So this is the story—"

Cayson held up his hand. "I want to hear it from Skye."

Slade shut his mouth then looked at me.

Cayson turned his eyes on me, and he didn't look happy. "What is it?"

I wanted to slap Slade right then. "Trinity and I were in the library this afternoon when Zack stopped by. He's pissed I'm dating you and he wanted an apology. Trinity kicked him a few times then Zack pinned her down. Slade came in then and chased him off."

Cayson's face was unreadable. He stared me down, his jaw clenched tight.

"It wasn't even a big deal. It was just annoying." I crossed my arms over my chest. "I was going to tell you but I wanted to wait until after dinner. It's not even worth discussing."

"Not worth discussing?" Slade snapped. "He's bothered you twice now. And he held Trinity down. That shit's not okay in my book."

"Slade, go home." Cayson didn't look at him when he said it.

Slade sighed then walked off. His footsteps were loud against the cold pavement. His engine revved as he hit the gas and drove away. When the sound of his tires was gone, I knew we were alone.

Cayson hadn't blinked once. "Why didn't you call me?"

"There wasn't any time. And Slade was there."

"What does that matter?" His voice was low and calm, but the ferocity was evident in his tone. "I'm your boyfriend, not Slade."

I rolled my eyes. "Don't overreact."

"Don't. Roll. Your. Eyes." He stared me down, his anger flashing.

The world suddenly became silent. The snow fell around us, masking us in a winter wonderland.

"Skye, I was annoyed that Zack bothered you before. But the fact he's done it again makes me uneasy. Really uneasy."

"He's annoying but not dangerous."

"It doesn't seem like it. Holding Trinity down is unacceptable."

"I'm not saying what he did was right. But he wouldn't actually hurt me or Trinity."

"You don't know that," he snapped.

"In a few weeks, he'll be over it and move on."

"And I'm just supposed to patiently wait until he's ready to move on?" he snapped.

"There's no other option. It's not like I can call the police. What would I even say? What evidence do I have?"

"We don't need the police," he snarled. "We need someone with the power to get rid of someone—no questions asked."

I knew what he was implying. "Don't you dare tell my father."

"I'm running out of options, Skye. I'd gladly kill him with my bare hands but I have a feeling you wouldn't like that very much."

"No one is going to kill anybody," I snapped. "Why is that the first thing you think of?"

"Because it's the best option."

"No, it's not! Zack isn't a threat. I can handle him."

"And what would you have done if Slade hadn't showed up?" Cayson asked.

"I was about to slam my ethics book right on his skull. I'm sure that would have knocked him out."

He ran his fingers through his hair, flustered.

"Leave my father out of this. I mean it, Cayson."

He stared into the distance.

"Cayson."

He turned his gaze back on me. "I'm not letting you out of my sight. I don't care if it pisses you off. If he thinks he can harass you again, he's in for a surprise."

This was the reaction I expected so I guess I couldn't be upset. "Fine."

"I'm glad we're on the same page." His jaw was still clenched.

"Cayson, I can take care of myself."

"I know you can. But you don't have to."

I kept my arms across my chest. "Now what?"

"I'm not in the mood to sit in a restaurant and pretend I'm fine. Let's order in." He walked toward the apartment.

I stayed in my spot before I trailed behind him and walked up the stairs.

When he reached the door he held out his hand. "Can I have my phone back?"

I handed it to him.

"Just for the record, I don't like hearing this shit from my friends. I want to hear it from you." Anger still lingered in his voice.

"I wanted to wait until after dinner. I already said that."

He walked inside then pulled off his coat. "I think that's more important than a meal."

"I just didn't want to watch you brood all night long."

"That's too damn bad. You're everything to me, Skye. I'm not going to let some guy harass you. The fact you're my girlfriend is irrelevant. I will not let some jackass treat you that way."

"Like I said, I can handle him."

Cayson was struggling to still his emotion. He turned away from me then headed to the couch, his shoulders stiff with tension.

I opened the drawer of take-out menus then found my favorite pizza place. I pulled out my phone and made the call. When I was done, the silence stretched in my apartment. Cayson still sat on the couch, staring at the blank TV screen.

I didn't want to spend our night like this. Cayson wasn't angry very often, and I hated feeling his fury linger in the air like the moisture after a heavy rain. I sat beside him on the couch then scooted close to him. I hooked my arm around his stomach and leaned close to him. My lips brushed his neck before I planted a kiss on the warm skin. Cayson didn't react to my touch. I continued to kiss him, tasting him. When my hand moved up his chest, I guided him against the back of the couch, forcing him to relax. He sighed but didn't push me away.

I moved into his lap then straddled his hips. I flipped my hair over one shoulder as I undid my scarf.

Anger still thudded in his eyes.

I pressed my chest against his then sought his neck with my lips, kissing him the way he liked.

He leaned his head back and closed his eyes. But his hands were idle by his sides, not touching me.

My hands massaged his shoulders and I gave him my best moves. I knew it would take awhile to loosen him up. When a quiet moan, almost unnoticeable, came from his lips, I knew I was getting somewhere.

I leaned back then pulled my sweater over my head. I wore a burgundy bra covered in lace. It showed the color of my skin but hid the most intimate parts.

He took me in. Desire burned in his eyes but the resentment still lingered behind.

I unclasped my bra and let it fall.

He swallowed the lump in his throat. "I admit you're beautiful, Skye. But this isn't going to make me forget how upset I am—"

I grabbed my chest with both hands and massaged my breasts, squeezing and rubbing them while I stared into his eyes.

He swallowed the lump in his throat again while he stared at my moving hands. Quickly, he was forgetting the heated conversation we just had. The Cayson I knew and loved was in there, coming back.

I stood up then pulled off my boots and jeans. I left my thong on before I moved back to his lap.

Cayson eyed my body without shame, his thoughts as easy to read as an open book.

I straddled his lap again, my hands moving to his shoulders. My breasts were in his face, and I felt his warm breath fall on my nipples.

Cayson's hands moved to my hips.

I had him.

His hands moved up the skin around my ribs. Then they moved to my chest, groping them. He leaned forward then pressed his lips against mine, giving me a gentle kiss. "I know I come off a little strong sometimes, but it's only because I love you like crazy, Skye Preston."

I stared into his eyes, feeling the emotion leak from every pore in his body. Of all the years I'd known Cayson, he never gave anyone the look he was giving me. And he never said those words, at least not like that. "I love you too, Cayson."

He hooked an arm around my waist then rolled me to the couch, shifting on top of me. His lips found mine and he kissed me gently, moving his mouth against mine purposefully. He breathed into my mouth, making me hot everywhere. I hooked my legs around his waist and pulled him closer to me, wanting more than he could give.

I gripped his shirt and yanked it off, wanting to feel his muscled chest against me. Then I moved to his jeans, getting them off. I took the boxers too, wanting all of him. He grabbed my thong and yanked it off, practically tearing it.

I wrapped my legs around his waist again, feeling his cock against my folds. I'd been thinking about being with him for a long time. We'd been together for months, longer in terms of our friendship, and I didn't want to wait anymore. He was mine and I was his.

Cayson gave me one last kiss before he pulled away and looked into my eyes. It was clear he was thinking the same thing I was. He breathed hard then brushed his lips against mine.

I moved one hand down his back until I reached his hip. I tugged him toward me, telling him what I wanted.

Understanding filled his eyes. He adjusted himself then pressed his mouth against mine. Then he pointed himself at my entrance, ready to enter me. I dug my nails into his skin, anticipating the pleasure I was about to feel. I had decent sex throughout my life but I knew Cayson would be different. It would be beautiful and wonderful. My soul would touch his, and his mine.

A knock on the door interrupted us.

We both flinched, startled by the sound.

Cayson broke our kiss and glanced toward the door.

"Forget it. It's probably a girl scout." I grabbed his neck and crushed his lips to mine.

The knock sounded again.

Cayson pulled away. "It's the pizza guy."

"Who cares about pizza?" I wanted Cayson, not food.

He smirked. "Skye, I have to get that." He left the couch then quickly pulled on his clothes.

I sighed then pulled the blanket over me, hiding my body.

Cayson answered the door and took the pizza. After he paid the guy, he set it on the kitchen table.

The magical moment was ruined.

Cayson placed the pizza on two plates then he brought me one.

I sighed then took the plate, feeling my stomach rumble. I was more than disappointed. I was totally crestfallen.

Cayson leaned toward me and kissed me on the cheek. "We have the rest of our lives, baby."

I sighed then took a bite of my pizza. "You're right."

He rubbed his nose against mine then took a bite of his pizza. "*I Love Lucy*?"

"Sure."

He leaned back against the couch then pulled me next to him. We watched TV together, like we used to when we were just friends, but now everything was different. He was the best thing that ever happened to me.

Chapter Thirty

Slade

My life was turned upside down.

After I slept with Trinity, I couldn't stop thinking about it. She was drunk and I was drunk. We were both out of our minds. We fucked against a wall in the snow like animals. I had a lot of wild sex but I have to say that was the wildest. I didn't even wear a condom.

And it was Trinity.

If anyone found out, it would ruin me. It would get back to Uncle Mike and I'd be as good as dead. My dad was easy-going and pretty much cool with everything, but I don't think he would be too happy about this. My mom would probably slap me. I'd been a jerk to everyone I knew, but I was never a jerk to my family. I crossed a line I could never uncross.

But one thing made it worse. She was the best sex I ever had.

Maybe I remembered history in a different way than it really happened. Since I was drunk and disoriented, maybe I thought it was better than it really was. What if it was sluggish and awkward? How long did it even last?

The guilt was eating me alive.

Trinity and I talked about it and we settled our differences. I was grateful she wasn't in love with me like Cayson was with Skye. That would just give me more problems. I didn't want a relationship, especially with her. I wasn't a one-woman type of guy. She knew that. Shit, everyone knew that.

But I couldn't stop thinking about it. Every time someone asked me about her, I felt like they were shining a light in my eye. Did they know? Did they hear something? I had a small panic attack every time.

Since Cayson was my best friend, it was hard to keep him in the dark. I told him everything, even if he didn't always want to hear about all my sexual conquests. And he told me everything he did with Skye. The decent thing would be to reciprocate with what I did with Trinity.

But I couldn't tell anyone about that—not a soul.

I was going through women quicker than usual. I picked them up left and right and had my way with them. But nothing hit the spot. They either just lay there and did nothing, or they just weren't good in bed—period.

I kept comparing them to my night with Trinity. Even though most of it was a blur, I still knew it was awesome. I would never admit it to Trinity. I'd take it to the grave rather than say it out loud. But I was definitely thinking it.

I ran into Roland in the hallway. "Going to Trinity's tonight?"

"What? Why? I'm not seeing her," I blurted.

He cocked an eyebrow. "She's having people over for game night. I just assumed you were going."

"Oh...yeah. Totally." *Totally? I've said that word twice in my entire life.*

Roland eyed me for a long time. "You okay, man?"

"I'm groovy." I walked away before he could ask me another question.

***

When I arrived at Trinity's house, I set the beer on the counter.

Everyone was seated on the couch, talking and watching TV. Trinity wore a burgundy dress with a pink scarf. The color looked good on her fair skin tone, and her blonde hair contrasted against it perfectly. The fabric clung to her hourglass figure and her perky breasts. She was thin and tall, but she was all curves in all the right places. She kept brushing loose strands from her face but they fell every time. Her fingernails were the same color as her dress. Black tights were on her legs slightly see-through and lacy. Black heels were on her feet, making her calf muscles more prominent. She dressed in a classy but elegant way.

Why was I noticing every little damn detail?

I put the bottles in the refrigerator and kept one for myself. I used my lighter to pop open the cap.

"I have a bottle opener."

I turned to see Trinity. Up close, I could see the light make up on her face. Gray eye shadow was over her eyes and black eye liner really made them noticeable. Her lips were red and shiny. "This works too."

"Yeah...but I don't want you to set off the fire alarm."

"This is the cool way to open it."

"And the dangerous way," she added.

I leaned against the counter and drank my beer. "Are you asking me to stop?"

"No. I'm just offering a better solution."

Our eyes met and a moment passed between us. I thought about our night fucking against a wall and I was pretty sure she did too. "Are you doing okay?"

"Why wouldn't I be okay?"

"Zack held you down in a library...that couldn't have felt good."

"Oh, that." She rolled her eyes. "I wasn't scared then and I'm not scared now."

"Has he bothered you or anything?" *If he did, I'd kill him.*

"No. But I usually wear heels so I'll give him a good kick in the nuts next time I see him."

"Leave him to me. I'll kill him instead."

"I'm sure Cayson will beat you to the punch."

I eyed Cayson and Skye on the couch. They were close and cuddly. Just as in love as ever. "I guess he got over it."

"I'm sure she did something with her titties and Cayson completely forgot."

I glanced at Trinity's breasts then looked away.

"Did you just check out my chest?"

She caught me? "No..."

"Slade, I saw you."

"I didn't."

"I was looking at you when you did it."

"Wow, you're conceited."

"I'm not conceited," she argued. "I know what I saw."

"You're absolutely hideous."

"It didn't seem that way when you were fucking my brains out," she snarled.

I glanced at everyone in the living room then turned back to her. "Shh! Keep your voice down."

She rolled her eyes. "They aren't listening to us."

"You better hope not."

"I'm the one who has something to be embarrassed about. So just chill out."

"See?" I said. "Conceited."

"I just know my value."

"If you did, you wouldn't let me screw you next to a dumpster."

"Maybe I like being screwed by a dumpster."

My cock hardened and twitched. What the fuck was wrong with me? "You've done it before?"

"Just because I don't talk about every sexual experience doesn't mean I don't have plenty."

"Sounds like you're a whore."

"Sounds like you're a sexist pig," she countered. Trinity was the only woman who argued with me like this. All the other women in my life listened to what I said and let me get my way. She called me out on my shit and told me off more times than I could count. I didn't realize it until that moment.

I finished my beer then grabbed another.

She held out the bottle opener.

Being defiant, I took out the lighter and burned the lid.

"You don't even smoke. It makes more sense to carry around a bottle opener instead of a lighter."

"Not really. You can do a lot with a lighter."

"Like burn down trees?" she said sarcastically.

"You're such an annoying brat."

"And you're a jerk. What's new?"

I stared her down, feeling annoyed all over again. "I'm going to walk away before I slap you across that pretty face."

"You think I have a pretty face?" she challenged.

I walked away before I did something stupid. I sat beside Cayson on the couch.

Cayson eyed me, seeing the annoyed look on my face. "So you and Trinity are back to normal?"

"Something like that." I drank my beer with a clenched jaw.

"Twister!" Trinity pulled out the box and set it up. "Let's do it."

"We aren't five," Conrad said.

"Come on," Trinity said. "It'll be fun."

"Let's do it." Silke straightened out the game on the floor.

"Whatever." Conrad rolled his eyes. "But then we're playing UNO."

They started the game but I didn't participate. Trinity put her hands and feet on the right dots. As much as I tried not to look at specific parts of her body, I couldn't help it. When her ass was directly in my face, I stared at it, remembering how good it felt in my hands.

They played a few rounds before we moved on to UNO. I stayed far away from Trinity and tried not to look at her. She was distracting and it was really getting under my skin.

Skye won three rounds in a row.

"God, you're annoying," Roland said.

"It's not my fault you suck," she countered.

Cayson gave her a fond look then rubbed his nose against hers.

"None of that," Conrad said. "It's gross."

"You're gross," Silke said. "Cayson and Skye are adorable."

Conrad rolled his eyes. "Girls…"

When we were tired of the board games, we watched TV. I leaned back in the chair and didn't finish my third beer. I didn't eat enough and they were going to my head. The last time I was around Trinity when I was drunk, it was a disaster.

My phone rang in my pocket and I saw the name on the screen. It was my dad. Why was he calling me? I walked out the backdoor and stood in Trinity's back yard. Then I took the call. "Yo."

"Yo," he said back. "What's going on?"

"You tell me. You called."

"I haven't talked to you in a while. Wanted to see what you were up to."

"You never check up on me," I countered.

"I know. I'm a horrible father," he said with a laugh.

"No. You're an awesome father."

My dad didn't have a response to that.

"Why are you calling so late?"

"Late? Aren't you a night owl?" my dad asked.

"Yeah." He had a point.

"So, what's new?"

"Nothing. Just school."

"There's got to be something else," he pressed.

"I've been getting pretty good with the guitar. I should drop out of school and join a band."

"Your mother would love that," he said sarcastically.

"And my artwork is getting better. I drew this piece of a tiger moving through stalks of grass. I want you to ink it on me."

"I'll take a look at it when you come down for a visit."

"So, what's new with you, Dad?"

"Nothing. The shop is doing well. Your mother has been busy with work, but that's not surprising."

"Why don't you guys retire?" I asked. "You're like a hundred."

"Do hundred-year-old guys get hit on left and right?"

"Rich ones do."

"Well, I'm not rich. So it's obviously just my looks and sex appeal."

"I'm going to tell Mom you said that."

He laughed. "You think she doesn't know this already?"

"I guess you're right," I said with a laugh.

"Well, I'll let you go. I'm sure you're up to no good and I'm interrupting."

I smirked. "You know me so well, Dad."

"I do," he said. "I'll talk to you later."

"Okay."

"I love you, kid."

"I love you too."

He hung up.

I put my phone back in my pocket then stepped inside.

Everyone was gone. Empty beer bottles were on the coffee tables and counters. The games were piled on the floor. Snacks and plates were littered everywhere.

How long was I on the phone?

I closed the door and stepped inside.

Trinity was piling garbage into a bag. "You're still here?"

"I was talking to my dad," I explained.

"What's he up to?"

"Nothing new." I watched her bend over and grab an empty beer bottle. "Everyone left?"

"You think they're all in the bathroom?" she said sarcastically.

"You know, I'm a jerk to you because you're a bitch to me."

She laughed. "Cut the shit, Slade." She threw the plates and napkins away then left the bag against the wall. "Well, thanks for coming over."

"Sure..."

She put her hands on her hips and stared at me.

"I guess I should go..." It was awkward being alone with her...in a house...with a bed.

"Yeah." She walked toward the door and I followed her.

She opened it. "I'll see you around."

"Yeah." I stopped and looked at her. "Thanks for having me over..." I wasn't sure why I said that. I was never polite.

Surprise moved into her eyes but she didn't say anything.

I didn't cross the threshold. I stayed on this side of the door, unsure what was keeping me there. I kept thinking about her long legs under her dress. When they were wrapped around my waist, it felt so good. I remembered how good it felt to be inside her. All the girls I'd been screwing didn't compare to her—at all.

She studied my face, her eyes guarded.

I needed to leave…

Trinity said nothing, just waiting.

Whatever. I was horny and I was going for it.

I pushed her against the wall then sealed my mouth over hers. The door was still open and the nighttime air came in but I ignored it. I gripped her hips then moved my lips against hers aggressively.

She didn't respond initially. Her mouth was immobile. She was probably in shock, unsure what was going on.

I kept kissing her, hoping for the best. I pressed my body against hers, my erection noticeable in my jeans. I felt her breasts against my chest and I wanted to feel them again. I wanted to taste them this time.

Then she kissed me back. Her lips sought mine like she was desperate for me. Her hands moved into my hair, fisting it while she deepened the embrace. She was an amazing kisser, one of the best I ever had. She knew when to use her tongue and when to pull away. Sometimes her lips would brush past mine, teasing me, and then she would kiss me again. Her hands moved down my shoulders and to my arms, squeezing the muscle. She breathed into my mouth, panting.

I used my foot to kick the door closed. It slammed so hard it shook the walls of the house.

Neither one of us noticed. I'd never been in her bedroom but I knew it was down the hall. Still kissing her, I guided her through the living room and around the couch.

She suddenly gripped my shoulders then jumped up, wrapping her legs around my waist. Like I could read her mind, I caught her ass and held her. Then I kissed her again while I walked down the hallway. I spotted a bed with a yellow bedspread with pink and purple pillows. White dressers were arranged in the room. I knew this was her bedroom.

I walked inside then laid her on the bed. I looked down at her, seeing the same desire in her eyes that burned in mine. My hands moved up her dress then yanked down her leggings. I got them off then tossed her shoes across the room.

Trinity undid my jeans while I grabbed the bottom of her dress and pulled it up. Like we'd done it a hundred times, we pulled each other's clothes away. I was desperate to see her, needed to see her.

When I was naked, I stood in front of her, my cock throbbing.

She eyed my chest, seeing all the tattoos that covered my arms and stomach. I had everything you could possibly imagine. I was a walking canvas. I was quickly running out of room and would have to add ink down below.

Trinity leaned forward, her face close to my waist. Then she parted her lips slightly and pressed a kiss to the head of my cock.

Oh my fucking god.

She grabbed the shaft then licked my tip like it was a lollipop. Her warm and wet tongue felt so good across my skin. Her breath fell on my cock, exciting me even more. Then she took me into her mouth—all the way in—and moved up and down.

I could hardly get girls to go down on me. And whenever I brought it up, they always acted like it was a chore. Trinity sucked me off like she liked it. A moan escaped her lips while she did it and I thought I'd come right there.

She pulled me out slightly then moved her tongue across the tip, giving it a kiss goodbye.

I was breathing so hard I thought I just ran a marathon. That was the best two minutes of my life. My cock twitched, wanting more. Now I wanted to be inside her. My level of desire had increased by tenfold.

At the speed of light, I pulled the rest of her clothes off then yanked her yellow thong off. I stared at her naked body, my cock getting harder with every passing second. I thought I might explode. I picked her up then moved her further up the bed. Then I separated her legs and pressed my face right in between.

She immediately moaned and fisted my hair.

I hated going down on chicks. It was the worst. But with her, I didn't mind. She made me feel unbelievably good and I wanted to make her feel the same way. I used my tongue to circle her clit then I slipped it inside her, making her cry out. My thumb rubbed her nub in a circular motion. Soon, she was panting for me, wanting me as much as I wanted her.

I moved up her body and separated her legs with mine. When she positioned her legs practically behind her head, my eyes widened. I had no idea she was so flexible. I was caught off guard, just staring at her.

She grabbed my neck and pulled my lips to hers. My cock moved past her folds, feeling the wetness and warmth. I was shaking because I was so excited to be inside her, and without a condom. I never knew bare pussy felt so good.

Trinity dug her nails into my back then gripped my ass with her other hand. Then she pulled me inside her, moaning the entire time.

Shit, she felt good.

I slid inside her slowly until I was completely buried. She felt even better than last time. She was warm and tight, creating just the right amount of friction. As soon as I started to move, I moaned. Sex had never felt this good in my life.

Her breasts shook while I rocked into her, and seeing her legs by her head was only making it more enjoyable. Quiet moans escaped her mouth. She bit her lip while she watched me pound into her. "God, you feel so good…"

I rocked into her harder, giving her all of me. I was moving so fast sweat was accumulating on my chest. I held my weight on my arms and used my hips to thrust inside her hard and fast.

"Slade…fuck me just like that."

"Fuck, you're killing me." When she talked like that, I wanted to come.

She gripped my ass with both hands and pulled me into her harder. "God, yes! Yes!" She was practically screaming, coming hard.

I gave it to her as hard as I could.

"Harder!"

"This is as fast as I go!" My cock was sliding in and out of her quicker than I could see.

Her head rolled back and she moaned, breathing hard. Then she spiraled down, releasing her nails from my ass. "That was nice…so nice."

Seeing the redness flood her face and the look of pure satisfaction in her eyes made me want to come. The idea sounded so good.

Trinity gripped me then rolled me to my back, still keeping me inside her. My head hit the pillow and I looked up at her. She kept her knees on either side of my hips and she rode me hard, using her thighs and ass to bounce up and down, not forward and backward. She took me over and over, her hands resting on my chest.

Watching her bounce on my dick shattered my inhibitions. I wanted to make this last as long as possible. I normally wanted to finish quickly but this felt so good. Every time I slid inside her, it was heaven. Fucking heaven.

"Come for me."

I was never into dirty talk but Trinity knew how to do it right. I felt my body tensing as the orgasm was about to happen. Trinity seemed to know because she increased her pace, riding my dick like a cowgirl.

I gripped her hips as the unbelievable sensation struck me. I moaned and bit my lip, and then I came inside her, filling her.

"Fuck…" I breathed hard as she kept riding me, making it last as long as possible. I closed my eyes as the sensation lingered for a second. Then it drifted away, making me feel tender.

Trinity rested on my hips, leaving me inside her.

I caught my breath, feeling winded. She did the same.

Then she moved off me then lay at my side.

I stared at the ceiling, still in my post-orgasm high.

Trinity got under the covers then sighed happily, obviously satisfied.

When the sensation started to wear off, I realized what just happened. I fucked her—again. And this time, I wasn't drunk and neither was she. We both knew what we were doing. The fact it was decided by free will disturbed me even more.

Fuck. Now what?

Trinity lay beside me and didn't say anything.

I couldn't look at her. I wasn't sure why. Was I awkward? Was I embarrassed? Was I angry? I couldn't tell.

Trinity sighed. "Let's just not talk about it."

I cocked an eyebrow and looked at her. "Just not say anything?"

"Yeah." She set her alarm then adjusted her pillow. "Good night, Slade."

That was the last thing I expected her to say. I figured we would have the conversation all women wanted to have. *Where was this going? Did that mean we were in a relationship*? But she didn't ask any of that. It didn't seem like she cared—at all. "Good night, Trinity."

Chapter Thirty-One
Trinity

What have I done?

Slade threw himself at me and I just couldn't stop him. And honestly, I didn't want to. I hadn't had good sex in so long I couldn't even remember it. And Slade definitely knew what he was doing. It was nice to be with a guy who knew where everything went.

But the fact he was a friend—in a way—complicated things.

What did it mean? I knew Slade only felt lust. There was nothing else there. And I felt the same way. I guess it wasn't a big deal. Neither one of us wanted anything more. As long as we didn't tell anybody, our secret would be safe.

This time, we didn't avoid each other. I saw him in the library and around campus often. But we never spoke to each other. Sometimes I caught him looking at me but he quickly turned away when I saw him. We weren't fighting anymore, and that didn't go unnoticed.

"What's going on with you now?" Skye asked from across the table.

"What are you talking about?" I asked while I flipped through a magazine.

"You and Slade. You guys aren't fighting anymore."

I felt my skin prickle. Did she know something was up? "I guess we ran out of ammunition. I thought you and everyone else would be relieved."

"It's just weird how quiet it is..." She eyed me for another second before she turned back to her textbook.

I guess I'd have to pick a fight with Slade next time I saw him to keep up pretenses.

***

"Ugh, I suck at bowling." I picked up the lightest ball I could find then headed to the lane. I aimed the ball but it sped into the gutter—like usual.

"You suck at life so it isn't that surprising." Conrad grabbed his ball then came up next.

"Shut up." I walked past him and sat down.

Slade was sitting beside me, sipping a soda.

We were both quiet, having nothing to say to one another.

"Baby, you're the best bowler I've ever seen." Cayson nuzzled Skye's neck while she sat in his lap.

"You don't even watch me," she said. "You just stare at my ass."

"It is a lovely ass." Cayson rubbed his nose against hers.

"You're going to make me gag," Slade said.

"Ditto," I added.

"Wow," Roland said. "You guys actually agreed on something for once."

I flinched at the accusation. "Slade could die for all I care."

"Dumb bitch," Slade muttered, half assed.

We still didn't look at each other.

They finally backed off and returned to the game.

Phew.

Slade's turn was up. He grabbed the ball and rolled a perfect strike. His thick arms were covered in bright and beautiful tattoos. I was never attracted to them before but know I couldn't stop staring. His shoulders were broad and strong, and his back was tightly packed with muscle. I remembered how he looked naked…it was a nice sight. And his package was pretty nice too.

Cayson tickled Skye while she sat on his lap.

"Stop," she said with a giggle. "You're going to make me pee."

"Please don't," Roland said with a cringe. He stood up and bowled his turn. He got a spare then sat down again.

"Come on, baby." Cayson slapped her ass. "Show us up."

She smirked at him then retrieved her ball.

"You fucked her yet?" Slade blurted.

Cayson glared at him.

"You do see me, right?" Roland asked. "Her brother? Her flesh and blood?"

Slade rolled his eyes. "You thought your sister was a blushing virgin?"

Cayson never answered. He ignored Slade.

"So that's a no," Slade said.

"I'm not having this conversation right now," Cayson whispered.

Slade rolled his eyes. "Ro, you care if Cayson sleeps with your sister?"

Roland left the table. "I'm going to take a piss..."

Cayson gave him a hard look. "He might be my brother-in-law someday. I'd prefer it if he liked me."

"He already likes you," Slade said. "Everyone does. And your life would be a lot simpler if you didn't give a damn what people thought of you to begin with."

Cayson stared at Skye while she bowled.

"Dude, what are you waiting for?" Slade asked. "Do the deed already."

"I will...soon. Now let's stop talking about this," Cayson said.

"Skye really wants to do it," I added. "Like, *really*."

Cayson's face flushed red and he ignored my look.

Skye came back and sat on his lap. "Did you see that? I hit one pin!"

"Good job, baby." He kissed her.

"Wow," Slade said. "You're worse than Trinity. I didn't think that was possible."

I wasn't sure if he wanted to pick a fight or if he was just doing it to keep people from being suspicious. I couldn't tell what was going on anymore. I decided to go along with it. "You suck at everything."

He gave me a glare but it didn't look genuine. "You're ugly."

"Likewise."

"There they are," Conrad said sarcastically.

We finished the game, and Cayson was the victor.

"When did you get good at everything?" Skye asked.

He smirked. "I used to let you win. You still haven't figured that out?"

"What?" Skye look shocked. "Then why did you stop?"

"I already have you. I don't have to do anything." He smirked at the appalled look on her face.

Roland nodded. "Good. My sister is too much of a brat anyway."

We turned in our equipment to the counter then walked to our cars. Slade walked close to me, his hands in his pockets.

Roland and Conrad got into the truck then drove away, waving. Skye and Cayson left in his car, just leaving him and I. Instead of walking to his car, Slade walked with me.

This was weird.

I stopped when I reached my car. "What?"

He leaned against the side and crossed his arms over his chest. He stared across the parking lot for a long time before he spoke. "What's going on between us? Like, what is this?"

"Slade, why are you acting like a girl?"

He rolled his eyes. "I'm not asking if we're in a relationship. Just...what is this? Like, are we going to keep doing it? Or...just at random times? Shouldn't we talk about this? Or should we stop?"

I shrugged. "I guess."

"What? That we should talk about this or stop doing it?"

"I don't know...what do you want to do? I didn't think we'd do it again after the first time but then you jumped my bones."

"Don't act like you didn't want it."

"You came on to me, remember?"

"And you sucked my dick then rode me like a damn cowgirl," he snapped. "Let's not play the blame game. You wouldn't have fucked me so easily unless you had thought about it before.

652

And you didn't drink at all that night so you were totally sober."

I didn't have an argument against that. "Well, what do you want to do?"

He shrugged. "What do you want to do?"

It seemed like neither one of us wanted to put our cards on the table.

He stared at me, waiting for me to respond.

I held his gaze and said nothing.

He sighed. "Fine. I'll go first." He paused for a long time, running his fingers through his hair. "Honestly, sex with you is pretty fucking fantastic. Of course I want to keep doing it."

"I like it too..." I crossed my arms over my chest, still acting indifferent.

"If we keep doing this, we should have some sort of system so we don't get caught. You agree?" he asked.

I nodded.

"Okay. I really don't want anyone to find out about us."

"That makes two of us," I agreed.

"So...this is a booty call situation, right?"

"That's fine."

"Alright. We'll text in code just in case someone sees the messages."

"What kind of code would this be?"

He shrugged. "'A' means come over. 'B' means can I come over?"

I shook my head. "And you don't think that would be suspicious if someone read it? Like Cayson?"

"Then what's your idea, genius?" he snapped.

"'Go to hell' means come over. 'I hope you die' means can I come over? That sounds a lot more believable coming from us."

"What if I want to call you?" he asked.

"Just call, idiot."

He rolled his eyes. "Do we have any rules?"

"What kind of rules?"

"Are we exclusive?"

"I assumed we weren't." I wouldn't stop dating and looking for Mr. Right just because I was fooling around with a jerk.

"That's fine with me. But are...we going to keep doing it...without wearing anything?"

"As long as you're clean, I don't care. It feels better anyway."

"Are you clean?" he demanded.

I glared at him. "I'm going to pretend you didn't ask that."

"Do you normally not wear anything with guys?" he asked.

I glared at him.

"Hey, I'm sleeping with you. I have the right to ask this."

"Never."

"Then why didn't you make me wear anything?"

"I don't know. There wasn't time. It all happened so fast. And since you didn't wear anything the first time, if you had something, I was already screwed. So why wear something a second time?"

"Well, I'm anal about my sexual health so don't worry about that."

"Do you always wear something?"

"Fuck yeah," he snapped. "I don't want to catch something or knock up some girl. They might say they're on the pill even if they aren't just to trick you."

"How do you know I'm not tricking you?" I questioned.

He gave me a look that clearly said, "Shut the hell up."

"Okay. So, we always wear something with other people. We only text in code. What else?"

"What about our friendship?" he asked.

"What about it?" I questioned. "We were never friends to begin with."

He smirked. "I guess that's true. But what about when one of us wants to end it?"

"Then we walk away. End of story."

"Just like that?" he asked incredulously. "You aren't going to start crying or beg me to stay?"

I cocked an eyebrow. "Slade, you're the kind of guy I like to sleep with, not *go* to sleep with. Believe me, we won't have a problem."

"Good, because I don't do the relationship thing and I never will."

"Shocking," I said sarcastically.

"I'm serious. Don't expect me to change for you."

"I don't," I said firmly. "I would never want something more with you—ever."

He seemed to believe me. "I'm glad we got that settled."

"Alright. Are we done here?" I was eager to go home and take a bath.

"Yeah." He moved away from my car and put his hands in his pockets.

"I'll see you later." I opened the car door then got inside.

He drifted away and found his car on the other side of the parking lot.

I couldn't believe I just had that conversation with Slade. We were fuck buddies now. Never in a million years did I think that would happen. I should have just said no, but I liked good sex. And Slade was at least good at that.

My phone vibrated so I looked at the screen.

It was Slade. *I hope you die.*

I smirked and stared at the screen. *See you soon.*

Chapter Thirty-Two

Cayson

I dropped the subject of Zack but that didn't mean I stopped thinking about it. The fact he bugged Skye twice got under my skin. He obviously planned it when I wasn't around. That meant he was watching her. That made me extremely uncomfortable.

What did he want from her? What was he trying to do? What was he trying to gain? I couldn't find an answer just and that made me panic. It seemed like he wanted revenge.

Maybe I was overreacting, but when it came to Skye, I was always like that. If it were any of the girls in my family, I'd be on edge. Harassment wasn't okay in my book. But since Skye was at a different level than every other person on the planet, that just made me more concerned about the situation.

What were my options? I could kick his ass but what would that accomplish? He would just come back, even more pissed off. I could kill him but I'd have to live with the guilt forever. Plus, I had to do it and not get caught. And I would be a prime suspect in the investigation. I could try to have an adult conversation with him and make him see reason, but Zack didn't strike me as a reasonable guy. I could walk Skye to every class and never leave her side, which was fine, but she wouldn't live that way forever. Knowing Skye, she would quickly get irritated by the constant watch. She would lash out at me and that would put a strain on our relationship.

I had to tell her father.

I knew she would be pissed but I didn't care. He was the only person who could make something like this disappear. He had the money and the resources to get away with pretty much anything. Skye would be pissed if she knew but I had to do it. I had to.

***

The bar was quiet tonight. Only a few guys hung around and watched a recap of a game from earlier that day. My beer sat in front of me but I didn't touch it. I just wasn't in the mood for alcohol, or anything. Skye thought I was playing ball with Slade. It seemed to be the most convincing excuse.

The door opened and a tall man in a suit walked inside. He headed to my place by the bar, walking with perfect posture. When he reached me, he unbuttoned his jacket then slid onto the stool. He looked at me with his menacing blue eyes but didn't say anything.

Uncle Sean never greeted me this way. It was always with a warm hug and a smile. But I knew he was on edge. My phone call didn't exactly make him happy.

"What's this about?" he asked quietly. He glanced around the bar discreetly, making sure no one was near us.

"Skye."

He tensed up noticeably and his eyes became more threatening. "Is my daughter okay?" He kept his voice low but his tone conveyed his concern. And his protectiveness was obvious.

"She's fine. She's sitting at home watching *I Love Lucy*."

He relaxed slightly. "Then what is it, Cayson?"

The bartender approached and gave him a beer.

Uncle Sean didn't drink it.

There was no going back. "Zack. He won't leave her alone."

He stared at me, his eyes guarded and his jaw clenched tightly.

"I kicked his ass the first time, broke his nose and unhinged his jaw. The second time Slade gave him a good pounding. But he won't stay away. He waits until Skye is alone then he harasses her. He keeps asking for an apology. Skye claims he isn't dangerous but I don't believe that. He sounds like a fucking psychopath to me."

He didn't react. He hardly moved. It was almost like he hadn't heard me at all. His Rolex shined on his wrist, and his wedding band reflected the dim lighting in the bar. "I'll take care of it."

"What are you going to do?"

"Kill him." He said it plainly, like he was discussing the weather.

"Skye is going to know it was you. I don't think that's a good idea."

He processed my words for a while. "I'll make sure he doesn't bother her, Cayson."

"What are you going to do?"

"I'll hire someone to give him a good scare. He'll shit his pants. Then I'll have a few guys tail him everywhere he goes, and they won't make their presence unknown. Zack will know he can't do anything without my knowledge. If he knows what's good for him, he'll knock it off and never speak to her again."

That was good enough for me. "Okay."

He finally sipped his beer, his eyes dark.

"Please don't tell Skye I told you."

He wouldn't look at me. "She should have told me herself."

"She thinks she can handle everything on her own. For the most part, that's true. But in this case...I'd rather not take the chance."

"I'll keep your secret, Cayson."

"Thank you." I could tell he was still in a bad mood. "I can take care of her myself. I haven't let her out of my sight. I just thought you would want to know—"

"I know you can take care of her, Cayson. I never doubted that."

"Okay. Because even now, Slade is sitting in his car in front of her apartment while I'm here."

Uncle Sean looked at me with approval in his eyes. "You have my respect. You've always had it. And keep in mind that most men don't. I have no doubt you're the right man for my daughter."

That meant the world to me. "Thanks."

He patted my shoulder then tossed some cash on the table. "I need to hit the road. My wife is waiting for me."

"I should get home too."

This time he hugged me and held it for a while. "Thank you for telling me. I only wish my daughter would turn to me more often."

"She knows how you get."

"I get that way for a reason—because I love my daughter more than anything." He pulled away then gave me a firm look. "I'll see you later."

"Bye."

He walked out and disappeared.

I stayed at the bar and finished my beer.

***

When I got out of my car, Slade got out of his. He rubbed his hands together and vapor escaped his lips.

"About damn time." He cupped his hands to his face and blew his hot breath on them. He was wearing a t-shirt and jeans even though it was snowing outside. "I've been freezing my ass off."

"Then turn on the heater."

"And waste the gas? I'm not rich, man."

"Then wear a jacket," I argued.

"Then you can't see my tatts."

"Were you expecting to run into someone while you sat in your car for an hour?" I asked sarcastically.

He shrugged. "It could happen."

I rolled my eyes then stuffed my keys into my pocket. "Did he come by?"

"No. He probably never will. I'm sure he knows you're hanging around like a bat in a cave."

I cocked an eyebrow. "What kind of comparison is that?"

"What? Don't bats always stay in one spot?"

"Because they have to be in the dark," I argued. "That makes no sense at all."

"Whatever. Fine. Zack knew you would be hanging around like a...shark."

"A shark?" I asked. "They are fish so they have to swim around. By definition, they can't linger in one spot."

He rolled his eyes. "Fine, like a sand fish. You know, those things that hide under the sand in the ocean and become camouflaged. Then they—"

"Okay. Just stop. I get your point."

"About time." He rubbed his hands together again. "So, what were we saying?"

"Zack didn't come by."

"Yeah, no sign of him. How was Uncle Sean? Was he pissed? Did he turn into the Incredible Hulk?"

"He was pissed but he didn't freak out."

"Is he going to kill Zack?"

"No. He's going to scare him off and have guys follow him everywhere he goes."

Slade nodded his head in approval. "Uncle Sean...the badass."

"I don't think he's a badass...he just cares about his daughter."

"Same difference." He leaned against the car door. "So, are you going to get laid tonight?"

Did he ever talk about anything else? "Why do you care?"

"You're my boy. You've been dating her for months. You deserve some action."

"I get plenty of action from her," I argued.

"Unless it's pussy, it's not the same thing."

I raised my hand. "Look, you can talk about the other girls I've been with like that, but not Skye. It's different with her. I mean it."

He rolled his eyes. "Whatever, Romeo. So, are you going to get it on or what?"

I leaned against my car door and faced him. "We almost did last week."

His jaw dropped. "What the hell stopped you?"

"The pizza guy knocked on the door."

"I'm not following... Why didn't you just take the pizza, slam the door, and then slip it inside her?"

"That's not exactly romantic."

"So?" He shrugged. "Sex isn't supposed to be romantic. It's sex."

"You've obviously never been in love with anyone before."

"What gave you that idea?" he said sarcastically.

"I just want it to be perfect, you know? This is the woman I'm going to spend the rest of my life with."

Slade gave me an incredulous look. "Aren't you jumping the gun?"

"You even said the same thing."

"Nothing is set in stone," he argued.

"Well, it's going to happen. I know it is."

"Then you have the rest of your life to make it romantic. Now get your dick wet," Slade said. He rubbed his arms to fight the chill.

"What did I just say?" I snapped.

"You're no fun anymore."

"And you need to grow up."

He crossed his arms over his chest and eyed her apartment. "Have you seen Jasmine since?"

"No...I feel bad."

He shrugged. "Whatever. You told her you were with Skye. It shouldn't be surprising."

"But Skye was all over me, practically rubbing Jasmine's nose in it." I ran my fingers through my hair. "I hated the pained look on her face. I felt like such a jackass."

"Hurting her will probably make it easier for her to move on."

"She's such a nice girl...she deserves someone really great."

"Well...do you mind if I get in on that action?"

I gave him a threatening look. "Don't even think about it."

"What?" He raised his hands in innocence. "If you aren't tapping her, somebody should. Ever since she said you fucked her on the dryer in your apartment building, I've been intrigued."

"I mean it, Slade. She's off limits."

He rolled his eyes. "Greedy..."

"Slade, do I have your word?"

He sighed. "Fine. Whatever."

"Thank you." I moved to my feet. "I should get inside." I eyed his pale skin. "And you should go home before you get hypothermia."

"I don't need to be told twice." He turned to his car.

"And get a jacket."

"No. I got these sleeves for a reason."

"Fine. Die for all I care."

"I'll see you in hell then." He shut the door and started the car.

I shook my head then walked up the stairs to her apartment. I used my spare key to get inside.

Skye was sitting on the couch with a bowl of popcorn in her lap. "How was hanging out with Slade?"

"Fine."

"Who won?"

"Who won what?" I asked.

"The game." She raised an eyebrow. "Didn't you play basketball together?"

Oh yeah. "I won," I blurted. "He was a big baby about it."

"Slade's a big baby about everything."

I moved to the couch beside her and grabbed a handful of popcorn. Then I shoved it into my mouth. "What have you been doing?"

"Just watching TV." She wore a t-shirt with her flannel bottoms. Even when she was wearing her pajamas, she still looked beautiful.

"I'm surprised you aren't studying for a test or something."

"I can only read a textbook for so long."
She munched on the popcorn until it was gone.
"I'm exhausted…"

"Why?"

"I don't know." She yawned. "I went on a jog earlier. I guess I'm really out of shape."

I stilled. "You went on a jog—alone?"

"It was only for a few miles."

"Skye, I told you not to leave my sight." My voice became full of anger.

"Well, I don't do whatever you tell me," she argued.

I knew where this was going. "I'm not trying to boss you around. With Zack giving you a hard time, I would prefer it if you didn't go around by yourself, especially at night."

"I'm not scared of him and I refuse to live my life that way."

"It's only temporary. Then you can go back to doing whatever you want. If you go on a jog, I'm more than happy to go with you."

She gave me a hard look. "You've known me your entire life, Cayson. You know what kind of girl I am. I'm not going to let that fly."

I knew I had to be firmer with her. "We can do this the easy way or the hard way. Your choice."

Her eyes narrowed. "Excuse me?"

I sighed. "I'm sorry, Skye. I hate to be this way. You know it's not in my nature. I just care

668

about you and I need to look after you...until I know he'll really leave you alone. Please don't make this harder for me."

She spotted the unease on my face. "Fine. But it's only temporary."

I sighed in relief then kissed her forehead. "Thank you."

She stood up then set the bowl on the table. "I'm going to bed. Are you coming?"

"Duh." I turned off the TV and followed her into the bedroom. I was more aggressive with Skye than I used to be. Now when I wanted something from her, I just took it. Judging the moans that escaped her lips and the way her fingernails dug into my skin, she liked it. I pulled her top off then unclasped her bra with lightning speed. I groped her breasts, loving how warm they felt in my hands. I loved her chest and now I wasn't afraid to admit it. She let me suck them and kiss them whenever I wanted...among other things.

I really wanted to take our relationship to the next level. I was ready and I knew she was too. But tonight didn't feel right. Since I just went and spoke to her father, something she specifically asked me not to do, I felt guilty. Another night of fooling around would have to suffice—for now.

Chapter Thirty-Three

Skye

"If Cayson thinks he's going to boss me around, he's got another thing coming." Zack tried to do the same thing, much more aggressively, and I wasn't a push over. I was a strong, independent woman. It was my way or no way.

Trinity smirked at me then sipped her coffee. "Honestly, Skye...I'm with him on this one."

We were sitting in a coffee shop right off campus. Students littered the tables and jazz music played overhead. I got a blueberry muffin but I only ate half of it. I stared at her incredulously. "Sorry, did I hear you right?"

"If Cayson just brushed off Zack's behavior, I would be worried. You can't blame him for wanting to look after you. I wish I had a guy that was so concerned for my well-being."

"I'm glad he's concerned. I just don't want to be bossed around. There's a big difference."

"He just asked you not to jog in the dark alone." She stared at me like I was crazy. "It's really not a big deal."

Trinity had been my best friend since we could speak. She had my back for everything—

except for this. "What happened to my sassy best friend?"

"She's just telling you how it is. It's not like Cayson is like that all the time. He just wants to wait until Zack stops obsessing over you."

"You know how hard it was for me to come to coffee with you?" I asked. "Without him?"

"Because you miss him?"

"No," I snapped. "Because he almost didn't let me come alone."

She shrugged. "I like Cayson. I wouldn't mind if he came."

I rolled my eyes. "That's not the point. I can hang out with my best friend whenever I want."

"And if Zack appears?"

"We'll kick his ass."

"Last time we tried that, he sat on me like a log."

"I had him," I hissed. "I was going to break his skull with my textbook."

"I still think it's better to avoid Zack than go head-to-head with him again. You must see the logic in that." She rested her elbows on the table while she stared me down.

"I guess..."

"Now cut Cayson some slack. He's the sweetest guy in the world. He would never boss you around. He recognizes your independence and it's one of the reasons he's so attracted to you. Just humor him for a few weeks."

I knew she was right. I was being too stubborn about this. "Okay. Fine."

"Good. Now invite him to coffee with us."

"No, I want to have girl talk with you."

"I'll say anything to Cayson that I say to you," Trinity said.

"It's still a lot more fun when it's just us."

"Well, of course," she said with a laugh. She sipped her coffee then flipped her hair over her shoulder. "Please tell me you've taken a ride on his cock."

"Trinity!" I pressed my finger over my lip. "Shh!" I glanced around the nearby tables to see if anyone had heard.

"Grow up, Skye. No one cares."

It seemed like no harm had been done.

"You better say yes," she pressed.

"No...it hasn't happened yet."

"What the hell is wrong with you guys?" She stared at me like I was crazy.

"It was going to happen the other night but the damn pizza guy ruined it."

"How did he ruin it?"

"He came to the door."

"So? Wasn't he only there for a minute?"

"But it ruined the moment," I said with a sigh.

"Ruined the moment?" she asked incredulously. "Wasn't he still hard? That's enough to keep going."

I laughed lightly. "Cayson wants it to be special."

"Well, if he keeps wanting it to be special, you're never going to have sex at all."

I laughed again. "I know, right?"

"You must be going crazy. It's been months."

I gave her a firm look. "I am going crazy. We fool around but I want everything."

"He satisfies you, right?"

"Oh yeah," I said immediately. "That's not a problem. But I want him, not his hand or his mouth."

"I hear you, girl."

I pulled my tea bag out of my cup then set it on a napkin. "Any men in your life?"

She looked down at her cup and blew the steam away. "No."

"How long have you been single?"

Trinity thought for a moment. Her gold earrings reflected the light, and her lip gloss was shiny. She had perfect features, and her make up only highlighted her stunning appearance. I definitely felt dwarfed by her beauty. "Almost a year."

"When's the last time you had sex?"

She sipped her coffee. "Uh...I can't remember. It's been a while though."

"We should go out so you can pick up someone."

She smirked. "It'll happen when it happens. No need to rush."

"I feel like we haven't gone out in so long." I felt guilty. Since Cayson and I got together, I hadn't been the closest friend to Trinity.

"We're going out now."

"It's not the same. We should hit a club." I didn't really have any interest in that. Now that I had a serious boyfriend, the idea of going out to a noisy club where a bunch of men would stare at my rack and Trinity's legs didn't exactly sound fun.

"We'll see." She looked out the window and watched people go by. Her eyes lost their light for a moment, seeming to disappear. Her lips pressed tightly together like she was thinking.

"Everything okay, Trinity?" I asked.

She turned back to me. "Yeah. I've just got a lot of homework and stuff..."

It still seemed like something was off but I didn't press her on it.

***

Cayson was leaning against my car when I walked outside the coffee shop. He was staring at his phone, hitting his thumb against the screen like he was playing a game. He wore dark jeans and a gray t-shirt. His muscled arms were noticeable under the winter sun. Hair started to come in around his chin, thick and brown. I loved it when he shaved but I also loved it when he didn't. I eyed his body for a moment, remembering how he looked naked on my bed. I wanted to run my tongue all over his body and taste him.

I shook my head and made the thoughts escape. Then I walked over to him. "Hey you."

He put his phone down then turned his gaze on me. His blue eyes suddenly looked brighter when he took me in. A grin stretched his lips. "I'm glad you're happy to see me, not pissed."

"Trinity talked me down."

"I've always liked her." He put his phone in his pocket then embraced me. One hand moved into my hair while he kissed me, making my lips burn. He always moved his lips against mine in just the right way. He clearly knew what he was doing. He steered me against the car door and pressed his body against mine while he continued the embrace.

Then he pulled away slowly. "I think this is getting out of hand..."

"A little." I glanced at his lips then returned my look to his eyes.

"Have a good time with Trinity?"

"Yeah."

"What did you guys do?"

"Talked."

"About?" he asked. "You guys always talk."

"Boys, sex, music...stuff like that."

"Did I come up?" he pressed.

"You always come up."

"Oooh...I hope good things were said."

"They were." I gave him a flirtatious smile.

"And I hope it wasn't just about my...size." A tint came into his cheeks.

"No." I started to blush too.

He stared at me for a moment before he moved his hands to my hips. "Have plans tonight?"

"With you, I assume."

"Can I take you to dinner?"

"You can take me anywhere."

"Good answer." He leaned in and kissed me. "I'll pick you up at seven."

"Okay."

"You want to sleep at my place tonight?"

Why did it matter? He never asked that. "Sure."

"Okay." He opened my door and helped me get inside. "I'll see you then."

"Okay."

He gave me another kiss. "Wear something nice." He shut the door and walked back to his car.

***

I wore a backless black dress with silver heels. A matching bracelet was on my wrist and diamond earrings were in my lobes. My pea coat was hanging over the chair. I wanted Cayson to see my dress before I put it on, just to see his reaction. I thought I looked pretty decent. Hopefully he liked the way I looked.

A knock on the door announced his presence.

"Come in," I called.

He stepped inside, wearing slacks and a button up shirt.

I whistled. "Someone looks like a million bucks."

He eyed my waist and legs. "I can say the same about you." He hooked one arm around my waist and rested his hand on my bare back. His fingers trailed down the skin. "I like this…"

"You do?" I was pleased by his words.

"I like your skin." He moved behind me then pulled my hair over one shoulder. Then he pressed a kiss between my shoulder blades, making heat move through my body.

"I like your lips."

He came back around me, his hand moving to my chin. "You look lovely tonight." His eyes moved down to my chest then back to my eyes. "But you're missing something."

"What?" I blurted. I checked everything.

He pulled a box out of his pocket then opened it.

Inside was a white gold bracelet. On the chain were moons and clouds. I stared at it for a moment before I picked it up. It was light and smooth in my hands. I turned it over and saw the engraving.

A billion stars in the Skye. Only one you.

My heart swelled at the sight. I looked back at him, at a loss for words. "Cayson…"

"Shh." He grabbed the bracelet then clasped it onto my wrist. He removed the one that was already there. "You don't need to say anything. I just want you to have it." His fingers stroked the skin of my wrist before he placed a gentle kiss there. "Now you're perfect."

My eyes watered. "I'm perfect with you."

Affection moved into his eyes then he stepped closer to me. "That's the truest thing I've ever heard you say." He cupped my neck and placed a gentle kiss on my forehead.

I rested my face against his chest, treasuring the moment. Cayson's sweetness always caught me by surprise. He did everything and anything to make me happy. "I'm sorry I was being a brat before…"

"It's water under the bridge." He kissed my lips gently then pulled away. "Are you hungry?"

"Have we just met?" I countered.

He gave me a fond look before he grabbed my coat and put it over my shoulders. "Ready?"

I nodded.

We left the apartment then headed to the restaurant. When we pulled up to the front, I realized it was an Italian place.

"I know how much you love pizza," he said. "This was my way of taking you to a nice place but giving you what you really want."

I smirked. "Genius idea."

We walked inside then moved to the table near the window. Like always, Cayson pulled out the chair for me and allowed me to sit down before he sat across from me. He handed a menu to me before he looked at his own.

"I don't know if I should get the eighteen inch or sixteen inch pizza..." I stared at the menu while I tried to decide.

He smirked at me. "Get the twenty inch and take the leftovers home. I know you like to munch in the middle of the night."

"So, you won't judge me?"

"Have I ever?" He looked at his menu again. "I'm getting the tortellini."

"Pizza is better," I blurted.

"You never order anything else." He said it in a condescending way but affection was in his eyes.

"Because it's good."

The waiter came to our table and took our order. The bottle Cayson ordered when we arrived was poured.

"This is a fancy evening," I said.

"I wanted it to be special." He looked into my eyes as he said it.

Then it hit me. When we went back to his place tonight, we wouldn't fool around and go to sleep. What I've been looking forward to was finally going to happen. I tried to hide my excitement but I had a feeling my face was giving it away.

We made small talk about school and our family. Our voices were low while we talked over the clanking glasses and moving plates. We drank our wine until the bottle was empty then ate our meals when they arrived. I would normally eat half of my pizza but tonight I didn't want my stomach to be too full. So, I just ate a few slices. Cayson didn't eat as much as he normally did. Perhaps he was nervous.

When the check came, he slipped the cash inside.

"Can I get the tip?" I asked.

"Nope." He pushed the tab away then placed the remainder of my pizza in the to-go box.

"You need to let me pay sometime."

"Nope," he said again. He stood up then pulled out my chair for me. "Let's get this pizza in the fridge." His arm moved around my waist and he led me out of the restaurant. Knowing what we were going to do when we got to his place made my heart race. I was excited and warm. My nerves were firing off and I was eager to feel him. I daydreamed about our rendezvous for the entire ride home, imagining how he would feel when he was finally inside me. By the time we pulled into the parking lot, I was wet.

After we walked inside, he put the pizza box in the refrigerator then came back to me. "Thank you for having dinner with me."

"Thanks for feeding me."

Silence.

He stared at me, his hands by his sides.

I met his gaze, suddenly feeling sweat on my palms. I was nervous, but not in a bad way.

Cayson moved his hands to my hips then bunched up my dress lightly. He eyed my body for a moment, his eyes lingering on my chest, and then he met my gaze. Desire was in his eyes, shining bright.

My lips parted on their own, my need guiding me. I pressed my chest to his then leaned my face near his. His warm breath fell on my cheek. Since I knew where this was going, it felt different. It was like the first time all over again.

Cayson stared at me until he finally closed the distance and kissed me. His embrace was gentle and purposeful. He took his time, not rushing. His hand moved up my stomach and my chest until he reached my neck. His fingers dug into my hair while he deepened the kiss. His tongue slipped into my mouth, lightly touching mine.

I was lost to him immediately. His kiss always swept me off my feet. The way his tongue felt against mine was unlike any experience I ever had. He was the best kisser I've ever been with, hands down. He put every other guy I dated to shame. My relationship with Cayson was different. It was beautiful, pure.

Cayson slowly led me down the hallway, stopping every few feet to give me a passionate kiss. He pressed me into the wall while his hands moved over my body. He would grip me tightly, like he never wanted to let go. Then he led me down the hallway again, heading for his room.

When we walked inside, there was a gentle glow from dozens of white candles. They flickered as we passed. He continued to kiss me as he led me to his bed. When I felt the frame behind me, I stopped.

Cayson stared into my eyes while he found the zipper at my side. He pulled it down, never looking at his hand. Once it was loose, he pulled it down, revealing my bare chest. I couldn't wear a bra with the dress so nothing was covering me. He got it off then picked me up and placed me on the bed. He grabbed each foot and slipped my heels off. Then he kissed my calves and knees, moving to my inner thighs. When he was between my legs, he grabbed my thong and pulled it off.

I lay back on the bed and felt a lump. I reached behind me and pulled out a candy bar. Rose petals and bite size candies were across the bed. "Candy bars?" I asked with a smirk.

"I know what my baby likes."

My heart swelled and I cupped his face. "I love you so much, Cayson."

His eyes filled with emotion. "And I you." He placed a gentle kiss on my lips before he moved down my body and to the area between my legs. His mouth moved over my folds and his tongue did wonderful things. He always touched me the right way, like he could read my mind. He pushed me to the edge but wouldn't let me fall over.

I leaned up and unbuttoned his shirt. I was eager for him so my fingers worked furiously. They shook slightly, my need obvious.

"Don't rush. Make it last." He kept his voice low while he stared at me.

My hands slowed down as I finished. I couldn't contain my excitement. I'd been waiting for this my whole life. When every button was undone, I pushed the shirt over his shoulders and let it fall to the floor. Then I pressed my lips to the skin over his heart, giving him a gentle kiss. His hand moved into my hair, a quiet moan that was almost inaudible coming from his lips.

My hands undid his jeans then pulled them down. I took his boxers too. Cayson kicked out of his shoes then tore off his socks. When he was naked, I stared at him for a second, taking in all his glory.

Cayson stared back at me before he scooped me up and moved me further up his bed, resting my head on one of his pillows. A few candy bars got in the way so we pushed them aside.

I wrapped my legs around his waist then dug my hands into his hair. His lips sought mine in the dim glow and he breathed hard into my mouth, setting it on fire. His hard cock lay against my stomach. It was thick and long, definitely impressive. I was eager to feel him. I knew it would be an experience I'd never forget.

Cayson opened his nightstand and pulled out a foil wrapper. Then he tore it open like he'd done it a hundred times.

I snatched it from his hands then threw it on the floor. "I don't want you to wear one." I always practiced safe sex but Cayson was different. I didn't want to be separated by latex for our first time.

"Are you on the pill?" he whispered.
"Yes."

"Good. I didn't want to wear one either." He moved back over me and separated my legs with his.

My hands moved to his arms, feeling the muscle, and then around to his back. I was shaking with excitement and I wasn't sure how to hold on. Cayson grabbed my legs then moved his arms behind my knees. We were as close as possible. His head was pressed to mine and then I felt his tip at my entrance. My hands moved to his arms and I squeezed them in anticipation.

Cayson slowly moved inside me, stretching me the second he entered me. I was wet so it was easy for him to slide through. He stared into my eyes as he inserted himself further, going until he was completely sheathed.

Damn, he felt good.

I breathed hard while he stretched me. My body took a moment to acclimate to his large size. My fingers dug into his skin of their own accord. I stared into his eyes, seeing the desire and love shine back at me.

Then he started to move, sliding in and out without shaking the bed. Every movement was precise, hitting me in the right spot. He didn't kiss me. Instead, he watched my face and locked his eyes with mine. He took his time, going slow.

My hands moved up his neck and into his hair. He already felt so amazing and I didn't want it to end. I enjoyed him in a way I never enjoyed another guy before.

Cayson continued to move and a moan escaped his lips. "Fuck, you feel good, Skye."

"You feel better." Sweat formed on my upper lip.

He leaned in and kissed me gently, using his tongue to tantalize mine. He moved at that pace for a long time, not in a hurry to reach the finish line. Then he pulled away and started to move faster. Sweat formed on his chest and I touched it with my hand, feeling the heat.

"Cayson..."

He moved harder and faster, pushing me into the bed with his strength.

I felt the distant burn in my stomach as his desire grew to a crescendo. My legs started to shake and I moaned incoherently. My nails dug into his skin, about to make him bleed. Then it hit me like a slab of bricks. My head rolled back as the explosion reached every part of my body, making my fingers and toes tingle.

"You're so beautiful," he said through his heavy breathing.

It lasted for almost a full minute, the longest orgasm I've ever experienced. The area between my legs grew tender as he continued to slide in and out. Even though I had already climaxed, it still felt good.

Cayson pressed his lips to mine then breathed hard. He started to tense up as he moved into me harder. A deep moan from the back of his throat escaped his lips then he tensed again, starting to fill me. "Skye..." He moaned again as he finished.

I moved my hands through his hair, feeling the sweat.

He stayed over me, still inside me. When he recovered from his moment, he looked into my eyes. An instant passed between us, unspoken but still acknowledged. I knew what it meant on his part, and I knew what it meant on mine.

Cayson kissed my forehead before he pulled out of me then lay in the bed beside me. He was hot and sweaty but he still hooked his arm around my waist and cuddled with me. "How was that for you?"

I rolled him to his back then leaned over him. "Wow...just wow."

He smirked with fondness in his eyes.

"I want to do it again," I blurted.

He laughed slightly. "I'd love to. Just give me a few minutes."

I kissed his chest and stomach. "You're really good at that. I can't believe we waited so long."

His hands moved through my hair. "It was worth the wait."

"I want to do it all the time," I blurted again.

"Can I get that in writing?"

I laughed then rubbed my nose against his. "Cayson, you're the perfect man. I was stupid for not realizing it before, but now that I do, you're mine forever. I'm never letting you go."

Fondness moved into his eyes. He stared at me for a long time. "The feeling is mutual."

"Good. Because you're stuck with me."

"And there's no one else I'd rather be stuck with."

We lay in the dark, touching each other and sharing quiet kisses. Silence stretched as our hands did all the talking. He moved his fingers through my hair then across my skin. I felt his chest, noting the feel of his muscles.

When an hour had passed, I crawled on top of him. "Round two."

A grin stretched his face. "Yes, ma'am."

Chapter Thirty-Four

Slade

When I saw Cayson on campus, he had a stupid grin on his face. "Why do you look like an idiot?"

He shrugged, the ridiculous grin still there. "It's a beautiful day."

I cocked an eyebrow. "A beautiful day? Are you a poet now?"

"You asked what I'm grinning about and I told you."

I studied his face, not believing him. Then it hit me. "You fucked Skye!"

"Keep your voice down," he hissed. He looked around the hall to make sure no one had heard. "I mean it. I don't want everyone knowing my business."

"I can't believe this. How was she?"

"Why do you think I'm grinning?" he countered.

I clapped him on the shoulder. "You're finally a man."

"I've been a man for a long time, actually."

"You aren't a real man until you've had Skye Preston, man."

I cringed. "Dude, for the last time, she's your cousin."

He ignored my words. "So, what position?"

"I'm not going into detail with you."

"Was she on top?"

"How lazy do you think I am?" I snapped.

"Was she ever on top?"

"Why does it matter?" I asked.

He shrugged. "If this is the girl you're going to spend the rest of your life with, you got to make sure she's not selfish in bed."

He rolled his eyes. "Well, we're good there."

"Did you buy her dinner first?"

"Yeah," he said. "And I had candles and rose petals in the bedroom."

"Cliché," I blurted.

"And candy bars," he added. "You know Skye has a sweet tooth."

"Okay...that's pretty cool," I agreed. "Wait until everyone hears about this."

"Slade, this stays between us. I don't want Roland to know."

Cayson could be annoying sometimes. "Dude, you've known Roland your whole life. He's never been the protective brother type. He doesn't care what Skye does."

"I still don't think he wants to hear about me having sex with her," he snapped.

"Whatever."

"Don't say anything to anyone."

690

"What about Trinity?"

"What? Why would you talk to her at all?"

Oh yeah. We hated each other. That's right. "I just meant in passing."

"I'm sure she knows anyway. Skye tells her everything."

"That's what normal friends do," I snapped.

Cayson looked at his watch. "I have to get to class. I'll see you later."

"Basketball tonight?"

"Sure." He disappeared down the hallway.

***

I went to a local bar and scouted the talent. Sipping my beer at the counter, I searched the crowd and tried to find a winner. A lot of cute girls lingered around. They were in packs, wearing short dresses with sparkly rhinestones. When it came to women, I was particularly attracted to long legs. I'd always been that way. A nice rack and ass were important too but I usually searched for legs.

I zoned in on one blonde in particular. She had a curvy waist and bright blue eyes. When she laughed, a full set of perfect teeth were noticeable. She was really cute. I wouldn't mind watching her breasts jiggle while I fucked her on my bed.

When I fast-forwarded through our evening together, I realized I'd have to wear a condom, a thick slab of latex that blocked the best sensations from my cock. Then she would want to snuggle and I'd have to push her away. Then I'd have to kick her out and she would call me a dick. It sounded like a lot of work.

My phone vibrated and I looked at the screen.

It was Trinity. *Go to hell.*

I smirked when I read the message. I was in the middle of catching tail, but Trinity was a good lay. I didn't have to wear a condom with her, I didn't have to pretend to care, I didn't have to kick her out, and I could be myself.

She was the clear winner.

I abandoned the blonde in the corner and drove to Trinity's house a few miles away. The lights shone through her windows and snow littered her lawn. I parked in her driveway then headed to her front door. After I knocked, she answered.

"You came quick."

"I was down the street," I answered.

She walked away and let me come inside.

I shut the door and locked it behind me. "Did you know Skye and Cayson finally fucked?"

"Yeah, she told me." Trinity walked into her bedroom. "About time. If she wasn't going to fuck Cayson, I was going to do it for her."

I followed her then saw her pull her shirt off. "You have a thing for Cayson?"

"Of course not. But I'm not stupid. He's clearly a catch."

"You think I'm a catch too?" I winked at her.

She rolled her eyes. "Sure, Slade." She unbuttoned her jeans then pushed them down. She stood in a purple bra and matching thong. Her long legs traveled for days. I eyed them for a long moment, excited to feel them wrapped around my waist.

I came closer to her then pulled my shirt off.

Trinity stared at the tattoos that marked my chest and arms. Her hand moved to my sternum while she stared at the artwork.

"I always knew you were into ink."

"It is pretty hot."

Wow, she actually paid me a compliment.

"Now, are we going to talk all night or get to the good stuff?"

Her forwardness surprised me. "I don't need to be told twice."

I lay beside her, trying to catch my breath. I never expected Trinity to be so good in bed. She knew exactly what she was doing and how to rock my world. Every kiss and every touch electrified me.

She pulled her pillow closer to her then sighed in satisfaction.

***

■■

I stared at her, watching her face. "You know what's weird?"

"Hmm?" She didn't open her eyes.

"This isn't weird."

"Why would it be weird? It's just sex. It's like two friends going for a jog together. It's just an activity like any other."

"I've never had a fuck buddy relationship like this."

"Really?" She opened her eyes and seemed surprised.

"Yeah. They always want more."

"Well, I think since we despise each other so much, we don't have to worry about that." She laughed lightly.

"Man, having sex without a rubber is heaven. I was going to pick up this girl tonight but the thought of wearing one made my hard-on disappear."

"It's that different?" she asked.

"Just take my word for it." I rested my hands behind my head and stared at the ceiling. Normally, I would leave a girl's house as quickly as possible but I didn't feel rushed. Trinity knew my visit didn't mean anything. "Meet anybody lately?" I wasn't jealous, just curious.

"No." She sighed sadly. "I'm not even bothering to look anymore."

"What do you mean?" I grabbed my beer from the nightstand and took a sip.

"All guys are jerks. I'm sick of expecting them to be anything more than that."

"I'm not a jerk."

She gave me a look that clearly said, "You've got to be kidding, right?"

"I'm not Prince Charming, obviously," I blurted. "But I'm not a liar or a cheat. With me, you know exactly what you're getting."

"Which isn't much," she said sarcastically.

"The guys that lie and treat you like you actually mean something to them then run around with other girls and spit out lies more than truths are the real assholes. I don't like hurting people so I avoid it. I get this reputation for being a jackass when all I am is honest. It gets old."

She processed my words for a moment. "I guess you have a point."

"Damn right I do." I took another drink.

She turned on her lamp and then grabbed a book from her nightstand. She sat up and began to read it.

"What are you reading?" I asked.

"*One Flew Over the Cuckoo's Nest.*"

"Are you reading it for class?"

"No." She continued to read through the words. "I like to read."

I eyed her bookshelf in the corner and saw all the books piled high. "That's an interesting choice for a girl."

She cocked an eyebrow and looked at me. "What's that supposed to mean?"

"I just don't think most girls would like to read that."

"And what should I be reading?" she demanded. "Jane Eyre?"

"No, I'm just surprised. That's all."

She closed the book and looked at the cover. "It's my dad's favorite book. He let me borrow it."

"Uncle Mike knows how to read?" I said with a laugh.

"He reads a lot, actually. He started a few years ago. We have our own father-daughter book club."

"That's actually really cute."

"Cute?" She looked at me like I was crazy. "I've never heard you use that word before."

"Doesn't mean I don't know it," I snapped. "I did get into Harvard after all."

"And how is still a mystery..." She opened her book again.

I rolled my eyes and let her comment go unchallenged. I eyed the window and watched the snow fall. Trinity kept her house particularly clean. You could eat soup off the carpet if you really wanted to. She always had flowers on every table, and candles were lit in the kitchen, her room, and the bathroom. It was peaceful and warm. "I'm too tired to go home."

She flipped the page and kept reading.

"Do you mind if I sleep here?"

"I don't care." She pulled her knees to her chest and rested the book on her thighs. "Just don't get in my way in the morning."

"I can do that." I took out my phone and played a game. "What's your favorite book of all time?"

She sighed and put her book down. "You aren't going to let me read, are you?"

"Let's be real; my company is far more entertaining than a psych ward full of weirdos and a murderous nurse."

"That's debatable." She put the book on her nightstand.

"You don't have a bookmark?"

"No."

"Then how do you know where you left off?"

"I remember it," she said with an attitude. She turned off the lamp then got comfortable under the covers.

I turned on my side and faced her, the comforter up to my shoulder. "So, what's your favorite book?"

"*The Odyssey.*" She said it without hesitation.

I didn't expect her to say that. "Isn't that the epic Greek novel that's a million pages long?"

"It is."

Trinity caught me by surprise. I never thought she was stupid but I didn't think she was smart either. "Why?"

"I like that it's a story that takes place over years and years. It's chronological and shows a man's life over time. I think that's how a story should be. Not every chapter is a synopsis of the good stuff. It tells everything, the good and the bad."

I processed her words for a moment. "Do you have any other favorites?"

"By definition, you can only have one."

"Then what are others you like?"

"Why do you care?" she snapped.

"It's the first time I've spoken to you and haven't hated you. I think we're making progress. Now answer the damn question, you annoying brat."

She smirked. "*Harry Potter.*"

"Wow...those books couldn't be more different."

"*American Psycho* is another favorite. My dad recommended it."

"About the guy who kills prostitutes?" I blurted.

"Yep. I'm guessing you've only seen the movie. Believe me, the book is a lot better."

"Your dad has interesting and violent tastes in literature."

She shrugged. "My dad can be a bit of a brute sometimes."

"So, are you going to ask me what my favorite book is?"

She laughed. "You know how to read?"

I narrowed my eyes at her. "Yes, I know how to read. Now ask me."

She stopped laughing. "Fine. What's your favorite book?"

"*Schindler's List*."

She gave me an incredulous look. "About the holocaust?"

"I'm a history major. It shouldn't be that surprising."

"But that's...so depressing."

"And your favorites aren't?" I asked. "I like it because it's real. What could be more terrifying, more meaningful, than something that horrific happening less than a hundred years ago? Isn't it weird to think about it like that?"

"I suppose." She stared at me while she thought about it. "And it's weird that slavery wasn't really that long ago."

"Right?" I asked. "It's really weird. That's why I like to read about it because nothing like that would ever happen now—thankfully."

"If you want to ink, why didn't you major in art?" she asked.

"I already know how to draw. I'd rather learn something new that I'm interested in."

She nodded. "I guess that makes sense."

"A lot, actually. Why are you majoring in business if you hate it?"

"I don't hate it."

I gave her a look that clearly said, "Cut the shit."

"Okay, I loathe it," she admitted. "I told my dad how I felt and he said I could pursue fashion if that's what I wanted."

"He wasn't mad?"

She shook her head.

"Wow. That's really cool. Then why are you still here?"

She shrugged. "I'm almost done with my degree. I may as well finish it."

"True. I can't deny the logic in that."

"So, you're really going to ink then? That's set in stone?"

"And I'm going to play in a band."

She smirked. "What band?"

"I don't know yet. But I'll find them."

"I've never heard you play guitar."

"I'm pretty damn good," I said.

"Cocky." She gave me a grin.

"I know I'm good. Why does admitting that make me cocky?"

"You could say it in a better way."

"How?"

"Like, 'I've been playing for a long time and I know all the chords.'"

"But that's pretty much what I said."

"But in a nicer way," she said.

I shook my head. "No. I'm blunt and honest and I'll never change."

"Fine. Be hated by everyone you meet."

"I'd rather be hated for who I am than loved for who I'm not. Besides, you hate me but you're sleeping with me."

She stared at me for a long time. "Slade, I don't hate you..."

"You don't? Because I hate you."

She hit my arm lightly. "No, you don't. I know you don't."

I avoided eye contact and stared at her comforter.

"I think there's more to you than you let on, Slade. But don't worry, I won't tell anyone. You can pretend to be shallow and rude all you want."

"I *am* shallow and rude."

"No. You just try to be. You can fool everyone else but you can't fool me."

"What makes you say that?" I asked.

"You've saved me twice now. And I didn't even ask you to."

"I would have done it for any girl."

"But I don't think you would have beaten the shit out of those guys for just any girl."

I guess she had a point.

"And you even said you couldn't stand the thought of something bad happening to me."

"Well...yeah. You're family."

"See?" She gave me a victorious look. "You are a good guy."

"A guy that uses his friend as a fuck buddy?"

"It's mutual. I'm using you as much as you're using me."

"Let me ask you something," I said.

"What?"

"You can have any guy you want. So why are you settling for this arrangement?"

Her eyes widened when she looked at me. "Did you just give me a compliment?"

"No. Not at all." *Did I? I'm pretty sure I didn't.*

"You just said I could have any guy I wanted."

"That's not a compliment," I argued.

"Yes, it is. It means you think I'm pretty. And not hideous."

"If you were hideous, I wouldn't be fucking you," I said.

She smirked. "Slade thinks I'm pretty." She said it in a high-pitched sing-song voice.

"No, I don't!"

"You think I'm pretty! You like my hair and my face. You like my body and my legs. You like my—"

I sealed my mouth over hers and gave her a hard kiss. My hand dug into her hair, gripping her tightly. I breathed hard into her mouth and she reciprocated that. Our lips crashed together and our tongues danced. Then I pulled away. "Stop talking."

The redness moved into her face and she kept her mouth shut.

"That's better." I settled down under the covers and got ready for bed. The room was dark and warm. Her bed was a million times more comfortable than mine.

She remained quiet on her side of the bed, her breathing even. She never answered my question and I didn't ask her again.

***

When I woke up the following morning, our bodies were tangled together. Her head was resting on my chest and my arm was around her shoulder. Her leg was hooked around mine and it felt smooth against my skin. When I realized what we were doing, I slipped away and got dressed without waking her. Then I left without looking back.

Chapter Thirty-Five

Trinity

Slade still annoyed me but he didn't irritate me as much as he did before. But the friendship and bond forming between us was creating a huge problem. When we were around the others, we didn't fight as much. We had to force it.

Slade looked at me, and his eyes darted back and forth while he was thinking. "I hate you."

Everyone looked up from their food. We were having dinner at a burger place down the street.

"That was random..." Roland eyed him suspiciously.

It sounded forced and unnatural. I could tell Slade was trying too hard. I decided to take the lead. "Cayson told me he beat you at basketball the other day. I knew you sucked."

"I don't suck," he snapped. "You suck."

I gave him a look that said, "I suck your dick alright."

"I mean, you're lame." He picked at his French fries.

"That was the weirdest fight I've ever seen the two of you have," Conrad said. "That was totally out of nowhere."

"Well, I'll always hate her and I never want her to forget it," Slade said.

We really needed to get better at this.

"Why don't you just try to get along?" Conrad asked. "Wouldn't that make everything easier?"

Slade shook his head. "Never."

I finished my fries and ignored him.

"So...I bet you guys are anxious to get home." Conrad gave Skye and Cayson a playful look.

Cayson glanced at Slade and gave him a merciless glare. "I don't know what you're talking about."

"Come on," Conrad said. "We all know you guys finally did the deed."

"Slade, I'm going to kill you," Cayson snapped.

"It wasn't me!" Slade said immediately.

"Who else would have said anything?" Cayson demanded.

"Uh...I did," I said. "Skye told me."

"Oh." Cayson looked apologetic.

"Are you mad I told her?" Skye asked fearfully.

"No, of course not." Cayson put his arm around her shoulders.

"Excuse me?" Slade demanded. "Don't I get an apology?"

"For what?" Cayson asked.

"For being called a liar." He pushed his food away, finished with it.

"Nah." Cayson turned back to Skye and rubbed his nose against hers.

Slade brooded from his seat. "Jackass…"

***

A few days later, I was in the library reading a book. It'd become a pastime that I loved almost more than anything else. Fashion was always my number one choice. But it was nice to get lost in a story that was different from my lame and boring life.

Slade pulled out the chair across from me then sat down. "Yo."

"Hi." I didn't look at him.

He was eating a sandwich, chewing loudly. "What are you reading now?"

"Same book."

He set his sandwich down then opened his backpack. "I got you something."

"If it's a sandwich, I don't want it." All he cared about was food and sex.

"No, it's not that." He placed a book in front of me. It was *Schindler's List*.

"Why are you giving this to me?" I examined the hardcover and the wear and tear along the pages.

"I want you to read it. I'll read The *Odyssey*."

What? "Are we in a book club now?"

He shrugged. "I just thought it would be cool. You can understand why I liked this book so much and I can try to understand why you like yours so much." He examined my open book. "And it looks like you're almost done with that one."

This was weird. Slade and I never did anything together except screw. "Seriously?"

"Yeah. Why not? Can you only be in a book club with one person?"

I guess there was no harm. "Okay. Come over tonight and I'll give you *The Odyssey*."

"We're going to have sex too, right?" he blurted.

I rolled my eyes. "If I'm in the mood."

He laughed. "You're always in the mood."

"Then maybe you should do a better job of keeping me satisfied," I jabbed.

"Hey, I always make you come!"

"Shh!" I narrowed my eyes at him.

He closed his mouth and fell silent just as Skye took a seat at the table.

"Hey," she said.

"Hi." I smiled at her.

"Yo." He grabbed his sandwich and kept eating.

Skye eyed our books. "Were you both reading?"

Uh… "No, these are both mine." I scooped them up and put them in my bag.

"*Schindler's List?*" Skye asked incredulously. "That doesn't sound like something you'd want to read."

"I'm trying new things," I blurted.

Slade kept his eyes glued to his sandwich.

"What's going on with you?" I tried to change the subject.

"Just school," she said. "And Cayson." A smile lit up her face.

"He's good in bed?" I asked.

"Like you wouldn't believe." Skye kept smiling.

"I taught him everything he knows." Slade said it while chewing a mouthful of food.

"I doubt that for some reason," Skye said.

Actually, I didn't. Slade really knew his way around the bedroom. I was never left unsatisfied. It was a nice change to be with a guy that could rock your world and give you exactly what you wanted without having to ask for it. Unfortunately, he was a jerk covered in tattoos and had a horrible attitude. So, the package wasn't pretty but the gift inside was exquisite.

"And if you think his dick is big, you should see mine." Slade shoved the rest of his sandwich into his mouth.

"How would you know unless you've seen his?" Skye argued.

"You look at Cayson's package?" I asked Slade.

"I just know, alright?" Slade said, annoyed.

"I think someone is into Cayson," Skye teased.

"Am not," Slade argued. "He's my best friend. I know everything about him."

"Yeah...everything." I loved teasing Slade. He would get so mad.

He rolled his eyes then crinkled up his wrapper. "I'm out of here."

"Thank god," I blurted.

"Shut up, Trinity." He left the table and put his backpack over his shoulder. Then he walked off.

Skye looked at her textbook then eyed me. "That's weird."

"What?" I asked.

"Slade's favorite book is *Schindler's List.*"

How did she know that? "Why do you say that?"

"He mentioned it to me once."

"Oh." *What else was I supposed to say?*

"Did he give it to you?" she asked.

I felt like she was cornering me. Sweat started to form on my palms. "No. It's mine."

She finally backed off and looked at her textbook.

Phew. I stared across the library and tried to gather my bearings while Skye wasn't looking. Sneaking around was becoming more stressful than I realized. I was never good at keeping secrets and I was a horrible liar.

While I stared across the library, I saw a familiar face. "Code red. Zack is in the building."

Skye sighed and slammed her textbook closed. "I'm going to beat him over the head with this if he comes over here."

Zack was approaching our side of the library. A book was under his arm and he was typing on his phone. When he looked up, he spotted Skye. Like he was scared, his eyes widened and he immediately turned around, practically running out of the library.

"No running!" the librarian yelled at him.

Skye turned to me, her eyebrows raised. "What the hell was that?"

"I don't know. It was like he was scared of you."

"But why would he be scared of me?"

I shrugged. "I wouldn't have believed that happened unless I'd seen it myself."

"That was...bizarre." She was quiet for a long time. "Zack would never be scared of me. The only person I know who can possibly make a grown man scared is..." She stopped in midsentence. Her eyes were wide. "My father."

I watched her face, seeing the emotion and anger come through.

Skye slammed her book down then packed her bag. Judging by her quick movements and the anger burning in her eyes, she was pissed.

"What?"

"Cayson told my father—even though I specifically asked him not to." She put her bag over one shoulder and stormed off.

Shit, I felt bad for Cayson.

***

I just took dinner out of the oven when I got the message.

Go to hell.

Slade texted me four times that week to hook up. I didn't mind. My mind wasn't used to having four amazing orgasms in a week but my body could get used to it.

Sure.

I finished preparing the vegetables and rice just as the doorbell rang.

"It's open," I yelled.

Slade walked inside. "I could be a murderer."

"I doubt criminals ring the doorbell before they rob someone."

He shut the door then joined me in the kitchen. He wasn't wearing a jacket, just jeans and a t-shirt. "You should still be smarter about it."

"I unlocked it because I knew you were coming."

"It takes two seconds to unlock the door and let me in. You better do it next time."

"If you want to get laid, I suggest you not be a dick to me."

"I've been worse and you still spread your legs," he countered.

I eyed his arms. "You really should wear a jacket."

"I'm fine," he growled.

I felt his arm and was surprised by the heat.

"Told you." He pulled his arm away from my grasp. He walked through the kitchen then sniffed the air. "Something smells good."

"Chicken, broccoli, and rice," I answered. "Would you like to join me?"

"Free food?" He sat down at the table. "Hell yeah."

I served the food on plates then put them on the table.

Slade cut into his food and stuffed it into his mouth. "Wow, this is good."

"Thank you."

"I wasn't complimenting you," he said quickly.

"Well, I did make it."

"I'm still not flattering you." He ate everything off his plate then moaned. "Even the green stuff was good."

"Again, thank you."

"Again, no compliment." He leaned back in his chair while he waited for me to finish. "Do you cook a lot?"

"About five times a week."

"How do you have time for that?"

"I make time," I answered. "Eating healthy is important."

"No wonder you have such a nice body."

I smirked. "You're giving me compliments left and right."

He shook his head slightly. "Don't let it go to your head."

"Too late." I finished my food then put my dish in the sink. "Since I cooked, you should clean."

He laughed. "Yeah right."

Why did I expect anything else? I put hot water in the sink then placed the dishes inside to soak.

"You got dessert too?"

"I wouldn't have a nice body if I ate junk all the time," I countered.

"I know there's a little fat girl deep inside."

A lot of fat girls, actually. I opened the freezer and revealed a Ben and Jerry's pint of chocolate ice cream.

He winked. "Now that's hot."

I grabbed two spoons then sat beside him at the table. We ate out of the same carton, our metal spoons tapping together as we tried to get to the large chunks of chocolate before the other.

"That shit was good." Slade left his spoon on the table. "If you cook every night, I'm coming over more often."

"I'll make sure the door is locked," I said sarcastically. I shoved the empty pint into the garbage can then walked into my bedroom. "Are we going to do this or what?"

"Right to the chase, huh?" He followed behind me, stripping his shirt off as he went.

When we were in my room, I turned around and looked at him. I never had a thing for guys with ink and it was something I never expected to find attractive. But seeing them on Slade made me hotter for him. His body was thick and toned with muscle, and that just highlighted the appearance of the different colors on his skin. He was a collage of different art, a canvas that was beautiful in a chaotic way. I'd had sex with Slade dozens of times, and every time we were together it was better. I found new ways of appreciating him, of understanding him. He could be the biggest dick I knew, but when we were alone, he lowered his walls. He was a much different person. There were layers unseen to the naked eye. He had more depth than he was willing to reveal. And in a complicated way, that made me like him more than I did before. It seemed like this odd relationship made us better friends, unexpectedly.

He crossed the room then pulled my shirt off, eager to see my naked body. He was aggressive with me, doing exactly what he wanted when he wanted. My previous partners were hesitant and slow. There was no heat in their eyes, not the way Slade had at least. He removed the rest of my clothes, practically ripping them. "I've been thinking about this all day."

"It didn't seem that way."

"Well, I was."

I kissed his chest. "How do you want me?" We'd done it in every position imaginable. It surprised me that they were all enjoyable. Only Slade could pull that off.

He smirked. "I like it when you give me the control. But I like it when you take it too. Most girls don't."

"You didn't answer my question." I sucked his bottom lip. Every time I touched him, I was lit on fire. The desire I had for him was paramount. I'd never wanted someone in such a sexual way before. Perhaps it was because there were no emotional feelings to dilute it. It was carnal, animal-like.

His hand moved down my back to my ass. "How about anal?"

"Okay," I said without hesitation.

His eyes widened. "You like that?"

"Yeah. Why are you surprised?"

"I just didn't expect you to have done it before."

I smirked. "I'm not sure what I did to give you the impression I was a good girl. Believe me, I'm not."

He took a deep breath and desire burned in his eyes. "You're good at hiding it."

"Just because I don't talk about my sex life like you do, doesn't mean I don't have one."

"Apparently." He squeezed my ass with his hand. "Man, we should have been doing this a long time ago."

"Yeah, we should have." I lowered myself to my knees and sucked him off.

He fisted his hands into my hair and moaned while he stared down at me. A moan escaped his lips every few seconds. Then I moved to the bed and got on all fours.

"What are you waiting for?" I asked with a sexy voice.

After Slade was lubed and ready, he was inside me faster than I could process.

***

"Oh my fucking god, that was good." Slade caught his breath beside me. "Best anal I've ever had."

"It was pretty good, huh?"

"Hell yeah, it was." He ran his fingers through his hair then sighed.

I lay on my side of the bed then got comfortable. Whenever I had a huge climax, like the one Slade gave me, I was exhausted and relaxed. My mind just wanted to drift in and out of reality. I almost felt high.

Slade stared at the ceiling, his chest still rising and falling with a quick pace.

I was in the mood for a bath. I liked to take them in the wintertime to stay warm. Candles lit the room. I closed my eyes and let my worries escape the surface of my skin. That's what I was planning on doing tonight before he came over. Since Slade would fall asleep soon, I decided to get up and head to the bathroom.

I drew the bath and added bubbles. Then I lit a few candles and got a stack of magazines to read. The mirrors on the wall started to fog from the humidity. When everything was ready, I slipped inside and felt my body relax as the heat surrounded me. I closed my eyes and thought about nothing in particular.

Slade walked in some time later. I wasn't sure when. My mind was on a different planet at the time. He lifted the toilet lid then took a piss.

"Do you mind?" I asked. "There are two other bathrooms in this house."

"Too far away." He held himself with two hands and filled the bowl.

I shook my head and ignored him. When he was finished, he flushed the toilet then came to the bathtub.

"What are you doing?" he asked.

I rested my head on a towel. "Taking a bath. What does it look like I'm doing? And did you wash your hands?"

He rolled his eyes then washed his hands in the sink. "There. Are you happy?"

"Much. Although, I'm concerned for your overall hygiene."

He eyed me in the water. "So, you're just sitting there in your own filth?"

"How dirty do you think I am?" I countered.

He sat on the corner of the tub. "I've never taken a bath before."

"Not even as a kid?"

"Well, not as an adult at least."

"They're wonderful."

He shrugged. "I prefer the shower. You can't have sex in a tub."

"Yeah, you can."

He eyed me for a moment, amusement in his eyes. "Really?"

I nodded.

"So, you've done it?"

I nodded again.

"You really are a whore."

"Hey." I gave him a firm look. "Just because I enjoy sex doesn't make me a whore. I don't sleep with married men, I don't cheat, and I don't accept money as payment. Don't ever call me that again. It's sexist and offensive."

He seemed to understand he shouldn't push me on this. For the first time, he backed off. "I'm sorry. I take it back."

Whoa...did Slade just apologize? "I've never heard you say that before."

"What?"

"That you're sorry."

"Because I only say it when I really mean it. And when your voice gets all firm like that, I know you aren't kidding around. You were actually hurt by what I said."

Maybe Slade knew me better than I thought. "Well, I appreciate it."

"Yeah..." He scooped up the suds with his hands then blew them back into the water. "That's some girly shit."

"It's really nice. Join me."

"It'll be a tight fit."

"Bend your knees," I said.

"Fine." He stood up then came to the rear of the tub. I scooted forward so he could move in behind me. When he was settled, I leaned back against his chest. It was cramped but we were both covered by the water. He leaned his head against the towel pillow I made.

"It's nice, huh?" I asked.

"It's not bad." Both of his hands hooked around my waist and he anchored me to his chest. He never held me like that before. It was something I wasn't used to. I didn't say anything and just let it play out. "What do you do when you're in here?"

"Read magazines. Think." I played with the bubbles on the surface, cupping them into my hand.

"Think about what?" he asked.

I shrugged. "My life. What I want to change. Where I'm going in life."

"And what have you decided?"

"One of the best parts of life is its wonderful unpredictability. So, I really don't know where I'm going."

"Where would you like to go?" he asked quietly.

"I just know I love fashion and I'd like to be a part of it."

"Be a model," he blurted.

I smirked. "I could get used to these compliments."

He chuckled. "I guess you aren't totally hideous."

I leaned my head back and looked up at him. "Just admit it. You think I'm pretty."

He stared into my face, and his eyes became darker. The change was so sudden it was hard to notice. He kept staring, like he was trying to find something. "I think you're beautiful."

I stopped breathing for a second because his response caught me off guard. That was the last thing I expected Slade to ever say, especially to me. No smartass comment came to mind. I couldn't think of a response.

It didn't seem like Slade wanted one. He leaned down and pressed a kiss to my shoulder where it emerged from the water. Then he leaned back and rested his head against the towel.

Did that just happen?

His hands were still wrapped around my waist, holding me to his chest. "Since you're so into fashion and appearances, I never expected you to be such a book worm. I didn't think you were so intelligent and witty. You continue to surprise me the more I get to know you. It's weird. I've known you my whole life but I never really knew anything about you."

"Yeah, me too. I feel like we're actually friends now."

He chuckled. "Yeah, I never expected that to happen."

"Me neither."

"I mean, you're still annoying and all that, but I definitely have a new respect for you."

"Me too." I felt his chest rise and fall, noting its power and strength.

"We have to start doing a better job of arguing in front of the others," he said. "I think we're losing our touch."

I laughed. "Yeah, it's getting hard. We could just get along and let them get used to it."

"No," he said immediately. "They'll know something is up, especially Cayson. That damn psychologist can analyze me like a bug under a microscope."

That reminded me of what Skye said that afternoon. "She knows Cayson told her father about Zack. And she was really mad."

He sighed. "Poor Cayson. It's going to be a long night for him…"

"I don't blame him for protecting her, but I understand why Skye is mad. She isn't going to just let this go. She's always been really obsessed about proving her independence to her father. I think this is the worst thing Cayson could have done to piss her off."

"She needs to get over it. Cayson did the right thing. I have his back on this one."

"Well, I'm not on anyone's side. I just want them to be together, to be happy."

"Yeah…" He moved his fingers against the skin of my stomach. "I was pissed that Cayson stopped spending as much time with me because of Skye, but I definitely want him to be happy. And that little brunette with a huge rack really makes him giddy."

I cringed. "Slade, she's your cousin."

"But I'm not blind to her most attractive feature."

"I don't think anyone is."

He adjusted himself in the tub then sighed. "This is nice."

"Told you."

"I guess sitting in your own dirt isn't so bad."

"It's not like I'm a gardener that just got off work," I snapped.

His hand moved down to my belly button piercing. "I really like this."

"You do?"

"It's hot." He touched it again before he pulled his hand away.

I touched his arm. "I like your tattoos. They're hot."

"Well, duh."

I chuckled. "Don't be cocky."

He moved his lips to my ear. "I'm glad you like them."

I felt my spine shiver when his lips touched the shell of my ear.

Slade massaged my thigh. "You're doing okay? I didn't hurt you, right?"

"No, definitely not."

"Good. Sometimes I'm afraid I'm too rough with you."

"If you are, I'll tell you."

"Thank you." He rubbed my shoulder. "I don't want this to end so I don't want to give you a reason to leave."

"I don't want this to end either."

He held me in the tub for several minutes, not speaking. His hand glided over my skin, making me feel warm and comfortable. I'd always taken baths alone, but I didn't realize how enjoyable they could be with another person. It was nice to cuddle under the water. It was an intimacy I never shared with another person. I'd had sex with countless guys but no one had ever held me this way, like they cared.

"Last week, I asked you a question and you never answered it."

I didn't know what he was talking about. "Refresh my memory."

"You can have any guy you want. So why do you settle for this type of arrangement?" He stared at the side of my face as he waited for me to answer.

This wasn't a conversation I ever had with anyone. But I guess I could have it with Slade since I was sleeping with him. "Ever since I was a little girl, my dad told me that I'd end up with a really great guy that would treat me like a princess. And he told me to never settle for anyone unless he was absolutely perfect. He would open every door for me, listen to my every thought, and always take care of me, even if he hurt himself in the process. And for the longest time, I believed that.

"My father has always been a great role model to me. He's smart, loyal, strong, and he treats my mom like he loves her as much as the day he married her. It's like he lives and breathes for her. I guess, in a twisted way, I've always compared every guy to my father. Does he open every door for me? Does he treat me right? Would he die for me?

"Then I grew up. With every date I went on and every guy I met, I realized none of them gave a damn about me. Some were better than others, but it was pretty clear they just wanted sex or a short-term commitment. And the ones who did want to be with me didn't treat me right. My only somewhat serious boyfriend cheated on me with a friend from high school. Men are all the same. I keep waiting to meet a guy who's different, who's right. I know Cayson isn't perfect, but when it comes to Skye, he is. I've quickly realized I'm wasting my time searching for that perfect guy, someone I can actually introduce to my father and not feel a single doubt. So, I stopped searching.

"I don't need a man in my life to be happy. I can take care of myself and do everything on my own. I refuse to settle for someone who can't give me everything I want, so I'm not going to do it. But I need sex. I love sex even if it's meaningless.

Which is why this relationship with you is so perfect."

Slade said nothing. Time stretched for a long time. I didn't expect him to say anything, but the quiet echoes in the bathroom were awkward. I spilled my deepest secret to him and now I wasn't sure why. Then he cleared his throat. "Trinity, I care about you—a lot."

I sighed. "It's okay, Slade. I know you're just using me and it doesn't bother me at all. I don't think less of you."

"But I really do care about you, Trinity. I do give a damn. I know I've been an ass to you a lot in the past—"

"A lot."

He smirked. "But you're important to me. And you do mean something to me."

They were just empty words but I didn't want to argue about it anymore.

"Trinity, you're one of the most beautiful women I've ever seen, on the outside as well as the inside. You're a strong woman who's too intelligent for her own good, and you're fun to be around. I know the right guy is out there, just waiting for you. And when he finally has you, he'll ask himself how he got so lucky. And when you compare him to your father, you'll realize he's better."

His words echoed in my mind long after he said them. Slade hardly said anything without a curse word in it, and I've never heard him say anything so heartfelt in my life. It pulled at my heartstrings and made me feel a twinge of hope. "Thanks…"

He held me close to his chest. "I'm right. I promise you."

"How can you make a promise like that?"

"I just can."

Chapter Thirty-Six
Cayson

I just got out of the shower when I heard someone ramming into my door like they were trying to break it down.

"Cayson! Open up!" It was Skye.

I panicked at the urgency in her voice. Was she okay? Did something happen? Just wearing a towel, I ran to the door then opened it. "Baby, what's going on?" I immediately looked outside and made sure there was no danger.

"What's going on?" Anger was heavy in her voice. "*What's going on?*"

What was she so mad about?

She pushed herself inside, forcing me back. "I specifically told you not to tell my father about Zack. I trusted you not to tell him. You even promised. And then a second later, you went behind my back and did it anyway!"

"I didn't promise anything," I said immediately. "When you asked me not to tell him, I didn't say anything."

That just pissed her off even more. "Seriously, you're trying to get out of this on a technicality?"

"I'm not trying to get out of anything," I snapped. "I know what I did and I take full responsibility for it. You may not always like the decisions I make, but that's too bad. I had to protect you. So if you're upset about it, fine. I would do it again in a heartbeat."

Skye looked like she might explode. "Cayson, if there's one thing you should know about me, it's how strongly I value my independence. I've spent my entire adult life proving to my father that I don't need his money, his protection, or his concern. I'm perfectly capable of taking care of myself. And you sabotaged that by snitching on me to him."

"I didn't snitch—"

"Shut up! I'm talking."

I pressed my lips together and clenched my jaw.

"I don't need a man to take care of me, whether that be my father or you. Alright? Do you understand that? I chose to go out with Zack and I got myself in this mess. I admit my mistakes and my poor judgment, but I will get out of this situation without my father or you. If you don't understand that, understand how important that is to me, then we shouldn't even be together."

Her words echoed in my mind long after she said them.

"I'm sick of my father constantly hovering over me. He did it all through my life. As a result, he never let me handle anything on my own. As soon as I got into trouble, he fixed it for me. But when it came to Roland, my dad turned his back and forced him to figure out everything on his own. As a result, Roland is stronger and more self-sufficient. I don't want to be babied anymore. I'm sick of it."

I tried to keep my anger back so I wouldn't push her over the edge. "I agree with you—for the most part. But Zack is a fucking psychopath. You claim he wouldn't hurt you but you don't know that for sure. And I'm sorry, Skye, but he's a guy twice your size and height. If he wants to hurt you, he will. You will never be strong enough to match him. I had to do what was right to protect you."

"Fuck you, Cayson."

My eyes widened. "Don't talk to me like that."

"Don't go behind my back and betray my trust!"

"It's not the same thing and you know it. If you don't want to be treated like a brat then don't act like one!"

Her eyes were smoldering in rage. "I can't believe you..."

"I stand by what I did and I won't apologize for it." I stood my ground and didn't back down. "Zack has left you alone ever since and I know he won't bother you again. I can sleep at night and so can your father. Now if you want to go for a damn jog in the middle of the night, you can. You have your independence back."

She gripped her hair in frustration. "I've never been so angry in my life!"

I said nothing, staring her down.

"I can't be with someone I can't trust, Cayson. I just can't."

My heart skipped a beat. "What did you just say?"

"You heard me, Cayson. I can't do this relationship anymore. Without trust, there is no relationship."

Now I was pissed. I marched to her so fast she almost tripped. I slammed her against the door with my body. "Take that back. Now."

Fear filled her eyes while she was pinned down.

"Don't you ever say that to me again." Spit was flying out of my mouth because I was so angry. "You're being a pain in the ass about this, Skye. I love you more than anything on this damn planet and I will do whatever it takes to keep you safe. If that means you can't trust me, fine. You'll just have to deal with that. You can throw a hissy fit and play the victim all you want, but I know without a doubt that if the situation were reversed, you would do the same for me. And honestly, I would judge you if you didn't.

"Now let's get something straight here. Do not ever treat me like this again. I've been the perfect damn boyfriend of the year to you. I do everything for you and break my back just to

731

make you smile. You do not have the right to say that to me. You do not have the right to get upset with me. Now shut up and deal with it."

She stared at me, breathing hard. Her eyes started to water.

I stepped back and gave her space. "Now get out of my apartment." I turned my back on her and walked into my bedroom. Then I slammed the door so hard it broke off the hinges.

***

Slade held the door while I used my screwdriver to put the door back into place. "So...you guys had a fight?"

I was still fuming about it. Skye and I hadn't spoken since the night before. She didn't call me and I didn't call her. I didn't go by the library during the day like I usually did. She owed me an apology and I wasn't going to do anything until I got it. "Something like that..."

"You guys didn't break up, right?" Fear was in his voice.

"No." I wouldn't let her go without a fight.

He nodded. "Is there something I can do to help?"

I shifted the door then drilled the hinge back into the case. "Just hold the door steady."

"I *am* holding it steady."

"Then keep doing it."

Slade fell silent while he waited for me to finish.

When I was done, I opened the door then closed it again. It didn't creak or shake. "It works."

"You ripped the door off like the Incredible Hulk or what?"

"No. I just slammed it too hard."

Slade kept staring at me like I might snap. "Damn...how hard did you slam it?"

"Pretty damn hard," I snapped.

Slade was usually full of jokes but today he kept them to himself. He knew I wasn't in the mood. "It's probably not the best time to bring this up but..."

"What?" *What more could possibly go wrong in my life?*

"My dad called and said the family is getting together at the ski lodge in Connecticut. We're staying at Sean's ski Chalet. Since it's a four day weekend coming up, they want to go then."

I really didn't want to deal with any of that right now. "Great."

"I think it'll be fun. I love snowboarding. None of that pretentious skiing bullshit."

I didn't give a damn about whether he preferred skiing or snowboarding. "I'm surprised my dad hasn't called me."

"I'm sure he will."

"Well, thanks."

"Yeah." He nodded then headed to the front door. "Cay, you want my advice?"

"Not even a little bit," I blurted.

"You're going to get it anyway," he said. "Chicks are always wrong. But always let them think they're right." He walked out and shut the door behind him.

I thought about his words for a long time after he left. Maybe he understood women more than I gave him credit for. I tested my bedroom door again when my father called.

"Hey, Son."

"Hey, Dad."

He knew something was off. "Everything okay?"

I didn't want to talk about Skye right now. "I just fixed my bedroom door and I'm a little tired from it."

"What happened?"

"Since you're a computer geek, you wouldn't understand."

"Very funny," he said sarcastically. "So, how's school?"

"Boring."

"And your lovely girlfriend?"

"She's lovely—like usual."

"Give her a kiss for me, please—on the cheek. None of that face-sucking stuff."

"Sure, Dad." I just wanted to get off the phone.

"We're skiing this weekend. Everyone is going. You're coming, right? Your mother and I would love to spend time with you."

Since Skye and I were going through a hard time, I didn't want the added pressure of family. But I couldn't think of a way to wiggle out of this one. "Sure."

"Great. We'll see you on Friday."

"Sounds like a plan."

"Okay, kid. I'll talk to you later."

"Bye, Dad."

"Bye, Son. I love you."

"I love you too." I quickly hung up then shoved the phone into my pocket. Then I sat down on the couch and stared at the blank TV screen. I wanted Skye to call me but she never did. I guess I would have to keep waiting.

Chapter Thirty-Seven

Skye

Five days had passed without speaking or seeing Cayson. I was starting to go through withdrawals. I missed my best friend. I missed looking at his ridiculously perfect face. His lips were unbelievably tasty. His hands fit my hips perfectly. I missed talking to him. Did he miss me?

But I was still so pissed at him.

I couldn't believe he deliberately went behind my back and pulled that stunt. And to make it worse, he wasn't even going to tell me about it. If he didn't get caught, I never would have known. I knew I was headstrong and stubborn, but I was particularly passionate about this subject.

We were going skiing in a few days with my family, and with the drama going on with Cayson, I knew I wouldn't have a good time. How would we act? Would we tell everyone we were fighting? Or would we pretend that nothing was going on?

Every time I was in the library, I hoped Cayson would stop by. He never did. Clearly, he was as pissed as I was. When I was home in the evenings, I always listened for a knock on my door. It never came. And my hand was glued to my phone, waiting for it to ring. It never did.

"Just talk to him," Trinity said. "You're being a big fat baby over this."

"Big fat baby?" I asked.

"Yes." She gave me a hard look. "It would be different if Cayson was trying to purposely hurt you but he's not. He was just looking out for you."

"He of all people should know how I feel about this."

"Which only proves how much he loves you," she snapped. "He was willing to piss you off in order to keep you safe. That's the most selfless thing I've ever heard."

"Trinity, just stay out of it."

"If you lose him, I will beat you up, Skye."

I gave her an incredulous look.

"I mean it. He's my family too, Skye. Just because we're related by blood, doesn't make me more loyal to you. If you hurt Cayson, I'll hurt you."

"I can't believe you're taking his side."

"I can't believe you aren't." She grabbed her bag and stormed off. "Pull your head out of your ass, Skye."

I growled then tried to focus on my textbook. But that was pretty much impossible.

Slade dropped into the seat across from me.

"Go away. I'm not in the mood to even look at you."

He had a serious look on his face. "Then I'll make this quick."

The last thing I wanted to do was talk to Cayson's best friend. "What?"

His eyes appeared lifeless and dull. He seemed sad and torn apart. "I just wanted to give you a heads up. I told Cayson I wouldn't say anything but I'm going to."

What was he talking about?

"Cayson doesn't think this relationship is going to work. He says he loves you like crazy but you're too headstrong for him. He understands you don't want anyone to take care of you, but he hates how difficult it is. He thinks it's best if he ends it now before it gets worse...and you can't be friends again."

My hands started to shake and I felt my heart fall into my stomach. It was a deathblow. I couldn't live without him. I just couldn't. When I suggested breaking up a few days ago, I didn't mean it. Cayson was the best damn thing that ever happened to me. I couldn't let him go.

Slade stood up again. "Since you're my cousin, I wanted to make sure you were prepared." He walked away without another word.

Fuck, I had to talk to Cayson.

I left the library then walked outside. When I looked at the time, I realized he just finished his class. He normally went to the library, but since he wasn't going there, he was probably going to his apartment. Or he would be with Slade but he clearly wasn't. I walked over there as fast as my short legs would carry me.

I was still pissed off at him for what he did, but I could let it go as long as I got to keep him. There was so much goodness to our relationship. Nothing was worth losing that bliss. He made me happier than I ever thought I could be. The idea of him being with someone else was sickening. It would be torture.

I arrived at his apartment and slammed my fist into the door, impatient. He opened it a moment later, his eyes guarded and his jaw clenched tight. He didn't speak, just staring me down like he loathed me.

Tears sprang from my eyes and I moved into his chest, wrapping my arms around him. "I'm sorry… I'm so sorry." I squeezed him hard, never wanting to let go.

Cayson pulled me inside the apartment then shut the door. Then his hands were on me. He rested his chin on my head then moved his fingers through my hair. He stood there, just holding me.

"I'm sorry about everything. Please don't leave me. Please don't go."

"Shh," he whispered in my ear. "I'm not going anywhere."

I clutched him harder. "I know I can be stubborn and annoying but I'll work on it. I know in my heart you were just trying to do the right thing for me. I know…"

"It's alright, Skye." His voice was gentle. His fingers soothed me, making me feel calm.

"Please don't go. I'll beg if I have to."

"Skye, I would never leave you."

I pulled away then looked into his eyes.

He used the pad of his thumb to wipe away my tears. "Ever."

"But Slade told me…"

His eyes narrowed. "Told you what?"

"That you were going to leave me…because you were sick of putting up with me."

Realization came into his eyes then he sighed. "I never said that, Skye. Slade must have said that to get us back together."

Now I felt like an idiot. But I was so relieved Cayson wasn't leaving me that I didn't care about my premature apology. "That jackass."

He smirked. "He's spent the week with me and he knew how upset I was. I'm sure he was just eager to get us back together."

"That's really sweet...but pisses me off at the same time." I wiped my tears away then chuckled.

"He's a jerk but he has a heart of gold."

"Apparently..."

He looked down at me. "Does that mean you're going to walk out again?"

"No...I miss you."

He sighed. "God, I miss you too."

"I'm sorry, Cayson. I just don't want to get my father involved in anything. It's really important to me."

"I know, baby. I never would have done it if I didn't have to."

I was scared to ask my next question. "What did he do to Zack?"

"He just scared him a little bit then had two guys tail him everywhere he went. I'm sure Zack is scared to death to be seen within a hundred feet of you. He won't bother you anymore, Skye."

That kind of protection was excessive but at least they didn't hurt Zack. And I didn't have to deal with him anymore. "Okay."

He cupped my cheek. "So...are we okay?"

I nodded. "I'm sorry about everything I said."

His eyes turned serious. "I never want you to say that to me again. And if you say it, make sure you really mean it. Because there's nothing worse you can do to hurt me."

I felt lower than dirt. "I'm sorry. I was just angry."

"That's no excuse."

"I know...it won't happen again."

"Good."

I was feeling worse by the second. "I'm sorry I keep messing this up. I'm not doing it on purpose."

"It's okay." He kissed my forehead. "It's water under the bridge."

"You always say that."

"With you, it'll always be water under the bridge."

I held him close and cherished the moment. He was still mine. I didn't mess this up too badly.

"Are you going skiing this weekend?" he asked.

"Yeah. Are you?"

"Like my parents would let me say no," he said with a laugh.

"It should be fun."

"It'll be a lot more fun without us fighting."

"Well, there is one good thing about fighting..."

"What?" He held me close.

"Make up sex."

His eyes sparkled. "I do like sex—any sex—with you."

"Well, let me make up for my behavior."

"That sounds like a good idea."

***

We piled our belongings into my SUV.

"Trinity, why do you always need to pack so much shit?" Conrad snapped. He tried shoving her final bag into the pile but it wouldn't fit.

"Because we're going skiing for four whole days." She crossed her arms over her chest and glared at her brother. "I need clothes."

"If you donated your wardrobe to a charity, they would have enough clothes to wear a different outfit every day for a year." Conrad tried to push the bag in again. It still wouldn't fit. It kept falling off. He dropped it on the ground. "Trinity, it's not coming."

"Find a place for it," she snapped.

He looked at her like she was crazy. "It. Won't. Fit."

"Rearrange the bags," she said.

"*You* rearrange the fucking bags," Conrad snapped.

Cayson kept his arm around my waist. "This will be a fun trip..."

Slade sighed then approached the back of the SUV. He pulled all the bags out and dropped them on the ground then started to rearrange them like a puzzle.

I shared a shocked look with Trinity. Roland looked at Conrad like he just saw a snake with wings. Cayson stared at Slade like he's never seen him before.

Slade managed to fit in every single bag. Not an inch of space was unutilized. The luggage was packed so high Roland wouldn't be able to see in his rearview mirror but everything was there.

Slade wiped his hands on his jeans. "Now shut up so we can get on the road." He wore a t-shirt and jeans. His breath came out as vapor against the cold.

Trinity looked at Slade but didn't say anything. It seemed like a silent conversation passed between them.

Did I just see that?

I must be seeing things.

"I sincerely hope you brought a jacket," Roland said. "Remember, we're going skiing."

"Snowboarding," Slade snapped. "And I don't fall so I don't need a jacket."

I knew where this was going. I decided to stop the argument before it started. "Where's Silke?"

"She's riding with Theo and Thomas," Slade answered. "She had something to do this morning."

"Oh. I just saw her the other day and she didn't mention that," I said.

"Not my problem," Slade said. "Now let's get on the road before it gets dark. I don't trust Roland's driving."

"I'm a fantastic driver," Roland argued.

"In the snow, no one's a fantastic driver," Slade said. He walked to the side of the SUV then got in.

"Alright, let's head out," Conrad said.

Roland got behind the wheel and Conrad sat beside him.

I moved to the back seat and scooted over so Cayson could sit beside me. Trinity moved to the middle row and sat by the window. When Slade got inside, he glanced back and forth between the empty seats next to Cayson and Trinity.

I assumed he would sit next to Cayson because he despised Trinity. It was weird to watch him debate it.

"I don't want to watch you guys make out for the whole drive." Slade took the spot next to Trinity and faced forward.

Trinity looked at him then stared out the window.

That was not the choice I expected him to make.

Roland left the city then got onto the highway. He turned on the radio but kept it low. He and Conrad talked about sports and a few girls they met at a bar.

Cayson put his arm around my shoulder and moved closer to me, his leg touching mine. With his other hand, he grabbed mine and caressed my knuckles. "What should we do on the drive?"

I gave him a knowing look.

"Okay, not that," he blurted.

I smirked. "What do you want to do?"

"I brought a deck of cards."

"We can play that."

"Okay." Cayson dug into his bag and pulled out the deck.

I stared at the back of Slade's head, noticing his gaze pointed toward his lap. Trinity was doing the same, clearly reading something. I sat forward and looked over the seat. They were both reading books.

What the hell? "Slade, you read?"

He flinched at my words. "What's it to you?" Aggression was in his voice.

"You don't strike me as the reading type," I said.

"Well, I am." He turned his gaze back to his book. "Now mind your own business."

"You're one to talk. You lied to me and told me Cayson was going to leave me."

"You're welcome, by the way," Slade snapped. "I just saved you a month of fighting over something so stupid. If you ask me, Cayson should leave you. He's the best damn boyfriend on the planet. Maybe you should appreciate him once in a while."

"Word," Roland said from the driver's seat.

"Ditto," Trinity added.

"Yep," Conrad said.

I sighed in annoyance. "Don't gang up on me, alright?"

"You fuck with one of us, you fuck with all of us," Conrad said.

"I'm your cousin," I argued.

"Well, Cayson is my brother." Conrad looked out the window.

I hated being singled out. "Whatever…"

Slade read his book again.

I looked at the title. "*The Odyssey*?" I didn't expect Slade to read at all, let alone an epic Greek novel.

"What?" he snapped. "I'm a history major. It makes sense for me to read this." He sounded defensive.

"That's Greek mythology," I argued.

"Based on historical events," he snapped.

I turned to Trinity. "Isn't that your favorite book?"

She flipped a page in her book. "It's an odd coincidence…"

"Can you leave us the fuck alone now?" Slade snapped. "Give your boyfriend a handy in the backseat."

Roland swerved slightly. "Please don't."

I leaned back against the seat and ignored Slade.

Cayson passed out the cards. "Ready to lose?"

"How about we just make out instead?"

His eyes darkened at the idea.

Roland swerved again. "Please don't."

Cayson returned to the cards. "Let's just play instead."

I sighed then gathered my cards. "I'm going to beat you this time."

"I'll let you win a few times." He gave me a smirk then played the game.

***

"Is this it?" Conrad stared at the wooden cottage. Lights were bright in every window. Snow was piled on the roof and the road. The lawn was completely white, covered with powder.

"It's a fucking mansion," Roland said.

"Well, there will be twenty people staying there," Trinity said.

"Check the address again," Roland said.

Conrad looked at his phone. "They match."

I looked through the window. "I see my mom's car."

"Alright." Roland drove over the snow then found a spot to park.

Trinity stared out the window. "It's beautiful."

Slade stared out the window too but held his comment. No smartass words came out.

"How's this going to work?" I asked Cayson.

"What do you mean?" he asked.

"How are we going to sleep together?" I asked. "Are you going to sneak into my room?"

He stared at me like I was crazy. "Is that a joke?" he blurted. "I'm not sleeping with you when your dad is around. I don't need a pistol blowing my brains out."

I rolled my eyes. "My dad loves you, Cayson."

"A father's love for his daughter makes him blind to everything else."

"He's not stupid. He must know we sleep together."

"But I doubt he wants to think about that when he's staying in the same house."

"He'll still have sex with my mom," I argued.

"Who he's married to..." Cayson gave me an incredulous look. "Forget it, Skye. I'm not sleeping with you."

"But I can't sleep without you," I argued.

"Neither can I but I'll deal with it."

"Is this an episode of *The Young and The Restless*?" Slade snapped.

Cayson ignored his comment. "Forget it, okay?"

I gave him my best pout. "Please..."

"No." He gave me a firm look. "We have the rest of our lives. Your dad likes me and I want to keep it that way."

"He'll always like you no matter what happens between us," I said. "He's your godfather."

"When it comes to you, anything can change. Believe me." He got out of the SUV and helped me out.

I always got my way with Cayson but I knew it wasn't happening this time.

We grabbed our bags out of the back. Cayson carried my bags and his own inside. He refused to let me touch anything. He always carried my stuff but I knew he was insistent because my father was there.

We walked inside and saw our parents sitting in the expansive living room in front of an enormous fireplace. A fire burned inside, crackling and licking the wood.

"About time." Uncle Ryan got up first then went to Slade and hugged him. "I'm glad you made it here in one piece."

"Me too." Slade eyed Roland. "Daredevil over there managed to not drive over a cliff."

"Where did I get this reputation as a bad driver?" Roland said.

"You didn't," Slade said. "I just know you're stupid like your sister."

Roland shrugged. "My sister is stupid…"

Uncle Ryan came to me next and hugged me. He was my godfather so I knew he saw me as his own daughter. "Beautiful like always."

"Thanks, Uncle Ryan."

He pulled away and patted me on the shoulder. "Are you ready for that tramp stamp? My door is open anytime."

"Just because you're my brother-in-law, doesn't mean I won't break your neck," my dad threatened.

"My baby will avenge my death," Uncle Ryan said. "You know my wife. That girl is a fucking ninja."

The parents greeted their kids with long-winded conversations and hugs. When my dad looked at me, affection was in his eyes like it usually was. "You look more like your mother every time I see you."

"Thank you." To me, that was a compliment. My mom still turned heads whenever she went to the grocery store. She took care of herself over the years and worked out every morning. She was curvy but still in great shape.

He hugged me for a long time. "Every time I say good bye to you, my heart breaks a little. But when I see you again, I'm so happy."

I wanted to yell at him for interfering with my personal life and Zack but I didn't have the heart to do it then. He seemed so thrilled just to hold me. "I missed you too."

He pulled away then kissed my forehead. Then he looked down at my wrist, noticing the white gold bracelet I wore. He examined the moon and the stars. "Where did you get this?"

"Cayson gave it to me."

"It's nice." He nodded his head in approval.

I flipped it over and showed him the engraving.

He nodded again. "Very nice." He swallowed the lump in his throat like he was moved.

"What's wrong?"

His face immediately returned to normal. "I'm just happy my daughter is taken care of even when I'm not around. It's every father's dream come true." He stepped away so my mother could embrace me. Then he headed to Roland.

"I'm so happy you're here." My mom gave me a big smile then hugged me.

My mom was my favorite person in the world. She had a warmth about her that couldn't match anyone else. I loved my father just as much, but we were so similar that we butted heads constantly. I always wanted to be more like my mother, with the grace to forgive anyone for anything. To love and never hate. Like my father, I was headstrong and aggressive. My mom was the only person I knew who never let her emotions dictate her actions. "I missed you."

"I always miss you, honey." She pulled away then gave me an affectionate look. "You didn't kill each other on the drive?"

I shook my head. "We survived somehow. But Cayson beat me at every round of poker."

"Well, Uncle Mike taught him how to play. You never stood a chance, honey."

I laughed. "I guess not."

"I'll show you to your room."

"Am I sharing with Trinity?"

"No. You guys can have your own room."

"Cool," I said.

My dad grabbed my bags and carried them to my bedroom. Roland carried his own things.

It was small with just a twin bed. A window overlooked the back of the house. Tall trees were covered with patches of snow. Several blankets covered the bed. There was a closet and a single dresser.

"There's a bathroom down the hall," my dad said.

I made a face. "I have to share it with the boys?"

My mom laughed. "I'm sorry, dear."

"Ugh. I have a feeling I'm going to throw up at some point on this trip," I said.

"We're having dinner in an hour," my dad said.

"Ooooh...what are we having?" I asked.

"Pizza." My dad gave me a fond look. "Your favorite."

"Yes!" I rubbed my hands together greedily.

My dad chuckled. "My girls are so much alike."

My mom shrugged. "She has good taste."

"I know she does." My dad put his arm around her. "Let's let her get settled. We'll be downstairs."

"Okay."

They closed the door and disappeared.

I stared at my tiny bed and the hardwood floor. Sleeping alone would be lonely and cold. I wished Cayson was more of a daredevil like Slade and would just sneak in during the night. But he was too good for that.

My door opened and Cayson appeared. He stared at the small bed then at me. "My room is pretty small too."

"At least we don't have to share."

Cayson sat beside me on the bed. "I heard we're having pizza."

"Me too." I patted my stomach. "I'm starving."

"Like always," he teased.

"Where's your room?"

He stared at me suspiciously. "I don't think I should tell you…"

I hit his arm playfully. "Just tell me."

"Last door on the left."

"Where are the old people staying?" I asked.

"The third floor."

My eyes widened. "This place has three stories?"

He laughed. "Apparently."

I snuggled close to him. "Then they'll never know…"

He scooted away. "Don't even think about it, Skye."

"Come on. We've barely had any sex this week."

"Whose fault is that?" he asked.

I gave him my best puppy eyes.

"Forget it, Skye."

"Well, I'll just sneak into your room…"

"Don't even think about it. I'll throw you out on your ass so fast."

I rolled my eyes. "Why can't you be more like Slade?"

"I can't believe you just said that," he said with a laugh.

"I guess my hormones are doing all the talking."

"I can tell." A smirk was on his lips.

"Let's go down to dinner. I'm about to eat your lips if I don't get something in my stomach."

"Then let's go. I need these bad boys to kiss you."

Chapter Thirty-Eight

Slade

Dinner was served at the long table. Ten boxes of pizza were ordered to feed everyone. Skye probably ate half of that herself because she's a fatty. My aunt Scarlet came in second place. I wasn't sure where they put all those calories because it didn't show.

Trinity and I didn't speak to one another. It was easier just to avoid each other. Just reading at the same time in the car sent out red flags. People were constantly watching us, finding any interaction between us to be abnormal. I never knew sleeping around with someone would be so difficult. If she weren't the best lay I ever had, I wouldn't bother.

At the end of the night, people drifted to their bedrooms. I was a night owl so I preferred staying up until the distant rays of the sun crested the horizon. My dad was the same way. He usually went to bed when my mom did, but I knew it was only to get laid. When she fell asleep, he got up and watched TV and drank beer. He'd been that way all through my childhood. Sometimes I wondered if he was an insomniac.

I poured myself a brandy then sat in the comfy armchair by the fire. My dad sat on the other couch, his glass in his hand.

"You excited for tomorrow?" he asked.

"Hell yeah. It's been too long since I've hit the slopes."

"Me too. Are you going to try to ski for once?"

"Duh. Only annoying, pretentious people ski."

He smirked. "I couldn't agree more." He drank his glass then refilled it. He rested his legs on the table, something he would never do if my mom were around.

"How's the shop?" I asked.

"Good. I'm thinking about opening another one in Times Square."

"Seriously?" I knew my dad was doing well, but damn.

"Tourists get crazy when they come to New York. They want it to be thrilling and exciting. It's a tourist trap."

"How are you going to work at two places at once?"

He gave me a serious look. "I figured I'd have my son run one of them."

My heart hammered in my chest. "Are you shitting me?"

"You're graduating soon. If it's still what you want to do, it's yours."

I sat up, my glass still in my hand. "That would be fucking awesome." My dad didn't care if I cursed. Actually, he was worse than I was.

"Are you sure it's what you want to do? You could pursue something with your degree, even continue your education."

I shook my head vigorously. "Inking is what I was meant to do. Why are you trying so hard to dissuade me from it?"

My dad drank from his glass then rested it on his knee. "It's not as glamorous as you think. There isn't a lot of respect for the institution. I love what I do but I've always felt like I wasn't good enough for your mom, an educated woman who works for a huge publishing house."

"Well, I don't care what people think. I never have."

Affection was in his eyes. "You have more wisdom than I give you credit for."

"I'm a genius but no one ever recognizes it." I rolled my eyes and put my feet on the table.

"You are a genius. But you get that from your mom."

"You're smart too."

He shrugged. "I have street smarts. Your mom is a bit of an airhead about that stuff."

"I'm going to tell her you said that." I smirked.

"Go ahead," he said. "I'll say it to her face."

My parents fought a lot but I never feared they would break up. It was obvious how much they loved each other even though it grossed me out most of the time.

"I'm thinking about getting another tat." I pulled up my shirt and pointed to the area over my ribs.

"What are you thinking?" he asked.

"I don't know. Something green. I think it would look cool."

"What about a tree?" My dad started talking with his hands. "Like, going up and curving around your side. A few leaves could be falling."

I nodded my head. "That sounds sick."

He shrugged.

"Why don't you have any tats, Dad?"

"I have this one." He held up his left hand. Around his ring finger was a tattoo of a black ring.

"Yeah, but that one is lame."

"Lame?" he asked with a laugh. "The fact I'm so committed to your mother that I permanently marked my skin so I can never remove it—even when death takes me? I think it's romantic as hell. So does your mother."

"I guess I don't do romance so it's not impressive to me."

"Still having fun I take it?"

"I told you, Dad. I'm a terminal bachelor."

"I said the same thing until I turned twenty-nine."

I raised an eyebrow. "What happened when you turned twenty-nine?"

"Your mother walked into my apartment." He finished his glass then poured another. He held his alcohol well, another reason why I looked up to him so much. He was a badass.

"And you just knew she was the one?" I asked incredulously. "I think that whole love at first sight thing is bullshit."

"I didn't say it was love at first sight," he said immediately. "The only things I noticed were her long legs and awesome rack. Don't get me wrong, all I wanted to do was fuck her."

I cringed. "I don't mind talking about my sex life, but I don't want to hear about yours...well, at least when it's about Mom. The others are okay."

He ignored my comment. "As soon as I got to know her, I was smitten. She was the best lay I ever had and I didn't want to have sex with anyone else. That's how I knew."

"You still feel that way? Twenty years later?"

He smirked. "Your mom has only gotten better with age."

I cringed again. "Anyway...I don't see me settling down for anybody."

"That will change."

"Nope." I finished my glass and poured another.

"All your uncles went through the same thing. And they all seem pretty happy."

"That's debatable..."

"Who are you juggling now?" he asked.

I usually had several girls at once. "Actually, just one." I'd never tell him it was Trinity. He wasn't just my dad, but my closest friend. But I knew how close he was to Trinity's father, Mike, and I wasn't stupid. My dad would beat the shit out of me if he knew what I was doing with her.

He cocked an eyebrow. "Just one?" Surprise was in his voice.

"She turned out to be pretty good in the sack. And she doesn't care that I'm just using her. Actually, she's using me just as much. And I don't have to make excuses to get away from her. I can be myself, and I don't have to worry about leading her on. She doesn't want a relationship any more than I do."

My dad processed my words for a long time. "How long has this been going on?"

I shrugged. "Over a month."

"And you haven't slept with anyone else?" he asked incredulously.

"No. Every time I think about it, I remember I have to wear a damn rubber. With this girl, I don't have to."

Alarm moved into his eyes. "Slade, don't fuck around like that. She could trick you into getting her pregnant."

"Believe me, she's not like that. I'm pretty sure she never wants to have kids—ever."

He calmed down slightly. "Still, be careful."

"I've known this girl for awhile. I trust her."

"Trust?" He stared me down. "You never trust people."

Was I making it obvious it was Trinity? "Well, I've known her all through college because we've had classes together. I know she's cool." *Did that cover my tracks?*

"And you only like having sex with her?"

"Well, she's really good and why would I go somewhere else when I know it's going to suck in comparison?"

My dad smirked at me, a knowing look in his eyes.

"What?"

"Nothing." He sipped his brandy and looked at the fire.

"I saw that look," I pressed.

"I think your bachelor days are almost over."

"No," I blurted. "Absolutely not. It's not what you think. Don't get your hopes up."

He shrugged. "I heard what I heard."

"Just because I'm sleeping with her now, doesn't mean I won't get tired of her and move on to someone else. I guarantee that will happen."

"You just said sex with anyone else wouldn't compare."

"For now."

He shook his head. "The definition of a monogamous relationship is when two partners only hook up with each other. And you've never been monogamous before..."

"I never said we were monogamous. We aren't. I just haven't slept with anyone. Big difference."

"Has she?"

"No."

"Would it bother you if she did?"

"I don't give a shit what she does," I blurted.

"Right..."

"What? I don't."

"Whatever you say, Son."

"I'm not lying," I argued.

My dad smirked but fell silent.

"You're a jackass."

"You're a cunt," he snapped.

I narrowed my eyes at him. "Go to hell."

"I'll see you there."

I leaned back in my chair and brooded.

"If you want that shop, you better be nicer to me."

"If you don't want me to tell Mom you drink like a camel, you better be nice to me."

He gave me a knowing look. "Your mother knows everything about me. I have no secrets from her."

"And she approves of you drowning your liver in alcohol?"

"She doesn't tell me what to do. Love is about accepting each other, not controlling each other. If I tried bossing her around, she'd slap me across the face."

"I know. I've seen it countless times."

My dad stared into the fire.

"You guys fight all the time..." The realization hit me hard.

"Yeah." He sounded bored.

"But...you guys still like to be around each other all the time." *Were Trinity and I like that?*

"Every relationship is different. But your mother and I are both headstrong and passionate. We fight a lot because we care so much. There are lines we never cross but we always speak our mind. Some people find it dysfunctional, and that's true, but it works for us. Believe me, even though I scream in her face, I love her more than I could ever put into words."

I processed his words for a moment. Then I sipped my drink. Trinity and I fought like we were going to battle. If we had guns, we would have blown each other to smithereens. We had no problem saying the most hurtful things to each other. But our sex was off the charts. *Did that mean something?*

"What are you thinking?" my father whispered.

My thoughts were shattered. I sipped my drink again and looked at the fire. "Nothing."

***

When I got back to my room, I texted Trinity. *Are you awake?*

Now I am.

Can I come over?

Our parents are upstairs.

Whatever. They aren't going to know.

It's risky...

Come on. I'm horny.

Slade, it's three in the morning. We're getting up in three hours.

Like I give a damn. I waited for her to respond. When she didn't, I texted her again. *I'll do that thing you like.*

There are a lot of things I like.

I'll do them all.

Fine. Make sure you aren't seen.

See you soon. I put my phone in my pocket then walked into the hallway. Just as I stepped out, I saw Skye step out in just a nightshirt. I froze, panicking. When she turned around, she saw me. Her eyes widened but she didn't say anything.

Fuck. Fuck. Fuck. *Why would I be up in the middle of the night?*

She stared at me then crossed her arms over her chest. "What are you doing?"

"What are *you* doing?" I countered.

"Um..."

I realized she was in front of Cayson's door. Then it hit me. "A midnight fuck?" I grinned at her.

"Shut up, Slade. Don't say anything."

"Maybe I will...maybe I won't."

"And what are *you* doing?" she demanded.

I went with the first excuse that came to mind. "Going to the bathroom."

She seemed to accept that. "Keep this to yourself."

"Then be nice to me."

"Go to hell." She walked into her bedroom then shut the door.

I stayed in the hallway, making sure she didn't come out again. Then I dashed into Trinity's room and shut the door quickly. The lights were off and I could barely see her. The outside light filtered through her window and allowed me to see her outline.

Wordlessly, I undressed then got into the bed with her.

"Be quiet," she said. "I share a wall with my brother."

"If he hears anything, just tell him you were fingering yourself."

"What makes you think I'm the loud one?" she demanded. "You're always the one moaning like you haven't had sex before."

"Shut up. Fucking bare pussy is totally different than regular sex."

She sighed. "Let's stop arguing and just screw already."

"Fine by me. I hate listening to you talk anyway."

"That makes two of us."

I moved on top of her then pulled her close to me. I slipped inside her without any problems. "You're already soaked."

She dug her nails into my back but didn't make a sound.

"I guess you wanted me more than you let on."

"Just shut up and fuck me."

Her words made my spine shiver. I pressed my face closer to hers and kissed her while I rocked into her. She breathed into my mouth while I breathed into hers. Her pussy was the best damn thing in the world. It felt so good that I wanted to explode the moment we started. Her long legs wrapped around my waist, only arousing me more. I loved her legs more than any other feature. I loved how smooth and toned they were.

I moved in and out without shaking her bed. We were both deadly silent. She moved under me slightly, clearly enjoying it. When she tensed around me, I knew she was hitting her climax. I crushed my mouth against hers and tried to keep her moans down. She was particularly loud during an orgasm. I usually didn't mind because we were alone, but I definitely didn't want her brother to hear it. When she was finished, her breathing returned to normal and I let myself go. I didn't try to make it last longer because of our situation. I just wanted to get off and go to bed.

I rolled off her then lay beside her. We both breathed hard, catching our breath. Trinity sighed loudly, the sound she usually made when she was satisfied. We didn't speak, having nothing to say. I stared at the ceiling then felt my eyes grow heavy. Then I fell asleep.

***

A knock on the door made my eyes snap open.

"Trinity, are you awake?" It was her dad.

Fuck. Fuck. Fuck.

Trinity and I were snuggling so close together we were practically one person. Her body was wrapped around mine and my arms formed a solid cage around her. I quickly sat up then kicked the blanket away.

Trinity sat up and pulled the sheet over her. She looked at me with fear in her eyes. Too scared to speak and be overheard, we just spoke with our eyes.

She pointed underneath the bed. "Hide," she mouthed.

I got down then moved under the bed, pulling my clothes with me.

Fuck, I was a dead man.

Trinity quickly pulled a shirt on. "Come in, Dad."

The door opened and he stepped inside. I could see his feet as he moved across the hardwood floor. I prayed he didn't see me. He would strangle me then crack my skull open with his gorilla hands. My dad wouldn't be able to protect me. Shit, my mom wouldn't even be able to. She'd probably help him.

He sat on the edge of the bed, the mattress sinking under his weight.

I took a deep breath, trying not to be heard. My heart was pounding so fast I heard it in my ears.

"Morning, honey." He spoke with a gentle voice I never heard before. He was always so stern and deep all the time. He joked around a lot but there was always a threat in his eyes. He was the kind of guy I wouldn't want to see in a dark alley. He was generous and compassionate, but he was also murderous. But he didn't act that way at all with Trinity.

"Hey, Dad."

"Sleep well?"

"Yeah. It's peaceful up here." She also spoke in a tone I'd never heard before. It was quiet, almost submissive. Whenever she spoke to me or anyone else in our group, there was a fire in her voice. And there was always an attitude. But her father didn't get that tone from her.

"Your mom has always liked the snow. Whenever it falls at home, she never wants me to shovel it off the driveway...even though it makes it nearly impossible for me to get to work."

She chuckled lightly. "But she always gets her way."

"And so do you."

What the hell? I didn't realize they were so close.

"You ready to go skiing today?" he asked.

"I'm excited. But I really want a cup of hot cocoa from the lodge. It's my favorite."

"We'll get one together. How about that?"

"We can't break tradition, right?"

"Never," he said. "Are you hungry?"

"A little."

"You want me to bring you something?"

"No, it's okay. I'll go down there after I get ready."

"Okay, Honey."

I heard him kiss her on the cheek or forehead.

"I'll see you soon."

"Okay, Dad."

He got up and walked to the door. "I'm excited to spend time with you this weekend."

"Me too."

He shut the door.

I waited until I couldn't hear his footsteps anymore.

Trinity got up then locked the door.

I slid from under the bed then got dressed as quickly as possible. "Shit, that was close."

She rounded on me like she might kill me. "Why did you sleep here?"

"I don't know. I always sleep with you."

"What kind of argument is that?" she hissed.

"What? I was tired and fell asleep. Get off my case."

"*Get off your case*?" she snapped. "We almost got caught, you stupid idiot."

"Shut up, daddy's girl."

"Is that supposed to be offensive?" she asked incredulously.

"If you weren't such a daddy's girl, he wouldn't have come in here."

"Don't blame him for saying good morning to me! You should have been out of my room as soon as we were done."

"Just calm down, alright? We didn't get caught so shut the hell up."

"You shut up!" She slapped me across the face.

I took the hit then clenched my jaw. For some reason, inexplicably, it turned me on. I grabbed her face then shoved her against the wall. Even though neither one of us had brushed our teeth, I didn't care. I kissed her hard, and to no surprise, she kissed me back.

A knock on the door made us break apart.

Then they tried the doorknob. "Trinity, why is the door locked?" It was Skye.

Both of our eyes expanded to the size of orbs. Since I was right next to the closet, I got inside then she shut the door quickly.

Trinity opened the door. "I'm getting ready. What do you want?"

"Wow...talk about attitude. Not a morning person, huh?"

"Skye, what do you want?" she asked firmly.

"Have you seen Slade? His dad can't find him."

"Why would I know where he is?" She said it a little too quickly and a little too defensively.

"I'm just wondering. They can't find him anywhere."

"Well, I don't know where he is, alright?" She shut the door quickly then locked it again.

Fuck, could this day get any worse?

Trinity opened the closet and looked like she might murder me right on the spot.

"I'll go out the window and pretend I was playing in the snow," I blurted.

"But you're wearing what you wore yesterday." She sounded hysterical.

"It's me," I said quickly. "No one will question it."

She ran her hands through her hair in a panic. "If we get through this, I'm going to kill you."

"Well, if we don't get through this, your dad is going to kill me. So I'm dead either way."

"Good," she snapped.

I opened the window then peeked around. No one was out and about.

"Duck under all the windows so no one sees you," she whispered. "Just walk through the front door."

"You act like I've never escaped out of a girl's bedroom before."

"We're on the second story, Sherlock."

"I've had worse, trust me."

"Shut up and go." She slapped my ass.

"Did you just slap my ass?"

"Just go, Slade!"

I put one foot through then looked back at her. "I'm coming over tonight, right?"

Fire burned in her eyes. "That better be a fucking joke."

"So yes? Great. See you then." I crawled out and shut the window before she could scream at me.

I ducked as I moved around the roof, making sure no one could see me. Then I moved to the edge and peeked at the ground. It didn't seem like anyone was around. I slid down a pipe then landed in the snow.

I stood up and brushed it off, proud of myself for not getting caught.

"What are you doing?"

I stilled when I recognized my dad's voice. *Oh shit.* I turned around and smirked. "Practicing my parkour. What else would I be doing?" I tried to act as normal as possible.

"On the roof?" he asked incredulously.

"You know me, I like a challenge."

He stared at me like I was crazy. "At six in the morning?"

"When else would I have time to do it?"

My dad seemed to accept my story. "Sometimes I wonder if your mother drank when she was pregnant with you."

"I wouldn't put it past her. Or maybe your sperm was soaked in brandy and that's where the problem started."

He shook his head slightly.

"So, you wanted to see me?"

He cocked an eyebrow. "How did you know that?"

Fuck. Fuck. Fuck. "Why else would you be outside? You must have seen me practicing." *Please buy it.*

He did. "I wanted to order our gear before we got to the resort. What size are you?"

Seriously? I jumped off a roof just because he wanted to know what size shoe I wore? "Eleven." I tried not to let my anger come out.

"Thanks." He took out his phone then made the call.

I rolled my eyes and walked inside.

Everyone was sitting at the table eating breakfast. When Trinity saw me, she glanced at me then looked to her food. I sat at the end of the table and piled food onto my plate. No one questioned where I was. And I ate like I didn't just almost die.

***

We got our equipment from the front then stood in a circle.

"Baby, Slade and I are heading to a black diamond." He kissed my mom quickly then pulled away.

"Be careful, Ryan." My mom gave him a look like she would kill him if he didn't come back alive.

776

"Mom, we'll be fine," I said. "We know what we're doing. Have fun on those sticks you call skis."

"Skis are a lot harder than snowboarding," Silke argued.

"No, they aren't. A two-year-old could ride on those," I snapped.

"Let's go before the kids pull each other's hair," my dad said.

"Good idea," my mom said. She wore a green beanie and her long blonde hair stuck out underneath.

"Be careful," he said to her.

"Dad, they'll be on the bunny hill. They'll be just fine," I said.

My dad held his board with one arm. "Let's go."

Everyone else was sticking with their parents. My dad and I were the only ones who preferred snowboarding over skiing. We were cool like that. We moved to the chair lift then let it take us to the very top of the mountain.

"You want to race?" I asked.

"Not really."

"Scared?" I teased.

"I just don't want to hurt your feelings. I know how sensitive you are."

I slugged him in the arm.

"Was that supposed to hurt?" he said sarcastically.

"Go to hell, Dad."

We reached the slope far in the back then finally got off the lift. Like pros, we moved off the lift easily then rode our boards out of the way of other people. We stopped when we reached a good part to drop in at. It was almost a cliff face. I smirked in excitement.

"I can't believe you aren't wearing a jacket."

"It's not even cold. It's sunny as hell."

"You should still wear one."

"Then how will anyone see my tats?" I argued.

"Maybe you should put them on your face if that's all you care about," he snapped.

I shrugged. "I guess that would be cool."

He rolled his eyes then buckled himself in. "Ready?"

I checked my boots then strapped myself in. "Let's do this."

"You first."

"Dad, you don't have to trail behind me. I'm a big boy."

"I like to know where you are. There's no reception up here."

"Whatever, Dad." I moved forward then pushed my weight into the dive. I picked up speed as soon as I took off. Like I'd done it a million times, I cut through the snow, shredding the fresh powder. My dad was close behind me. I could see him in my peripheral vision. He was pretty good, just as good as I was. There's no one I'd rather go with than my dad. He was the only one who could keep up with me.

I was going fast down the slope, faster than I ever had. It made me feel alive, exhilarated. When I cut through the snow, I felt like I could do anything. I didn't think about school or life. I just thought about the moment I was in. Personally, that's how I thought life should be lived.

When I reached hard snow that was practically slush, I lost control then slipped down the mountain. I was going so fast that I couldn't stop. I dug my board in to slow down but it was too hard. It must be an area where it melted overnight and refroze as ice. There was no friction so I kept going. I dug my hand into the snow so I would stop. My skin burned from scraping against the ice.

When I flew off the trail and into the trees, I started to panic. I'd never done that before.

Fuck. Fuck. Fuck.

When I was about to hit a tree, I managed to swerve out of the way.

Shit, that was close.

"Slade, I'm right behind you!"

My dad was there. *Thank god.* "I can't stop!"

"Dig your board into the snow!"

"What do you think I'm doing?" I screamed.

"Slade! Stop! Cliff!"

Shit, did he just say cliff?

Fuck. I tried to grab onto anything.

All of a sudden, I felt something heavy land on top of me. I was pulled to an immediate halt. I felt hands grip both of my arms.

"Son, are you alright?"

I looked up and my dad was looking down at me with concern in his eyes. His nose was bloody.

"Yeah...I'm fine." I sat up then rubbed my head. "What happened?"

"I landed on you." He said it like it was no big deal.

"How did you manage that?"'

"I don't know. I wasn't thinking. There's a cliff fifty feet away. If I didn't do something, you were going to fall."

Holy shit.

He wiped the blood from his nose then caught his breath.

"Thanks..."

"Yeah. Be a little more careful next time."

"I don't know what happened. I just hit an ice patch."

Then I heard a sound that made me even more terrified than I've ever been in my life.

A bear roared.

My father and I both moved to our feet with a quickness that belied our ability. Twenty feet away was an enormous grizzly bear. He was on his hind legs and didn't look happy to see us.

Could this get any worse?

"Give me your lighter." My dad said it calmly.

"Why?"

"JUST DO IT!"

I dug my hand into my pocket then threw it at him. "What the fuck are you going to do with it?"

My dad cracked a branch off a tree then held the lighter to it. It caught flame in a few seconds. Then my dad marched to the bear with the stick raised. The bear started to back away. My dad swung it at the beast, the heat searing its fur. Then it turned around and ran away.

My dad turned around then dropped the branch in the snow. "Let's get back to the slopes. Now."

I didn't need to be told twice. I grabbed my board then walked alongside my father, looking around to make sure we were alone. When we made it back to the main lift area, I started to breathe again.

I looked at my dad. "We almost died. Twice."

"Say a word to your mother and I will kill you."

"Your secret is safe with me."

"Good." He ran his fingers through his hair but he still seemed calm. My dad saved my ass twice and he didn't even freak out over it. It was like nothing phased him.

"Dad, you're a badass."

He looked at me, his eyes dark. "No. But I would give my life for my son. It's called being a parent." Seriousness was in his voice.

We stood there, saying nothing. No other riders were on the slope. We were there alone, listening to the silence.

"Want to hit the bunny hill?" I asked.

He laughed. "I thought you'd never ask."

Chapter Thirty-Nine

Trinity

We spent the entire day skiing. My brother was pretty good and so was my father. My dad grew up skiing so he was practically a pro. My mom had never skied before she met my dad, so she and I sucked equally.

My ass was sore from falling down more often than standing up. Every time I fell, my dad waited for me to get back on my feet. I would slide down a few feet before my face was in the snow again. My dad showed me a few tricks but I could never grasp it. By the time we went to the lodge and had lunch and cocoa, I was exhausted. My brother and I didn't even argue because we were so tired. I needed a nice nap right then.

When the sun went down, we finally returned to the house. Everyone else was already back, probably passed out on the couch or asleep in their beds. The first thing I did was take a shower to warm up. Then I went downstairs and shoveled twice as much food as I normally would onto my plate. I sat down on the couch and ate quietly, too exhausted to talk to my family.

A lot of people were in the other living room, watching TV. But I sat on the couches in front of the fireplace, enjoying the silence. I could practically hear my muscles screaming because they were so exhausted.

My dad sat in the seat next to me, his plate in his hand. "You doing okay?"

"Just exhausted."

He nodded. "Skiing is harder than it looks."

"But I think I'm more tired from falling than actually skiing." I laughed at my own comment.

"You'll get better."

I noticed my dad always teased everyone else mercilessly. He was particularly harsh with his own brother. But when it came to me, he treated me in a different way. He never teased me when I failed at something. He always tried to make me feel better. He wasn't that way with Conrad, just me. "Dad, it's okay to say it. I know I suck."

"I never said you didn't. But you will get better."

At least he didn't lie to me. I ate my potato salad then moved on to my chicken.

"How's school going?"

"It's okay."

He ate quietly and slowly. "Have you decided what you want to do yet?" He stared at his plate while he said it.

"I want to go into fashion. There's no doubt about that."

"Then are you going to drop out?"

"No," I said with a sigh. "I'm almost done. I'd rather finish."

"Honey, do whatever you want. Don't worry about pissing me off."

"You spent so much money on my—"

"And you know I don't care about that. Don't let money be a factor."

"But I might be able to use my business degree for what I want to do."

"Which is?"

"Running my own clothing line."

He nodded. "It will be helpful. And your old man has a lot of experience to help you." He gave me a smile before turning his attention back to his food.

"Not according to Uncle Sean," I teased.

"Well, that guy is an idiot. Don't listen to him."

I finished my food then left the plate on the table.

"There's pie. Do you want me to get you a piece?" he asked.

"No. As odd as this sounds, I'm too tired to eat."

He chuckled. "You need to exercise more often."

"I jog."

"Not the same. You need to do some weight training."

"I don't even know the difference between a bench press and a squat."

"I can show you," my dad offered.

"Nah. I'll stick to running on a treadmill."

My dad finished his food. "Did you finish that book I gave you?"

"I did."

"Did you like it?"

"Actually, I did."

He crossed his foot at the ankle. "We should watch the movie sometime. It's a classic."

"Sure." I settled into the couch and pulled my knees to my chest.

My dad grabbed a blanket then placed it over me, tucking me in like he used to when I was a child.

"Thanks."

"Yeah." He stared at the fire while he rested his hands in his lap. "Anything new in your life?"

I immediately thought of Slade. I spent a lot of time with him, more than I expected to. "No, not really. Skye and Cayson bring a lot of drama to the group but that's not surprising."

"Well, Skye is Sean's daughter," he teased.

I laughed. "She can be too stubborn sometimes."

"Just like her dad."

"But they're good together," I said. "I know they're going to last forever."

"You think?" he asked.

"I know." I was jealous when I thought about it. Skye had a guy that loved her more than life itself.

"You're going to find that someday too." It was like my dad could read my mind.

"You think?" I was already twenty-two and I hadn't found anyone who came close.

"I know. You're a beautiful girl who's smart and fun. Believe me, you have admirers even if you don't know it."

The only admirer I had was a tattooed bad boy that just wanted to have sex. "Maybe."

"No, not maybe." He said it firmly.

I decided not to argue with him.

"I finished your book," he said.

"How did you like *The Count of Monte Cristo*?"

"It was good. Too many characters to keep track of but good."

"Totally different than the movie, huh?" I asked.

"Yeah. But I like the ending in the movie more."

I gave him a smile. "I did too. I'm a sucker for happy endings."

"I guess I am too." His hand moved through my hair for a second before he dropped it.

Companionable silence stretched between us. We could spend hours sitting together without saying anything. It wasn't awkward at all. Skye and I did the same thing countless times. My dad was my dad, he always would be, but he was also my friend. I knew he babied me a lot. When it came to Conrad, my dad was strict and firm. He pushed him a lot more than he pushed me simply because Conrad was a man. Sometimes I wished he didn't do it, but there were times when I absolutely loved it. My dad had unique and special relationships with each of us. I never felt like he loved me more or less than my brother.

My eyes were growing heavy and I couldn't keep them open anymore. "I'm sorry, Dad. I'm so tired…"

"It's okay, honey. Go to sleep."

***

My phone vibrated on my nightstand and woke me up. I was tucked in my bed. I was wearing what I wore earlier except my shoes were gone. My dad must have carried me up and put me to bed. That wasn't surprising.

I squinted at the clock and realized it was three in the morning. Then I looked at my phone.

Are you awake? It was Slade.

Stop waking me up in the middle of the night! I'm tired.

And I'm horny. Cry me a river.

Good night, Slade. Leave me alone. I turned off my phone so he wouldn't wake me up again.

Just as I fell asleep, my bedroom door opened.

Ugh.

Slade took off his clothes then got into bed beside me. "Hey," he whispered.

"We have to wake up in three hours. I'd rather go to sleep than have sex."

"I didn't come here to have sex. I want to talk."

Did I hear him right? "What?"

"You'll never guess what happened to my dad and I today. We almost died—twice."

I sat up. "What?"

Slade told me he almost fell off a cliff but his dad saved him. And then a bear almost ate them but his dad used his lighter to scare it off.

It was almost too ridiculous to believe. "Are you making this up?"

"No! Don't tell my mom. My dad doesn't want her to know."

"But...that's crazy."

"I know! I almost died twice in one day. It was so awesome."

"Awesome?" I asked incredulously.

"How many people can say something like that?"

"How many people *want* to say something like that?"

"I just had to tell you."

"Me? Why me?"

"Because..." He seemed to be at a loss for words. "I don't know. I just wanted to tell you."

Silence stretched between us but it was a little tense.

"How was your day?" he asked.

Slade never asked me stuff like that. I turned on my side and faced him in the darkness. His hand rested on my hip. "It was okay. I suck at skiing."

"What's new?"

I hit his arm lightly.

He chuckled. "It's okay. I can teach you if you want."

"No, it's fine. My dad shows me but I just don't get it. I've fallen on my face so many times that it's sore as hell."

"Your face?" he asked incredulously. "Is it even possible for it to be sore?"

"Yes, it is," I said firmly. "I just found that out. And my ass is killing me."

"That's sore too?" he asked.

"Yeah."

Slade undid my jeans and pulled them off.

"What are you doing?"

"Who the hell sleeps in jeans?"

"Who the hell doesn't wear a jacket in the snow?" I countered.

His hand moved to my ass and he started to massage it.

I winced in pain then it started to feel amazing. I moaned quietly and closed my eyes.

"Your ass is really tense."

"I'm not surprised," I said with a sigh.

He rubbed the other cheek then moved down to my thighs.

"You're good at that. You should be a masseuse."

"I know the female body pretty well." He gave me a cocky wink.

"Shut up, Slade."

He chuckled then kept rubbing me. "Other than that, how was your day?"

"Well, it wasn't as exciting as running away from a grizzly bear and almost falling off a cliff."

"Well, your day will never be as exciting as mine was," he said with a laugh.

"The highlight of my day was when my father and I got hot cocoa and discussed the books we just finished reading."

"Wow...that's lame."

I hit him in the arm.

"You want me to stop rubbing you?" he snapped.

I quickly rubbed his arm. "Please don't stop."

He smirked. "I've heard you say that several times—but in a very different context."

"Go to hell, Slade."

He laughed then rubbed my calves.

"It's nice to talk about stuff like that with my dad. We discuss politics and economics, and we talk about fictitious characters and storylines. I can't have those kinds of conversations with anyone else but him."

Slade stared at me for a long time. "You guys are really close."

"Yeah..."

"It's actually really cute."

"Cute?" That was the second time he used that word.

"Yeah. I've known Uncle Mike my whole life and he's always been fun and aggressive. He tells more jokes than my dad. He's the life of the party but he can be a brute like a gorilla. But when he's alone with you...he's totally different. He's gentle, quiet, and thoughtful. He treats you like....like a princess."

"Pretty much," I whispered.

"And you're different around him too, a completely different person."

"You mean I'm myself?"

"Is that the real you?" he asked. "Because I've never seen it before. You're always so sarcastic and have a hot-headed attitude."

"Well, I know my dad would never hurt me. It's totally different. He would never make fun of me for saying something stupid. I can say anything and he won't judge me."

He stopped rubbing me. "You can say anything to me… We talk about books and stuff."

I eyed him, unsure of his meaning. "What are you saying?"

He was quiet for a long time. "I'm not sure what I'm saying, actually."

I didn't either.

"I guess…I feel like I could tell you anything." He didn't look at me when he said it. His hands rubbed me again, removing the aches and sores.

When I thought about it in retrospect, I realized I told Slade a lot more than I told anyone else. Perhaps this arrangement brought us closer together as friends. I was close to everyone in my circle, especially Skye who was my best friend, but I never told her any of that. "I could tell you anything too."

He looked into my eyes. "Wow…I never thought this would happen."

"What?"

"You're like…a really good friend to me. Cayson has always been my best friend but…I don't tell him every thought that runs through my head. With you, I do."

"Are you saying I'm your best friend?" I asked.

"I guess. Isn't that what a best friend is?" he asked. "Someone you can say anything to? You can be yourself without any fear of judgment or repercussion?"

"Yeah..." That's exactly how I described my relationship with my father.

He shrugged. "I guess sleeping together was the best decision we ever made."

My hand moved to his bicep, the muscle I grabbed more often than not. Slade had a particular smell to him, cologne mixed with his natural scent. I recognized it so well that I could tell where he sat on a couch even after he left the room. I'd grown accustomed to his company. We spent over half the week in the same bed. Now I was used to his morning routines before we left for school. He always made toast in the toaster then left new bread inside so all I had to do was turn it on. I hated him for the longest time but...now I really cared about him. "I think you're right."

Chapter Tourty

Skye

I hadn't cornered my dad about the episode with Zack. We were having a lovely weekend hitting the slopes and bundling up to stay warm. There was never a good time to unleash my rage.

After spending most of the day on the hill, we headed to the ski resort for lunch. We grabbed our trays and piled them with food. Naturally, my tray had the most items.

My brother eyed it. "You're such a fat ass."

"No, I'm not," I argued. "I've been running around all day."

"Maybe your ass will get smaller then." He walked to a table near the fire and sat down.

I held my tongue and imagined ripping his eyes out.

"He teases you because he loves you." My mom stood behind me while my dad pulled out his wallet and paid for the meal.

"Mom, I know you're right about a lot of stuff...but this time you aren't."

She smirked. "Your uncle Ryan and I are the same way."

"You guys tease each other in a completely different way."

My mom laughed. "Actually, we don't."

We took a seat at the table. Roland was already eating his pizza and fries.

My dad had a salad, like usual, and my mom was eating a burrito.

I ordered a hot cocoa because it was freezing outside. The sun was out most of the day but then the sky became hazy with clouds. A few snowflakes sprinkled the ground.

My dad eyed my mom. "You like your food, baby?"

She already ate half of it. "It's delicious. How's your...salad?" She smirked while she stared at it.

He grinned. "It's...decent."

She laughed. "You look like a man but you eat like a rabbit."

"But you like the way I look, right?" he asked. "And I don't want you to run off anywhere..."

"Like she would," Roland said. "You'd put a bullet in her new man's head."

I knew my brother wasn't joking. That honestly sounded like something Dad would do.

My dad gave him a dark look. "Don't joke about stuff like that."

"Because you're afraid Mom will cheat on you?" he asked.

"No." My dad remained calm. "Guns aren't a good subject over lunch."

"And you talking about having sex with Mom is?" Roland questioned.

"Shut up and eat your food, Roland Preston." My dad stared at him from across the table.

That shut my brother up.

"I don't want to go home," my mom said with a sigh.

"We can stay," my dad blurted. He'd do anything to make her happy.

"No," she said. "You need to get back to work. I'm more sad about the kids heading back to school."

I wasn't looking forward to it either. I loved spending time with my parents, even if they were a little annoying and overly affectionate sometimes.

"I hate school," Roland said. "The only good about it are the girls."

"But don't you prefer them married?" my dad jabbed.

Roland rolled his eyes. "I'm never going to live that one down…"

"Probably not," my dad said.

My mom shook her head slightly. "We all make mistakes as we age. But you better not repeat that one."

Roland shoved his pizza into his mouth and stayed quiet.

"Have you seen Cayson much this weekend?" my mom asked.

Just at night. "No. We've been busy with our families all day. But that's fine. I see him every day at school."

"So, everything is great between you two?" my mom asked. "Because your father and I really love Cayson."

"Who doesn't?" I blurted. "Yeah, we're great."

"When Skye isn't fucking it up left and right," Roland said with a mouthful of food.

I kicked him under the table.

"Argh!" He kicked me back.

"Fucking it up?" My dad raised an eyebrow while looking at me. "What's that mean, Skye?"

Great. My brother put me right on the spot. "We've had a few fights...nothing major."

"You almost dumped him," Roland said.

"Why don't you shut up and mind your own business?" I kicked him as hard as I could under the table.

"Bitch," he mumbled.

My dad's hand snatched his throat from across the table quicker than I could see. He pulled Roland toward him and lowered his voice. "Never talk to your sister like that again." He released him then leaned back.

Roland would normally argue but this time he didn't.

Awkwardness set in at the table.

My dad knew we teased each other often, but there were certain rules he had. We weren't allowed to say anything unforgiveable or hateful to one another. Everything else was fair game.

"Anyway…" My mom cleared her throat. "Skye, is that true? You almost dumped him?"

When I looked at my dad, I felt my anger come out. "Cayson betrayed my trust and tattled on me to Dad about Zack. I'm perfectly capable of taking care of myself and handling my own problems. But Cayson seemed to disagree. I told him I couldn't be with someone I didn't trust implicitly. We quickly made up and moved on."

"Such a stupid thing to get upset about," Roland mumbled. "He was just looking out for you."

My dad kept a stoic expression on his face. I couldn't tell what he was thinking. "He did the right thing coming to me. I wouldn't want him to be with you if he made any other judgment call."

"You and everyone else I know," I mumbled.

"I made sure Zack will never bother you again," my father said. "Now Cayson and I can both get some sleep at night."

"He was never a threat to me," I snapped.

"Cayson didn't agree. And I'd take Cayson's opinion over yours any day." His eyes narrowed while he stared me down.

When it came to this topic, my dad was aggressive and mean. He always pinned me down and wouldn't let me get the upper hand. Just like me, he was stubborn and argumentative. He would never let me win, no matter what, and he would put his foot down over and over. He had the patience of a sloth and the adrenaline of a coyote.

"Than your own daughter's?" I snapped.

"I admire your independence and intelligence. I really do." My dad's voice was calm the entire time. We were in a crowded room full of people so he acted normal, like we were discussing the lotto numbers that were announced the evening before. But his eyes gave his rage away. "I would never want you to be any different. Just like your mother, you're strong and understand your self-worth. But you're blind to your own safety and foolishly think you're invincible. You have no idea what this guy is thinking, and as strong as you might think you are, he's twice your size and could take you down with one throw of a fist.

"You know why I'm such a successful businessman?" He asked it like a question but I knew it was rhetorical. "How I grew a large company into an international empire? It's

800

because I'm proactive, not reactive. I don't take chances when it comes to stuff like this. I'm always on the offense, not the defense. If this guy isn't leaving you alone and he held down Trinity—a fucking red flag—then I don't want him anywhere near you. Being angry with Cayson is immature and petty. You're lucky he loves you as much as he does to put up with your naivety. Not all men are like me, your uncles, your cousins, and Cayson. There are men who will rip you apart the first chance they get. It's a lesson I thought you already learned."

I looked away and stared at the fire in the stone hearth. My dad always got under my skin when he made speeches like this. He never got emotional, but he did get angry. He somehow reduced me to a shadow, stripping my confidence and my strength. He did it every time, leaving me defenseless and raw.

"Don't be so hard on her," my mother whispered.

"Baby, stay out of this." His voice was full of threat.

My mother backed off.

I left the table and abandoned my food then stormed outside. I didn't want to look at my father or my family. I wanted to hide my face. Moisture bubbled under my eyes and they burned as they touched my cheek. I finally made it outside and stood away from the windows, getting some privacy.

I hated crying. It was weak and pathetic. I quickly wiped the tears away, refusing to be anything but strong. Sometimes I felt like I was screaming as loud as I could but no one was listening. I was lucky I had a father who cared so much about me, but for once, I wanted him to trust me enough to take care of myself. He treated Roland that way. Why should I be treated differently?

The door opened again and I felt someone come near me. Judging by the cologne in the air, I knew it was my father.

I turned my back to him, not letting him see the redness around my eyes. I should have held my tongue and not gone head-to-head with him in the middle of a crowded room. It wasn't smart to corner him when we were on a family trip. Perhaps I was stupid after all.

My father stood behind me but didn't touch me. "Skye, I'm sorry I upset you."

"You didn't." I said it with a strong voice, hiding my vulnerability. "I just needed to get away from you."

"Then why are you crying?"

How did he know that? I decided not to answer.

He came closer to me then rested his hand on my shoulder. "Skye, I love you so much. Please know that everything I say comes from a good place."

"I know..."

He sighed then dropped his hand. "Pumpkin, look at me."

Since he already knew I was upset, I turned around and faced him head on.

He stared at the redness around my eyes. He took a deep breath, the self-loathing coming into his features. "I'm sorry I made you cry. Please tell me what you're thinking."

"I'm just sick of you babying me, Dad. I can take care of myself but how will I prove that if you won't let me?"

"I know you can take care of yourself. I've always known that."

"It doesn't seem like it."

"You know what our problem is—both of us?"

I crossed my arms over my chest and listened.

"I'm too overprotective—I admit it. But you're too proud."

"Proud?"

"You will never ask for help even if you're drowning. That's the reason why I'm like this. You're so determined to do everything on your own that I fear you won't reach out to me or anyone else for that matter when you need to. And that scares the life out of me, Skye."

I processed his words then looked at the ground.

"Correct me if I'm wrong."

I knew he wasn't.

"Does that explain my behavior a little better?"

I nodded.

"Do you honestly see Zack as nonthreatening? Be honest, Skye."

He did threaten to hurt Cayson but I thought he was just being an ass. And he did hold down Trinity. And he did spend six months lying to me just to be with me. He was controlling when we were together, trying to get me to follow his rules. Perhaps he had psychopath written all over him. Maybe I was wrong about the whole thing. "No..."

My dad didn't gloat. There was no victory in his eyes. "Then I'm really glad Cayson came to me. But Skye, it should have been you."

"I know... I just...you've babied me my whole life and—"

"You're my one and only daughter. I can't begin to explain how much I love you. I understand you're going to get hurt. That's how life is. As much as it pains me, I accept that truth. But when it comes to stuff like this, serious stuff, I have to intervene."

"I know, Dad."

"I promise I'll be better from now on. If you ask me to back off and leave you alone, I promise I will. But I want a promise in return."

"What promise?" I asked.

"That you will come to me when you need help. You will not be proud and try to figure it out while you're drowning. You will not try to prove anything to me. Skye, you've already proven how amazing and self-sufficient you are. I don't need anything else."

I nodded.

"Can I have that promise? I know you'll mean it if you give it to me."

"I promise."

He breathed a sigh of relief. "Thank you."

"I'm sorry, Dad…about everything."

"I'm sorry too, Pumpkin." He came to me then held me close. "But I'm glad this happened. I feel like we've really covered new ground here. I feel a lot more comfortable knowing you'll make the right decisions even if I'm not around."

"And I'm glad you know I can take care of myself."

"You're just like your mother." He cupped the back of my head with his hand and held me close. "In every good way possible."

"That's a big compliment."

"It was meant as one."

He pulled away then stepped back. "Are you ready to head back inside?"

"Yeah. I want to finish the rest of my food."

He laughed. "That's my girl."

***

Cayson and I sat in front of the fire with cups of cocoa.

"How was your day?" he asked.

"It was okay. My dad and I got into a fight."

"It seems like that's all you ever do," he teased.

"Well, we are a lot alike."

He smirked. "And I know how you are…"

"We talked about the whole Zack thing."

"I'm sure that went well," he said sarcastically.

"He made a lot of good points…but I think we're better off because of it. He made me realize how proud I am."

"Wow…you finally admit it."

I gave him a hard look.

"Sorry," he said quickly.

"And he admitted he's too overprotective. We agreed to work on our shortcomings."

He nodded. "A compromise…I like it."

I sipped my hot cocoa then tried to get a few marshmallows into my mouth. The fire burned in front of us and snow fell outside. Everyone had gone to bed already. It was just he and I.

"No sex tonight," he said quietly. "It's a miracle we haven't gotten caught."

"It's our last night and it's so romantic. Let's just do it."

"No. I feel like I'm going to have a heart attack every time your father looks at me."

"He's not a mind reader," I snapped.

"He could be. Maybe he developed some technology that allows him to do that."

"My dad is smart...but not *that* smart."

"I'd rather not risk it."

"I'll sneak into your room anyway. And when I start doing stuff you like, you won't be able to get rid of me."

He glared at me. "You're such an evil enchantress."

I smirked. "I know."

We heard footsteps from the stairs and were joined by Theo and Thomas.

"Hey." Theo had a leftover slice of cold pizza in his hand.

"Hey," I said. "How was your day on the slopes?"

"I got sunburned," Theo said. "Can you believe it?"

"I told you to put on sunblock, man." Thomas sat on the couch then sunk into it.

"Well, I never listen to you for a reason," Theo said.

Then Silke joined us. "Why is everyone awake?"

"We're plotting to kill you," Theo said without looking at her.

"That's so ironic because I was planning to do the same to you." She held a pint of ice cream and started to eat directly out of it.

"So much for a romantic evening by the fire," Cayson said sarcastically.

"Go upstairs and screw like snow bunnies," Theo said. "What's more romantic than that?"

I gave Cayson a flirtatious look. "I couldn't agree more."

He ignored my comment and stared at the fire.

Slade came downstairs with Trinity. "It's a full house tonight."

"Why are you two together?" I asked.

"We aren't." Slade took eight steps away from Trinity. "It was just a coincidence."

"An unfortunate one." Trinity looked through the fridge until she found a leftover sandwich. Slade dug out his own then joined us in the living room.

"Why are we all huddled here?" Slade asked.

I shrugged. "Cayson and I wanted some alone time...but we clearly aren't going to get it."

"Like fucking in the middle of the night isn't alone time," Slade snapped.

I glared at him. "So much for keeping quiet about it."

"Hey, I didn't tell any of the old people," he argued. "They are the only ones that count. None of us give a shit."

Roland and Conrad came down the stairs next.

"You guys are talking so loud that I can't sleep." Roland plopped down on the armchair by the fire and started to rock it back and forth.

Conrad took a seat on one of the couches. "I'm so glad we're going home tomorrow."

"Why?" Trinity asked.

"I'm sick of seeing Mom and Dad," Conrad said. "Dad keeps talking about the company and what I need to be prepared for. And then Mom keeps bugging me about settling down with a nice girl who will give her grandkids. I'm only twenty-one. Give me a break…"

"I don't want to go home," I said. "I like seeing my parents."

"Me too," Cayson added.

"You guys are the worst suck ups ever," Silke said.

"I'm not sucking up," I said. "I really do like my parents."

She rolled her eyes. "Whatever."

"I want to order a beer and wings," Slade said. "And watch a game. All they have is cable here."

"It's nice to take a break from the rest of the world," I said.

"God, you're annoying," Slade said.

Trinity ate her sandwich. "I'm horrible at skiing so I'm not too upset to leave the resort. But I will miss my parents."

"Another suck up," Silke said.

We fell into comfortable silence by the fireplace. Cayson held me close to him and wrapped his arm around my shoulder. My hot cocoa was abandoned for his warmth. Theo fell asleep and started to snore. Silke pulled out her phone and was typing away. Roland started to snore when he dozed off. It was late so we should have gone to bed but nobody moved. Just being together was comfortable enough. We were together constantly, but there was a reason for that. We were family, allowed to be ourselves in front of one another and still be loved. It was something I took for granted once in a while. But when we took trips like this, knowing exactly where we belonged, I cherished it. A lot of people hardly had any family in the world. But I had a huge one. And even though they teased me relentlessly and often told me to shut up, I knew they loved me.

And they always would.

Forever and Ever:
Volume Two

Available Now

Did you enjoy Forever and Ever: *Volume One*?
Leave a review on
Amazon

CPSIA information can be obtained at www.ICGtesting.com
Printed in the USA
BVOW06s1828260916

463338BV00016B/82/P

9 781537 541563